Titus Maccius Plautus

Mostellaria

Titus Maccius Plautus

Mostellaria

ISBN/EAN: 9783337411886

Printed in Europe, USA, Canada, Australia, Japan

Cover: Foto ©Andreas Hilbeck / pixelio.de

More available books at **www.hansebooks.com**

T. MACCI PLAVTI

MOSTELLARIA

WITH NOTES CRITICAL AND EXEGETICAL

AND AN INTRODUCTION

BY

E. A. SONNENSCHEIN, M.A.,

PROFESSOR OF CLASSICS IN THE MASON COLLEGE, BIRMINGHAM.

CAMBRIDGE:
DEIGHTON, BELL, AND CO.
LONDON: GEORGE BELL & SON.

1884

PREFACE.

In adding another play of Plautus to the series inaugurated by the late Prof. W. Wagner, Ph.D., of the Johanneum, Hamburg, I have little to say by way of preface beyond explaining the relation of this volume to the volumes that have preceded it (the *Aulularia*, the *Trinummus* and the *Menaechmi*) and to acknowledge my obligations both to writers of books on my subject and to personal friends who have helped me in my work.

Wagner's edition of Plautus with English notes shared the fate of so many other Plautine schemes; it was interrupted by death. The present volume is a contribution to the undertaking, and it is my intention to follow it up by other plays. The principles by which I have been guided, and by which I was guided in my edition of the *Captivi* (1880), are those of the school of criticism to which Wagner belonged, and which now rules the field, practically without a rival.

It would have been satisfactory had I been able to rely to some considerable extent upon material of

Wagner himself. Unfortunately he left very little in MS.; one short fragment ('Critical Notes on the Mostellaria') has been found among his papers; but it is mainly a collation from the *apparatus criticus* of Ritschl, contains very few conjectures by Wagner himself, and is limited to the first hundred lines of the play. The publishers have been unable to obtain from Wagner's executors any copy of Plautus with marginal notes by his hand.

But if I have had to dispense with aid from Wagner himself, I have every reason to be grateful for the very ready help that has been given me by other scholars. To my friend and former teacher Mr Robinson Ellis, I am indebted not merely for his valuable comments upon the *Mostellaria* published in the *Journal of Philology*, but also for the great trouble which he has taken in reading through the proof sheets of the whole play, and sending me many new suggestions of his own; he has also added a special Excursus upon the difficult fifth and sixth *Cantica* (see pp. 153—158). Mr J. S. Reid has also been so kind as to read through my proof and send me notes of his own upon a number of passages. Some of his conjectures I have adopted, but space prevented me from profiting by many of his notes, which I hope may find their place if I ever reach a second edition. My best thanks are also due to Professors A. Palmer, H. Nettleship and Minton Warren for occasional suggestions, and to Dr. Theodor Gottlieb of

Brünn, the Rev. A. J. Smith of the Camp Hill Grammar School, and Mr C. M. Dix of the Oratory School, Birmingham, for reading through part or the whole of the proof: the latter gentleman has also kindly made a full index to the notes.

My text is the result of a careful study of the play, extending over four years. I have had the editions of Ritschl, Ramsay, Lorenz, Bugge and Ussing constantly before me, and have tried to keep pace with other recent Plautine literature of Germany. Several valuable articles in periodicals by Brix and Langen have received the consideration due to anything that comes from their pens. I hope too that I have been able to contribute something myself to the improvement of the text. In a play so corrupt as the *Mostellaria*, there is plenty of room for conjecture even after the labours of the above-mentioned scholars; in every dozen lines there is a passage in which the question is not whether an emendation should be admitted but which particular emendation should be preferred. In such places the editor who emends need not fear to rush in where so many wise men have already trodden. Occasionally (as in lines 469, 1042) I have ventured to suggest a correction in a passage not usually regarded as corrupt. At the same time the critic will, I hope, find in my work signs of a careful study of the MSS., and an effort to protect their tradition where possible. In some passages I have been more conservative than Ramsay himself. I have, in fact, tried to

emulate the principle of the most recent school of Plautine criticism in Germany, which is, briefly, respect for
the MSS., subject only to greater respect for well es-
tablished laws of language, metre and logic.

In the explanatory notes my obligations are mainly
to the first edition of Lorenz: his second edition reached
me after my work was in great part finished; but I
have not hesitated to gather from it what seemed to me
valuable. From Ramsay and Ussing I have also derived
help, and have occasionally drawn upon Lambinus,
whose edition remains still the best complete commentary on Plautus. In writing the Metrical Introduction,
I have relied mainly upon the *Prolegomena to the Trinummus* of Ritschl and the *Metrik der Griechen und
Römer* by Christ (2nd Edition, 1879).

BIRMINGHAM,
November, 1884.

INTRODUCTION.

The Mostellaria[1], like other plays of Plautus, is founded on a Greek original called Φάσμα 'The Ghost' (see the didaskalia, or notice appended to the play by the grammarians). There were several plays of this name belonging to the νέα κομῳδία; probably the one in question was written by Philemon (cf. note on 1149), from whom Plautus borrowed the plot of his Trinummus and Mercator.

The scene is laid in a public street in Athens (cf. 30, 66, 1072) in which stand the houses of Theopropides and Simo. The time is midday (cf. 579 *circiter meridiem*, 651, and note on *merenda* 966). Between the two houses, which occupy the back of the stage, is a narrow street (*angiportus* cf. 1045), employed in several passages of the play as a place from which the conversation on the stage may be overheard. The stage is approached by two side doors, that on the left of the spectators leading to or from the harbour, that on the right to or from the town (*forum*); see Menaechmi 555 f., Amphitruo 333.

Before Simo's house stands the usual altar (cf. Aul. 598).

I. THE PLOT OF THE DRAMA.

During the absence abroad of Theopropides, an Athenian merchant, his son Philolaches has been sowing his wild oats. He has fallen in love with a slave-girl named Philematium and after purchasing her from her master with borrowed money, has presented her with her freedom; his days are being spent in riotous living. In Act I, Scene 4 we are introduced to a drinking bout and make

---

[1] The word is a feminine adjective derived from *mostellum*, the diminutive of *monstrum*: *Mostellaria* (sc. *fabula*) then means 'A Ghost Story.'

the acquaintance of one of his friends, Callidamates, who
has come with his sweetheart Delphium. Philolaches is
aided and abetted in his prodigal career by the clever
and unscrupulous Tranio, one of his father's slaves.

This state of things is interrupted by the news that
Theopropides has suddenly returned and is already in the
Piraeus, at the very time when the banquet above referred to is in full swing. At this critical moment Tranio,
the ˙dissolute and pampered slave (cf. *urbanus scurra,
deliciae popli* 15) steps forward and assumes the direction
of affairs and the position of hero of the piece. No time
must be lost, if detection is to be avoided. The house is
promptly locked up. Philolaches, Callidamates, Philematium and Delphium retreat indoors and are enjoined
to keep strict silence: Tranio remains on the ground to
meet the enemy. The old gentleman is now made the
victim of the slave's inventive genius. He is informed
that the house has been shut up for seven months, owing
to the discovery that it was haunted. In an admirable
scene Tranio pretends that Theopropides has himself
incurred the resentment of the Ghost by knocking at
the door of his house, and so converts the ghost-story
into a matter of present and patent fact; Theopropides is
only too glad to be able to escape with his head wrapped
up in his cloak (*capite obuoluto* 424).

But so far only the first difficulty has been overcome.
Theopropides returns when he has recovered from his
fright, having made enquiries of the person from whom
he bought the house: the latter has indignantly denied
the whole story. The situation is complicated by the appearance of the money-lender Misargyrides, who demands
payment of interest long overdue. Tranio finds himself
between two fires. But he is equal to the occasion. He
advises Theopropides to go to law with the refractory
vendor of the house. The debt he does not deny, but
explains it as a necessary means of raising money *to buy
another house*, when the old one had to be abandoned.
He even induces Theopropides to promise payment next
day, and Misargyrides departs pacified.

'Where then is this new house?' asks Theopropides.

Tranio is in doubt for a moment, but decides to locate it next door. Philolaches, he says, has bought the house of his neighbour Simo, and at a ludicrously small figure. The delight of the old man of business knows no bounds; his son is a chip of the old block. Yet another awkward demand of Theopropides—that he should be shown over the house—is met by the reminder that there are ladies therein, whose permission must first be asked. (That Philolaches is not in present possession of the house, but in the country, is not explicitly stated in the text as we have it, but seems rather to be assumed or inferred; cf. note on 929.) Theopropides promises to wait until Tranio has spoken to the present occupant, Simo, and leaves the stage.

In the interview with Simo that follows Tranio pretends that his master wishes to inspect the house with a view to imitating certain parts of it: he is himself, says Tranio, about to build an additional wing to his own. Simo remarks ironically that he might have chosen a better model, but consents, and also promises not to breathe a syllable about the misdemeanours of Philolaches. Tranio now summons Theopropides. He informs him that Simo regrets the bargain he has made, and begs him to say nothing about the purchase *out of consideration for his neighbour's feelings*. Thus primed for the interview, the two old men are allowed to meet and the inspection of the house takes place, without either of them discovering that he is a puppet in Tranio's hands. The latter is all the while on the alert to twist any ambiguous phrase into evidence that makes for his story of the purchase. So far Tranio has been entirely successful: when his master orders him to go to the country to fetch Philolaches, he employs this, his first moment of leisure, to release the rioters from the 'state of siege' (1048) by means of a back gate leading into the *angiportus*.

But the whole device is, after all, only a temporary measure. Theopropides must ultimately discover that Simo has not really sold his house. This truth Tranio recognizes in 1054:

nam scio equidem nullo pacto iam esse posse haec clam senem.

The discovery has indeed been already made through an untoward incident. According to a custom frequently alluded to in the plays of Plautus, slaves called *Aduorsitores* (cf. on 313) come to fetch their master Callidamates from the banquet and knock loudly at the door of the house supposed by Theopropides to be haunted. Theopropides warns them off, but is only laughed at for his pains: from the lips of these slaves, to whom he is a perfect stranger, he learns that for the last three days his house has been the scene of one long debauch. He hastens to Simo, who, in answer to his anxious enquiries, denies explicitly that he has ever had any business transactions with either Philolaches or Tranio. The whole truth dawns upon the unhappy father: the ghost-story is a fabrication. His mind is now filled with one purpose—he will have his revenge on the slave who has so impudently hoaxed him. Simo enters into his plans and lends him a number of flogging-slaves (*lorarii*), with whom he lies in wait for Tranio. The day of reckoning has now come; but the indomitable Tranio rises once more to the emergency. Instead of running away, he meets his master with a smiling face and innocent manner; and the moment the latter shows signs of bringing out the *lorarii*, calmly seats himself upon the altar in front of the house of Simo—a place of refuge from which social and religious feeling forbade Theopropides to drag him. Meanwhile Callidamates arrives as peacemaker. He promises that Theopropides shall not be out of pocket by his son's extravagance and makes profession of deep contrition in the name both of himself and his friend. Theoproprides is partly pacified. But Tranio shall not escape unpunished. The slave himself certainly does not contribute to bring about such a result. He assumes an air of provoking indifference and answers the threats of Theopropides with light banter and impudent taunts. But Callidamates is importunate. He will not yield in his entreaties that Tranio be pardoned. Tranio's last speech is a bright idea. 'Pardon me? why not indeed?' he says: 'I shall be sure to get into some scrape to-morrow and then you can punish me for both things at once.'

Such a miscreant is irresistible, and the play concludes with the promise, extracted from Theopropides, that bygones shall be bygones.

The Mostellaria must be considered as one of the best of the plays of Plautus. The characters are drawn with a masterly hand : Tranio is almost an Iago in his architectonic faculty for intrigue ; Philematium is one of the most charming figures in Plautus. Her pretty simplicity of character and girlish delight in dress are portrayed with effective naturaluess, and her faithful devotion to Philolaches raise her above her class. Simo too is a very well drawn character. He belongs to a class often ridiculed in Plautus—husbands of old, ugly and bad-tempered wives whom they have married for the sake of their money. His unhappiness shows itself in cynical sneers and a certain malignity of temper. He has no moral indignation for the misdeeds of Tranio and Philolaches ; he even takes pleasure in the idea of keeping his neighbour in the dark about them. But when there is a chance of seeing Tranio flogged, he is quite ready to lend his *lorarii*. He is totally without the capacity for sympathy, and remains a mere outsider to the action. Theopropides[1] is the narrow minded, mercantile Philistine, the chief notes of whose character are avarice, superstition, and childish vindictiveness. His only grievances are the pecuniary loss he fears he may suffer, and the wounding of his *amour propre*. Callidamates claims sympathy by his frank good nature ; the reader is willing to condone his vices. The minor characters are none of them colourless. Grumio the honest but uncourageous peasant, Scapha, the sceptic of human nature and would-be temptress of Philematium, the merry Delphium, the pampered and effeminate Phaniscus, the jealous *aduorsitor* have all their clearly marked traits, and stand out as living figures. Perhaps the least effective character in the drama is the prodigal son, Philolaches.

The management of the plot and humorous business deserves all praise. But in criticizing the play as a whole,

[1] The name ('prophetic') is probably ironical : its owner is unable to see an inch before his nose.

it is impossible to conceal certain defects. We are not quite clear about the ultimate fate of Tranio. But what about Philematium? The thread of her destiny is completely lost. Without attempting to prescribe a happy ending for the love-story, such as that suggested by Lorenz, the reader notes that Philematium could not, as a freedwoman, become the wife of her liberator. The interest excited in the couple remains thus unsatisfied. Tranio has become so completely the hero, that Philematium and Philolaches are forgotten, and their faithfulness not rewarded.

Nor is the tone of the piece as a whole a high one. It is the old story—repeated over and over again on the Latin stage—of successful knavery. The old father is regarded as fair game for the pleasure-loving son and the astute slave. That Theopropides is himself a man of low type is an accident and not consciously present to the poet's mind as warranting the mortification that he suffers. There could not be any stronger evidence of the wholly non-ethical character of the comedy of Plautus than the fact that the love of Philolaches and Philematium, which in reality raises them so far above many other pairs and which has its romantic side, is never pleaded as their justification, or as mitigating their fault. The story need not have been different, had the relation of the two been as low as that of Menaechmus and Erotium. That they are true lovers is a detail. There are all the elements of high class comedy in the plot of the Mostellaria; but the author, whether Greek or Roman, has contented himself with writing a farce.

The Mostellaria has been frequently imitated. *I Fantasmi* by Bentivoglio (Venice, 1545), *Les esprits* by Pierre la Rivey (1550—1600), *Le Comédien poète* by Montfleury (1640—1683), *Le Retour imprévu* by Regnard (1655?—1709), *Abracadabra* by the Danish playwright Holberg (1684—1754) are all founded upon it[1]. In English we have the *Alchemist* of Ben Jonson (first acted 1610): in this play *Face* the housekeeper excludes

---

[1] See Lorenz, *Einleitung zur Mostellaria*, pp. 34—40.

Lovewit from his house by means of a made up story;
his prototype, both in action and character, is Tranio;
and that the Mostellaria was present to the author's
mind is shown by some direct quotations, e. g. Act V,
Scene 1,
'Nothing's more wretched than a guilty conscience'
cf. Most. 544
nihil est miserius quam animus hominis conscius,
a line which in this edition is excluded from the text.
The English Traveller by Thomas Heywood (1633)
contains a bye-plot in which the young prodigal *Lionell*
and his servant *Reignald* hoodwink *Old Lionell* by a
story of a haunted house. Other characters too are
taken from the Mostellaria: *Robin* stands for Grumio,
Blanda for Philematium; *Scapha* is the name for the
old servant in both plays.

That Shakspere knew the play seems to be shown
by his employment of the names Tranio and Grumio in
his *Taming of the Shrew;* in at least one passage he
appears to have taken a hint from Plautus; see note on
18 (and also on *Personae* p. 5).

II. THE TEXT.

For an account of some of the principal MSS. (*A, B,
D*) on which the text of the Mostellaria is founded, the
reader is referred to Introduction to Captivi pp. 16, 17.
The palimpsest (*A*) is far more copious in this play than
in the Captivi, being available in *vv.* 576—613, 653—
723, 759—796, 826—858, 893—1030, 1044—1073.
Another MS. of which mention must be made here, is
the *Codex Decurtatus* (*C*) belonging to the 12th century,
and at present at Heidelberg. It is of similar importance to *D*. *J* does not contain the Mostellaria.

In the present edition clarendon type and the symbol
M are employed to denote the reading of the three
Vatican or Palatine MSS. *BCD*, minor discrepancies
being neglected. Where the differences are of import-
ance, the MSS. are referred to singly as *B, C* and *D*.
The readings of *A* are given in clarendon capitals.

An inferior MS. to which occasional reference is made is *F*, the *codex Lipsiensis* (15th century). It contains many conjectures, and representing as it does the views of Plautine language and prosody held by scholars of the time at which it was written, is of similar authority to *Z*, the *Editio Princeps*, by Merula (printed at Venice, 1472).

The critical notes in this edition do not form a complete *apparatus criticus*, but are designed to illustrate and, so far as possible, to justify the readings adopted in the text by reference to MS. authority[1] and the conjectures of previous scholars. Mere orthographical variants are not as a rule given: the student who desires minute information about the MSS. must go to Ritschl or Ramsay. Nor has it been thought necessary to cite all the conjectures even of eminent critics : only those are inserted which seem deserving of special consideration[2]. On the other hand it is hoped that everything of importance has been gleaned, and that the notes have been brought up to date. Owing to the intimate connection between prosodical and metrical questions on the one hand, and questions of reading on the other, remarks on these topics are given side by side.

The numbering of lines in the margin is that of Ritschl[3] : at the head of each page are given the Act,

[1] Words, or parts of words, printed in italics in the text, are *omissions* (not merely errors) of the MSS. The words '*omitted in M*' are usually added in the critical notes : sometimes however this is not expressly stated (if the matter be of secondary importance), but left to be inferred from the italics in the text.

[2] A reading adopted in the text is always attributed to its author, and the names of the modern editors who have adopted it are also given. About readings merely mentioned in the notes and not admitted to the text, less full information is usually given. In a few cases in which the MSS. confuse the distribution of parts, or omit the name of a speaker, it has not been thought necessary to mention the author of an obvious correction.

[3] It cannot be denied that systematic adherence to Ritschl's numbering gives rise to occasional difficulties. Thus in such passages as 205—206, 457—467, where Ritschl transposed the lines and I have reverted to the order of MSS., I have nevertheless been compelled to employ Ritschl's numbers. This may

Scene and Verse according to the traditional description in the Vulgate[1].

This play has suffered seriously by transposition of pages in the archetype (and the archetype of the archetype) from which BCD are derived. The result is that in these three MSS. a large part of the text is dislocated. A glance at the edition of Parens (A.D. 1619, 1623) who followed them, will make this clear: 802—841 (Par. IV 1, 29—69) are placed *after* 842—883 (Par. III 3, 20—IV 1, 28): further, 601—646 (Par. IV 2, 3—44) follow after 885 *a* (Par. IV 2, 2), and 647—685 (Par. V 2, 18—60) after 1065 (Par. V 2, 17). Camerarius, the great German student of Plautus of the 16th century, utilizing the labours of previous scholars, restored all these passages to their proper places[2]; but in one point he went too far. He transferred the whole scene beginning *Quid tibi uisumst mercimonium* (904) from its present position and inserted it between the scene ending 857 and the scene beginning 858. The order of Camerarius was followed by the Vulgate, so that this scene bears the traditional description III 3. Ritschl restored it to its present position, which is also its position in the MSS.

cause some difficulty to the young student: but consistency in this matter seemed imperatively necessary.

[1] The division of the play into three Acts (cf. pp. 57, 110) is due to Lorenz. The reader may be referred to my note in Introduction to Captivi, pp. 1, 2, where I have adopted the same principle of division for that play: the three acts contain the statement, the complication and the solution of the problem, respectively. The traditional division into five acts is due to the Italian editors at the time of the Renaissance.

[2] The palimpsest (not, of course, known to Camerarius) has escaped this error of transposition.

METRES OF THE MOSTELLARIA[1].

IAMBIC METRES.

The iambic metres of Plautus are based upon the double iambus (*dipodia iambica*).

$$\smile - \smile -$$

But the double foot does not always retain this, its pure form; instead of either iambus the Latin comic writers admit a tribrach, a spondee, a dactyl or an anapaest (except at the close of the verse: see below), thus proceeding further in license even than Greek comedy. The Plautine *dipodia iambica* may therefore exhibit any of the following forms:

$$\begin{matrix} \smile\smile & & \smile\smile \\ \bar{\smile} & \perp & \bar{\smile} & - \\ & \swarrow\smile & & \smile\smile \end{matrix}$$

The proceleusmatic ($\smile \smile \swarrow \smile$) is not common, but it is sometimes admitted, especially in the first foot, e. g. Trin. 66 (cf. Asin. 71, 430, 482).

  sĕd hŏc ănĭm' ăduōrt' ātqu' aŭfĕr rīdĭcŭlărĭă,

so in the second foot, Most. 19

  nūnc, dŭm tĭbĭ lŭbĕt, lĭcĕtquĕ pōtā, pĕrdĕ rēm,

cf. Most. 131 (*-tĕnŭs ăbĕ-*), Aul. 330, 657.

The position of the ictus should be carefully observed. In iambic verse the dactyl, for instance, has always the form $- \swarrow \smile$, never $\swarrow \smile \smile$. The second half of each dipodia has a minor ictus in corresponding places.

[1] This sketch is intended for the student who is approaching the subject of Plautine verse for the first time; it makes no pretension to originality.

The most common iambic metre—indeed the most common of all the metres of Plautus—is the

Iambic Trimeter

or *Senarius*, so called because it is composed of six iambi, or three *dipodiae iambicae* (hence the Greek name τρίμε-τρος): it bears three principal ictus, one on the first arsis of each *dipodia*.

Although other feet are admitted instead of the iambus, as explained above, yet certain restrictions are observed :

(*a*) The last foot must always be pure.

(*b*) The fifth foot should be a spondee; an iambus is however permitted when the verse ends with a cretic, diiambic or polysyllabic word, or when the final iambus is preceded by a word of the form of a 4th paeon: the following verse-endings are therefore legitimate (the upright lines mark the beginning and end of a word) :

$$\smile \mid - \; \smile \; - \mid$$
$$\mid \smile \; - \; \smile \; - \mid$$
$$\mid \smile \; \smile \; \smile \; - \mid \smile \; -$$

(*c*) The use of the anapaest is limited: as a rule the three syllables of the anapaest belong to one word, or to two words that are closely connected, as in Trin. 759

pŏtĭn' ĕst ăb ămīc' ălĭcŭnd' ēxōrārī? pŏtĕst.

(*d*) The dactyl is employed under the same limitations as in trochaic verse (see p. xxii.).

(*e*) On the prosodical license by which, especially in the first foot, a bacchiac or cretic is allowed to stand for an iambus, see Introduction to Captivi A (ii), (v).

The caesura is more carefully preserved by the Latin than by the Greek comic poets. The principal caesura is the penthemimeral, i.e. the division of the verse after the fifth half-foot : Most. 1, 2 :

ēx' ē cŭlīnā | sīs fŏrās, mūstīgiă,
quī m' īntēr pătīnās | ēxhĭbēs ārgŭtĭās.

Occasionally the hepthemimeral caesura is found: Most. 27 f., cf. 36, 41, 67, etc.

hōcĭnĕ bŏn' ēss' ŏffĭcĭŭm | sēru' ēxīstŭmūs
ŭt ĕrĭ sŭī cōrrŭmpăt | ēt r' ēt fīlĭŭm.

Frequently the hepthemimeral and the trihemimeral are

found combined, in place of the single penthemimeral caesura: Most. 24, 502, etc.

părăsĭtōs: | *ōpsōnătĕ* | *pōllūcĭbĭlĭtĕr*
dĕfŏdĭt | *ĭnsĕpŭltŭm* | *clăm ĭn hĭsc' aedĭbŭs.*

The iambic trimeter is the suitable vehicle for ordinary, unimpassioned dialogue, being of all metres the most like prose. This was observed by Aristotle Poet. IV μάλιστα γὰρ λεκτικὸν τῶν μέτρων τὸ ἰαμβεῖόν ἐστιν. σημεῖον δὲ τούτου· πλεῖστα γὰρ ἰαμβεῖα λέγομεν ἐν τῇ διαλέκτῳ τῇ πρὸς ἀλλήλους: similarly Cicero (Orator LVII § 191) speaks of iambic verse as '*orationi simillimus*' and Horace (A. P. 81) as '*alternis aptus sermonibus.*' On the same principle we find in Plautus that when a letter is read aloud on the stage, or a formula (e.g. an oath) is recited, the metre changes to senarii cf. Bacch. 1007, Pers. 501, Pseud. 998, Rud. 1338; cf. on Most. 887 f. A scene written in this metre was never accompanied by music and was called *Diuerbium* ('dialogue').

On the difficult question of hiatus in the principal caesura of senarii and other metres, the reader may be referred to Intr. to Aulularia G. pp. lix—lxiii, Intr. to Trinummus (2nd Ed.) pp. vi—viii, and Intr. to Captivi D.

Iambic Tetrameter Catalectic.

This metre (called in Latin *Iambicus Septenarius* and by Prof. Key the 'Laughing Metre') consists of four iambic *dipodiae*, the last being catalectic:

The proceleusmatic is excluded in the last *dipodia*.
This verse is subject to the same limitations in regard to the employment of the tribrach, spondee, dactyl and anapaest as the Iambic Trimeter.

The principal caesura falls after the fourth foot; from which, in this case, the spondee and its representatives are excluded; cf. Most. 168, 173:

quĭd tŭ t' exōrnās, mōrĭbūs | *lĕpĭdīs quōm lĕpĭdă tŭt'ēs*
uĭrtŭtĕ fŏrm' ĭd ĕuĕnīt | *t' ŭt dĕcĕăt quĭdquĭd hăbĕās.*

But caesura after the thesis of the fifth foot is occasionally permitted as a substitute. There is no example of this caesura in the Mostellaria. One line in this play is found without either caesura (183).

At the end of the second *dipodia* the license of the *syllaba anceps* is permitted: cf. Most. 158:

$$n\bar{e}c \; qu\breve{o}m \; m\bar{e} \; m\breve{e}l\breve{u}' \; m\breve{u}\breve{a} \; Sc\breve{a}ph\breve{a} \; | \; r\breve{e}\breve{a}r \; \acute{e}ss\breve{e} \; d\bar{e}f\breve{\imath}c\bar{a}t\breve{a}m.$$

Here *Scăphă* stands for an iambus: so too in 170, 174. Cf. 169 where *-ĕrĭs* (*mulieris*) stands for ◡ – : cf. critical note. Hiatus too is occasionally found in the caesura, cf. Asin. 653

$$\bar{\imath}d \; p\breve{o}t\breve{\imath}\breve{u}s \; . \; u\bar{\imath}\bar{g}\bar{\imath}nt\breve{\imath} \; m\breve{\imath}n\bar{u}\bar{e} \; | \; h\bar{\imath}c \; \acute{\imath}ns\bar{u}nt \; \bar{\imath}n \; cr\breve{u}m\bar{\imath}n\breve{a}.$$

Most. 230, 236 exhibit hiatus, according to the reading of the MSS.; but emendation is easy in both cases.

Scenes written in this metre were accompanied by music and called *Cantica* in the wider sense of the term [1].

Iambic Tetrameter Acatalectic.

This verse (called in Latin *Iambicus Octonarius* and by Prof. Key the 'Swearing Metre') is composed of four iambic *dipodiae*. Caesura is found after the thesis of the fifth foot, or, less frequently, after the arsis of the fourth foot: for the former see Most. 118, 131, 143, Capt. IV 4, 1–14; for the latter Most. 107, 128, 132, 146. In this metre, as in the *Septenarius*, the fourth foot is regularly pure.

Iambic Dimeter Acatalectic.

This verse is composed of two iambic *dipodiae*, and employed as a *clausula*. It occurs, among other places, in Most. 885 *a*, 886 *b*.

Versus Reizianus.

The exact constitution of this metre is still a matter of dispute among the Germans: Reiz, after whom the verse is called, Hermann, Studemund, Wagner, Christ and Spengel take different views. Ellis has expressed

[1] Cf. note on p. xxiv.

himself on the subject in Excursus II at the end of this volume. In the present edition Studemund, to whom Bugge, Lorenz and Kayser give their adherence, has been followed. According to him (Festgruss der philologischen Gesellschaft zu Würzburg, 1868, pp. 51—56) the verse consists of two parts, (i) an iambic dimeter acatalectic, (ii) an iambic dimeter catalectic and syncopated (i.e. in which the second arsis is lengthened so as to be equivalent to the time of three short syllables):

$$\cup \perp \cup - \cup \perp \cup - \;\; | \;\; \cup \perp \cup - \perp \cup$$

According to Studemund, this metre is found in Most. 858, 860, 880 and we have in the line which Ritschl numbered 874, two short lines, each identical with the second half of the *versus Reizianus*. I have also introduced it in vv. 891 b + 892, 893.

Spengel, who, like Wagner and Christ, accepts the constitution of the first half of the verse as an iambic dimeter, relegates the second to the category of anapaestic rhythm[1]. Wagner and Christ (Metrik, 2nd Ed.) regard it as an iambic *tripodia* catalectic: $\sigma - \cup - \sigma$ (or $\cup\cup - \cup - \sigma$, or $\sigma - \cup \cup - \sigma$): cf. Aul. 412—442.

TROCHAIC METRES.

The trochaic metres of Plautus are based upon the double trochee (*dipodia trochaica, ditrochaeus*),

$$- \cup - \cup$$

But the tribrach, the spondee, the anapaest and even the dactyl are freely admitted in place of either of the pure trochees (except at the close of the verse: see below).

The Plautine *dipodia trochaica* may therefore exhibit any of the following forms:

$$\cup\cup \; . \qquad \cup\cup$$
$$- \qquad\qquad -$$
$$\perp \quad \cup \quad - \quad \cup$$
$$\perp\cup \qquad \cup\cup$$

The proceleusmatic ($\perp \cup\cup\cup$), which is excluded by the Greeks from trochaic verse, is sometimes admitted by

---

[1] He calls it a hypercatalectic anapaestic monometer.

Plautus, especially in the first foot, c.g. Men. 119, Mil. 451

nĭmĭ' ĕgŏ t' hăbŭī dḗlĭcātăm . nănc ădĕ', ūt făctūrŭs,
dīcăm.
dŏmĭcĭlĭŭmst, Ăthénĭs dŏmŭs ēst . ăt ĕrŭs hīc . ĕy' ĭstắm
lŏmăm.

Cf. Most. 384, 396, Aul. 587 (Wagner); so in the second foot Capt. III 1, 33.

Observe carefully the position of the ictus, comparing its place in iambics; see p. xvi. The second trochee has a minor ictus on the first syllable.

The most common Trochaic metre is the

Trochaic Tetrameter Catalectic

or *Trochaicus Septenarius,* which is composed of four *dipodiae trochaicae,* the last being catalectic and pure:

$$\text{⏑ ⏒}$$
$$\text{⏒ ⏑}$$

The natural caesura is after the thesis of the fourth foot, e.g. Most. 248

cĕdŏ mĭ spĕcŭl' ēt c' ŏrnāmēntĭs | ărcŭl' āctūtăm, Scăphă.

But sometimes the comic poets substitute a caesura after the arsis of the fourth foot, e.g. Ter. Phorm. 863

pŏn' ādprēndĭt păllĭō, | rĕsŭpīnăt : rēspĭcĭō, rŏgō.

Cf. Most. 304, 306, 310 f., etc.

Occasionally verses are found without either of these caesurae, e.g. Trin. 1145

nēu quī r' ĭpsăm pŏssĕt ĭntēllĕgĕrĕ, thēnsaūrŭm sŭŏm.

A second caesura (*caesura minor*) is often found after the first dipodia, e.g. Men. 957

ăbĭĭt sŏcĕrŭs, | ăbĭĭt mĕdĭcŭs: | sŏlŭs sŭm, prō Iŭppĭtĕr.

Hiatus in the principal caesura of this verse is not uncommon, especially when there is a pause in the sense or change of speakers, e.g. Men. 219,

spŏrtŭlăm căp' ătqu' ārgēntŭm: | ĕccōs trĭs nŭmmōs hăbĕs.

So too Most. 380, 398, 821, 952: but sometimes without any pause, cf. Most. 389, 394. Change of speakers justifies hiatus at any place of this, as of other kinds of verse: cf. on Most. 567.

Scenes written in this metre were called *Cantica*, in the wider sense of the word, and were accompanied with music.

Although the first three *dipodiae* may assume any of the above mentioned forms, certain restrictions are observed:

(*a*) If the caesura falls after the thesis of the fourth foot, that foot must be either a trochee or a spondee (never a tribrach, a dactyl or an anapaest), and if it falls after the arsis of the fourth foot, the third foot must be either a trochee or a tribrach.

(*b*) The seventh foot being pure, a spondee is preferred in the sixth, as a kind of counterpoise (cf. the usage in *senarii*, p. xvii *b*).

(*c*) The dactyl is not employed in any but the first foot, except under certain limitations:

1. It must not be composed of a single trisyllabic word.

2. It must not be divided so that the first two syllables form a trochaic word (or the trochaic termination of a polysyllabic word). On these principles the lines

síc hunc dēcĭpĭs . ĭmm' enim uer' Ántiph', hic me décipit
iám nisi quidem suo quícquĕ lŏco m' erĭt situm suppelléctilis

are faulty (cf. Ter. Phorm. 528, Plaut. Stich. 62—according to the conjecture of Ritschl). But the following (Mil. 1137) is correct

séquiminī: sĭmŭl circumspicite, nĕ quis adsit árbiter.

So too are the following (Epid. 673, Cas. III 2, 31)

ápag' ill' a me . n' íllĕ quĭdem Volcán' iratist fílius
n' ég' aliquid contráhere cupio lĭtigi' ĭntĕr ĕós duos

for the words *ille quidem*, *inter eos* are so closely connected that they are treated as a single word. An exception too must be made for the fifth foot, in which a dactylic word is allowed to represent a trochee: cf. Trin. 1127

n' éxaedificauĭsset m' ex hisce aédĭbŭs, ạpsque tĕ foret,

where Wagner (following Ritschl) reads *apsque tĕ fŏrĕt, ex hisce aédibus* in order to avoid the dactylic word. So too in Mil. 721

cénser' emorī: cecidisset ĕbrĭŭs aut d' equ' úspiam.

Another trochaic metre is the

Trochaic Tetrameter Acatalectic

or *Trochaicus Octonarius,* which consists of four trochaic *dipodiae,* and is subject to the same laws as septenarii. The hiatus in the principal caesura is permitted, e.g. Men. 594

néc măgĭs mănĭfésť ĕǵ hŏmĭnḗm | úmqu' ūllūm tĕnḗrī
uīdī.

Examples of this metre in the Mostellaria occur in lines 862 + 863 *a,* 877 and possibly also in 321 + 322, 335.

Besides these metres there will be found in the text of this edition two instances of the

Trochaic Dimeter Acatalectic

hí sŏlḗnt ēsse ĕrĭs ūtĭbĭlēs
stúltă sĭbi ēxpĕtúnt cōnsĭlĭă

(Most. 859, 861); but it is quite possible that these lines should be scanned otherwise: see Excursus II p. 153.

Mention must also be made of the

Trochaic Tripodia Catalectic

$$\text{‿‿} \quad \text{‿‿}$$
$$\perp \; \smile \; \perp \; \smile \; \times$$
$$\smile\,\smile \quad \smile\,\smile$$

which is found repeated in verse 345 (possibly too in 333) and in combination with a cretic dimeter frequently (e.g. 108: see below under cretic metres).

BACCHIAC METRES.

The bacchiac foot (‿ ⊥ –) in Plautus exhibits the following forms:

$$\smile\,\smile$$
$$\smile \; \perp \; -$$
$$- \quad \smile\,\smile$$
$$\smile\,\smile$$

i.e. Plautus admits, as representatives of the bacchius, the molossus and the ionicus a minore, the long syllables of each being liable to resolution into two shorts.

c 2

Bacchiac metres are very common in the cantica[1]; the chief of them is the

Bacchiac Tetrameter

composed of four bacchiac feet, e.g. Most. 120

prīmŭmdŭm părēntēs făbrĭ lībĕrŭm sŭnt.

The following verses contain instances of resolution of one or both of the two long syllables, or of the ionicus a minore: Most. 91, Trin. 240 (Wagner), Aul. 132 (Wagner), Most. 89 *b.*

nŏuăr' āedĭ' ĕss' ārbĭtrŏr sĭmĭl' ĕg' hŏmĭnĕm
dēspŏliātŏr lătĕbrĭcŏlār' hŏmĭnŭm cŏrrŭmptŏr
quĭn pārtĭcĭpēm părĭtĕr ĕgŏ t' ĕt tŭ m' ŭt făcĭās
sĭmĭl' ĕss' ārbĭtrārēr sĭmŭlăcrŭmqu' hăbērĕ.

A metre admitted into the text of this edition, but not accredited by Spengel, is the

Bacchiac Trimeter

(three bacchiac feet); see Most. 89 *a*, and cf. critical note on 123—125. It would be impossible to discuss the

---

[1] By *Cantica* are here meant *Cantica* proper. It seems to be certain that scenes written in *septenarii*, whether trochaic or iambic, were declaimed to music in the style of recitative, and also called *Cantica:* (they are usually marked *C* in early MSS., to distinguish them from the *Diuerbia* or *senarii*, marked *D*). But the *canticum* proper was, according to most of the grammarians, a lyrical monologue, which was sung (not merely declaimed or recited) by the actor or else by a special *Cantor*, the actor meanwhile gesticulating to suit the words. [We must however include the lyrical scenes which are not monologues: there are four of these in the Mostellaria, i.e. I 4; III 2, 1—57; 96—116; IV 2, 1—23.] The problem of determining the metrical structure of the *Cantica* is an extremely difficult one. At first sight they seem to present a fortuitous congregation of the most heterogeneous metres: nor has criticism yet succeeded in discovering any clear principles in the structure of many of them. There appears to be only imperfect coincidence of changes of rhythm and logical arrangement of matter. But it is possible that the poet and the musician were working together in a way no longer determinable by us. The main metres employed are bacchiacs, cretics, trochaics and iambics.

question within the limits of this Introduction, but it may be mentioned that this metre is accepted by Ritschl (e. g. in Trin. 261 f., Most.[1] 317, 319, 322, 331 f., 344), by Brix (Trin. 261 f.), by Lorenz (Most. 89 *a*, 319) and by Goetz and Loewe in Poen. 259 f. The catalectic trimeter (also rejected by Spengel) was admitted by Wagner in Men. 579 f.

Spengel accepts as a test of bacchiac rhythm the law of Seyffert (De uers. bacch. p. 15 f.) that bacchiac verses which contain no pure thesis (i.e. short mono-syllable) are not genuine.

In bacchiac, as in cretic verse, there is far less prosodical license than in iambics and trochaics. The following phenomena are however found:

(*a*) Archaic long vowels: Poen. 260 *excĭdĭt ŭt ĕg' ŏpīnōr*, Amph. 652 *hăbĕt ōmnĭ' ădsūnt*, Trin. 226 *exercĭtŏr ănĭmŭ' nŭnc ēst*, Capt. iv 2, 2 *auctĭŏr ēst ĭn ănĭmō*, etc.

(*b*) Loss of final -s: Capt. iv 2, 1 *mĕŏ mägĭ' uŏlŭtō*, Men. 769 *uĕrŭmst mŏdŭ' tămĕn*; perhaps too Most. 85 *rĕcŏrdātŭ' mŭlt' ēt*.

(*c*) Shortening of a final long syllable under the influence of the ictus on a preceding short syll. (Intr. to Capt. A i) is denied by Spengel, but admitted by Ritschl, Brix and Wagner, cf. Trin. 261 (*fŏrŭm f.*), Aul. 131 (*mĕtŭm m.*): the scansion in Pers. 816 *căuĕ sĭs m' ăttĭgās nē* (Intr. to Capt. A ii) is not questioned by Spengel.

(*d*) Synizesis is not unfrequent in the arsis: cf. Capt. v 1, 2 *reddŭcĕm tŭŏ pătrī*, Rud. 906 *grătĭās mĕŏ pătrŏnō*, 908 *quŏm m' ĕx suĭs lŏcĭs*: synizesis in the thesis is denied by Spengel (but cf. Aul. 133 *ĕŏ nŭnc ĕgŏ*).

(*e*) Hiatus after a monosyllable that forms the first syllable of a resolved arsis (see Intr. to Capt. D iii, Intr. to Aul. p. lxiii) is unobjectionable: cf. Cas. iii 5, 39 *quĭd cŭm ĕā nĕgŏtī*. But hiatus and *syllaba anceps* after the second foot are questionable. Ritschl and most editors

---

[1] i.e. according to his constitution of the text.

have accepted it and it is admitted by Christ, who quotes
Pers. 789, Pseud. 256, 1253, 1272, Cas. iii 5, 60, etc.;
cf. too Men. 968 (Brix³); but Spengel rejects it. The
fact that the bacchiac tetrameter does not possess, like
the cretic tetrameter, a regular caesura after the second
foot is an argument against the admissibility of this
hiatus.

CRETIC METRES.

Cretic metres (employed in the Cantica: see note on
p. xxiv) are built up of a certain number of cretic feet.
In place of the cretic foot ($- \cup -$), the Latin comic poets
admit occasionally a molossus, and even a choriambus.
Resolution of the first or second long syllable is common.
The foot may therefore assume the following forms:

$$\begin{array}{l} \cup\cup \quad \cup\cup \\ \acute{} \cup - \\ \acute{} - - \\ \acute{} \cup\cup - \end{array}$$

The following are examples of verses composed of pure
cretics (Most. 715 f.):

> hóc hábēt . réppĕrī quī sĕnēm dūcĕrēm
> quō dŏl' ā mē dŏlōrēm prŏcūl péllĕrēm.

The following verses exhibit more or less divergence from
this norm: Most. 106, 110, Pseud. 1332, 1248 f., Most.
882, Asin. 133

> cŭm pĭgrā fămĭlĭ' ĭnmūndŭs ĭnstrénŭŏs
> dŏmĭnŭs ĭndĭlĭgēns réddĕr' ălĭás nĕuŏlt
> tĕ sĕquŏr . quĭn uŏcās spéctātōrés sĭmŭl
> n' hérclĕ sĭ cĕcĭdĕrō uŏstr' ĕrĭt flăgĭtĭŭm
> mălĕ cāstĭgắbĭt ēos éxŭŭĭs bŭbŭlĭs[1]
> péllĕcĕbraē pérnĭcĭēs ădŭlēscēnt' éxĭtĭŭm.

The admissibility of the choriambus is denied by Spengel
(Reformvorschläge, pp. 21—35).

_____

[1] The MSS. give *bubulis exu-*
uiis; this would throw the choriambus into the last foot, where
it is less excusable; cf. however
Capt. ii 1, 14, Bacch. 659.

The most common cretic metre is the

Cretic Tetrameter

$$\overset{\_}{\underline{}}\,\cup\,\overset{\_}{-}\,\overset{\_}{\underline{}}\,\cup\,-\;\Big|\;\overset{\_}{\underline{}}\,\cup\,-\,\overset{\_}{\underline{}}\,\cup\,-$$

which has the caesura after the second foot; see instances quoted above (two of them Most. 716, 106 have not this caesura). Occasionally we find hiatus or *syllaba anceps* in the caesura, e.g. Most. 718 (cf. 149), Asin. 134, 137 :

sắluōs (or *sắluŏ'*) *sīs Trắnĭō.* | *ắt uắlēs . nōn mắlĕ.*
nắm mắr' hauid ēst mắrĕ, | *uŏs mắr' ắcĕrrūmām.*
quāē dĕd' ēt quŏd bĕnĕ | *fĕc' : āt pōsthắc tĭbī.*

But in no case is the resolution of the final long syllable of the second cretic permitted.

In general it may be remarked that cretics are governed by stricter laws, both in regard to metre and to prosody, than either iambic or trochaic verse. Synizesis is rare (instances are however found in Most. 711 (*tu͡os*), 882, Capt. II 1, 45). Dropping of a final -s takes place only occasionally, e.g. Epid. 322, Cas. II 2, 16 :

nĭmĭ' dĭū mắcĕrōr : sĭtnĕ quĭd nĕcnĕ sĭt
ĕm, quĭd ēst? dĭc ĭd' hōc: nắm pŏl hauid sắtĭ' mĕō.

So too may be scanned Most. 113 (*factu'*), 697 (*somnu'*), 711 (*abitu'*), 718 (*saluo'*). Shortening of a long final syllable under the influence of the ictus on a preceding short syllable (Intr. to Capt. A i) is comparatively rare; but it occurs Cas. III 5, 7, II 2, 4, Pers. 758, Trin. 272 :

cắuĕ tĭbī, Clĕŏstrăt' : ābscĕd' ắb ĭsť, ŏbsĕcrō
nam ŭbĭ dŏmī sŏlắ sūm, sŏpŏr mắnūs cắluĭtŭr
ĭtĕ fŏrās, hĭc uŏl' ānť ŏstĭ' ēt iắnuăm
bŏnĭ sĭb' haūec ēxpĕtūnt, rĕm fĭd' hŏnŏrĕm
(cretic dimeter + trochaic dipodia).

A monosyllabic word ending in -*m* or a long vowel may, as in iambic and trochaic verse, be shortened (not elided) before a succeeding short vowel and so form the first syllable of a resolved arsis; cf. Intr. to Capt. D iii (Hiatus): so Most. 334, Men. 115, Most. 881

> quŏ ĕg' ĕ'; ăn scīs? scī': īn mēntēm uēnĭt mŏdŏ
> quŏ ĕg' cām, quăm r' ăgām, quĭd nĕgōtĭ gĕrăm
> hŏc dĭē crăstĭnī quŏm ĕrŭ' rēscĭuĕrĭt.

Cretic Tetrameter Catalectic

$$\overset{\shortmid}{\,} \smile - \overset{\shortmid}{\,} \smile - \mid \overset{\shortmid}{\,} \smile - \overset{\shortmid}{\,} \smallsmile$$

is found in two verses of the Mostellaria (329, 347): cf. Trinummus 244 ff., 266 ff., 293 ff.

Spengel, who denies the existence of catalectic cretics (and there is certainly considerable doubt about the matter), scans Most. 329, 347 as anapaestic dimeters:

> sĭ cădĕs, nōn cădĕs quĭn cădām tēcŭm
> d' ăb Dēlphĭō cĭtŏ cănthărŭm cĭrcŭm.

Cretic Trimeter

is a very rare metre; Spengel indeed throws doubt upon its existence in Plautus. However there are at least six verses, which have a prima facie appearance of belonging to this class: Most. 338, Pseud. 1119, 1277, Pers. 802, Bacch. 622, Cas. ii 1, 7:

> iăm rĕuōrtăr . dī' ēst i' ĭd mĭhĭ
> uĕr' ŭb' īs nōn uĕnĭt nĕc uŏcăt
> ĭd' ămīcāē dăbăm mĕ mĕāē
> lŭdōs mē făcĭtĭs ĭntēllĕgō
> quĭ pătrī rĕddĭd' ōmn' aŭr' ămāns
> ănĭm' ămōrĭsquĕ cāūsā sŭī.

Cretic Dimeter

is found, as a clausula, Most. 320, according to the reading adopted in the text: so too in Pseud. 262, 1122, Pers. 797, Epid. 85—98 (in alternate verses), Curc. 113 b, etc.

The verse $\stackrel{\angle}{\smile} \smile - \stackrel{\angle}{\smile} \smile - \mid \stackrel{\angle}{\smile} \smile \stackrel{\angle}{\smile} \smile \stackrel{\vee}{\smile}$

must be regarded as a combination of a cretic dimeter
and trochaic *tripodia* catalectic (see above p. xxiii); it is
frequently found in the Mostellaria, 108, 113, 116,
133—136, 690—692. Hiatus or *syllaba anceps* is not
uncommon after the cretic dimeter, Most. 342, 710:

ắnd' ắgīs t'. ắnd' hŏmŏ | *ĕbrĭắs prŏbĕ*
pēiŭ' pŏsthắc fŏrĕ | *quắm fŭĭt, mĭhĭ.*

The inversion of this metre

$\stackrel{\angle}{\smile} \smile \stackrel{\angle}{\smile} \smile \stackrel{\vee}{\smile} \mid \stackrel{\angle}{\smile} \smile - \stackrel{\angle}{\smile} \smile \stackrel{\vee}{\smile}$

has not been proved to exist in Plautus. It was assumed
by Ritschl in Most. 315 (with hiatus):

n' ĭll' ŭbĭ fŭĭ, | *ĭnd' ĕffŭgĭ fŏrās*

and is maintained by Lorenz and Bugge in 111 f. (see
critical notes), but is given up by Brix in the third
edition of his Captivi (II 1, 10). On the whole Spengel
seems right in casting doubt upon this metre (see Reformvorschläge pp. 95—102).

The verse $\stackrel{\angle}{\smile} \smile - \stackrel{\angle}{\smile} \smile - \mid \stackrel{\angle}{\smile} \smile \smile \smile -$

must be regarded as belonging to a different category
from the last: but its first half is a cretic dimeter. It is
found Most. 336—341, 344, 693, 696 f., 702, 706 and
in other plays, as Spengel (Reformvorschläge pp. 86—95)
has shown.

ANAPAESTIC METRES.

Anapaestic rhythm is one of the most thorny problems of Plautine criticism, and it would be out of place
to discuss it here. The extreme views on opposite sides
are taken by Ritschl, who avoided the metre so far as
possible and did not admit more licenses than in his
trochaic octonarii, and by C. F. W. Müller, who employed

it as a sort of Home for Incurables[1]. Spengel, in his recent *Reformvorschläge zur Metrik der lyrischen Versarten bei Plautus* (1882) takes up a mean position, which how- ever approaches in some respects to that of Müller.

For the purposes of this edition (anapaests occur only in 887 *a*, 887 *b* + 888, 889, 895 + 896, 901 *a* − 903) the following brief statement may suffice. The basis is the anapaestic *dipodia;* in place of the anapaest, Plautus admits the spondee, the dactyl, the proceleusmatic, and perhaps, in the first foot, the fourth paeon:

$$\acute{\cup}\cup \qquad \cup\cup$$
$$\cup\cup\acute{}\qquad \cup\cup-$$
$$-\qquad -$$
$$\cup\cup\cup\acute{}$$

Prosodical licence transcends the limits observed in iambic and trochaic metres. Synaloephe (e.g. *aurê̄*, *tertiūst* Stich. 25, 30, *gaudiīs* Trin. 1119) is common: cases of shortening of syllables long by position are found which cannot be explained by the laws set forth in Intr. to Capt. A i, ii (i.e. as due to the ictus on a preceding or succeeding short syllable); e.g. *sĕptŭmās* Pseud. 597.

We have the

Anapaestic Tetrameter Acatalectic

in Most. 887 *b* + 888 and 895 + 896. It is composed of four anapaestic *dipodiae*. Half of the anapaestic tetra- meter acat. forms the

Anapaestic Dimeter Acatalectic

which occurs Most. 318, 319, 887 *a*, 889. This metre when catalectic is called the

.

[1] In order to justify the ex- pression which I have used, I would call attention to the con- stancy with which Müller solved troublesome questions of metre by calling the verse anapaestic —a kind of metre in which he permitted all possible licenses. In Persa 497 for instance he scans *aŭfĕrās* as an anapaest!

Paroemiacus

$$\cup \cup - \cup \cup - \cup \cup - \underset{\vee}{\wedge}$$

a verse which is sometimes employed as a *clausula*, and is found Most. 901 *a*—903.   The verse has no regular caesura after the second foot; cf. Men. 360, 366

> *nūnc ĕ' ădīb', ădlŏquăr últrō*
> *nĕquĕ tĭbĭ iămst ūllă mŏr' íntŭs*

and Most. 901 *b* + 902 *a*, 902 *b*: but the caesura is sometimes found: Most. 901 *a*, 903, Men. 355, 368.

ABBREVIATIONS.

A = Codex Ambrosianus (Ambrosian palimpsest).
acc. to = according to.
Acid. = Acidalius.
Ald. = Aldus.
Anal. Plaut. = Analecta Plautina (by Schoell, Goetz and Loewe, 1877).
Ang. = Angelius.

B = Codex Vetus (the figures 1, 2, 3 above the line denote the first, second and third hands respectively).
Bent. = Bentley (many of the readings quoted are derived from MS. notes in the British Museum and Bodleian libraries, published by the present editor in an edition of the Captivi, 1880, and a volume of the *Anecdota Oxoniensia*, 1883).
Bo. = Bothe.
Bossc. = Bosscha.
Br. = Brix.
Büch. = Bücheler (Lat. Decl. = Grundriss der lateinischen Declina-tion, 2nd ed. by Windekilde, 1879).
Bug. = Bugge.

C = Codex Decurtatus.
Cam. = Camerarius.

D = Codex Ursinianus.
del. = delevit.
Diom. = Diomedes.
Dou. = Dousa.

edd. = Ritschl, Ramsay, Lorenz, Bugge, Ussing, (rec. edd. = recent editors, Lorenz, Bugge, Ussing).
Ell. = Robinson Ellis.

F = Codex Lipsiensis.
Fl. = Fleckeisen.

Gepp. = Geppert.
Gron. = Gronovius.

Grut. = Gruter.
Gul. = Gulielmius.
Guy. = Guyet (from the edition of Plautus by M. de Marolles, 1658).
Gz. = Goetz.

Herm. = Hermann.

Intr. to Aul. = Introduction to Aulularia (by Wagner, 2nd Ed.
 1876).
Intr. to Trin. = Introduction to Trinummus (by Wagner, 2nd Ed.
 1875).
Intr. to Capt. = Introduction to Captivi (by E. A. Sonnenschein.
 1880).

Lachm. = Lachmann.
Lamb. = Lambinus.
Lang. = Langen (Beiträge zur Kritik und Erklärung des Plautus,
 1880).
Loew. = Loewe (Prodr. = Prodromus Corporis Glossariorum Latin-
 orum, 1876).
Lor. = Lorenz.

M = BCD.
Madv. = Madvig (the §§ refer to Madvig's Latin Grammar, Engl.
 Trans.).
Müll. = C. F. W. Müller (Plautinische Prosodie, 1869).

Non. = Nonius.

om. = omitted.

Par. = Pareus (Lex. = Lexicon Plautinum, 1634).
Pi. = Pius.
Pist. = Pistoris.
Pyl. = Pylades.

Quich. = Quicherat.

Rams. = Ramsay.
Rl. = Ritschl (Neue Pl. Exc. = Neue Plautinische Excurse; Opusc.
 = Opuscula).

S. = the editor.
Salmas. = Salmasius.
Scal. = Scaliger (Some of the readings of Scaliger are taken from
 MS. notes in his copy of Sambucus, 1566, now in the Bodleian
 [Auct. S. 5. 21]. This copy bears the inscription 'Scaliger
 Heinsiadae, Heinsiades Dikio, Dikius mî').
Schwarzm. = Schwarzmann.
Sciopp. = Scioppius.
Seyff. = O. Seyffert.

Speng. = Spengel (Reformv. = Reformvorschläge zur Metrik der
  lyrischen Versarten bei Plautus, 1882).
Stud. = Studemund.

Turneb. = Turnebus.

Uss. = Ussing.

Vahl. = Vahlen.
Vulg. = Vulgate (1669, 1684).

Wagn. = Wagner (Some of the conjectures quoted on the first
  hundred lines are from a MS. entitled 'Critical notes on the
  Mostellaria': see Preface).

Wei. = Weise.

Z. = Editio Princeps (1472).
...... = a lacuna in MSS. (In statements about A, the number of
  dots = the number of letters which appear to have been lost).

EDITIONS QUOTED.

Aulularia (2nd Ed. 1876) ⎫
Trinummus (2nd Ed. 1875) ⎬ Wagner.
Menaechmi (1878) ⎭
Miles Gloriosus, Tyrrell (1881).
Captivi, E. A. Sonnenschein (1880. In this play the Act, Scene
    and Verse in the scene are cited).
Bacchides ⎫
Persa   ⎬ Ritschl (1848—1854).
Pseudolus ⎭
Amphitruo ⎫
Asinaria   ⎪
Curculio   ⎪
Epidicus   ⎬ Loewe, Goetz, Schoell (1878—1881).
Mercator ⎪
Poenulus ⎪
Stichus   ⎪
Truculentus ⎭
Rudens, Fleckeisen (1850).
Casina   ⎫ Weise (1842, 1847).
Cistellaria ⎭

T. MACCI PLAVTI
MOSTELLARIA

GRAECA ΦΑΣΜΑ

S. P. M.

ARGVMENTVM.

Manumísit emptos súos amores Philolaches,
Omnémque apsente rém suo apsumít patre.
Senem, út reuenit, lúdificatur Tránio:
Terrífica monstra dícit fieri in aédibus,
Et índe pridem *esse* émigratum. intéruenit   5

THE most important MSS. together with Nonius and Priscian
give the form **Mustellaria** as the name of the play. Loewe (Prodr.
p. 282) quotes a gloss '*φάσμα*: *mostellum, mustellum.*' The whole
weight of evidence is in favour of *Mustellaria*. *Mostellaria* appears
only in the acrostich (no very great authority) and in editions since
Pylades.

5. *esse* Rl., om. in M. The question of the admissibility of
hiatus in the principal caesura of the trim. iamb. is one of the
most difficult in Plaut. criticism ; the question of its admissibility
in the 'Argumenta acrosticha' is perhaps more difficult, but not
worth solving. On the whole it appears best to treat these on the
same principles as the text, though we know that they were written
at least a century after the death of Plaut.

The DIDASKALIA is restored
according to Festus pp. 162 and
305 (ed. Müll.), where two verses
of the play are quoted as taken
e Plauti Phasmate.—**Graeca** (sc.
fabula) Φάσμα (sc. *uocatur*) 'the
Greek original is called Φ.': cf.
Intr. p. vii.

1. **manumitto** is an unplautine word ; Plautus always says
manu emittere (975) or *emittere*
(perh. *mittere* Capt. II 3, 48)

manu or (seldom) *emittere* alone
(Pseud. 994, 1183).

On the date and composition
of the Arguments see on Trin.
Arg. (p. 3, 2nd Ed.).—**amores**
'mistress'; so Mil. 1377, Stich.
737 etc. (also in Cicero and
Ovid, *peregrinos addis amores*
Hor. ix 47, cf. Virg. *delicias
domini* (παιδικά) Ecl. II 2) ; in
Pseud. 64 *amores* is used differently, = 'loves', 'toyings'.

1—2

Lucrípeta faenus faénerator póstulans,
Ludósque rursum fít senex: nam mútuom
Accéptum dicit, pígnus emptis aédibus.
Requírit quae sint: aít uicini próxumi.
10 Inspéctat illas: póst se derisúm dolet,
Ab súi sodale gnáti exoratúr tamen.

7. *Ludusque* is a schoolmaster's correction, admitted by most edd. from the time of Saracenus and Pius. *Ludum facere aliquem* is unplautine: early Lat. knows only the phrase *ludos facere aliquem* (*ludos facere alicui* 427 f., with different sense). May not *ludos fieri* be good Lat. for the passive, 'to be made fun of'? So we have it (with the subject however in the accus.) in Pseud. 1168 *adeo donicum ipsus sese ludos fieri senserit;* and Bacch. 1090. To read *ludus* is to make the Argum. more unplautine than it already is. That *ludos facere* is really to be regarded as a sort of compound verb (= *ludere, ludificari*) seems to be shown by Men. 405 *iam amabo desiste ludos facere* (where there is no object) and the phrase *ludos dimittere aliquem* Rud. 791: *facere aliquem ludos* is in fact not parallel to *facere aliquem consulem*. With the passive we may compare *nugas fieri* in Varro (quoted by Nonius 355) *quod si Actaeon occupasset...non nugas (nugasset* MSS.) *spectatoribus in theatro fieret.* It is difficult to believe that *nugas*, which Charisius treats as an indeclinable noun of three genders, was originally anything but accusative of *nugae*.

6. **lucripeta** (from *lucrum* and *peto*, cf. *lucrifuga* Pseud. 1132, *agripeta* Cic.) a substantive formed for the occasion; to be joined as adjective with *faenerator*, cf. *turba incola* Ov. Fast. iii 582, *bellator equus* Virg. G. ii 145. Madv. § 60 c. obs. 3.

7. **mutuom** 'a loan,' here absolutely (generally as adj. with *argentum*), cf. Stich. 255 *Immo tu ut aps te mutuom nobis duis,* Amph. 819 *saltem...sumas mutuom.*

8. **acceptum** 'raised'.—**dicit** 'the slave says': note the change of subject.—**pignus** cf. 978 'part-payment' 'earnest-money', = *arrabo* 648, 1013.

9. **requirit,** ... **ait,** ... **inspectat** (10). The subject changes with each of these verbs.

PERSONAE

TRANIO SERVOS
GRVMIO SERVOS
PHILOLACHES ADVLESCENS
PHILEMATIVM MERETRIX
SCAPHA ANCILLA
CALLIDAMATES ADVLESCENS
DELPHIVM MERETRIX
PVERI
SPHAERIO SERVOS

Tranio is prob. a significant name ("redender name" Lessing, i. e. a name which suggests a type of character, like 'Malaprop', 'Absolute' in Sheridan); but the derivation is not clear. Uss. draws attention to line 1115 *Ne faxis : nam elixus esse quam assus soleo suauior* and hints that *Tranio* may be derived from the name of some fish: Lor. quotes also 1070 *Non ego illi extemplo hamum ostendam, sensim mittam lineam*, and suggests θρανίς, θρανίας 'sword-fish' as the Greek original; others derive from θρᾶνος 'bench' (of rowers) or τρανός (τρανής) 'keenwitted.' For the bye-form *Tranius* see on 560.

Grumio: not to be derived, says Rl., from *gruma* (*groma*), = an instrument for measuring land, but rather from γρυμέα, γρυμαία 'a bag for old clothes' (Opusc. III 307).

It is interesting to observe that the names Tranio and Grumio, which Shakspere employed for two waiting men in the Taming of the Shrew, appear to have been derived direct from the Mostellaria; they do not occur in the Taming of a Shrew (A.D. 1594), the origi-

nal of the Shaksperian drama. Possibly Shaksp. may have seen a representation of the Mostellaria, or he may have read the Italian translation of Geronimo Berardo (1530). Cf. the passage quoted on 18.

Philolaches (φίλος, λάχος 'lot'). Gen. either *Philolachetis* or *Philolachis*, or *Philolachae* (374).

Philematium (φιλημάτιον cf. *meum suauium* as a term of endearment in Poen. I 2, 156) 'Kissy', a common name in later Greek literature.

Scapha is an aged waiting woman. In 213 the MSS. show traces of the word *lena*, applied to Scapha; but, if *lena* be the true reading, it was only used as a term of reproach, and not as a description.

Callidamates is a further (Plautine) development of Καλλιδάμας 'he who subdues by beauty'; cf. δαμάτειρα. The penultimate is short, as Speng. shows (cf. ἀδάμᾰτος, δαμάσίφρων), and not long as Rl. assumed. In 311, 373 we might scan with long or short penult.; cf. 341.

Sphaerio. This name rests on Scyffert's clever emendation in 419, where see crit. note.

THEOPROPIDES SENEX
PEDISEQVI
MISARGYRIDES DANISTA
SIMO SENEX
PHANISCVS ADVORSITOR
ADVORSITOR
LORARII

Observe that the order of persons is that in which they appear in the successive scenes.

Theopropides (θεόπροπος 'prophetic'). This, the true form of the name, was restored by Bergk, and is now generally accepted. Rl., who at first opposed Bergk's view (Most. Praef. xvi), was led afterwards to accept it (Opusc. iii 344). The MSS. have as a rule, **Theuropides** and this form was consequently adopted in all editions down to 1852; it was supposed to be a latinised form of Θεωρωπίδης (Lachm. Lucr. p. 313). But this is a very questionable Greek name, and the MSS. themselves contain traces of a different form: thus A gives **THEO-** (**TEO-**) as the first part of the word in 784, 962, 904 (superscription of scene, Gepp.); in 784, 962 B has **-propides** (-em) as the second part; the forms **Theutropides** (B, 690), **Teutropides** (D², 532) are also found. The form *Theoprŏpides* suits the metre just as well as *Theu-*

rŏpides in all passages except 784, which admits of easy emendation.

Pedisequi, see ii 2.

Danista a latinised form of the Greek δανειστής, cf. *poeta* from ποιητής, *sucophanta* from συκοφάντης, *mastigia* from μαστιγίας etc. It is not certain whether **Misargyrides**, which occurs only in iii 1, 41, is intended as the real name of the money-lender or as a nickname invented for the occasion by Tranio; it means 'hateful son of money', 'Macmoneygrub'; the explanation 'Son of a hater of money', *per ἀντίφρασιν* = 'Son of a miser', suggested by Donatus on Adelph. i 1, 1, and adopted by all recent commentators, is laboured and unnatural. Such compounds appear to assume either active or passive sense: cf. *bucaeda* 884.

Aduorsitor, see on 313.

Lorarii appear v 1.

ACTVS I.

GR. Exi é culina sís foras, mastígia,
qui mi ínter patinas éxhibes argútias.
egrédere, erilis pérnicies, ex aédibus.
ego pól te ruri, sí uiuam, ulciscár probe.
exi ínquam, nidor, é pupina. quíd lates?   5
TR. quid tíbi, malum, hic ante aédis clam*it*átiost?

3. **permicies** CD; but see Gz. and Uss. on Asin. 133.
5. *nidor, e pupina* Löwe (Anal. Plaut. p. 215), **nidore cupinam**
M., *nidor, e culina* (cf. Juv. v 162, Martial I 92 [93], 9) Pyl., Lor[1].,
Bug., *mando, recupito animum* Reid, *nidoricape. nam quid hic
lates?* Rl. (*nidoricape* = κνισσοδιώκτης 'roast meat sniffer').
6. *clamitatio est* Acid., Rl., rec. edd., **clamat iosi** M.

1. Grumio, who is standing
in the street outside the house,
calls to Tranio, who is within.
This is an excellent scene, opening up the whole situation. It
should be compared with the
first scene in the Aulularia.—
Exi 'come out'; cf. *is* 547: in
Aul. I 1 *exi* is 'get out'.—**sis** lit.
'if you please' contr. fr. *si uis*,
as Cic. (or. 45, 154) says. *Sis* is
often used in Plaut. where the
feeling is the reverse of polite,
cf. 569 *Abi sis, belua*, Aul. 46
and note: in effect *sis* = 'confound you'.
2. **argutias** 'sharpness'.
4. **si uiuam** (fut.) 'if I live'
(i.e. if I shall live); *si uiuo*
1067 is rather different; see

note.—**probe** strengthens the
verb (*ulciscar probe*, also Poen.
v 4, 58), 'I will revenge myself
finely', cf. 342, 473, 736, 870,
1067, 1108, 1179.
5. "**nidor** et **pupina** contemp-
tui dicta sunt: *nidor* = fetor
('stench'); *pupina* uolgariter
pro *popina*, idque uocabulum
uilem ac sordidam coquinam
significat; cf. Vaticani 1468
glossam 'gurgustium: pupinam
sordidam, uel ubi porci includun-
tur'" Löwe Anal. Plaut. p. 215.
6. **malum** 'interiectio sto-
machantis' Lamb. (**quid malum**
'Why the mischief?'). It is found
only in questions cf. 34, 368, Aul.
426, Capt. 531, Men. 390, Mil.
446.—(**quid**) **tibi clamitatio est?**

an rúri censes te ésse? apscede ab aédibus.
abi rús: abi dierécte. apscede ab iánua.
9, 10 cm: hocíne uolebas? GR. périi. quor me uérb-
                                          cras?
TR. quia tú uis. GR. patiar. sine modo aducniát
                                       senex:

8. Since Rl. edited the Trinummus it has been usual to regard *dierectus* (*dierecte* etc.) as trisyllabic by synizesis (see Brix on Trin. II 4, 56): but Palmer (Hermathena No. x, 1884) has shown that in at least 5 of the 13 passages in which it occurs in Plaut. it is (acc. to MS. reading) four syllables with the two first long (*dïĕrectus*): Bacch. IV 1, 8, Merc. I 2, 72, Men. II 3, 87, Poen. I 2, 134, Rud. IV 4, 126; so too in Varro Eumenides (quoted by Nonius) *Apage in dierectum á domo nostra istam insanitátem*: cf. Most. 850.
   9. *Em* Br., Bug., Uss., Lor²., *En* BD (In C), Rl., Lor¹.
   11. *tu uis* Cam., Rl., Lor., Bug., **tui uis** D, **uiuis** B, Uss., **uiuus** C. Rl. remarks '*exspectes potius* lubitumst *uel* meritu's': Uss.

lit. 'what is your bawling?' = *quid* (*quor*) *clamites*? 'what business have you to bawl?' This use of the verbal subst. in -*io*, esp. in angry questions, is a very favourite idiom in Plaut.; cf. 377 and see further on 34.
   8. **dierecte.** The generally accepted explanation of this difficult Plautine word is that it is the vocative of a participle, derived from *di* (=*dis*) and *erectus* = lit. 'raised up asunder' i.e. 'stretched on the cross (or *patibulum*)'; so Brix on Trin. 457, Lor. on Most. 850, Rams. on Most. I. 1, 8. Nonius (followed by Lamb.) says '*Dierecti dicti crucifixi quasi ad diem erecti*'; to him the word suggested the cross, though his derivation from *diem* is absurd. Paul. Diaconus (p. 69 ed. Müll.) '*Dierectum dicebant per ἀντίφρασιν, uolentes significare malum diem*' which is still more absurd. It is to be remarked that in all passages except two *dierecte, dierectus* (nom.), *die-*

recta, are connected with a verb of motion; thus *abi dierecte* Most. 850 (cf. Trin. 457), *abin dierectus* Merc. 756 (cf. Cas. I. 15), *i dierecta* Rud. IV 4, 126, *i dierectum cor meum* Capt. III 4, 103 (emended), *recede hinc dierecte* Bacch. IV 1, 7; in one passage we find the accusative after *ducere, ducit lembum dierectum nauis praedatoria* Men. 442; in another, we have *lien dierectus est* Curc. 240. (Perh. here we should read διαρρηκτός, 'my spleen is burst'.) The true origin of *dierectus* is still involved in some obscurity; it may also be doubted whether *dierecte* is not an adv., cf. *macte* (*uirtute esto)*: the instances quoted above show that in effect *dierecte, dierectus* are always adverbial.
   9. **em** (different from *hem*) is another form of the demonstrative particle *en*, cf. 297, 314, 333, 804, 1180, 1144. Trans. 'take that' (beating him).
   11. **quia tu uis** 'because it's

sine módo ucnire sáluom, qucm apsentém comcs.
TR. nec uéri simile lóqucre nec ucrúm, frutex,
comésse quemquam ut quísquam apsentcm póssiet.
GR. tu urbánus uero scúrra, deliciaé popli,   15

defends *uiuis* (perh. 'because you're not yet dead': cf. Cas. II
3, 11). But *uolebas* (10) and *patiar* (11) support *uis*.
    12. *Ne modo* Non.   *saluo(u)m* Non., edd., saluo(u)s M.
Note the change of accent in *sine módo* as compared with *sine modo*
of 11, and see Herm. De R. Bentleio eiusque edit. Terentii p. xxx :
"*ubi repetiti uerbi uel maior est uel minor uis, uel quocumque
denique modo alia ratio, etiam pronuntiari debet aliter*". Here
the emphasis of the first clause lies on *aduenit*, of the second on
saluom. But even apart from any '*alia ratio*', we find the accent
constantly varied, when a word is repeated in the same or
following verse. Thus we have 168 *lepidis...lépida*, 170 *lepidást*,
171 *lépide*, 181 *uérum...uerúm*, Aul. 412 *ténẽ tenế*, 647 *mánẽ manế*,
Men. 281 f. *párasitúm...parasitum*, 346 f. *récte...rectẽ...récte*, Amph.
530 *actútum...actutúm*. Analogously in the hexameter, e.g. Ovid
Met. XIII 607 *Et primo similis uolucri mox uera uolúcris*, VI 246
Ingemuere simúl, simul incuruata dolore.
    13. *rupex* ('clown') Guy., Rl. Bug., Uss. Lor²., put a : or . at
end of this line, and a ? at the end of next.
    14. *possiet* Pyl., posset B¹C, posse[t] B², possit D.

your own wish': i.e. why do you
not go away? For the sense cf.
Rud. 873, 4.
    12. quem comes 'whose sub-
stance you are devouring' (οὗ τὴν
οὐσίαν κατεσθίεις), cf. Pseud. IV
7, 24 *iamne illum comessurus
es?*—In the verb *edo* and its compounds (*comedo* etc.) Plaut. and
Ter. use the contracted forms
exclusively; thus *comẽs = comẽdis*
(*ẽs = ẽde* Cas. II 3, 34, Mil. III
1, 81, Pseud. I 2, 7), *comest =
comedit* Most. 559, Trin. 250,
Truc. 593, *estis (comestis)=edi-
tis (comeditis*) Most. 63, Truc.
155, *este = edite* Most. 65, *esse
(comesse) = ẽdere (comedere)* 14,
889, Capt. 463 (?), Trin. II. 1, 25.
Men. 627 (where correct note of
Wagn.), 918, 919; in the passive
we have *estur = ẽditur* Most. 235,

Mil. 24, Poen. IV. 2, 13. These
forms arise by dropping the
connecting vowel and changing
the dental of the root into *s*.
The forms *ẽdim, ẽdis, ẽdit* etc.
are always subjunctive in Plaut.
(equiv. to *edam* etc.); prob. it was
the only form of the subj. which
he employed (cf. however Poen.
III. 1, 31, Stich. 554).
    13. uerisimile loquere....ut.
Bug. by putting a colon at *frutex*
(see crit. note) makes the next
line an independent question
('how could any one'). But
perh. *uerisimile loquere ut = uerisimile est ut*, the phrase re-
producing the lax idiom of
every-day speech: ' 'Tis not
likely...what you talk, that any
fellow could etc.'
    15. uero, like *ain?*, expresses

rus míhi tu obiectas? sánc hoc credo, Tránio,
quod te ín pistrinum scis actutum trádier.
cis hércle paucas témpestates, Tránio,
augébis ruri númcrum, genus ferrátile;

16.   hoc B², Bug., om. by B¹CD, Rl., Rams., Lor., Uss.
17.   *scis* FZ, edd., **sis** M.

astonishment, 'What!'. For its
position third in the sentence cf.
Aul. Prol. 18; in Cas. ii 5, 5 it
stands in the fourth place.—
urbanus scurra 'city lounger'
'town-bred idler (loafer)'. The
word *scurra*, as used by Plaut.,
is defined Trin. 202 (*urbani ad-
sidui ciues quos scurras uocant*),
where see note.—**deliciae popli**
(=*populi*) 'darling of the popu-
lace' 'minion of the canaille',
cf. Othello i 2, 68 'the wealthy
curled darlings of our nation':
for *populus* =' the lower orders'
cf. *prostibulum popli* Aul. 283,
decus popli Asin. 655, and Livy
i 17, 8, ii 27, 5 and 12 *consilio
magis principum quam populi*
(almost = *plebis*) *clamore*. In
Curc. 29 *populus* =' the public',
' the general'.
16.   **mihi tu** are both emphatic.—**hoc** (abl.)...**quod** 'for
the reason that', cf. 51 and
Rud. 388 *hoc sese excruciat
animi, quia* etc., Pseud. iii 2,
33 *hoc...quom* (cf. iii 2, 18).
—**credo** is parenthetical; 'I
think'.
17.   **tradier** (=*tradi*). Plaut.
frequently uses the present for
the future infinitive (here *tra-
ditum iri*) after the verbs *dico,
promitto* etc.; see 633, 1084,
1087, 1132, Asin. 366 *dixit operam se dare*, 377 *promitto hostire*,
442 *aibat reddere*, 604 *minatur
sese abire*, Curc. 597 *nego me*

dicere, Pers. 401 *iuratus est se
dare*.—**in pistrinum tradier** 'to
be put to work in the mill', i.e.
in the country. This form of
labour, like that in the stone
quarries (cf. Capt. iii 5, 63—68),
was considered almost to amount
to torture.
18.   **cis** here of time; the only
other instances are Truc. 348,
Merc. 158 (emended).—**tempestates** here perhaps 'months',
but the time is marked as indefinite: in Cic. Divin. i 25 *tempestas* = a day, in Livy i 5, 2
multis ante tempestatibus = many
years before, in Lucr. i 179
tempestates = the seasons.—**Tranio**. There is something threatening in the repetition of the
name; so 'Φίλιππος' in Demosthenes. Cf. the *entreating* ef-
fects in Taming of the Shrew i 1
' Tranio, I burn, I pine, I perish,
Tranio. | Counsel me Tranio;
for I know thou can'st : | Assist
me, Tranio, for I know thou
wilt'.
19.   **augebis** 'add one more
to', cf. Virg. Aen. vii 211.—
ruri numerum, genus ferratile
'the people in the country, the
gang that works in irons' (cf.
ferratus Bacch. 781); *genus ferr.*
is governed by *augebis*, but also
forms a loose apposition to *numerum*. Strictly speaking, a
dat. is required after *augebis
numerum*.

nunc, dúm tibi lubet licétque, pota, pérdc rem, 20
corrúmpe erilem *spém*, adulcscentcm óptumum :
diés noctisque bíbite, pergraecámini :
amícas cmite, líberate : páscite
parasítos : opsonáte pollucíbiliter.
haecínc mandauit tíbi, quom peregre hinc ít, senex? 25
hocíuc modo hic rem cúratam offendét suam ?
hocínc boni esse offícium scrui exístumas,   -
ut erí sui corrúmpat et rem et fílium ?
nam ego illúm corruptum dúco, quom his factís
studet.

20. *tibi lubct*, a proccleusmatic, representing an iambus
(◡◡◡◡), see Intr. p. xvi. Guy., Rl. delete *tibi*. On *lŭbĕt l.* sec Intr.
to Capt. A (i)., Intr. to Aul. p. xxxiv.
21. *spem* Ell., om. in M, *erilem filium adulcscentulum* Bug.;
Rl. reads *erilem nostrum adulescentem optumum*, suggesting also (in
crit. note) that *ad. opt.* may be a gloss, which view Lor. adopts.
25. *it* Bo., edd., *iit* M.

22. **pergraecamini** 'play the
Grcck', 'be merry': cf. the
gloss in Paul. Fest. 215 *epulis
ct potationibus inseruite*. We
have the same word again 64,
960, and in other plays. It
expresses the contempt of the
Roman for the vices of the
typical Grcek of later times :
cf. Ben Jonson, The Fox iii 8
Let's die like Romans,
Since we have lived like Gre-
cians.
(quoted by Thornton).
In Horacc (Sat. ii 2, 11) *grae-
cari* is 'to live a life of effemi-
natc ease'. Strictly, of course,
the expression is impossible
in the mouth of a Greek; but
it is not uncommon to find the
persons of the *comoedia palliata*
talking like Romans: cf. on 56.
25. **peregre** 'abroad' with
sense of motion *towards;* so

976 ; On the other meanings of
peregre sec note on Capt. i 2,
64 and cf. Most. 374, 611, etc.
('from abroad').—*it*. For the
hist. present in Plaut. after
quom, postquam etc., see on
156.
26. **curatam** cf. 107 *bonae
quom curantur male.*
29. **quom his factis studet**
'now that he gocs in for this
sort of thing': *quom*, whether
temporal or causal regularly
takes the indic. in Plaut. Cf.
107, 149, 168, 251, 432, 588,
695, 858, 1128, 1156, and see
Lübbert (Die Syntax von *Quom*,
1870), who shows that wherever
the subj. is found it has some
potential, deliberative or conditional force, or else results from
subordination, and is not due
to *quom:* cf. on 149.

30 quo némo adaeque iúuentute ex omni Áttica
antehác est habitus párcus nec magis cóntinens,
is núnc in aliam pártem palmam póssidet—
uirtúte id factum túa et magisterió tuo.

30. *iŭuĕntute;* see Intr. to Capt. A (i), Intr. to Aul. p. xliv.
and cf. *pŏtĕstatem* Capt. v 1, 13, *sătĕllites* Trin. 833, *simĭllumae*
Asin. 241. (We have the similar phenomenon *iŭuĕntŭte* in Amph.
154, Curc. 38.) Or, as Lor. says, *iuuentute* may become trisyllabic,
by synizesis of the first two syllables (*iŭntute*), just as in Mil.
1359, Rud. 542 *obliuiscendi*, *diuitias* must be pronounced (and perh.
should be written) *oblĭscendi, dĭtias ;* cf. Aul. 809 (Gz.), and see
Intr. to Capt. C. In cases like this it is impossible to dogmatize ;
for synizesis of two vowels separated by *u* is a familiar phenomenon
in Latin (cf. *iunior, prudens, noram, consueram*); still, in view of
the frequency of such cases as those quoted Intr. to Capt. A (i),
(ii), Intr. to Aul. p. xliv, which can only be explained as due to
the influence of the accent, it seems better here to write *iŭuentute*
and to regard it as a case of the same law.

31. *Antehac* is dissyllabic, by synizesis ; so 731, 933. This
word may be added, as an instance, in Intr. to Capt. C, Intr. to
Aul. p. lix.—*măgĭ' cónt.,* see Intr. to Aul. pp. xxxi f., Intr. to
Capt. A (ii) : (for *măgĭ'* cf. 831).

33. So M, Rams., Uss. ; Lor.[2] omits et without reason ; Rl.,

30. quo nemo etc. 'one who
ere this hadn't his equal for
thrift or his superior in so-
briety '.—**adaeque** is a specially
Plautine word (=*aeque*), used
only in negative sentences; cf.
Cist. I 1, 57 *neque munda adaeque es ut soles*, Capt. v 4, 2
*nulla adaequest Accheruns atque
ubi ego fui in lapicidinis.* In
the text the second member of
the comparison is expressed by
the ablative (*quo*='as he '), cf.
Cas. III, 5, 45 *neque est neque
fuit me senex quisquam amator
adaeque miser* (*me*='as I'); for
the abl. after *aeque* cf. Amph.
293 *nullus hoc metuculosus aeque*,
and Curc. 141. This phrase
appears strange on first acquaintance, but is really the same
phenomenon as the abl. after a
comparative ; both comp. and
adaeque may be followed by *quam*
(cf. Stich. 274, 217) and *therefore* by the abl. (which expresses
the *standard* in both cases). In
Capt. IV 2, 48 (where see note)
and Merc. 335, we have a
comparative combined with
adaeque, aeque (*adaeque fortu-
natior, miserior aeque*) and followed by the abl.

32. Note the alliteration and
cf. 111, 143, 164 f., 245 (pro-
nounce *Pilolakes*), 312, 353, 536,
550, 963, 976, 1171. For alli-
terations with other letters see
notes on 41, 135, 170, 218, 352,
733.—**in aliam partem p. p.**
'bears the palm for the very
opposite '.

33. uirtute tua 'thanks to
you', 'owing to you'; so Truc.

TR. quid tíbi, malum, me, aut quíd ego agam, cu-
                rátiost?
an rúri quaeso nón sunt quos curés boues?   35
lubét potare, amáre, scorta dúcere:
mei térgi facio haec, nón tui fidúcia.

in accordance with his dictum in Trin. Prolegg. p. cix 'omissionem uerbi *est* et *es* omnino esse alienam [a sermone Plautino],' (to which rule however he admitted some exceptions p. cxi, Opusc. ii pp. 608—618) wrote *tuast*, *mag.*, and Bug. inserts *est* after *factum*: see explan. note.

741 *de eo nunc bene sunt tua uirtute* and cf. Most. 173 *uirtute formae*, Aul. 164 (note) *uirtute deum*, Trin. 355, 643, Mil. 676. *Virtute* is not to be taken εἰρωνικῶς as Lamb. says it may be.—**factum.** This seems to be one of those sentences of a semi-interjectional character, in which the usage of Plaut. was to *omit* the verb substantive; (trans. 'all this owing to you and your tutoring'); cf. 207 *bene hercle factum* 'one to me!' 'right I was', Persa 774 *tua factum opera* 'all owing to you!' Bacch. 295 *sapienter factum a nobis* 'a sensible thing to do!' Trin. 429 *factum* 'too true!' Stich. 375 *nimis factum bene* 'capital!' cf. Pseud. 361, 1099; so Capt. i 2, 67 *facete dictum* 'very good!' In such cases as Trin. 127, where *factum* is in reply to the question *dedisti argentum?* the omission of *est* gives a certain rhetorical colouring ('I did', 'even so') to the answer. For other cases of omission of *est* see on Most. 279.
    34. **malum** cf. 6.—**quid me curatiost.** In Plautus phrases formed of *esse* and a verbal sub-stantive in -*io* are equiv. to a simple verb. So *tua indicatiost* Pers. 586 = *tibi indicandum est*: here *quid curatio est = quor cures* (dub. subj.) and is transi-tive, governing *me* and *quid ego agam*. The dative represents the subject of the clause. Thus we have *quid hanc tibi digito tactiost?* 'what right have you to lay a finger upon this woman?' Poen. v 5, 29: simi-larly with dat. of 1st person *Quid mihi scelesto tibi erat auscultatio?* 'what did I want to listen to you for, confounded fool that I was?' Rud. 502: see note on 6, Aul. 420, and cf. Trin. 709.
    36. **ducere** 'keep company with'.
    37. **mei tergi fiducia** 'at the peril of', 'on the responsibility of', cf. Bacch. 752 *mea fiducia* ('on my own responsibility') *opus conduxi, et meo periculo* ('at my own peril') *rem gero. Fiduciam accipere* is a legal phrase, meaning 'to accept security' (for payment), e.g. in Cic. Pro Fl. 21; *fiducia* is that which is pledged or mortgaged (ὑποθήκη). Here then there is strictly a legal metaphor; 'my

GR. quam cónfidenter lóquitur! fu! TR. at te Iúppiter
dique ómnes perdant: óboluisti *tu* álium
40 germána inluuies, stércus, hircus, hára sui*s*,
cacnó κοπρῶν commícte. GR. quid uis fíeri?

38. fue BD, fut C, *Pfui* Uss.—Rl. is responsible for transfer-
ring the word to the next line (*fu, oboluisti:* trans. 'faugh'); he is
followed by Gz. and Loew. who read *fufae oboluisti* (*fufae=fu*),
and Lor. Uss. seems quite right in following M. The ejacu-
lation is necessary in the mouth of Grum. to explain the impreca-
tion of Tran.; besides Rl.'s reading creates a difficulty about the
perfect *oboluisti*, (not removed by Lor.); it would have to be
equivalent to a present.

39.   I have inserted *tu* (cf. note of Rl.) to remove the hiatus
after *oboluisti*. Lamb. read *perduint* with same object; but this
destroys the caesura. We might also read *oboluisti mi alium;*
cf. for dat. Men. 384, Aul. 214 (?).

40.   *stercus* Leo, **rusticus** M ('quod interpretis esse certum est'
Rl.). Rl. proposed *rus merum*, (cf. Truc. 269), which however
is not very good metre; Usener *rullus* 'vagabond' ἀγύρτης,
(restored also Pers. 169), and this Bug. adopts; Wagn. *rus stips*
(but doubtfully: *stips=stipes*, cf. Petron. 43, 5), Speng. *rustica*
(agreeing with *inluuies*); Ell. *ruscus*, cf. Ball. Gloss. '*rusticus* (i.e.
ruscus another form of *ruscum*): *genus herbi aut uirgulti*' and Virg.
Ecl. vii 42; Reid *rudus*, cf. Colum. x. 81 ff.

41.   *caeno κοπρῶν commicte* Leo, **canem** (-æm) **capram** (-an)
commixtam M, *canes capro commixta* Scal., Rl., and rec. edd.
fieri. For the quantity cf. Intr. to Capt. A (v).

back is the security which I
give to Fate in this matter'.
38. **quam confidenter** 'with
what assurance'.—**fu**, a sort of
whistle 'whew!', or='pshaw!'
so in Ter. Adel. 412, where it is
generally spelt *phy* acc. to *A*.
(cf. Diom. i p. 412, who says
'ironiam significat', Prisc. xv
7, 41 p. 1024). In Pseud. 1294,
where *B* has *Pfui*, we should
prob. give the word to Pseud.
reading PSEUD. *Fu!* SI. *I in
malam crucem!* (as Speng. Reformv. p. 80 suggests); the
sound there appears to be that
of a man belching.
39. **oboluisti tu alium** 'your

breath reeks of garlic': for the
accus. (*alium*) cf. 42, 278, Men.
170 and Madv. § 223 b. The
perfect seems to refer to the
action which accompanied *fu!*
(38): cf. note on 89 *b*.
40. **germana inluuies** 'you
proper filth' ('essence of filth'
'unmitigated filth'), cf. Lear
iv 2 'Proper deformity seems
not in the fiend So horrid as in
woman'.—**hara suis**, 'you pig-
sty'.
41. **commicte** from *com-
mingo* cf. Pers. 407 *Commictum
caeno stercilinum publicum.*
Note the alliteration *c. k. c.* and
cf. 55, 201, 311 f., 986, 1065,

non ómnes possunt ólerc unguenta exótica,
si tu oles, neque superius † accumbere   43, 44
neque tám facetis, quám tu uiuis, uíctibus   45
* * * * * *

tu tíbi istos habeas túrtures, piscís, auis :   47
sine me áliato fúngi fortunás meas.
tu fórtunatu's, égo miser : patiúnda sunt.

43, 44. **superios** M, i.c. *superius* (defended by Gandino),
superior Rl., Lor.[1], *superbe* Bug. The verse is corrupt: B alone
has an attempt to fill the lacuna, **quam erus** (approved by Bent.),
out of which Rl. made *cum ero* ('by the side of Master'). Leo reads
lubidost cum ero, Reid *cupediis* cf. Stich. 712.
45. A line seems to have been lost here, as Rl. supposes; Pyl.,
Bo. propose *uiuis uiuere*, Uss. *uiuere uictibus*, Leo *uiuo uictibus*,
in order to complete the sense in 45.
47. *tib' istos*, see Intr. to Capt. A (i), (ii) and cf. Most. 58, 70,
252, 372, 516, 851, 939, 961, 988, &c. It would also be possible to
write the word *stos* (as Lor.[1]), and in 58 and 70 *stuc;* cf. Intr. to
Capt. (v).
48. *alliato* F, Turneb., Rams., **aleato** M, *alliatum* Saracenus,
followed by Rl., rec. edd. (*aliatum*); Gronov. has *alliato*, without *me*.
49. *fortunatu's* Rl., and rec. edd. (*fortunatus's* Uss.), **fortunatus** M : cf. on 33.   **TR. patiunda sunt** D²F.

1114 and note on 32.—**quid uis
fieri?** 'que voulez-vous?' 'what
would you have?' The phrase
occurs also in Aul. 734 ('what
would you have?'), Amph. 702.
42. **olĕre.** Plautus uses
sometimes *olĕre*, sometimes
olĕre, as in next line: in 268
we have the pres. subj. *olant*
cf. 278, Poen. 268, Mil. 41 (71)
with Most. 273, 277: cf. note
on 836.
43. Gandino trans. **superius**
'in luogo elevato' 'in a place
of honour', which must also be
the sense of Rl.'s *superior :* but
see crit. note.
45. **facetis uictibus** 'dainty
fare' 'choice meats'. For *uictibus* cf. Mil. 739; in Bacch.
1181 we have it opposed to *uino*
and *unguentis:* cf. Most. 730.
For the sense of *facetis* ('dainty')

cf. Hor. Sat. ı 10, 44, and
facete Stich. 271. The sense
'witty' is more common in
Plaut.
48. **aliato** abl. of manner,
'on a garlic salad' (or perh.
'cibo alio condito' as Lamb.
says). If we read *aliatum*, it is
best to trans. as an adj. (formed
like *unguentatus*, *patibulatus* 56)
agreeing with *me*, lit. 'covered
with garlic' i.e. 'smelling of garlic'.—**fortunas** : for accus. after
fungi see note on Trin. 1 (*fungi*
=*pati*, 'to resign myself'). *For-
tunae* (pl.) in Plaut. never has
the sense of 'riches' 'posses-
sions', so common in Cic., but
always that of 'fate' 'destiny';
cf. Mil. 125 *conqueritur mulier
mecum fortunas suas*, Rud. 523,
etc.
49. **fortunatu's** = *fortunatus*

50 meúm bonum me, té tuom mantát malum.
TR. quasi ínuidere míhi hoc uidere, Grúmio,
quia míhi benest et tíbi malest. digníssumumst.
decét me amare et té bubulcitárier,
me uíctitare púlcre, te miserís modis.
55 GR. o cárnuficium críbrum, quod credó fore :
ita té forabunt pátibulatum pér uias

50. mantat Bent. (approved by Minton Warren), maneat M.
55. carnuficium Pyl., Rl., and rec. edd., carnificum M,
carnificinum Scal., Cam., Lamb., Bent.

es cf. 176, 194 etc.—patiunda sunt, 'amen', 'things must be endured', =patiundum est. The same phrase occurs Amph. 945; Plaut. is fond of the plural in some expressions in which the singular might also stand; thus mira sunt ni Capt. iv 2, 25 (=mirum est ni ibid. 44), Trin. 661, Amph. 283, palam istaec fiunt te me odisse Merc. 764 : cf. too note on 54.

51. quasi etc. a colloquial phrase, 'you seem to kind of envy me'.—hoc...quia, see note on 16.—quia (52)=quod (after a 'verbum affectus'), see on Capt. i 2, 44, and on Trin. 290 (cf. too Aul. 415).

52. dignissumumst, ἀξιώ-τατόν ἐστι, 'it is quite as it should be'. Here we have the sing.: cf. on 49.

54. miseris modis cf. in-dignis modis 1033, multimodis (=multis modis) 785; cf. also 1146. A similar phrase is pes-sumis exemplis 192 (cf. on 1040). See note on 49.

55. carnificium, gen. pl. for carnificum which Plaut. else-where employs (Asin. 311): cf. artificium, iudicium, supplicium, aruspicium, which are well at-tested by MSS. or inscriptions, though not so common as the forms in -um. It would also be possible to take carnificium as an adj.; cf. meretricius 190. carn. cribrum 'you sieve of car-rion' lit. 'of the executioners'; i.e. the executioner shall turn you into a sieve, by 'perforating your hide' (te forabunt 56).—quod credo fore, 'as I believe you will be'. Note the omission of the subject accus. (te) before fore, a favourite Plaut. construc-tion. Sometimes, as in 1079 quia negat nouisse uos, the subj. of the infin. is the same as the subj. of the governing clause (=se nouisse), cf. 633, 1024 : sometimes, as in the present passage, they are different : (ego) credo (te) fore. So in 205, 272, 278, 420 f., 752, 821, 954, 989, 1139.

56. ita 'so thoroughly', cf. 213, 565, 656, 685, 996.—patibu-latum 'fixed (nailed) to the cross beam (gibbet)'. The patibulum [pateo] was a piece of wood, fixed, like a milkman's yoke, over the shoulders of the slave to be punished : to this his arms were fastened, cf. Mil. 360 dispessis manibus patibulum quom habebis

stimulís *carnuflces* si húc senex reuénerit.
TR. qui scís, an tibi istuc éueniat prius quám mihi?
GR. quia númquam merui: tú meruisti et núnc
                                               mercs.
TR. orátionis ópcram conpendí face,   60
nisi té mala re mágna mactarí cupis.

. 57. *carnuflces* Leo, *si huc senex reuenerit* S. (cf. Men 880),
stimulis (stimuliis B¹) **si huc reueniat senex** M, giving an incomplete line. *Stimuleis terebris, huc si* Rl., Lor., Bug. (*terebra* =
'gimlet', i.e. 'goad', cf. Men. 951 *fodiam stimulis*. Reading thus,
we must supply a subject to *forabunt*, 'they will perforate'),
Stimuleis stimulis, huc si Ell., *Stimulatum stimulis, huc si* Speng.
   58. *tib' istuc*, cf. on 47 (*stuc* Lor.¹).

and note on *dierecte* 8. To be
fastened to the *patibulum* was
to undergo the first stage of
crucifixion: bearing it the condemned slave was driven, sometimes with whips or goads (*stimulis* 57), through the streets
to the place of execution 'outside the city wall' (*extra por-
tam* Mil. 359, Pseud. 331; cf.
ἔξω τῆς πύλης Hebrews XIII 12),
and there hauled up and fastened, by nails driven through
the feet, to an upright pole
called *palus, stipes* or *crux*.
The *patibulum* thus formed the
cross beam of the *crux*. The
following quotation from Nonius
221, 12 *Patibulum ferat per
urbem, deinde affigatur cruci*
shows clearly what the process
was: see Marquardt, Römische
Privalterthümer v 1, 193 f.—
It should be observed that this
is one of those passages in which
Plaut. describes *Roman* manners
and customs, though the scene
is laid in Greece; cf. on 22 and
on Capt. I 1, 22. Greek masters
did not treat their slaves in this
way.
   58. **qui** old abl. = *quomodo*

(here interrogative): cf. Capt.
Prol. 28, I 1, 33, Trin. 14, in
which places it is relative.
   60. **orationis operam conpendi face** 'spare yourself the
labour of a speech', cf. Pseud.
1141 *operam fac conpendi quae-
rere* 'save yourself the trouble
of asking'; for **operam** cf. Bacch.
994 *aurium operam tibi dico*
'I promise you the service of
my ears' (i.e. to listen), and
the common phrase, *operam
dare* 'to be at the service of'.
For **conpendi face** cf. on Capt.
v 2, 12 : **face** is a common form
of the imperative in Plaut. cf.
Aul. 151, Trin. 800, Men. 946;
but *fac* is also found e.g. Pseud.
1141, Trin. 1008; so *dice* Capt.
II 2, 109, *dic* Truc. 941; *duce*
Most. 324, 794, 843, Trin. 384,
duc Aul. 360, Amph. 854.
   61. **mala re magna mactari**
'to be visited with a fine fla-
gellation'. Note the alliteration, and cf. 352, Aul. 479. *Malo
et damno mactare* with acc. of object 'to inflict misery and loss
upon' occurs also Aul. 527: *te
macto infortunio* 'I invoke a
mischief upon you' Trin. 993.

18   MOSTELLARIA.   [I. 1. 59—64.

Gr. eruóm daturin' éstis, bubus quód feram?
dare sí potestis, ágite, porro pérgite,
quoniam óccepistis: bíbite, pergraccámini,
65 este, écfercite uós, saginam caédite.
Tr. tace átque abi rus: ego íre in Piraeúm uolo,
in uésperum paráre piscatúm mihi.

    62. *daturin'* Pyl., edd., **daturi** M.
    63. *Dare si potestis* S., **Data** (-te) **es in(h)onestis** (-te) M, *Date aes, si non est* (sc. *eruom*) Uss. (after Cam.), *Date, si non estis* (= *editis*, sc. *eruom*) Rl., Bug.; Lor. marks the passage as corrupt. The difficulty of the transition to *agite, porro pergite*, which Rl. tried to meet by reading *ceterum* (i.e. 'for the rest') *agite pergite*, I have attempted to obviate by connecting the first part of the line with the second: *dare* would be very like *date* in M.
    65. *effercite* Cam., edd., **ec feri(u)te** M. The genuineness of *saginam caedite* is open to doubt. Scal. suggested *saginam tendite* (after Ausonius Ephemeris 7 *nimiaque tendis mole saginam*), Rl. *sagina condite*, Madv. *ecfercite uos sagina, caedite*.
    66. *abi rus:* cf. 8 and Intr. to Capt. A (ii).

Amph. 1034, Ter. Phorm. 1028. On **mala res** 'punishment' cf. 700, 858, 867, Aul. 479, Trin. 63.
    62. Here Grumio states the real object for which he has come: for **daturin' estis** cf. 604.
    63. The sense is: 'if you can satisfy my legitimate demands, then I give you leave to ruin yourselves as much as you like': cf. 69, where Tr. affects surprise that Gr. is not silenced by his promise to send the *eruom*. — **porro pergite**, 'go ahead', cf. 963, Asin. 472 *perge porro*.
    65. **este**, cf. on 14.—**saginam** 'provender'. This word means (i) 'the process of fattening', 'cramming', cf. 236, Trin. 722, Mil. 845, Cic. pro Flacc. vii 17, (ii) 'food' e.g. *gladiatoria sagina*, Tac. Hist. ii 88, and cannot mean 'ipsum animal sagina pinguefactum' (Forc.).—**caedite**, not 'kill', as Forc. thought, but prob. 'de-

vour': similar verbs are sometimes used to describe the havoc made by a hungry man among the eatables: e. g. Stich. 554 *meum ne contruncent cibum*, Hor. Epist. i 12, 21 *seu porrum et caepe trucidas*. Goetz compares the word *cibicida* 'a bread consumer' used by Lucilius, and also Trin. 741 *ut inimici bona istic caedant*. The phrase **caedere saginam** seems to have been current: it occurs at any rate in Symmachus Epist. i 7 *Nam comitibus uestris utpote sobriis caedundae saginae cura posterior est* ('give less thought to gorging'), which passage may however be an imitation of Plaut.
    66. **in Piraeum**, see on Trin. 1103.
    67. **uesperum** 'the evening meal', cf. 700 and Mil. 995, Rud. 181.—**parare** = *paratum* ('in order to prepare'), see on Trin. 1015.—**piscatum** 'fish', so 730; prop. 'fishing'.

eruóm tibi aliquis crás faxo ad uillam ádferat.
quid est quód tu me nunc óptucre, fúrcifer?
GR. pol tíbi istuc credo nómen actutúm forc.   70
TR. dum intérea sic sit, ístuc 'actutúm' sino.
GR. itanést? sed unum hoc scíto: nimio célerius
uenit quód molest*umst*, quam íllud quod cupidé
petas.

69. This line might also be scanned *Quid ést, quod tu me
núnc optuére, fúrcifer?* In this case *optuére* will be 3rd conj., cf.
837, 836, 838, 840.
70. *tib' ístuc*, cf. on 47 (*stuc* Lor.[1]).
72. *Itanest?* Speng., Lang. (or *Itane?*), **Ita est** M, Rams., Uss.
(but this hardly makes sense here), *Ita fit* Rl.
73. *Venit quod molestumst* Bent., Lor.[2], **Venire quod moleste** M,

68. **faxo adferat**=*faciam ut
adferat:* cf. 1133 and note on
Trin. 60, 62; Madv. § 115 f.,
§ 372 obs. 4.
69. **quid est quod...optuere**
'What do you mean by staring?'
For the indic. cf. 1062: but
Plaut. also uses the more regular (classical) subj. in this phrase,
see Trin. 310, Aul. 201; similarly he varies between subj.
and indic. after *fuit quom*, cf.
note on 158.—**furcifer** 'jail-
bird'. The *furca* was a ᴧ
shaped piece of wood, to which
the arms of the slave to be
punished were bound, very much
in the same way as to the *patibulum* (cf. on 56), excepting that
the *furca*, while it involved dis-
grace, did not always involve
torture. The point of Tranio's
question is seen by reference
to 63, where see note.
70. **istuc nomen** sc. *furcifer*.
—**actutum** 'bye and bye'.
71. **sic** 'as it is' i.e. *bene*.
'Meanwhile so long as things
are as they are' etc.; cf. *sic ar-
matus* 'armed as he was' Livy
II 10, 11, *sic nudos* 'naked as

they are', Cic. pro Rosc. Am.
XXVI 71.—**istuc actutum** 'your
(threat of) bye and bye': *istuc*
is like Greek τό: cf. Xen. Cyro-
paed. v 1, 21 τό 'Εὰν μένητε, ἀπο-
δώσω 'the promise "if you remain, I will repay you"'.—**sino**
'I don't mind'.
72. **itanest?** 'Don't you?'
'Quite sure?' 'Is that your
drift?' The phrase expresses
surprise or indignation: cf. Pers.
219 f., Rud. 971 (*Itane uero?*),
747 (*Itane impudens?*).—**nimio**
=*multo* 'far', cf. 145, 442, 1103,
Capt. III 3, 1, and on Trin. 387.
So *nimis* (*nimium*) is often
scarcely more than *multum* e.g.
511; in 176 *nimis stulta's* is 'you
are quite too foolish': so 947.
The common phrase *nimio plus*
(Hor., Livy) is a development
of this conversational idiom,
and ='far too much' (*plus*='too
much', *nimio* is not abl. of comparison: Orelli is wrong in explaining as '*plus etiam quam
nimium*').
73. **petas** 'one wants'; for
the 2nd pers. sing. subj. imply-
ing an indefinite subject ('any-

TR. moléstus ne sis: núnciam i rus, te ámouc.
75 ne tu hércle praeterhác mihi non faciés moram.
Gr. satin ábiit neque quod díxi flocci cxístumat?
pro di ínmortales, ópsecro uostrám fidcm,
facite húc ut redeat nóster quam primúm sonex,
triénnium qui iam hínc abest, priusquam ómnia
80 periérc, et aedes ét ager. qui nisi húc redit,
82 paucórum mensum súnt relictae réliquiae.

Venire quod tu nolis (omitting *cupide*) Rl., *Venit quod nolis* Bug.,
Uss.   Bent.'s emend. anticipates the last result of German
criticism.   On *uenĭt quŏd* cf. Intr. to Capt. A (ii).

     74. *nunciam rus* Rl., Lor., Bug., regarding *i* as an addition
arising from a misunderstanding of *te amoue*, which is a synonym
for '*go*', as in Ter. Phorm. 566.

     75. *Ne tu hercle* Bent. (another proof of his insight), rec.
edd., **ne tu erres hercle** M, *ne tu erres non mihi praeterhac f. m.* Rl.

     76. *Gr.* Cam., om. in M.   In C this line is written after 77.

     80. *nunc* (for *huc*) Rl., Bug., Lor.[2]; Rl. supposes a line to have
dropped out between 80 and 82.

one and everyone', the *ideal
second person*) cf. Epid. 718 *sed
ut acerbumst, pro benefactis
quom mali messim metas* (so Pers.
856); and see Roby §§ 1544,
1546, Madv. § 370.   Thus *dicas*
in Hor.=*dicat aliquis* and *cre-
deres* in Livy=*crederet aliquis*.
—**cupide petas,** cf. on 316.

     74. **molestus,** with reference
to *molestum* 73 'don't *you* be a
nuisance (yourself)'.—**nunciam**
(three syllables) is a more emphatic *nunc*, cf. Trin. Prol. 3.
It is probably a compound of
nunc iam, in spite of the prosody:
cf. on Capt. ii 1, 26, where I
followed Brix in deriving from
nunci (=νυνί) and *-am* (an old
adverbial ending).

     75. **ne** (sometimes incor-
rectly written *nae*) is an inter-
jection='verily' (ναί), and does
not, of course, involve the subjunctive: cf. Trin. 62, Men. 256,
Mil. 571. —**praeterhac** = *post-*

hac.
     76. **satin abiit?** 'So he has
gone!' more lit. 'Has he really
(positively) gone?'   This use of
satin, almost equivalent to an
interrogative particle, here *num*
or *an,* springs from the sense
'quite': thus in 166 *satin haec
me uestis deceat?* 'is this dress
quite becoming to me?', 650
satin intelligis? 'do you *quite*
understand?', Trin. 1177 *satine
saluae* [sc. *res tuae*]? 'is all
quite right?', Men. 510 *satin
sanus es?* 'are you quite in your
right senses?' It is but a slight
step to such cases as Trin. 925
(where see note) *satine latuit?*
'is it possible that?', and the
present passage.   The phrase
always has an emotional character, expressive of indignation
or joy.

     82. **mensum.** So the gen.
might have been used in the
original Greek, ὀλίγων μηνῶν.—

nunc rús abibo : nam éccum erilem fílium
uideó, corruptum *iam* éx adulescente óptumo.

――――――――

PHILOLACHES.

Recórdatus· múltum et diú cogitáui,　　　85
argúmentaque ín pectus *méum* multa instítui,　86

83. **equum** (with c over the e) B, *hic quom* Rl., who supposes
a line to have been lost after 84.
84. *iam* S., om. in M, *ita* Rl., *ex adulescented* Rl. (Neue
Plaut. Exc. p. 72), *ex adulescente olim* Müll., Lor.², *ex adulescen-
tulo* Bug., Wagn.
85—156. The First Canticum falls naturally into four main
sections. Predominant rhythms:—*A* (85—104) bacchiac, *B* (105—
119) cretic, *C* (120—132) bacchiac, *D* (133—156) cretic. On the
meaning of the word *Canticum* and the metrical structure of the
lyrical passages in Plaut., see Introd. p. xxiv.
85—104. Section *A*. Bacchiac rhythm.
85—90. Subdivision I. Bacchiac tetrameters except 89 *a* (bacch.
trim.) and 90 (iamb. dim. cat.): a short line like this closing
a series is called a *clausula*.
86. *meum* Fl., Lor.², Wagn., om. in M, *institiui* Reiz., Rl.,
Speng.
M have here two lines
Ego atque in meo corde si est quod mihi cor
Eam rem uolutaui et diu disputaui
which are bracketed by Rl. and rec. edd. (except Uss.) as dittographies.

relictae reliquiae, λέλειπται
λείψανα 'figura etymologica',
see on Capt. ii 1, 54, 57, 'there
are only leavings, enough for a
few months, left'.
83. **eccum**=*ecce eum*, 'be-
hold him!' 'here he comes!',
Ital. '*ecco*', used parenthetically and without influence on
the construction : so in 1120 *sed
eccum tui gnati sodalem uideo
incedere*, cf. Ter. Eun. 967 *ecce
autem uideo rure redeuntem senem. Ecce* is perh. an imperative from √ oc (*oculus*) and=
'see'; cf. ἰδού (Curtius Gr. Etym.
457). The person referred to by
eccum stands as subject of the

clause in 311, 611, etc. : see
further on 560.
85—104. Subject: Introductory passage and enunciation of
the simile of the house.
85. **Recordatus** 'cudgelling
my brains' 'pondering', not 're-
membering': cf. Ovid Her. x
79 *non tantum quae sum passura
recordor* ('think over'). *Recordatus* has here the force of a
present participle (=*cogitans*,
reputans), as often in deponent
verbs (e.g. *ratus, lapsus*).—Join
multum et diu 'deeply and long
have I reflected' (*cor* =intellect;
but cf. 149 *cor dolet*).
86. **argumenta**　'reason-

89   { hominém quoius reí, quando nátust,
      { similem ésse arbitrárer simulácrumque habére.
90   id réppcri iam exémplum.
nouárum aedium ésse arbitrór similem ego hó-
minem,

89 *a.* Read *quoiŭ' rei̅* (*rei* is monosyllabic : cf. on Trin. 522):
Speng., disbelieving in the bacch. trim., scans as anapacst. dim.
hominém quoius rei | quandó natust.
89 *b.* *haberem* Herm., Lor.²
91—98. Subdivision II. Four bacch. tetrameters, followed by

ings''theories''considerations'.
The ground meaning of the
word is 'scheme of thought'
'principle': so in Truc. 169
Ast. *Amator similis oppidist
hostilis :* Din. *Quo argumento?*
'on what principle?' 'according
to what line of thought?' So
Asin. 302, Rud. 1022. Sometimes *argumentum* is the 'plot'
of a story (ὑπόθεσις). In Amph.
1087 *De ca re signa atque argumenta paucis uerbis eloquar*
we may trans. 'evidence'. In
Most. 92 *ei rei argumenta dicam*
'I will explain the principle of
the matter', 99 *argumenta ad
hanc rem* 'considerations bearing upon this matter', 118 *argumenta aedificiis* 'story of the
building'.—**in pectus institui**
'marshalled in my mind' cf.
Rud. 936 *in mentem instruere.*
89 *a.* **quoius** = *cuius.* Plaut.
always uses the gen. (never dat.)
after *similis.*
89 *b.* **similem esse arbitrarer**
'(asking myself) to what I
should compare (dubitative
subj.)', = *similis esset* (*sit*).
For this roundabout way of
speaking compare 158, 278 and
see on Capt. II 2, 18, Aul. 67—
69, Trin. Prol. 2 *finem fore quem
dicam nescio.* So even in Cicero:
legatis accusantibus, quod pecu-

*nias praetorem accepisse argue-
rent* (= *quod praetor accepisset*),
de Fin. I 8, 24.—Note the se-
quence of tenses: *cogitaui* corresponds to Eng. *present* perfect
(= 'I have reflected') and yet
takes the sequence of a secondary tense; cf. 715, Truc. 681 *Intellexisti lepide quid ego dicerem*
'you have twigged my meaning
very neatly', Ter. Eun. 932 *me
repperisse* ('that I have discovered'), *quo modo adulescentulus
posset noscere*, etc.: so in final
clauses, Aul. 134 *te seduxi* ('I
have led you aside') *ut loquerer*,
etc., Epid. 500 *ueni* ('I am
come') *ut cantarem.* The Lat.
idiom, in fact, makes these perfects aoristic (*intellexisti* = κατέ-
μαθες, *repperisse* = εὑρεῖν, κατα-
νοῆσαι). So Cic. in Verr. I 2,
de Off. II 1 and Caes. de Bell.
Gall. IV 1 *sub fin.*—**simulacrum
habere** = *similem esse*, pleonastically, as in Aul. 189 f.
90. **id exemplum** = *eius exemplum* 'an illustration of the
matter', as in Virg. Aen. II 171
*nec dubiis ea signa dedit Trito-
nia monstris* (= *eius rei signa*):
cf. Cic. de Am. 2 *eum sermonem*
= *sermonem de ea re* and Reid's
note. Uss. says '*id* = *quod quae-
rebam*'.

quandó natus ést.   ei rei argúmenta dícam.   92
atque hóc uosmct ípsi, sció, proinde utí nunc 96
ego ésse autumó, quando dícta audiétis
    mea, haud áliter id dicétis.
auscúltate, argúmenta dúm dico ad hánc rem :·
simúl gnarurís uos uolo ésse hanc rem mécum. 100

an iamb. dim. cat. (*clausula*). These verses form a correspondence
to 85—90.   93—95 are probably interpolations (so Rl. etc.).
    91. **arbitro** B¹. It is quite possible that this, the old form of
the verb, is right here, and that we ought to read *arbitrarem* in 89 b.
    92. **Quando hic** M, but *hic* is meaningless.—*ei rei:* both words
are monosyllabic (cf. Scyff. in Studemund's Studia Plaut. p. 25).
M have here three lines which edd. bracket as dittographies—

    Atque hoc haud uidetur ueri simile uobis?
    At ego id faciam esse ita ut credatis;
    Profecto ita esse ut praedico uera uincam.

Bent. proposed *creduatis*, but this does not make the verse metrical,
without further change.
    98. *aliter hau dicetis* Rl., *id haud aliter dicetis* Müll., Lor.², in
order to avoid the complete disappearance by elision of both
syllables of *Mea;* but the latter order is less rhythmical.
    99—104. Subdivision III. Three bacch. tetram., followed by
an iamb. dim. cat. and two iamb. octonarii. The last two lines
form a sort of flourish, finishing off the first (bacchiac) section of
the Canticum.
    99 and 100 are bracketed by Rl.
    100. *rem esse* (for *esse hanc rem*) Bent.

92. **ei rei argumenta**=*eius
rei arg.* 'the principle of the
thing'; the same phrase occurs
Trin. 522. For the dat. cf. *argumenta aedificiis dixi* 118, and
Madv. § 241 Obs. 3 and 4, where
it is shown that such a construction is not unknown in
classical prose, e.g. Livy II 30
is finis populationibus fuit: with
esse this phrase is very common
in Plaut. and Ter. Thus we
have *custos esse alicui* Mil. 271,
pater esse alicui Most. 962, Ter.
Ad. 126 *meo sum promus pectori*
'I keep the keys of my own
heart', Trin. 81 *uerbis falsis ac-
ceptor fui* 'I was the endorser

of their lies': so in classical
prose *dux esse alicui.* The common construction *est mihi liber*
is different: for there the dative
contains the logical subject of
the clause.
    96. **uosmet ipsi.** The speaker
turns to the spectators: cf. on
Capt. Prol. 10.
    98. **id** repeats the *hoc* of 96,
cf. Aul. 54 f.—**haud aliter** is a
kind of anacoluthon ; we should
expect *ita esse inuenietis;* cf.
Trin. 65.
    99. **ad** 'bearing upon'.
    100. **simul   mecum** 'with
me', 'as well as I do (am)': (so
Parcus in Lex. '*simul* πλεονάζει');

aedés quom extempló sunt parátae, expolítae,
  factaé probe examússim,
laudánt fabrum atque aedís probant: sibi quísque
  inde exemplum éxpetunt.
sibi quísque similis uólt suas: sumptum óperam *non*
  parcúnt suam.
105 átque ubi illo ínmigrat néquam homo, indíligens,
  cúm pigra fámilia, inmúndus, instrénuos,
hic iam aédibus uitium ádditur, bonaé quom curantúr
  male.
  átque illud saépe fit: témpestás uenit,

104. **simile suo is sua sumptu(-tum** CD) M, *similis uolt suo
sumptu:* Rl., *similis uolt suas: sumptum* Speng., Bug. *non* Herm.,
Rl., Bug., om. in M.   Rl. and Lor. bracket the line; but this
seems unnecessary. It is common enough in the Cantica to find
the thought developed at great length and with some tautology.
  105—119. Section *B*. Change to cretic rhythm.
  105—107. Subdivision I. Two cret. tetrameters followed by
an iamb. octon.
  105. *Atqui* Lor., Bug., Uss. (*Atque*='and then'). **indiligens-
que** M, with the excrescent -*que* so common in MSS., see on Capt.
iii 2, 5, iv 2, 11.
  108—113. Subdivision II.   108, 109 cret. dim. acat. + troch.
trip. cat. ⏑⏑‒⏑⏑‒ | ⏑⏑‒⏑⏑; 110, 111, 112 cret. tetram.; 113 = 108.

in Men. 748 *noui cum Calcha
simul*='I know you as well as
(I know) Calchas'; here *mecum*
represents a nominative : cf.
1037.—**hanc rem** is a curious
object after *gnaruris esse=no-
uisse:* cf. Pacuv. in Gell. i 24,
4 *hoc uolebam nescius ne esses,*
where *esses nescius* governs *hoc;*
instances in which an adj. governs an object are common
enough in Greek: thus Aesch.
Prom. 904 ἄπορα πόριμος, Suppl.
594 τὸ πᾶν μῆχαρ οὔριος Ζεύς.
  101. **quom extemplo** 'the
moment that', ἐπεὶ τάχιστα.
  104. **sumptum operam** 'expense and trouble'. The uniting
of two terms without a conjunc-

tion (asyndeton) is thoroughly
Plautine; cf. Rud.Prol. 23 *donis
hostiis,* Most. 105 f., Capt. ii 3,
46 *rebus in dubiis, egenis,* Asin.
223 *oratione uinnula uenus-
tula,* etc. For the connection
of ideas cf. 127 *suo sumptu et
labore.*
  105—119. Subject: the new
house under a bad master and
exposed to a storm.
  107. **aedibus uitium addi-
tur** etc. 'the house gets dam-
aged, being a good house but
badly looked after'. *Vitium* is
a 'flaw' 'blemish', cf. 275 and
Cic. Top. iii 15 *si aedes corrue-
runt, uitiumue fecerunt:* on indic. after *quom* see on 29.

cónfringit tégulas ímbricésque : ibi
dóminus indíligens réddere aliás neuolt.   110
uénit imbér, lauit párietes : pérpluont ;
tígna putéfacit, pérdit operám fabri :
néquior fáctus iamst úsus aédium.
átque *ea* haud ést fabri cúlpa, sed mágna pars
mórem hunc induxérunt : si quid númmo sarcirí potest, 115

111. *Vĕnit imber, pĕrlauit* Rl.; Lor. and Bug. keep reading of
M, and, in order to make *uenit* present, assume a form of verse
♉‿⌣ | ♉‿⌣‿ (inversion of 108), the existence of which is
uncertain (see Intr. p. xxix).
112. *putefacit* Rl., **putrefacit** M, Rams., Lor., Bug., Uss.,
which (*pŭtrefacit*, for mute and liquid never make position in
Plaut.) involves the form of verse mentioned on 111. Ritschl, in
the Rhein. Mus. vII p. 610 f., Opusc. II pp. 618—621, gives a
brilliant defence of *pŭtĕfacere*. He shows (1) that *putĕrc* is a
Plaut. word (see 146), (2) that *pŭtĕfacere* like *contăbĕfacere, perfrī-
gĕfacere* is quite right, side by side with *călĕfacere, commŏnĕfa-
cere, mădĕfacere* (cf. Most. 143), *pătĕfacere* etc., the principle being
the same as that on which we find *hăbĕ* (imperative), *mŏnĕ*, but
rĭdĕ, mĭscĕ never *rĭdĕ, mĭscĕ* : i. e. the short *e* is due to the accent
on the preceding short syll.; Intr. to Capt. A (i).—*perdit operam*
Bergk, Lor., Bug., Uss., **per operam** M, *aer operam* Cam., Rl.,
Rams.
114—119. Subdivision III. 114 cret. tetram., 115 troch.
septen., 116 = 108, 117 troch. septen., 118 iamb. octon., 119 troch.
septen.
114. *ea* Herm., Rl., Uss., Lor.[2], om. in M.
115. *Morem* edd. since Lamb., **Moram** M, Rams. ('permit a
stoppage (delay)' but?).

110. **reddere** = *reponere, re-
stituere:* 'put up (others) in
their place'.—**neuolt** = *non uolt:*
cf. Trin. 361: *ne* is the older
form of the negative: *non* = *ne
unum* (*noenum* Aul. 67), cf. Eng.
'not' [nă-wiht], Germ. 'n-icht'.
Compounds of *ne* and *uelle* are
common in Plaut., e.g. *neuis*
(762, 1176) = *non uis.*
111. **uĕnit** etc. 'suppose the
rain has come; it washes' etc.
Cf. Georg. II 519 *Venit hiemps,
teritur Sicyonia baca trapetis.*—

perpluont i.e. *parietes :* 'they
leak', 'let in water'; so Trin.
323, Quint. vI 3, 64 *cum cenacu-
lum eius perplueret.* In 164 we
have *perpluit* = 'rained through'
with the *rain* (*Amor et Cupido*)
as subject.
112. **putefacit** 'makes rotten'. — **operam** = *opus* 'work'
(more usually 'trouble' cf. 60) :
so Asin. 425 *operae araneorum*
'cobwebs'.
113. **usus** 'utility'.
115. **morem hunc indux-**

úsquc mantánt ncquc id fáciunt, dónicum
párictcs ruont; aédificantur aédes totac dénuo.
hacc árgumcnta cgo aédificiis díxi: nunc ctiám uolo
díccrc, ut homincs aédium cssc símilis arbitrémini.

120   primúmdum paréntcs fabrí libcrúm sunt,

116. *sarciunt* Bent., Crain, *farciunt* Palm.; these readings
make the verse a cret. tetram.; but *id faciunt* is good Lat., see
explan. note, and the metre does not require change.
117. *ruont: tum aedificant aedes totas* Rl., 'cum *ruont* uix
posse monosyllabum esse uideatur'. But we may scan *ruont aéd.*
(Intr. to Capt. A ii).
119. *Dicere homines aedium esse ut* Rl. ('fortasse'), cf. Bacch.
III 1, 3; V 1, 21.
120—132. SECTION *C.* Change to bacchiac rhythm.
120—125. Subdivision I. 120—124 bacch. tetram., 125 iamb.
dim. cat.

erunt, 'adopt this practice':
gnomic perf., Madv. § 335 b.
obs. 3.—For the pl. (κατὰ σύν-
εσιν) after *pars* cf. Capt. II 1,
39 *maxuma hunc pars morem
homines habent*, and see on
Trin. 35. Again *ubi quisque
uident* Capt. III 2, 3.—si=*etiam
si*, so 351, Asin. 164, Capt. II
1, 31.—nummo 'for a trifle',
so Capt. II 2, 81 *praeterea unum
nummum ne duis* 'a single farthing more', so Most. 357.
The word *nummus* in Plaut.,
standing without an adj., has
two main senses: (1) a definite
Greek coin, generally the δί-
δραχμον=about 2 denarii (20
asses) (so clearly in Pseud. III
2, 20, Truc. 562), but sometimes
the δραχμή=1 denarius (Aul.
445) and sometimes even the
τετράδραχμον (in Persa). (2)
vaguely, 'a small sum', suggesting to a Roman audience
their own coin the sestertius
=¼ of the denarius: see passages from Capt. and Most.
quoted above. For the *aureus*

nummus (*Philippeus*), a gold
coin struck by Philip II of
Macedon and called after him
(cf. French 'Napoléon'), see
Poen. I 1, 37, Asin. 153 etc.:
for the *plumbeus nummus* see on
892.
116. id faciunt, τοῦτο ποι-
οῦσι 'do so' i.e. *sarciunt*. The
phrase looks at first sight questionable Latin, because of its
similarity to the modern idiom
(cf. on Aul. 478). But cf. Asin.
67 where *id facere=facere obse-
quentiam* (65), Cic. de Amic. III
10 (*id faciam = mouear desi-
derio*), XXI 81 etc.
119. dicere ut, cf. on 14;
arbitremini is dubitative subj.;
'say how (why) you are to (may)
consider'.
120—132. Subject: points of
similarity between the building
of a house and the education of
a young man.
120. liberum = *liberorum*
(121). So *nummum* regularly
in Plaut. for *nummorum*, cf.
357.

et fúndamentúm supstruónt liberórum :
extóllunt, paránt sedulo ín firmitátem.
et in úsum boni út sint et ín speciem pópulo
sibíque, *h*aud matériae repércunt, nec súmptus
    sibi súmptui esse dúcunt.   125
nitúntur, ut alií sibi esse illórum similis éxpetant. 128
ad légionem adminiclum eís danunt tum iam áli- 129,
            quem cognatúm suom. 130

121. *Ei* Gul., Rl., Lor., Bug., Uss., Et M, Ell., Speng.
123—125. M have

> **Et ut in usum (usu B) boni et in speciem**
> **Populo sint sibique aut materiae reparcunt**

(B¹ adding **ne-** above re-, see Reformv. note p. 235; Rl. is mistaken)

> **Nec sumptus ibi sumptui esse ducunt.**

I have been guided by Ell. and Speng. We might also read,
if the bacchiac trimeter be admissible (see Intr. p. xxiv f.),

> *Et in úsum ut bonis inque spéciem*
> *Populó sint sibíque, haud matériae repércunt,*
> *Nec súmptus ibi sumptui sibi esse dúcunt.*

Rl., Lor., Bug. have *neparcunt* in 124, which is interpreted to mean
non parcunt, cf. on 110, 240 (if so, *sibique aut m. = nec sibi nec m.*).
But the word is very questionable, as Ell. says.--On the spelling
repercunt see Truc. 376, where A has *repercis,* BDZ *reparcis.*
Following line 125 M have

> **Expoliunt docent litteras iura leges**
> **Suo sumptu et labore**

which most edd. since Rl. regard as interpolated.
128—132. Subdivision II. (iamb. octon.).
129. After *legionem* M have **comita** (t. **tum** B³), for which
an old emendation was *quom itur* (F). Scyff. struck the word out,
as a gloss to *adminiculum.* So Speng., uniting the 2 vv.

122. **in firmitatem** ' to be
strong', cf. *in speciem* 'to be an
example' 123, *in sumptus* 538,
in usum 123, 145.
124. **materiae** 'their building materials' (properly 'tim-
ber') i.e. 'their means'.—**repercunt** 'grudge', cf. Truc. 376,
Lucr. I 667.
125. **nec sumptus sumptui**
etc. 'and think no expenses too

expensive for them' ; lit. 'think
expenses not an expense'.
128. **nituntur** 'it is their
ambition'. — **ut expetant sibi
esse** 'to be bent on having';
cf. 103. For the plethora of
words cf. on 89.—**similis** (acc.)
illorum 'children like those (of
like character)'.
130. **tum iam** 'then immediately', cf. *hic iam* 107.

eátenus abeunt á fabro. unum ubi émeritumst
stipéndium,
igitúr tum specimen cérnitur, quo euéniat aedificátio.
nám ego ad illúd frugi usque ét probús fui,
ín fabrorúm potestáte dúm fui.

131. *Protenus* Rl. *fabro* Speng. (cf. 114), **fabris** M.   **unum
ubi** M (see Speng. Reformv. p. 380. The collators seem to be all
mistaken). The words *Eatenus—fabro* have a very suspicious
look, see explan. note. Are they not a gloss intended to mean 'to
this extent they behave differently from the builders' i.e. 'there
was nothing to correspond to this in the case of the house-
building'?

133—156. SECTION D. Change to cretic rhythm.

133—143. Subdivision I. 133—136=108, 137 and 139 cret.
tetram., 140 f. =108, 143 iamb. octon.

133. *Năm ĕg.*, with hiatus, cf. 258, 311, 956, 965, Intr. to
Capt. D (iii).

131. 'So far (only) are they
removed from the care of the
smith', i.e. to the extent of
entering the army under the
charge of some relative, as As-
canius is entrusted to Epytides,
Aen. v. But it must be admitted that this is very strange
Latin.

132. **igitur tum**: *igitur* in
Plaut. is often merely a particle
of emphasis, 'look you': sometimes it marks the entrance of
the apodosis, see on Capt. IV
2, 91, and cf. Most. 689, Trin.
676, and Lucr. II 677; *tum igitur* or *igitur tum* is like τότε
δή or δὴ τότε (Homer). We have
igitur in the protasis in 393
(see note), 1093; in 380 *igitur
demum=tum demum*, where *igitur* is practically a temporal
particle; so Rud. 930, Amph.
301, 473. On *ergo igitur* 848,
cf. on Trin. 756.—**specimen cer-
nitur** 'proof is seen'.—**quo eueniat** 'as to how the building is
to turn out'. The subjunctive

is really deliberative or dubitative; so Mil. 1097 *quid me
consultas, quid agas?* ('what
you are to do'), etc. Hence the
reference to the future; cf. Virg.
Georg. I 29 where *uenias*='art
to be'. This usage will explain
many of the cases in which the
present subjunctive seems to be
used with future sense. For
quo euenire cf. τελεῖται δ' ἐς τὸ
πεπρωμένον Aesch. Agam. 68,
desinere in (Hor. A. P. 4).

133—156. The pointing of
the moral.

133. **nam** i.e. 'Don't be surprised at my speaking about a
*specimen, quo eueniat aedifica-
tio:* for' etc. The sentence is
a kind of sigh over what might
have been. See on Trin. 25
and Capt. III 1, 4 for this use
of *nam* (='I say this, for') and
cf. Most. 874, 1044.—**ad illud
usque dum**=*usque eo dum* 'for
so long a time as': he means
till the year of service was begun
(or ended?).

póstea, quom ínmigraui íngenium ín meum,   135
pérdidi upcrám fabrorum ílico óppido.
uénit ignáuia: *haec* míhi tempestás fuit: 137
haéc uerecúndiam mi ét uirtutís modum   139
déturbauít detexítque me ílico.   140
póstilla optígere me néglegéns fui:
continuo pro imbre amor aduenit †in cor meum.

135. *Postea quom* Guy., Rl., Lor., Bug., **Posteaquam** M, Uss.
ingenium in Both., **in ingenium** M.
137. *haec* Spcng., Lor.², **ea** M.   After this line M have
Mi aduentu suo grandinem imbremque attulit.
Rl. reads *Quae mi aduentu suo grandinem, imbrem attulit.* But it
has been well maintained by Crain and Brix (Jahrb. 1870 p. 427)
that the verse is a gloss; it is unmetrical and destroys the
symmetry of the passage: for there ought to be no mention of
rain till 142: *Ignauia* is the *tempestas* (cf. 108), *Amor* is the
imber (cf. 111), and the two stages of the uncovering of the roof
and the coming in of the rain should be kept distinct. Koenig
transfers the line to 142; q.v.
140. *detexitque me* Leo, *texit detexitque a me* M, *Detur-
bauitque detexitque a me* Kampmann, Spcng., Lor.²
141. *optigere me* Lor., **opticere eam** M, *me obtigere* Lamb.
As Lor. says, the sense demands *obtigere me ea* (sc. *uerecundia* or
uirtute); it is not his *uerecundia* but himself that requires roofing
in; Spcng. understands *eam* as *operam fabrorum* (136).
142. **in cor meum** (M) is very improbable; cf. ending of
next line: *guttis grauidis grandibus* is substituted by Spcng. in
spite of the warning of Rl. (Bug. *grandibus guttis pluens*), from a
passage in Fronto: '*nam illius quidem, ut Plautus ait, amoris*

135. **ínmigraui.** Cf. Livy
Praef. § 11 *nec in quam tam
serae auaritia luxuriaque immi-
grauerint.* But the metaphor
is confused: in 133 the young
man is the house, but in 135 he
is the slovenly tenant, his *ingenium* taking the place of the
house. 'When I took up my
lodging in my natural disposi-
tion': so *pro ingenio* Trin. 303
'in heart' (note).—Observe the
alliteration with *in-*.
136. **oppido** [perh. from *op-*

pedom, op-pedo, ἐπὶ πέδον]=*prorsus,* 'utterly'; so in 165.
139. **uirtutis modum** 'vir-
tuous self-control'.
140. **mi deturbauit** 'dis-
lodged my': cf. *deturbabo illum
de pugnaculis* Mil. 334, *ita
omnis de tecto deturbauit tegulas*
Rud. 87.—**detexit me** 'stript
me bare.'—**ilico** 'in a moment'.
141. **postilla** (*postillac* Men.
685 where see note)=*postea*
'after that'.

is úsquc in pcctus pérmanauit, pérmadcfecit cór
meum.
núnc simul rés, fidcs, fáma, uirtús, decus
145 déseruerunt: égo sum in usum fáctus nimio néquior.
atquc édcpol ita tigna únide putént hacc, non uidcór
mihi
sarcíre posse aedís mcas, quin tótae pcrpetuaé ruant,
quom fúndamenta périerint, nec quísquam esse auxilió
queat.
cór dolet, quóm scio, ut núnc sum atquc út fui:

*imber grandibus guttis non uestem modo permanauit, sed in medullam
ultro fluit'.* Koenig inserts 138 here, striking out *pro imbre* as a
gloss : *Cóntinuo Amor áduenit; | Mi áduentu suo grándinem im-
bremque áttulit.*
144—148. Subdivision II. 144 cret. tetram., 145 troch.
septen., 146—148 iamb. octon.
145. *Me deseruerunt* Fl., which would turn the line into iamb.
octon.   *usum* Lamb., Uss., Lor.[2], usu M; the acc. agrees bettcr
with 113 and 123.
146. *tigna humide putent haec* Bo., Speng., Lor.[2], **haec tigna
umide (-da) putant (-tent)** M, *tigna umide haec putent* Rl., with
hiatus in diaeresi.   *uideor* Cam., Rl., Rams., Lor., Uss., **uideo** M.
148. *Quom fundamenta* Crain, Bug., Uss., Lor[2]. (cf. 121),
Quin cum fundamento M, *Quin fundamento* Speng.
149—156. Subdivision III. 149=108 (or cret. tetram. with
hiatus after *scio*, justified by caesura), 150 cret. tetram., 151—153

144. **decus** 'respectability'.
145. **nimio nequior** 'far too
dissipated', cf. on 72.—**in usum**
'for any good purpose' lit. 'for
scrvice'.
146. **ita umide putent...non
uideor** 'so damp and rotten are
these timbers, I do not think':
with parataxis instead of hypo-
taxis ; so Capt. III 2, 7 *ita me las-
sum reddiderunt, uix miser iam
eminebam;* Mil. IV 2, 57 *ita me oc-
cursant multae, meminisse haud
possum:* cf. on Men. 94, Aul.
Prol. 9, 10.
147. **sarcire quin** 'patch
(repair) ... to prevent'. — **totae
perpetuae** 'entire, from top to
bottom': cf. *perpetuom diem*

'the whole day' 765; cf. Aen.
VIII 183 *perpetui tergo bouis*
'the whole chine of an ox' (νώ-
τοισι διηνεκέεσσι Il. VII 321).
148. **quom perierint**; see
note on 29. The subjunctive is
due to subordination to a clause
with the subjunctive (*quin......
ruant*), as in Aul. 784 *nullust
tam parui preti, quom (quin* B)
pudeat, quin puriget se 'as not
to excuse himself, when he is
put to shame', Men. 543 *ut te
libenter uideam, quom ad nos
ueneris,* Capt. II 3, 74, III 1, 13
etc. see Lübbert p. 233.
149. **scio** 'when I reflect';
in Capt. III 1, 24 *sciui*='I saw',
cf. 434, Mil. 828 *nisi uerum scio*

quó neque indústrior dé iuuentútc erat   150
  *   *   *   *   *
árte gumnástica, dísco, hastís, pila,   ⎱ 151-
cúrsu*ra*, armís, equo. *haud* uíctitabám uolup. ⎰ 153
pársimonia ét duritia díscipulinac aliís cram ;
óptumi quique éxpetebant á mc doctrinám sibi.   155
núnc, postquam nihilí sum, id uero meópte ingenio
                                    répperi.

=108 (or cret. tetram. with hiatus after *disco*), followed by cret.
tetram., 154—156 troch. septen.
   150. M mark no lacuna after this verse: but a second member
introduced by *neque* is needed. Bug. reads *nemo* for *neque*, which
however is less good metre: two *neque* clauses would be thoroughly
in the manner of Plaut.
   151—153. *pila* Z, and in margin of B, **filia** M. The hiatus
after *disco* might be explained by the loss of ablatival *d* : but the
verse probably contains further corruption. *Cursura* Speng. cf.
862, Asin. 327, Bacch. 67. *haud* Acid., Speng., Uss., om. in M.
After *equo* B has an erasure.
   156. *mĕŏpt' ing.* In cases like this it seems better to explain

'unless I *am told* the truth',
Persa 234.—**ut sum.** In Plaut.
dependent questions take sometimes the indic., sometimes the
subjunctive; cf. for former 460,
572, 614, 626, 1040, 1172 etc.,
and see note on Men. 207 *scin
quid uolo.* This idiom, in which
the question clause is in reality
co-ordinated to the principal
clause, gradually disappeared
from Latin. It is far less common in Ter. than in Plaut.;
and is only found in isolated
passages or phrases in the
golden age, cf. Virg. Ecl. iv 52,
v 7, Georg. i 57; more frequently in Propertius, e.g. iii (ii)
33, 33—38, iv 5, 25—40.
   150. The general sense of
this and the next (lost) line
must have been : 'no one of all
the youth was either more ener-
getic or took greater pleasure

in athletics'.—**industrior.** The
form is ante-classical; cf. on
442.
   154. **discipulina** is the old
form of *disciplina*, from *disci-
pulus* (cf. *uinclum, periclum* for
uinculum, periculum). The word
here = 'rule', 'pattern', cf. Asin.
201 *eadem nos discipulina uti-
mur*, Mil. 187, Pseud. 1004, and
Cic. in Cat. i 5, 12 *quoniam id,
quod maiorum disciplinae* ('rule
of our ancestors') *proprium est,
facere nondum audeo.*
   155. **optumi quique** = *opti-
mus quisque;* so occasionally in
Cic. e.g. de Amic. x 31; cf.
proxumae quaeque de Off. ii 21,
75, Livy *proxumi quique* i 9, 8
and Tacitus.
   156. **nunc postquam sum**
'now that I am', so Bacch. 531
*nunc ego illam me uelim | Conue-
nire, postquam inanis sum* 'now

PHILEMATIVM.   SCAPHA.   PHILOLACHES.

PHILE. Iam prídem ecastor frígida non láui magis
lubénter,

by synizesis than to assume the shortening of a syll. (*ŏpt-*) under
the influence of the preceding accent (*mĕŏpt' ĭng*), as Bug., etc.
157. *mágis l.* perh. to be pronounced *mage.*

that I am penniless'. Here
sum refers to present time only.
In other instances the force of
the present after *postquam* is
different; thus Most. 925 *tibin'
quicquam postquam tuos sum,
uerborum dedi* 'ever since I *have
been* your slave', Men. 234 *hic
annus sextust, postquam ei rei
operam damus* 'since we *have
been* engaged on this business'
(=*sextum iam annum damus*).
Thirdly the present is often
historical, e.g. Capt. III 1, 27,
Mil. 124, Curc. 683, Men.
Prol. 24. The same tense and
usage is also common after *ubi*
and *quom*, cf. on Capt. Prol. 24,
and add Most. 164, 1051, Amph.
1061, Capt. III 2, 3. — **nihili**
'good for nothing', a gen. of
price; so *homo minumi preti*
Epid. 494; cf. *est tanti* (Cic.)
'it is worth while'.—**id** involves
a slight anacoluthon 'for that I
have my own nature to thank'
(cf. 135). **id uero**=*id quidem*
'well, for that', with slight
pause after *sum:* cf. *ille uero*
Aul. 18.—**repperi** is true (present) perfect.
    Scene 3. Philematium, ra-
diant in the beauty of youth,
health, and elegant attire, together with her attendant, Scapha, comes out of the bathing
establishment belonging to the
house of Philolaches (cf. 191,
238); Scapha, doubtless an ugly
old woman, carries the apparatus of the toilette table (cf.
248, 258, 267). Philolaches, at
the opposite side of the stage,
listens to their conversation,
which, turning as it does upon
considerations of prudence in
love affairs, may be compared
with that of Clärchen and her
mother in Goethe's Egmont.
    157. **Iam pridem non laui.**
'This long time (this many a
day) I have not bathed etc.'
Here *iam pridem* = 'within a
long time' (cf. *anno hoc* 'within
this year' 690); the more common meanings are also found in
Plaut.: ii 'long ago', e. g. Pseud.
I 5, 7 *id iam pridem sensi* 'I no-
ticed it long ago;' ibid. I 3, 108,
Ter. Hec. 219; iii (with the present tense) 'during (for) a long
time', e.g. Bacch. 1157 *istuc iam
pridem scio* 'I have known that
for long', Rud. 963 *noui ego iam
pridem hominem*, Pseud. I 5, 51.
—**non laui magis libenter** 'I
have not enjoyed my cold bath
more (so much)': laui is true
(present) perfect. Note the active **lauare** in the intrans. sense,
=*lauari*, as so often in Plaut.—
frigida (*aqua*) 'in cold water',
opposed to *calida* (*calda*) 'in
warm water'.

nec quóm me melius, méa Scapha, rear ésse deficátam.
Sc. euéntus rebus ómnibus*t*, uelut hórno messis
                                            mágna*st*.
PHILE. fu! quíd ea messis áttinet ad méam laua-
                                    tiónem? 160
Sc. nihiló plus quam lauátio tua ad méssim.
                        PHILO. o Venus uenústa,
hacc íllast tempestás mea, mihi quaé modestiam
                                            ómnem

---

158. **quom** M, *quod* Rl. 'collato v. 691'. On *Scaphā* for ‿‿
see Intr. p. xxix. and cf. 170, 174.
159. *omnibust* Rl., Lor., Bug., **omnibus** M.
160. *fu!* Ell., **fuit** M, *Quid ea nam messis* Rl.

---

158. **nec quom**, etc. There
is a slight anacoluthon ; the
clause proceeds as if *nunquam
fuit quom lauerim* had gone before ; an exact parallel may be
found in Ter. Haut. 559—561
*Nunquam commodius unquam
erum audiui loqui, Nec quom
male facere crederem mi impu-
nius licere* 'I have never heard
Master speak more sensibly, nor
when I felt that I had more
free scope for mischief' i.e.
'there never was a time when
I heard... nor when etc.' cf. too
691 and note.—**rear me melius
deficatam esse** 'I have been
more thoroughly scoured, I
fancy': *deficatam = defaecatam*
cf. Aul. 79; for the subjunctive
rear after (*fuit*) *quom*, cf. Capt.
III 3, 1 *illud est, quom... ma-
uelim* and Ter. Haut. 1024: so
regularly in classical Latin, e.g.
Cic. de Orat. I 1 *Fuit cum mihi
quoque initium requiescendi fore
iustum arbitrarer*. But Plaut.
also knows the indic. after *est
quom* (*niduitas nos tenet* Rud.
665). The **present tense** (*rear*)
is to be ascribed to the peculiar

periphrasis, remarked upon in
the note to 89 *b*, *rear me deficatam esse* standing for *deficata
essem* (*fuerim* cf. Haut. 1025),
ut reor. Lor. regards *rear* as
hist. pres., like 25; but this
seems less good.
159. **euentus**, etc. 'All things
turn out somehow or other; for
instance we have a fine harvest
this year'.—For **uelut** = 'for instance' cf. 705, 876, Aul. 159,
Rud. 596.
160. **fu!** 'pshaw', see on 38.
161. Scapha's pert answer
implies that there is more in
her *messis* than appears at first
sight. She is thinking of the harvest which Philem. might make
out of Philolaches.—**Venus ue-
nusta**, 'lovely Love', cf. *grates
gratas* Trin. 821, *amoena amoe-
nitate amoenus* Capt. IV 1, 7.
162. **illa** 'of which I spoke'.
The simile of 137—143 is
slightly confused; instead of
ignauia, we have here *Philematium* figuring as the *tempestas*.
—**modestiam** 'good behaviour',
'self-control' (σωφροσύνη), cf.
Trin. 317.

detéxit tectus quá fui, quom míhi amor et cupído
in péctus perpluít meum : neque iam úmquam optigere póssum.
165 madént iam in corde párictes: periére haec oppido
acdes.

PHILE. contémpla amabo, méa Scapha, satin haéc
me uestis déceat.
uolo mé placere Philolachi, meo océllo, meo patróno.
Sc. quid tú te exornas, móribus lepidís quom lepida
túte's ?

163. *quom* Rl., **quam** M, *qua* 'by which road' Br., (holding
that *quom* introduces confusion into the order of events; but
cf. explan. note).
164. *eam* (for *iam*) Bug., in order to provide an object to
optigere; but *eam* would be ambiguous (*tempestatem* or *modestiam ?*).   *usquam* Acid., Rl., but cf. explan. note.
168. *Quid* Bo., Rl., Rams., Lor., Bug., **Quin** M, Uss., with
comma at *lepidis.*

163. **quom perpluit ;** see on
156; 'at the time when love
and desire trickled like rain
into my heart'. This clause
is not subordinate to *qua tectus
fui,* as Brix (Jahrb. 1870, p.
427) seems to think, but to
quae......detexit. There is no
intention of marking the time
of *perpluit* as prior to that
of *detexit;* the two acts of un-
roofing and raining through are
treated as simultaneous.
164. **perpluit** is present: cf.
on 25.—**neque iam umquam**,
etc. 'nor can I any longer for a
moment'. *umquam* is scarcely
a temporal particle here, but
rather serves to strengthen the
negative (*neque umq.* = *neque
prorsus;* cf. Asin. 630 *nunquam
ad uesperum uiuam,* Amph. 700
nunquam factumst 'it is a lie';
Donatus on Ter. Andr. 384 remarks '*numquam* plus habet
negationis quam *non* '; so often

nullus = *non* or *ne,* cf. T:in. 606
nullus creduas, Ter. Eun. 216,
Hec. 79 ; so too *totus* = *magno
opere* e.g. *totus doleo* Aul. 405.—
optigere without object, 'put
on a roof'. Transitive verbs
are occasionally found in re-
flexive sense in Plaut., cf. *laui*
157, and add Bacch. 1106 *unde
agis ?* (sc. *te*), Mil. 583 *irae len-
iunt* (sc. *se*), *res habet* (sc. *se*)
Cas. II 5, 30.
166. **contempla** = *contempla-
re;* again 172, 282; so in 473 *aucupet* = *aucupetur;* cf. *pergraeco*
960, *ludifico* 832, 1151, *proficisco*
Mil. 1329, and *arbitro, opino,
uenero,* all of which are Plaut.
(old Lat.) forms for the depo-
nents.—**amabo** 'please', 'as
you love me'; lit. 'I will love
you' (parenthetically).—**satin** =
num, cf. on 76.—**deceat,** a clear
case of subj. in depend. question ; cf. on 149.
168. Cf. Poen. 300 *Lepidi*

non uéstem amator múlieris amát, sed uestis fártum.
PHILO. ita mé di ament, lepidást Scapha: sapít
scelesta múltum. 170
ut lépide omnis morés tenet senténtiasque amántum.
PHILE. quid núnc?
SC. quid est? PHILE. quin me áspice et contémpla, ut haec me déceat.
SC. uirtúte formae id éuenit, te ut déccat quidquid
hábeas.
PHILO. ergo ób istuc uerbum té, Scapha, donábo ego
hodie áliqui,

169. *amator mulieris amat* Bo., **amatores amant mulieris**
M, Uss. (defended by Ell., who scans *mŭly̆éris* as dactyl), *amantes*
mulieris amant Lach., Rl., Lor., Bug. For the short syll. (-*is*)
in the diaeresis cf. 224, Asin. 632, 652, and see Introd. p. xxix.
171. *mores* Bergk, **res** M. *res autumat* Reid, cf. Men. 760.
172. *deceat* Cam., Bent., edd., **decet** M.
174. *ob istuc* Bug., Lor., Uss., Lang., **ob hoc** M, *hoc ob* Cam.,
Hercle ego ob hoc Rl.—*ób istuc* cf. on 47.—**hodie** M, Uss., (scan
hŏdie, as Büchcler says), *hoc die* Bo., Lor., *hocedie* (= *hodie*) Bug.,
Bergk, *hodied* Rl. (Neue Plaut. Exc. p. 90). Cf. 999.

mores turpem ornatum facile
factis comprobant.—**moribus le-**
pidis 'by your pretty ways'; in
such phrases *mores* approaches
very near the sense of 'qualities':
so Trin. 30 *mores mali* = 'wicked-
ness', 647 *stulti mores* = 'folly',
Rud. 1251 *sapientes mores* 'wis-
dom': *mores* is used differently
in 171 ('moods') and diff. again
in 286.
170. **sapit scelesta multum**
'she's a very knowing one, the
hussy': *multum* is prob. object
after *sapit*; but it might be adverbial to *scelesta*, cf. Aul. 124
multum loquaces, and Hor. Sat.
I 3, 57 *multum demissus homo*.
Note the alliteration with *s* and
cf. 250.
171. **mores** 'fads', 'whims'.
172. **quid nunc** 'I say!'—
quid est, 'Well?'—**quin aspice**

'*Do* look', almost = *quin aspicis!*
The imperative after *quin* is peculiar to comedy. Cf. 187.
173. **uirtute formae.** 'Thanks
to your beauty': cf. on 33. Prof.
Sellar quotes Burns:
'And then there's something
in her gait,
. Gars ony dress look weel'.
174. **ob istuc uerbum** 'for
saying that' explains and en-
forces *ergo:* cf. Amph. 378 f.
Ergo istoc magis, quia uanilo-
quo's uapulabis 'For saying that,
you shall be flogged all the more
soundly, I mean because you
are a braggart', Aul. 478, Mil.
1233; but cf. on 972.—**aliqui**
old abl. of *aliquis* (cf. Aul. Prol.
24, *si qui* = εἴ πως Trin. 120),
serving for all genders and either
number: so *qui* = *qua* (fem. re-
lat.) 258, = *quibus* Capt. v 4, 6,

3—2

175 nec pátiar te istanc grátiis laudásse, quae placét mi.
PHILE. nolo égo te adsentarí mihi.
         Sc. nimis tú quidem stulta's múlier.
177, 178 cho, *an* máuis uituperárier falsó quam uero extólli ?
equidém pol uel falsó tamen laudári multo málo,
180 quam uéro culpari aút meam speciem álios inridére.
PHILE. ego uérum amo : uerúm nolo mihi díci : men-
                                     dacem ódi.
Sc. ita tú me ames, ita Phílolaches tuos té amet, ut
                                     uenústa's.
PHILO. quid aís, scelesta ? quómodo adiurásti ? ita
                                  ego istam amárem ?
184 quid ? 'ita haéc me' id quor non ádditumst ? infécta
                                     dona fácio.

175.   *nec* Reid, **neque** M.   *gratiis* Bent., edd., **gratis** M.
176.   *nĭmĭ' tŭ* cf. 31.
178.   *an* Rl., rec. edd., om. in M.   *uituperarier* Bo., edd.,
uituperari M.
183.   *amarim* Guy., Rl., but wrongly.   '
184.   **id** B²CDF, Bug., Uss.; om. in B¹ and by Rl., Lor.

quicum?=quocum? Most. 519.
So in class. prose, where both
relative and interrogative senses
are found: e.g. de Fin. XXVI 85,
pro Rosc. Am. XXVII 74, de
Amic. VI 22.

178.   **falso** 'undeservedly',
uero 'deservedly': *uero* is here
not the adversative particle, but
a modal abl., lit. 'according to
truth', 'on true grounds'; so in
Capt. III 4, 35 ('in reality'),
Asin. 568.

179.   **uel** 'even' (*equidem uel
multo malo* 'I for my part go so
far as to greatly prefer': note on
299. Lang. here trans. 'wenn's so
beliebt'.—**falso tamen**=*quamuis falso*, cf. Capt. II 3, 44, Stich.
99 *quom tamen absentis uiros proinde habetis, quasi praesentes
sint*, Ter. Eun. 170 *tamen con-
temptus abs te haec habui in*

memoria. So Virg. Ecl. VIII 20
*extrema moriens tamen alloquor
herba;* cf. Thuc. VII 75 ἡ ἰσο-
μοιρία τῶν κακῶν, ἔχουσά τινα
ὅμως κούφισιν, οὐδ' ὡς ῥᾳδία ἐδοξά-
ζετο. The παρὰ προσδοκίαν is
like 1007—'to get praise, even
tho' undeserved, than blame well
merited'.

183.   **ita amarem** is the reported form of *ita Philolaches
tuos te amet*, the tense being
determined by *adiurasti*, as Uss.
says: Ell. trans. 'What oath is
that you swore—As truly as I
was to love her?' comparing
Hor. Sat. II 2, 124 *ac uenerata
Ceres, ita culmo surgeret alto*,
the reported form of *ita culmo
surgas alto.* Cf. note on 301.

184.   **ita haec me** sc. *amet.*—
infecta etc. 'I revoke my presents'.

Sc. equidém pol miror tám catam, tam dóctam et bene
te edúctam 186
nunc stúltam stulte fácere.
PHILE. quin mone quaéso, si quid érro.
Sc. tu ecástor erras, quaé quidem illum exspéctes
unum atque ílli
morém praecipue síc geras atque álios aspernére.
matrónae, non meretríciumst, unum ínseruire amán-
tem. 190
PHILO. pro Iúppiter! nam quód malum uorsátur meac
domi íllud ?

After this verse there is in M the foll. line

  Periisti quod promiseram tibi dona (-no B), perdidisti

which Fl., followed by most edd., pronounces to be an interpolation.

  186. *catam* Pius, edd., **captam** M. *et bene te eductam* Bent.,
Rl., Lor., Bug., **te et bene doctam** M. Seyff. proposes *tam coctam
te et bene doctam* cf. Poen. III 2. 9 *hodie coctiores iuris non sunt.*
  187. *Nunc stultam* Bo., Rl., Lor., Bug., **Non stai tam** M,
Non stultam B (margin), *Istaec tam* Uss.
  188. *exoptes* Acid., Rl., Bug. Reid suggests *aspectes* 'look
with desire upon'. Uss. and Lor.[2] follow M.
  190. *meretricis* Guy., Rl., in order to introduce uniformity
with *matronae*.

186. **doctam** 'clever'.
187. **stultam stulte** 'in such
a silly silly way'. The effect of
the combination is that the adj.
and adv. mutually strengthen
one another: but the total effect
is here prob. adverbial, as in Rud.
426 *bellam belle tangere* 'to give
a sweet sweet embrace' and
Curc. 521 *sequere istum bella
belle* 'follow him, like a good
good girl', cf. Asin. 676. So in
Spenser (quoted by Munro on
Lucr. III 889) 'Poorly, poor
man, he lived; poorly, poor man,
he died'. In other instances
the total effect is adjectival; see
Mil. 1015 *firme firmus* 'a trusty

friend', Aul. 312 *parce parcum*
'a stingy wretch'. Stich. 11
and Asin. 208 might be regarded
as coming under either heading.
—**quin mone**; cf. on 172.
188. **exspectes** 'look to', 'are
at the beck of'.
189. **praecipue sic** '(show
favour) so marked'.
190. **unum** : for the accus.
after *inseruire* cf. 216 and Poen.
IV 2, 105.
191. **nam quod** 'Why what',
cf. Georg. IV 445 *Nam quis te,
iuuenum confidentissime nostras
Iussit adire domos?* and Aul. 42,
44, Asin. 41. Wagn. and Lor.
regard *nam quis* as exactly

di deaéque omnes me péssumis exémplis interfíciant,
nisi égo illam anum interfécero sití fameque atque
                      álgu.
PHILE. nolo égo mihi male té, Scapha, praecípere.
                  Sc. stulta's pláne,
195 quae illúm tibi aetérnúm putes fore amícum et bene-
                          uoléntem.
moneo égo te: te ille déseret aetáte et satietáte.
PHILE. non spéro.
       Sc. insperata áccidunt magis saépe
                   quam quae spéres.
postrémo, si dictís nequis perdúci ut uera haec crédas

192. *me omnes* Rl., which has the advantage of removing the
ictus from the last syll. of *omnes*.—On the synizesis of *deae* cf.
Intr. to Capt. C. In the nom. and abl. pl. (*di, dis*) later Lat.
knows only the monosyllabic forms.
    194. *mihi* rec. edd., **mei** M, *Ego nolo mei* (monosyllabic and
dat. =*mihi*, a form common in MSS. from Plaut. to Cic., see Büch.
Lat. Decl. § 291 p. 112) Ell., *Nolo ego mi male te, mea Scapha* Rl.

=*quisnam*, but this is not certain. Cf. note on 258.—**uorsa-**
tur. The verb *uorsari* in Plaut.
is, as Lang. remarks, never used
in the later sense of 'to be engaged with (upon)': it has always
a strictly local sense; here 'to
take up one's abode', 'to nestle'.
—**illud,** with a gesture 'yonder':
cf. Amph. 543 *lucescit hoc iam,*
where *hoc* corresponds to the
gesture of pointing to the sky.
    192. **pessumis exemplis,** so
212; cf. notes on 49, 54. Phrases formed with *exemplis* and
modis are nearly equiv. to emphatic adverbs: *miris modis*
'strangely', 'in wondrous wise',
indignis modis (1033) 'shame-
fully'; *pessumis exemplis interf.*
'to put to a horrible death'.
    196. **aetate et satietate.**
Note the jingle: 'when you are

older and he is colder'. *Aetas*
is here used absolutely for 'old
age' (*aetas senecta,* Aul. 251,
Trin. 43, *aetas mala,* Men. 758),
so in 840; sometimes it is used
absolutely for 'youth' (=*aetas
integra* Pseud. 1 2, 69, or *aetatula* Most. 217, Rud. 894), *haud
aetati optabile fecisti* Bacch.
161, *aetas et corpus tenerum*
'youth and a delicate body'
Afranius. In classical Lat. both
senses are found; see Dict.
    197. **non spero** 'I hope not',
cf. 798 *haud opinor* 'I think
not', 146, 270, 820 *non uideor*
'I think (that) ...... not', 978 f.
non aio 'I say no': so in Greek
οὐ φημί =*nego*, οὐ θέλω =*nolo*, οὐχ
ἥδομαι = *doleo*.— **insperata** etc.
'it is the unexpected that always
happens' (Lord Beaconsfield).—
speres 'one expects', cf. on 73.

mea dícta, ex factis nósce rcm : uidc, quaé sim et
　　　　　　　　　　　　quae fui ánte.
nihilo égo quam nunc tu *mínus* sum amata, atque
　　　　　　　　　　　úni gessi mórem, 200
qui pól me, ubi aetate hóc caput colórem commutáuit,
relíquit deseruítque me. tibi idém futurum créde.
PHILO. uix cómprimor, quin ínuolem illi in óculos
　　　　　　　　　　　　　stimulatríci.
PHILE. solam ílli soli cénseo esse opórtere opse-
　　　　　　　　　　　　quéntem : 205
solam ílle me solí sibi suo *súmptu* liberáuit.　　　204
PHILO. pro di ínmortales, múlierem lepidam ét pudico
　　　　　　　　　　　　　ingénio. 206

---

199. So Bent. read and punctuated the linc, taking *uidc*
(**uides** M), from Sciopp.; Rl. considering that *Mea dicta* is awkward
after *dictis* removed the words, reading *Ex factis nosce rem : uide,
ego quae sim et quae fui ante*, with hiatus 'in diaeresi': Speng.
puts a full stop at *uides* and makes the exclamatious which follow
independent.　Lor.[2] gives *Ex factis nosce : me uides, quae sim : at
quae fui ante!* which introduces a very questionable hiatus after
sim. Mea dicta, however awkward, is prob. what Plaut. wrote.
　　200. *minus* Müll., rec. edd., om. in M.　**uni modo** M: *modo*
del. Bent., Rl., rec. edd.
　　202. *crede* Acid., Bent., **credo** M.
　　205. *illi soli* Guy., Bent. (who also proposed *ei me soli*), **illi
meo soli** M, *me soli* Rl., *Illi me soli* Fl., rec. edd., but against this
see Asin. 163—5 (quoted in explan. note): part of the point lies in
the repetition of *solam...soli* in each line.—Rl., followed by Lor.
and Bug., transposes this and the foll. line : but as Uss. says the
reason may be perfectly well put after the sentiment.
　　204. *sumptu* Bent., *aere* Bent. (as alternative), Rl., *argento* Fl.
sumptu seems to have the advantage as being alliterative.

---

199. **sim ... fui.**　Note the
change of mood and cf. 969 and
note on 149.
　　202. **me** is superfluous, but
gives additional emphasis: cf.
tu in 15 f., *mihi* Aul. 543 f.
　　203. **stimulatrici,** 'temptress', 'fire-brand of a woman'.
　　205. With this and foll. line

cf. Asin. 163—5.
AR. *Sólus solitúdine ego ted
　　útque ab egestate ábstuli:
Sólus si ductém, referre
　　grátiam nunquám potes.*
CL. *Sólus ductató si semper só-
　　lus quae poscám dabis.*
Note the omission of subject of
infin. and cf. on 55.

bene hércle factum, et gaúdeo mi níl esse huius
　　　　　　　　　　　　　　　　　　　　caúsa.
Sc. inscíta ccastor tú quidem es.
　　　　　　　　　　Phile. quaprópter?
　　　　　　　　　　　　　　　Sc. quae istuc *cúres,*
ut té ille amet.
　　　　Phile.　quor ópsecro non cúrem?
　　　　　　　　　　　　　　　　Sc. liberá's iam :
210 tu iám, quod quaerebás, habes: ille té nisi amabit último,
　id, pró tuo capite quód dedit, perdíderit tantum
　　　　　　　　　　　　　　　　　　　argénti.

208—223 are by many critics regarded as spurious; (see Goetz,
Dittographien im Plautus-Texte, in the Acta Soc. Phil. Lips. vi
p. 251 f.) and Lor. is perhaps right in removing them altogether
from the text. They certainly overburden the scene, and contribute
nothing to the development of the action.

208.　*cures* Pyl., edd., om. in M.

209.　*té ill.* (with hiatus); or accent *te ill.* (with elision).

210.　*ni amarit* Bent., *te nisi ille* Müll., Bug., Lor.². But the
change is unnecessary: *ille* is often a pyrrich, apart from all considerations of the incidence of accent or ictus on a preceding or succeeding syll.; see Intr. to Capt. A (v), on the words *ille, iste, unde,
inde, nempe* (add *ecce, ecquis, immo*); if *ille* may stand as a
pyrrich at the commencement of the iambic trim. (cf. Trin. 137,
Asin. 637 etc.), there is no reason why it should not also so stand
at commencement of second half of iamb. tetram. cat.—Sometimes
we find these words shortened even when the accent or ictus falls
on the shortened syll. e.g. Trin. 853, Mil. 262, 713, 830, Capt. iv
3, 1, etc.　It is well known that the word was often written *ile*
before the time of Ennius.

211.　*pro tuo capite* Bent., **pro capite tuo** M, Uss., *tuo pro
capite* Bo., Bug., Lor., *Pro capite tuo quantum* Rl.

207.　For omission of verb
subst. cf. on 33.—**mi nil esse**
etc. 'that I've ruined myself for
her sake'.

210.　**ultro** 'into the bargain', i.e. after having given
you your freedom (*quod quae-
rebas*), cf. Pers. 327 *et mulier ut
sit libera, atque ipse ultro det
argentum* 'that he himself may

have to pay money *into the bargain*'. Uss. explains 'uel sine
mutuo tuo amore' i.e. 'without
any trouble on your part' and
compares Men. 359.

211.　**perdiderit,** 'will find
that he has thrown away'.—
id tantum argenti 'all that
money'.

PHILO. perii hércle, ni ego illam péssumis exémplis
enicásso.
ita hánc corrumpit múlierem uití malesuada léna.
PHILE. numquam égo illi possum grátiam reférre,
ut meritust dé me.
Scapha, íd tu mihi ne suádeas, ut illúm minoris
péndam. 215
Sc. at hoc únum facito cógites : si illum ínscruibis
sólum,
dum tíbi nunc haec aetátulast, in sénecta male
querére.
PHILO. in ánginam ego nunc mé uelim uorti, út
ueneficae ílli
faucís prehendam atque énicem sceléstam stimula-
trícem.
PHILE. eundem ánimum oportet núnc mihi esse,
orátum ut inpetráui, 220
atque ólim, priusquam id éxtudi, quom illí sub-
blandiébar.

212.   ég' íll., cf. 214, Intr. to Capt. A (i); but see on 210.
213.   *Ita* Bonnet, Illa M, edd.   *uiti malesuada lena* S., **male-suada (-am) uitilena (Vttilena)** M, *uiti malesuada plena* Speng., Lor.[1], *malesuada uitíque plena* Crain, Lor.[2], Tyrr., *m. uetula lena* Br., Bonnet, *m. multum lena* Bug., *m. multilena* Ell., *m. futtili'* (*futtile*) *lena* Reid, hac (for *hanc*)...*malesuadâ cantilenâ* Uss.
217.   sénécta : Intr. to Capt. A (i). Rl. and Lor. suppose the first syll. to be suppressed (*s'necta*).
220.   *oratum* Palmer, **gratum** M.   *impetraui* Z, edd., **impetrauit** M.
221.   *fuit quom illi subblandibar* Müll., Bug.

212.   **enicasso** old fut. perf. = *enicaueso* = *enic(enec-)auero* (cf. Asin. 921 *enicauit=enicuit*): cf. *seruasso* 228 and on Capt. I 2, 40.
213.   **ita,** cf. 56 and note.— **uiti malesuada** 'that tempts to vice', cf. Acn. vi 529 *hortator scelerum Acolides.*
215.   **ne suadeas:** cf. on 468. —**minoris p.** ' think less of' i.e. than I do.

216.   **inseruibis** = *inseruies* ; cf. *congredibor* 783, *scibo* 997.
217.   **aetatula,** 'pretty age', 'youth', cf. Rud. 894 and on 196.
220.   **oratum ut impetraui** 'now that I have gained my petition'; cf. Amph. Prol. 33 *iustam rem et facilem esse oratam a uobis uolo* (Palmer).
221.   **id extudi** 'got it out of him '.

PHILO. di me *ét deae* faciant quód uolunt, ni ob
ístam oratiónem
tc líbcrasso dénuo et ni *té*, Scapha, cnicásso.
Sc. si tíbi sat acceptúmst, fore tibi uíctum sempi-
térnum
225 atque íllum amatorém tibi propriúm futurum in uíta,
solí gcrundum cénseo morem ét capiundas crínis.
PHILE. ut fámast homini, exín solet pecúniam inueníre.
ego sí bonam famám mihi seruásso, sat cro díues.
PHILO. si quídem hercle uendundúmst, pater ueníbit
multo pótius,

222. *et deae* S., om. in M. *Diui mc* Bo., Seyff. (cf. Schöll in
Truc. 701, Wagn. on Aul. 50), *Di pol me* Rl., *At (Ita) di me* Ell.
(who disbelieves in *diui*), *Qui di me* Bug.—For the synizesis of
deae (in thesis) cf. 463, 684, Pers. 831.—*uelint* Bug.
223. *ni te, Scapha* Reid, **nicaspam** M; edd. read *ni Scapham*
(after Cam.) with hiatus ' in diaeresi' after *denuo.*
226. B¹ preserves thc fem. **capiendas** to which Non. p. 202,
29 bears cxprcss testimony; **capiendos** M (the testimony of A is
wanting).
229. In Plaut. thc *si* in *si quidem (siquidem)* is long, as Bent.

222. **di me et deae.** Philol.
is fond of beginning his speeches
with an oath: cf. 161, 170, 191,
206. For thc order of words
cf. 463, 684, and Hor. Od. I 8,
2 *per omnes te deos oro.*—**me** abl.
'(make) of me', cf. 636 *quid eo'st
argento factum?* and on Capt.
v 1, 31.
224. **tibi sat acceptumst**
'you fecl assured'. *Satis accipere (dare, exigere)* are legal
terms = 'to take (give, exact)
security'; cf. Stich. 508.—**uictum sempiternum** 'provision
for lifc'.
225. **tibi proprium** 'your
own for ever', cf. Aen. I 73
*Connubio iungam stabili, propri-
amque dicabo.*
226. **capiundas crinis** ' assume thc matron's hair' or (freely) 'put on the matron's cap',

i.e. 'marry'. At marriage the
hair of a Roman maiden was
arranged in six plaits (called
crines) with the so-called *hasta
caelibaris;* cf. Festus p. 339
Senis crinibus nubentes ornantur
and Mil. 789—792. The custom,
which was a specially *Roman*
one, is alluded to by Browning,
Sordello Bk. II
    A Roman bride, when
      they'd dispart
  Her unbound tresses with the
      Sabinc dart,
  Holding that famous rape in
      memory still,
  Felt creep into her curls the
      iron chill.
227. i.e. according as his
credit stands high or low.—
exin...**ut**=*proinde ut* cf. 96,
Capt. II 2, 57.
229. **si quidem uend.** 'if I

quam té me uiuo umquám sinam *aut* egére aut men-
dicáre. 230
Sc. quid illís futurumst céteris, qui té amant?
PHILE. magis amábunt,
quom *mé* uidebunt grátiam reférre *bene* merénti.
PHILO. utinám meus nunc mórtuos pater ád me
nuntiétur,
ut ego éxheredem méis bonis me fáciam atque haec
sit héres.
Sc. iam istá quidem apsumpta rés erit : dies nóctis-
que estur, bíbitur, 235
neque quísquam parsimónias adhibét: sagina plánest.
PHILO. in te hércle certumst príncipe, ut sim párcus,
experíri :
nam néque edes quicquam néque bibes apud me *hís*
decem diébus.
PHILE. si quíd tu in illum béne uoles loqui, íd loqui
licébit :
nec récte si illi díxeris, iam ecástor uapulábis. 240

declared (see my ed. of Capt. p. 160); hence Wagn.'s scansion *si
quidem hĕrcle* is to be preferred to Lor.'s and Bug.'s *sĭ quidem hĕrcle;*
cf. Intr. to Aul. p. xlvi, note (p. 51), and Most. 671, 1075, 1147.
uendundumst, pater Cam., Rams., **uendundum si pater** M,
uendundust pater, Rl., rec. edd.
    230. *aut* Bent., to avoid hiatus, om. in M. *indigere* Reid.
    232. *me* Grut., edd., om. in M. *referre bene merenti* Bent., Rl.,
rec. edd., **referr...i** B, referenti CD.
    234. *bonis me faciam* Cam., Bent., Rl., Lor., Bug., **me bonis
faciam** M, except C which has me faciam bonis (so Uss.).
    235. *quidem absumpta* Z, edd., quidem absumpta quidem M.
    236. *parsimonias* Reid (cf. Trin. 1028), parsimoniam M.
    237. *principe* Bent., Bo., Rl., rec. edd., principium M.
    238. *his decem* Bent., Bo., edd., isdec B, isdem CD².

do have to sell'; **hercle** belongs
to *uenibit,* see on Aul. 48.
    230. **sinam** pres. subj., as in
847, 884; cf. on Capt. III 5, 30
praeoptauisse quam is periret.
    231. **illis** cf. on 636.
    235. **estur** cf. on 12.
    236. **sagina** cf. on 65.
    238. 'for (lit. 'within') the

next ten days'; for abl. cf. Madv.
§ 276 obs. 5.
    239. **si uoles** 'if you will
be so good as to' cf. 790.
    240. **nec recte dicere** = *male-
dicere,* so in Asin. 155, 471 etc.;
on the old form of the negative
ne or *nec* cf. 110.

243 PHILO. edopól si summatí Ioui illo argénto sacrufi-
cássem,
244 pro illíus capite quód dedi, numquam aéque id bene
locássem ;
241 ut uídeo eam medúllitus me amáre. oh, probus
homó sum :
242 quae pró me causam díceret, patrónum liberáui.
245 Sc. uideó te nihili péndere prae Phílolache omnis
hómines.
246 nunc, ne éius causa uápulem, tibi pótius adsentábor.
248 PHILE. cédo mi speculum et cum órnamentis árculam
actutúm, Scapha,
órnata ut siém, quom huc ueniat Phílolaches uoluptás
mea.

243, 244, 241, 242 is the order of M, also followed by rec. edd.;
Rl. rearranged the passage as indicated in the margin.
243. *si summati Ioui illo* Speng., si summo ioui bo B[1], si
summo ioui ioui (uiuo) M, *si uel summo Ioui eo* Rl., *si summo
Ioui bouem illo* Bug. (*boues argento eo*, 'accedente ipso Buggio')
Uss., Lor.[2], *ego si summo Ioui de uiuo* ('from the principal') Ell.
244. *locassem* Guy., Bent., edd., collocassem M.
241. *uideo* Bug., Uss., Lor.[2], uideas M.
242. *patronam* Guy., Bent.
246. After this verse M have Is acceptum sat habes tibi fore
illum amicum sempiternum, which Acid. and edd. have expelled
as a mere repetition of 224.
248. The *assentatio* begins (cf. 246) and the metre changes to
trochaic septenarii.
249. *siem* Bent., Bo., Uss., sim M, *sim quom huc adueniat* Rl.,
Lor., Bug.

243. summati 'supreme'.
Cf. Cist. I 1, 26 *summatis matro-
nas* 'high-bred', Pseud. 227 *deliciae summatum uirum*, Stich.
492 *summates uiri*. That the
word can also be used of gods
and goddesses is shown by Apul.
Met. II p. 267 *praecepta summatis deae*.
241. ut. In such phrases *ut*
becomes almost causal, 'since'
'now that', cf. Engl. 'as'=

'considering that': see further
on 268.—probus homo sum 'a
knowing fellow am I!' *Probus*
not in the moral sense, as in
133, but like *uictu probo* 730,
'fine fare'; cf. on *probe* 4.
242. patronum quae 'a
woman to..., a very advocate'.
246. eius causa 'on account
of him 'i. e.' for speaking against
him'.

Sc. múlier quae se súamque aetatem spérnit, speculo
ei úsus est : 250
quíd opust spéculo tíbi, quae tute spéculo speculum
es máxumum ?

PHILO. ób istuc uerbum, né nequiquam, Scápha, tam
lepide díxeris,
dábo aliquid hodié peculi tíbi, Philematiúm mea.

PHILE. súo quique loco uíde capillus sátin compositust
cómmode ?

251. *quom tute speculo's specimen* Rl., Lor., Bug. ('the com-
pletest pattern of beauty for a mirror to reflect'). Rams. and Uss.
follow M.
252. **nequiquam** BCD[1,2], **nequicquam** D[3]F: see Wagn. on
Trin. 440, 565. The spelling *nequiquam* is preferred by Keller in
Hor. and Dietsch in Sall. But good MSS. also support *nequicquam; cf. Most. 290, 1176, and Neue Lat. Formenl. II 642.
253. *peculi* Cam., cdd., **peculi (ferculi)** M.
254. *uide capillus satin* Müll., Bug., Uss., **uiden capillus satis**
M, *Suon quicque locost? uide capillum, satin* Rl.(after Acid.),
Lor., cf. explan. note. Non. has the curious note 'capillus...neutri,

250. **muller quae...ei** = *mulieri quae;* cf. 985 f., Capt. I 2, 1
istosquosemi...hisinditocatenas,
Trin. 137 *ille* (= *illum*) *qui mandauit, exturbasti ex aedibus?;*
so Virgil Aen. I 573 *urbem quam
statuo uestra est.*—**aetatem** 'person', cf. Rud. 1346 *Venus era-
dicet caput atque aetatem tuam,*
and the common phrase *Vae
aetati tuae* 'confound you'.
251. **speculo speculum** 'when
the looking glass has the best
of looking glasses in yourself
(and your eyes)'; i.e. you are
yourself 'the glass of fashion
and the mould of form'; cf.
Henry IV Pt II 2, 3 'he was indeed the glass wherein the noble
youth did dress themselves'.
253. **peculi** 'metal to look at'.
Note the pun (*speculum, peculium*) and cf. on 268. From an
article in Phillipps' Glossary

4626 *peculum : speculum,* it
might seem that the *s* of *speculum* was sometimes not pronounced.—**Philematium.** Note
the sudden apostrophe from Scapha to Philematium. Since
Scapha has made such a pretty
speech, he will reward—Philematium.
254. **suo quique** (= *quóque*)
loco 'in its own proper place'.
The simpler expression would
be *suo quisque loco* 'each in its
own place'; but it has been
proved by Madvig on Cic. de
Fin. v 17, 46 (*cuiusque partis
sua quaeque uis = sua cuiusque
partis uis*) that the attraction of
quisque to the case of *suus,* by
which *suus quisque* becomes
practically a single word, is good
Latin. So in Poen. 1178 *Tanta
ibi copia uenustatum aderat in
suo quique* (where *quicque,*

255 Sc. úbi tu commodá's, capillum cómmodum esse
crédito.
PHILO. uáh, quid illa pote péius quicquam múliere
memorárier ?
núnc adsentatríx scelestast, dúdum aduorsatríx erat.
PHILE. cédo cerussam.
Sc. quíd cerussa nám opust ?

Plautus Mustellaria, *uide, capillum satin' conpositum sit* (or, *sati'
conpositum est*) *conmode'*, and Lew. and Sh. cite this passage
as an instance of a neuter subst. *capillum;* if so, we should read
uide capillum satin compositumst. At any rate Non. supports *uide.*

256. **mulieri** B, Lor., unnecessarily; cf. *in 'Alidĕ Polyplúsio*
Capt. v 2, 20, *dúcerĕ medicum ǎn fabrum* Men. 887, see too 402
(*aĕdibŭs*), and Br. on Mil. 27 (accentuation of dactylic word).

258. *nam opust? Malas qui* Rl., Lor., Bug., **opus (opust) nam?**
PH. qui malas M, Uss.

though found in one MS. and
that the Ambrosian is impossible) *loco sita munde;* cf. Stich.
62 where the question is more
difficult to decide. We have
the idiom in Cic. e.g. Acad. II 7,
19 *in sensibus sui cuiusque gene-
ris* and in Virg. Ecl. VII 54 *Strata
iacent passim sua quaeque sub
arbore poma* (acc. to MSS. and
Non.). A large collection of
instances is given by Lachm. on
Lucr. II 371, where he (followed
by Munro) reads *quoduis fru-
mentum...Quique*(MSS. *quidque*)
suo genere.

255. **commoda...commodum**
'so long as you yourself are
gracious, you may be sure there's
a grace in your hair'. Sc. plays
upon the word *commodus*, which
has two senses in Plaut. (i) of
things 'all right' '*comme il
faut*' so Trin. 1117 *commoda
cueniunt,* Asin. 725 *minae com-
modae* 'of full weight', Most.
254 *commode* 'neatly' 'tidily';
cf. on Trin. 400: (ii) of persons
'accommodating', 'obliging', e.g.

Mil. 642 *conuiua commodus* 'a-
greeable', Cic. de Amic. § 54
mores commodi, etc., Most. 853
commode 'kindly'. *Incommodus*
has corresponding senses; for
(i) ' not as it should be' cf. Most.
418'unpleasant (consequences)',
807 'inconvenient'; for (ii) 'dis-
agreeable', cf. Asin. 62 *inpor-
tuna atque incommoda,* etc.; so
Hor. Epist. I 18, 75 *incommodus
angat.*

256. **uah** here an exclamation of disgust, 'Ugh!' cf. Aul.
294, 640; in Most. 457, 890
it is rather an expression of
horror or pain, cf. too 648. In
Trin. 1137 it is colourless.—
quid...quicquam: for the pleonasm cf. Aul. 803 *quis me Athe-
nis nunc magis quisquamst homo
quoi di sint propitii ?*—**pote**
(*potis*) without the verb *esse*
often = 'to be able'; thus here
pote = potest, Trin. 352 *pote =
potes,* cf. Virg. Aen. III 671,
where *potis = potis est.*

258. **quid...nam** = *quidnam;*
nam is frequently separated by

PHILE. malas qui óblinam.

Sc. úna opera *te* ebur átramento cándefacere póstules.

PHILO. lépide dictum de átramento atque ébure. euge,

plaudó Scaphae. 260

PHILE. túm tu igitur cedo púrpurissum.

Sc. nón do : scita's tú quidem.
nóua pictura intérpolare uís opus lepidíssumum?
nón istanc aetátem oportet pígmentum ullum attín-

gere,

néque cerussam néque mélinum néque aliam ullam

offúciam.

cápe igitur speculum.

PHILO. eí mihi misero : sáuium speculó dedit. 265
nímis uelim lapidém, qui ego illi spéculo dimminuám

caput.

Sc. línteum cape átque exterge tíbi manus.

PHILE. quid ita, ópsecro?

Sc. út speculum tenuísti, metuo né olant argentúm

manus :

259. *te* Müll., Lor.², om. in M.
260. *euge, adplaudo, Scapha* Bo., Rl., Lor.¹ But Uss. rightly
remarks that we have *euge* in Epid. 9 acc. to M, and A constantly
writes EUGAE. The quantity of εὖγε in Greek may well be different.
261. **purpurissimum** M, cf. gloss quoted by Loewe Prodr. p.
267 *purpurissimum: genus aedilis* (the last word is corrupt).
inscita's Müll., Bug.
262. *Nóuā* (abl.), cf. Intr. to Capt. A (i).
264. *mēlīnum*, not *mēlĭnum* as Lew. and Sh. (following Rl.'s
mēlĭnumue) say: *nēquĕ mēl-* form an anapaest.
268. *olant* Rl., rec. edd., oleant M.

one or more words from the interrogative in Plaut., e.g. Aul.
135 *quis east nam optuma?* 424;
so Virg. Ecl. IX 39 *Quis est nam
ludus in undis?*
259. **una opera** 'just as well'
cf. Men. 794 and on Capt. III 4,
31 ; for a different sense cf.
Men. 525 ('at the same time').—
postules te c. 'you might expect to' etc., cf. on Trin. 237,
Capt. III 5, 81 *cur ego me esse*

saluom postulem? With this
usage, cf. 1023 and contrast
omission of subject-accus. in 55.
262. **noua pict. interp.** ' to
daub with streaks of fresh paint ';
cf. 'to paint the lily': *interpolare*=vamp up anew: see Key
L. G. § 1342. 1, and cf. 274.
268. **ut tenuisti** 'After holding, as you have': cf. Pseud.
661 *nam ut lassus ueni de uia,
me uolo curare* 'having arrived

ne úsquam argentum te áccepisse súspicetur Philolaches.

270 PHILO. nón uideor uidísse lenam cállidiorem ullam
álteram.
út lepide atque astúte in mentem uénit de speculó
malae.

PHILE. étiamne unguentís unguendam cénses ?

         Sc. minume féceris.

PHILE. quápropter ?

 Sc. quia ecástor mulier récte olet, ubi níhil olet.
nám istae ueteres, quaé se unguentis únctitant, intér-
poles,

275 uétulae, edentulaé, quae uitia córporis fuco ócculunt,
úbi sudor cum unguéntis sese cónsociauit, ílico
ítidem olent, quasi quom úna multa iúra confudít cocus.
quíd olant nesciás. nisi id unum : ní*mis* male olere
intéllegas.

274. *istaec* Ald., Rl., Lor.[1], Bug.
275. *occulunt* Cam., edd., **occultant** M, an obvious gloss, like
that quoted by Loewe Prodr. p. 267 *occulunt: occultant.*
278. *olant* Rl., rec. edd., **oleas** M. *nimis male* S., **ni male** M
(**nimale** B), *male ut* Rl., Lor., Bug., *ut male* Uss. I also put a full
stop at *nescias*, and a colon at *unum*, where commas are found in
other editions.

wearied ', 278 *atque in pauca, ut*
occupatus nunc sum, confer quid
uelis; Amph. 329, Bacch. 106,
Merc. 371. So in Virg. Aen.
VIII 236 *Hanc, ut prona iugo*
laeuom incumbebat ad amnem,
Impulit, 'leaning, as it was',
Tac. Ann. IV 53 *poma, ut erant*
adposita, laudans; cf. line 241—
and Madv. § 444 a. Obs. 4.
—**olant**, cf. on 42 and 836.—
argentum. The mirror is supposed to be made of silver.
272. **unguendam** sc. *me;* cf.
on 55.
274. **istae ueteres** 'your old
ones'. — **interpoles** cf. Loewe
(Prodr. p. 267), *interpolis: ues-*
tis, quae ex uetusta fit quasi

noua. Here therefore properly
'furbished up', 'trimmed up',
like an old dress.
275. **uetulae edentulae** 'poor
toothless crones'.
278. **nisi id unum,** 'only
there is one thing'. For this
phrase cf. Mil. 24 *nisi unum:*
epityrum illi estur insanum bene,
1166 *nisi modo unum hoc: hasce*
esse aedis dicas dotalis tuas,
Men. 616. *Nisi* is in these
instances almost=*sed*; cf. further Mil. 378 *nisi mirumst faci-*
nus 'only it is a strange thing',
Trin. 233, Sallust Jug. XXIV 5.—
nimis male cf. Aul. 206.—**intel-**
legas is hypothetical subj.

PHILO. út perdocte cúncta callet: níhil hac docta
dóctius.
uérum illud esse máxuma adeo párs uostrorum in-
téllegit, 280
quíbus anus domi súnt uxores, quaé uos dote mérue-
runt.
PHILE. ágedum, contempla aúrum et pallam, sátin
haec deceat míhi, Scapha.
Sc. nón me istuc curáre oportet.
PHILE. quem ópsecro igitur?
Sc. éloquar.
Phílolachem: is ne quíd emat, nisi quod tíbi decere 284,
cénseat. 285
nám amator meretrícis mores síbi emit auro et púrpura.
quíd opust, quod suom ésse nolit, íd ei ultro osten-
tárier?

279. *doctiust* Rl., Lor., Bug.; see on 33.
280. *esse* (without stop) Gell., Bent., Rl., Uss., **est** M.   **maxima**
(**-um**) M (B has erasure after *maxima*), *maxuma id* Lang., Lor.[2]
281. *meruērunt* cf. *subegērunt* Bacch. 928, *iocauērunt* Pers.
160, etc.
282. *mihi* S., om. in M.   Cam. and edd. insert *me* after *haec:*
cf. on 284.
283. *istuc curare* Guy., Rl., rec. edd., **curare istuc** M.
284, 285. *decere* S. (see explan. note), **placere** M, edd.; Rl.
supposes a line to have been lost between *nisi* and *quod.*   Reading
placere it is certainly difficult, as Lor. says, to explain the logical
connection of ideas.
287. *nolit id ei* Rl., rec. edd., **nollitte** M.

279. **nihil...doctius**; cf. *ni-*
hil hoc simili similius Amph.
446, *nihil inuenies hoc certo*
certius Capt. III 4, 109. Such
phrases are to be regarded as
exclamatory: hence the omission of the verb *esse:* cf. too
nihil hoc confidentius Men. 618,
nihil hoc homine audacius ibid.
627; and on Most. 33.
280. Philol. turns and addresses the audience.—**adeo**
'what is more.'—**uostrorum**
partitive genitive=*uostrum*, as

Stich. 141 *neutram uostrarum,*
etc.; see on Aul. 319, and cf. the
old prayer in Livy VIII 9, 6 *diui,*
quorum est potestas nostrorum
hostiumque.
284. **tibi decere.** For dat.
cf. Amph. 820 *istuc facinus...*
nostro generi non decet, ibid.
1007 *ornatum capiam qui pŏtis*
decet, so Pers. 214; cf. on Ter.
Haut. 965.—**decere censeat** i.e.
deceat; cf. on 89 b.
287. **quod suom esse nolit**
'what he doesn't want to pos-

púrpura aetati óccultandaest, aúrum turpc múlieri.
289 púlcra mulier núda crit, quam púrpurata, púlcrior.
292 nám si pulcrast, nímis ornatast.

           PHILO. nímis diu apstineó manum.
quíd hic uos agitis?

           PHILE. tíbi me exorno ut pláceam.

           PHILO. exornatá's satis.
ábi tu hinc intro atque órnamenta haec aúfer. sed,

                        uoluptás mea,
295 méa Philematiúm, potare técum conlubitúmst mihi.

           PHILE. líbet et edepol técum mihi; nam quód tibi

                      lubet, id míhi lubet.

    288.   *aetati occultandaest, aurum turpe mulieri* after Bug. who
gives *aetati occultandae et aurum turpi mulierist*, **aetate** (**aetas** B
in marg.) **occultanda est aurum turpe** (-i) **mulieri** M, *aetas occultanda* (' the necessity of concealing years') *et auro turpe mulieri*
Bent., whom Lor.[2] follows in first half of line; *aetas occultandast:
aurum turpest mulieri* Rl., Lor.[1]   Might we not read *aetate occultanda* ('by concealing beauty and youth' cf. on 196) *et aurum turpest
mulieri* after M?
    289.   After this line M have

        **Postea nequicquam exornata est bene si morata est male
        Pulchrum ornatum turpes mores peius caeno continunt,**

which are quite unsuitable in the mouth of Scapha; the second
line is transcribed from Poen. 306.
    292.   *si* Cam., edd., **nisi** M.   *manum* FZ, edd., **manu** M.
    293.   *uos* Rl., Uss., Lor.[2], **uos diu** (due) M, *uos duae* Cam.: but
diu seems to have crept in from the last line.   *exornata's* Ell.
Rl., Uss., Lor. leave an hiatus.—*Quid hĩc* see Intr. to Capt.
A (i) p. 10, and cf. *quid hoc* 444, *Séd ĕst* 310, *quíd ĕst* 458, 742.
    296.   *tecum mihi* S., **mihi tecum** M.   *id* S., **idem** M.   Bent.,
Rl., and rec. edd. strike out *Libet*, Ell. om. *tecum*.   Müll.,
Bug., Lor.[2] read *mihi idem* for **idem mihi**.   See note on 509.

sess' i.e. jewels and dresses: he
wants the *person*.—**id ei ultro
ostentarier** ' be gratuitously
paraded before his eyes'.
Scapha means that there is no
reason to suppose that Philol.
wishes his bargain cancelled.
    288.   **aetati occultandaest.**
For the dat. of the gerundive

after *est* Bug. compares Livy
xxx 6 *ea, quae restinguendo igni
forent.*—**turpe**: viz. by imply-
ing that her charms are not suf-
ficient in themselves.
    292.   **nimis diu apstineo ma-
num** ' it is time to approach
them'.   Lamb. compares the
phrase *adire manum* Aul. 376.

PHILO. ém : istuc uerbum, méa uoluptas, uílest ui-
gintí minis.
PHILE. cédo amabo decém : bene emptum tíbi dare
hoc uerbúm uolo.
PHILO. étiam nunc decém minae apud te súnt : uel
rationém puta :
tríginta minás pro capite túo dedi.
PHILE. quor éxprobras? 300
PHILO. égone id exprobrém, qui mihimet cúpio id
opprobrárier,

297. So Br., Rl., Lor., **Mea uoluptas eam** (em B², *iam* F) **istuc
uerbum** M. Rams. following FZ and older editors gives the words
Mea uoluptas to Philem.   *Mea uoluptas, istuc uerbum* Uss.

297. **em** 'There now!' cf.
on 9.
298. **bene emptum** 'cheap'
so Pers. 587 *uin bene emere?*,
Cic. Att. 1 13 fin.; so *male emptum* 'dear' cf. 799, Pseud. 133,
Amph. 288, Cic. Att. 11 4, 1; *bene
uendere* 'to sell dear' Curc. 520.
299. **etiam nunc apud te
sunt** 'you have at the present
moment in hand'.—**uel** 'if you
like', cf. Trin. 964 CH. *Heus,
Pax, te tribus uerbis uolo. SVC.
uel trecentis* 'three hundred, if
you like', Bacch. 831 f. CH.
Sequere hac me tres unos passus.
NI. *uel decem;* so Stich. 426,
619, Pseud. 322, 345. Here the
disjunctive sense ('or') has almost disappeared. The other
characteristic meanings of *uel* in
Plaut. are: (ii) 'or rather', cor-
recting or withdrawing a statement, e. g. 921, 1091, Men. 177
feri: uel mane etiam; (iii) 'for
instance' e.g. Men. 1042, Mil.
55 *Qui sis tam pulcer: uel illae
quae heri pallio me reprehende-
runt;* cf. Virg. Ecl. 1 3, 50 *Au-
diat haec tantum—uel qui uenit,*

ecce Palaemon; (iv) 'even' as
so frequently in later Latin,
Most. 179, 984, Trin. 746 *atqui
ea condicio uel primariast* (see
Wagn.), esp. with numerals,
Pseud. 302, 829. — **rationem
puta** 'balance the account',
putare = prop. 'to clean, prune':
cf. Eng. 'to clear one's debts'
'ἐκκαθᾶραι τὸν λογισμόν' and
notes on Aul. 520, Trin. 417.
300. **quor exprobras?** cf.
Trin. 318 *quid exprobras bene
quod fecisti?*
301. **egone exprobrem?** 'I
reproach you?' cf. Capt. 11 1, 15
Nos fugiamus? 'What! we run
away?', ibid. 111 4, 24 *quid ego
credam huic?* 'Believe what?'
Most. 183 *ita ego istam amarem?*
(see note), Pseud. 288 *surruperet
hic patri, audacissume?*, ibid.
486 *abs te ego auferam?* This
idiom might be called the subj.
of indignant quotation: cf. the
slightly different instances in
note on 556.—**opprobrarier** almost = *exprobrarier*, but is perhaps rather more forcible: 'that
this should be cast in my teeth'.

néc quicquam argentí locaui iám diu usquam acqué
bene ?
PHILE. cérto ego, quod te amo, óperam nusquam
mélius potui pónere.
PHILO. béne igitur ratio áccepti atque expénsi inter
nos cónuenit :
305 tú me amas, ego té amo : merito id fíeri uterque exís-
tumat.
haéc qui gaudent, gaúdeant perpétuo suo sempér bono.
PHILE. áge accumbe igitur. cédo aquam manibus,
púere : appone hic ménsulam :
uíde, tali ubi sint. uín unguenta ?
PHILO. quíd opust ? cum stacta áccubo.
310 séd estne hic meus sodális, qui huc incédit cum sua
amíca ? is est.
Cállidamates cúm amica *eccum* incédit. euge, oculús
meus :

302. *iam* Cam., edd., **tam** M.
308. *puere...mensulam* Priscian iii p. 618, **puer...mensam** M.
After this verse M have
Qui inuident ne umquam eorum quisquam inuideat prosus
commodis
which most edd. have put after 306, but which Lang. has proved
to be unplaut. (*commoda* in Plaut. never = 'advantages', cf. on 255,
and *inuidere* takes a dat. of the *person* only; *prorsus* too is obscure).
310. *cum sua amica ? is est* Fl., Lor., Bug., **cum amica sua** |
(311) **Is est** M, Rl., Rams., Uss.

303. **certo** 'I am sure that'
= *certum est me nunquam potu-*
isse, cf. Epid. 540 *certo east =*
certo scio eam esse, Aul. 804,
Amph. 332, cf. Most. 953 (*certo*
scio).—**quod te amo** 'in loving
you' cf. Mil. 504 *Quod meas*
confregisti imbrices et tegulas,
Quodque inde inspectauisti etc.,
Capt. iii 4, 54—**operam** etc. 'I
have disposed of my heart in
the best possible way '.
308. Water for washing the
hands, dice, ointments and gar-
lands (not here mentioned) were

regular accompaniments of a
drinking bout.—**puere** is a voc.
of *puer* (old nom. *puerus*) cf. 843,
947, 949, 990 f. Philem., herself recently manumitted, loftily
addresses the slaves, as *pueri.*
Slaves did not call one another
by this name.
309. **cum stacta accubo** 'I've
oil of myrrh at my side', a com-
pliment to Philem.
311. **eccum** cf. on 83.—**ocu-**
lus meus is addressed to Philem.
cf. 325. The nominative for
the vocative is common in old

cónueniunt manupláres eccos, praédam participés
petunt.

CALLIDAMATES. DELPHIVM (CVM ADVORSITORIBVS).
PHILOLACHES. PHILEMATIVM. PVERI.

CA. Aduórsum ueníri mihi ád Philolachétem
uoló temperi. aúdi : em, tibíst imperátum.
nam illi ubi fui, inde ecfugi foras :　　　　　315
ita mé male conuíui sermónisque taćsumst.

The Second Canticum falls into two main sections. The
rhythm in SECTION *A* (313—335) is at first bacchiac, but varies
considerably and is often doubtful; in SECTION *B* (336—347) the
predominant rhythm is cretic (with admixture of trochaics).
SECTION *A*. 313—317 bacch. tetram. (315 is uncertain), 318,
319 anapaest. dim., 320 cret. dim., 325 iamb. octon., 328 iamb.
octon., 329 cret. tetram. cat., 330 bacch. tetram., 333 troch. trip.
cat., 334 cret. tetram.: in verses 315, 321—324, 326, 327, 331, 332,
335, I have abstained from marking the ictus, as various scansions
are possible but none certain. Speng. is inclined to scan 323
(reading *face* for *facere*), 324 (*sta* for *asta*), 326, 327, 329, 331 (*ma-
madere*), 332 as anapaestic dim.
　313. *ueníri* Dous., Rl., rec. edd., **uenire** M. *Philolachetem*
Herm., Crain, Speng., Lor.[2]
　314. *tibist imperatum* Herm., Rl., Speng., Lor.[2], **tibi imperatum est** M.
　316. *me male* Lor.[2], **me ibi male** M, Rl., Rams., Uss., *Itá male*
Speng.

Latin and in the poets, cf. Poen.
366 *meus ocellus*, 367 *meus mol-
liculus caseus*. Livy I 24, 7
Audi tu, populus Albanus, Lucr.
I 45, Hor. A. P. 292. In Asin.
664 we have both nom. and voc.,
*da, meus ocellus, mea rosa, mi
anime, mea uoluptas*.
　312. **manuplares** 'the companions in the service'.—The
praeda is the property of Theopropides.
　Enter Callidamates, accompanied by Delphium and his
servants (*pedisequi*); he has just
left another party, and has already drunk deeply. His first
words are addressed to the *pedisequi*. Philol. and Philem. take

no part in the conversation till
336.
　313. **aduorsum uenire** (*ire*
876, 880 etc.) 'to come (go) to
fetch' cf. Intr. p. x; in IV 1 the
pedisequi appear as *aduorsitores*.—**ueniri** is impersonal.
　314. **tibi**, perh. said to his
favourite slave Phaniscus.
　. 315. **illi**=*illic*, so 327, 787,
792; so *isti*=*istic* 741, 1064,
1143.—**illi ubi...inde** cf. on *mulier quae...ei* 250.
　316. **male taesumst** 'got
horribly bored'; for the adv. of
cognate meaning cf. on *di te bene
ament* Capt. I 2, 29, and Aul.
186 *perspicue palamst*, 'it is
quite clear', Most. 495 *inepte*

nunc cómmissatum íbo ad Philólachetem, ubí nos
hilari íngenio et lepide áccipiet.
ecquíd tibi uideor má-madere?

320 DE. sémper istóc modo
321, moratus uita*m* degebas.   CA. uisne ego te ac tu me
322   amplectare?
DE. si tibi cordist facere, licet.   CA. lepida's.
duce me amabo.
                        DE. caue ne cadas: asta.
325 CA. o ó! ocellus és meus! tuós sum alumnus,
                                                 mél meum.
DE. caue modo, ne prius in uia accumbas
quam illi, ubi lectust stratus, quo imus.
CA. siné sine cadere mé.
                        DE. sino.
                        C*A:* sed *né sine* hoc, quod
                                        mi ín manust.
DE. sí cades, nón cades, quín cadam técum.

---

317. So Lor., Bug., Speng.; in M *ubi nos* belongs to next
verse.
318. *lepide* Cam., Rams., rec. edd., **lepida** M.
319. *ma-madere* after Bo., **mammam adire** M.
320—322. So Speng., Lor., **uite debebas** M, *moratus uiuis,
haud uti debebas* Bug., *more alio uti debebas* Uss. *amplectare*
Pyl., Rl., rec. edd., **amplectere** M. The reading in these lines cannot be considered certain.
324. *Duc* Herm., making cret. tetram. cat.
327. *quo imus* Uss., **coimus** M, *nos coimus* Rl., *eo coimus* Ell.
328. *sino. CA. sed ne sine hoc* Rl. (after Herm.), Lor., Bug.,
Speng., **sinos et hoc** M.

stultus = 'extremely dense', 911
longe longissima 'far the longest'.
319. **ma-madere** 'to be ti-
tipsy'. Something of the effect
of a stammer is also given in
Pseud. 1297 *non uides me ut
madide madeam* (for *madide* cf.
also on 316).
321. **uitam degebas** cf. *aetatem degere* Cist. 1 1, 79, *dego
diem* Most. 534.

324. **duce** = *duc.*—**asta.** Delphium supports him in her arms.
325. **alumnus** 'your baby.'—
mel meum: cf. the Irish expression 'my honey' (*mo mhil*).
326. **in uia accumbas** 'sit
down in the street'.
327. **lectus**, the *triclinium.*
Trans. freely 'the table is laid'.
328. **ne sine hoc quod** etc.,
i.e. 'not without *you*'.

CA. iacéntis tollét posteá nos ambo áliquis.   330
DE. madet homo.
        CA. tun me ais ma-ma-madere ?
DE. cedo manum : nolo equidem te adfligi.
CA. ém tene. *DE.* age, í simul,
quó ego eo ; an scís ?   CA. scio : in méntem uenít
                         modo :
nempe domum eo commissatum.
DE. immo istuc quidem.   }335
        CA. iam memini.
PHILO. núm non uis, me óbuiam hisce íre, anime mi ?
ílli ego ex ómnibus óptumé uolo.
iam reuortar.
      PHILE. diu est ' iam ' id mihi.

330. *ambo* Herm., Rl., Lor., Bug., **ambos** M.
331. *CA.* FZ, edd., om. in M. *me ais* Scal., edd., **meam uis**
(his) M, *me uis* Reid. **mammam adere** M : cf. 319.
333. *i* Speng., rec. edd., ii M, *i i* Rl., Lor.[1] In M the whole
verse is given to DE., and the distribution is confused to the end
of the scene.
334. *eo* S., **eam** M, Herm., Rl., Rams., Lor., Bug. (making the
subj. depend on *an scis :* but *an* must stand first in its clause, as
Uss. says); *CA. quo ego eam?* *DE. an nescis* Gertz, Uss.
336—347. SECTION *B.* 336 cret. dim. + ⌣–⌣–≈, 337 = 108, (338
is uncertain), 339—341 = 336, 342, 343 cret. dim. + troch. trip. cat.
(= 108), 344 = 336, 345 ⌣–⌣– | ⌣–⌣–≈ (two troch. trip. cat.), 346
troch. septen., 347 cret. tetram. cat.
336. *hisce ire* FZ, Herm., Lor., Stud., Speng., **his eire** M
(see Speng. Reformv., note on p. 93). Leo proposes *bitere* for *ire*,
scanning as = 108.
337. *Illi ego* Cam., edd., **Ilico** M.
338. *id iam* Bug., Lor.[2], scanning as = 108; the line as it
stands in M is a cret. trim.; cf. Intr. p. xxviii.

330. **iacentis** 'where we lie'.
333. **age, i simul** ' come
along, do '.
334. **quo ego eo** ' (to the
place) where I am going '.—**an**
almost = *nonne.*
335 *b.* **istuc**, with a gesture;
' to your friend's '.
338. ' **iam** ' **id** ' that word
soon '; cf. *istuc actutum* 71.

For the order, which is certainly
unusual, cf. Ter. Andr. 264 '*in-
certumst*' *hoc* = ' this word *incer-
tumst*,' Martial v 58, 1, 2 (and
again 3, 5, 6)
*Cras te uicturum, cras dicis, Pos-
tume, semper.*
*Dic mihi cras istud, Postume,
quando uenit.*

CA. écquis hic ést?

PHILO. adest.

CA. eú, Philolaches.

340 sálue, amicíssume mi ómnium hominum.

PHILO. dí te ament. áccuba, Cállidamates.

únde agis te?

CA. únde homo ébriús probe.

PHILE. quín amabo áccubas, Délphiúm mea?

ílli da quód bibat. CA. dórmiam ego iam.

345 PHILO. núm mirum aút nouom quíppiám facit?

DE. quíd ego hoc faciam póstea, mea?

PHILE. síc sine eumpse.

PHILO. age tu ínterim

dá cito ab Délphio cántharum círcum.

341. *PHILO.* FZ, edd., om. in M.

342. Hiatus after cret. dim. : cf. Intr. p. xxix.

343. I have followed Seyff. and Lor.[2] in giving the line to Philem., instead of to Philol., cf.*on 385. M omit name altogether.

344. *illi da* Speng., Lor.[2], **da illi** M. *CA.* Uss., Speng. (In B a space is left for the name).

346 I have assigned to Delph. and Philem., instead of to Philol. and Delph. as Rl., Rams., Lor., Bug.; *quid—mea* would be discourteous in the mouth of Philol., as Uss. says.

347. *cito ab Delphio* Herm., Rl., Lor., Bug., **ab Delphio cito** M, Speng., who scans as an anapaestic line, and regards the alliteration (*c. c. c.*) as intentional: cf. Intr. p. xxviii.

339. **eu** (εὖ) 'Bravo!' 'Well done!' is rightly described (by Brix (on Mil. 394) as 'particula laetantis et laudantis': it is exactly equiv. to *euge* (cf. 686).

342. Cf. Bacch. 1106 *PH. et tu, unde agis te? NI. Unde homo miser atque infortunatus.*—**probe** cf. on 4.

344. **illi** i.e. to Callid., who refuses the offered cup.

346. Delph. addresses Philem. in reply to her invitation (343).—**hoc**, cf. on 636.—**mea** 'dear'.—**sic sine eumpse** 'leave him by himself, where he is'; for *sic* cf. on 71.— **eumpse** = *eum ipsum.*—**tu** is said to a slave.

347. **ab Delphio** 'beginning with Delphium', as the visitor.

ACTVS II.

TRANIO. PHILOLACHES. CALLIDAMATES.
PHILEMATIVM. DELPHIVM. PVERI.

TR. Iúppiter suprémus summis ópibus atquc in-
dústriis
mé perisse et Philolachetem cúpit erilem fílium.
óccidit spes nóstra: nusquam stábulumst confidéntiae. 350
néc Salus nobís saluti iam ésse, si cupiát, potest ;
íta mali maeróris montem máxumum ad portúm modo
cónspicatus sum. érus aduenit péregre : periit Tránio.
écquis homost, qui fácere argenti cúpiat aliquantúm
lucri,
quí hodie sese éxcruciari méam uicem possít pati ? 355

355. *meam uicem* Pyl., edd., **meamui** (mea uice) M.

Enter Tranio as *seruos cur-*
rens, in hot haste from the harbour (i. e. by the stage-door to
the left of the spectators cf. Intr.
p. vii). His first speech (348—
362) is delivered to the audience.
   348. **summis opibus atque**
industriis 'with all his might
and main': for *opibus* cf. Merc.
111 *ex summis opibus uiribusque*
experiri, Stich. 45, Cic. Tusc.
III 11, 25 *omnibus uiribus atque*
opibus repugnare; in Plaut. the
sing. *ops* is only used in the
sense of 'help'. The plur. *in-*
dustriis is prob. determined by
opibus.
   349. **perisse**, stronger than
perire, 'to be a dead man'.
   350. **stabulumst conf.** 'can
assurance find a home'; cf.

Capt. III 3, 8 *nec confidentiae*
usquam hospitiumst nec deuorti-
culum dolis.
   351. Cf. Capt. III 3, 14 *neque*
iam Salus seruare, si uolt, me po-
test.—**si cupiat, potest,** a slight
anacoluthon, = *neque potest, ne-*
que possit, si cupiat ('even if she
wished' cf. on 115).
   352. **mali maeroris montem**
'mountain of monstrous misery';
cf. 61. For *mali=uehementis*
(adj. of cognate meaning) cf. on
316 and Capt. I 2, 29.—**ad por-**
tum 'by the harbour' cf. *ad*
forum 'in the market-place' 844,
999.
   354. **lucri facere** is like *con-*
pendi facere 60 'to earn' 'to
clear'.

úbi sunt isti plágipatidae, férritribacés uiri,
357 uél isti, qui hosticás trium numnum caúsa subeunt
súb falas?
359 égo dabo ei taléntum, primus qui ín crucem ex-
cucúrrerit :
360 séd ea lege, ut óffigantur bís pedes, bis brácchia;
úbi id erit factum, á me argentum pétito prae-
sentárium.
séd ego sumne infélix, qui non cúrro curriculó
domum?
PHILO. *tándem* adest opsónium : eccum Tránio a
portú redit.

356. *ferritribaces*; cf. *flagritrĭba* Pseud. 138, *tympanotrĭba*
Truc. 611. Compounds of τρίβειν have, in Greek, a short penult.
(from the verbal stem), but in Lat. the verbal and present stems
seem to have been confounded.
357. *hosticas trium nummum* Rl. (on Trin.² 152), rec. edd.,
hastis trium nummorum M. *falas* Cam., edd., **falsa** M.
After this line M have **Vbi (Vel B¹) aliqui quique denis hastis corpus transfigi solent (solet)**. (*Vel ubiquomque* Rl., Lor.², *Vel alii
qui* Bug., after Scal., *Vel aliquo unde* or *Vbi alicunde* Ell., *Vel
ubiquomque abiegnis hastis...solet* Leo). But the line seems to be
an interpolation, suggested perh. by the word *falas* and the passage
of Livy (xxi 8, 10) quoted by Leo; *falarica erat Saguntinis, missile
telum hastili abiegno: ferrum autem tres longum habebat pedes, ut
cum armis transfigere corpus posset.* Possibly 357 is also an interpolation; (*subire* does not occur elsewhere in Plaut., see Lang. p.
218).
362. *sumne* Pyl., Bent., Rl., rec. edd., **sumne ille** M.
363. *Tandem* Herm., Bug., Lor.², om. in M, *En* Rl., Lor.¹,
Euge Uss.

356. **plagipatidae** 'sons of
the whip', again Capt. iii 1, 12,
where see note.
357. **uel** 'or rather', since
356 seemed to point to *slaves*;
here the reference is to Greek
mercenaries. Cf. on 299 (ii).—
nummum is the regular gen. pl.
in Plaut.; cf. on Trin. 152. For
sense of *mummus* cf. on Most.
115 (2); the *tres nummi* of the
Trinummus stand for any small
sum. There is therefore no reference to the daily pay of the
Roman legionary, which was
3 (and ⅓) *asses* at the time of
Polybius.—**fala** a high wooden
tower, from which the missiles
called *falaricae* were thrown.
359. **excucurrerit** 'makes a
sally upon'.
362. **curriculo** 'at full speed'
=*cursim;* for the *figura etymologica* cf. 45 *uiuere uictibus*, 985
misere miseret, 1158 *ludo ludere*,
Capt. ii 1, 54 *honore honestare*,
Men. 93 *uincire uinculo* etc.;
cf. too 930 *curriculo uenire*.

Tr. Phílolaches.
    Philo. quid ést?
        Tr. *et* ego et tu—
        Philo. quíd et ego et tu?
            Tr. pérïimus.
Philo. quíd ita?
    Tr. pater adést.
    Philo. *hem* quid ego ex te aúdio?
        Tr. apsumptí sumus: 365
páter inquam tuos uénit.
    Philo. ubi is est ópsecro?
        Tr. *in portú iam* adest.
Philo. quís id ait? quis uídit?
    Tr. egomet ínquam uidi.
        Philo. uaé mihi.
quíd ego ago?
    Tr. nam quíd tu, malum, me rógitas, quid
                 agas? áccubas.
Philo. tútin uidisti?
    Tr. égomet, inquam.

364. *et* Dous., edd., om. in M. *periimus* Pyl., Rl., rec. edd.,
perimus M.
    365. *hem* Seyff., Lor.², om. in M, *ex ted* Bo., Rl., Lor.¹
    366. *in portu iam* Rl., rec. edd., om. in M.
    368. *ago?* *TR. nam* Dous., edd., **agas TR. num** M.   *accubas*
Cam., edd., **accubans** M.   Scan *málñ' me.*
    369. *PH. tutin uidisti* Fl. (cf. Mil. 290), Lor., Bug., **tu nuidisti**
B, **tui inuisti** C, **tuun uidisti** D, *tun uidisti* Rl., Uss., *tutin uisti* Koch.

365. **quid ita?** 'why so?' cf.
267, 472, 644, 1094: similarly
quid iam 465, 1081.
    368. **quid ago?** = *quid agam?*
cf. 774 *eon?* = *eamne?*, Trin.
1062. Tran. pretends to misunderstand him.—**nam quid** cf.
on 191.—**malum** cf. on 6.—
accubas 'you're sitting at table'.
    369. **tutin** = *tute ne*, cf. *us-
quin* = *usque ne* 449, and the
common forms *istic* = *iste-ce*,
illic = *ille-ce.*—**certe.** Lang. re-

gards this word as adv. to *uidisti* = 'distinctly' [cf. Lucr. IV
760 *certe ut uideamur cernere*]:
but in Asin. 722 we have *certe
inquam*, unconnected with a verb
of seeing, and in Merc. 186 *certen
uidit?* must mean 'is it certain
that he saw her', as Lang. admits. Here then perh. trans.
'Sure?' 'Upon your word?' (as
an asseverative particle), cf. 571,
720, 952.

PHILO. cérte?

TR. *certe*, inquam.

PHILO. óccidi,

370 sí tu uera mémoras.

TR. quid mihi sít boni, si méntiar?

PHILO. quíd ego nunc faciám?

TR. iube haec hinc ómnia amolírier.

quís istic dormit?

PHILO. Cállidamates. súscita istum, Délphium.

DE. Cállidamates, Cállidamates, uígila.

CA. uigilo: cédo bibam.

DE. uígila: pater aduénit peregre Phílolachae.

CA. ualeát pater.

375 PHILO. uálet ille quidem atque *égo* disperii.

CA. bís peristi? quí potest?

PHILO. quaéso edepol *te*, exsúrge: pater aduénit.

CA. tuos uenít pater?

iúbe *eum* abire rúrsum. quid illi réditio huc etiám fuit?

certe inquam Cam., edd., **inquam** M.
370. *mentiar* Pyl., Bent., edd., **mentirer** M.
372. **Quid** CD.   *suscita istum* D. are given by edd. since
Lamb. (except Uss.) to Tranio; but unnecessarily.
373. *bibam* Bent., Rl., rec. edd., **ut bibam** M, Rams.
374. *Philolachae* Lamb., Rl., Rams., Lor., Bug., **Philolache** M,
Philolachis Z, Uss., *Philolachi* Reid (dat. commodi).
375. *ego* Pyl., edd., om. in M.   *CA. Disperisti* F, Rl.
376. *te* Rl., rec. edd., om. in M.
377. *eum* Rl., rec. edd, om. in M.   *huc etiam* Cam., Rl.,
Rams., Lor., Bug., **etiam huc** M, Uss.

371. **haec** i.e. the apparatus of the banquet.—**amolirier** is prob. pass., as *apiscitur* Trin. 367, *meditatus* 'practised' Mil. 903; but it might be active with the obj. of *iube* (i.e. *seruos*) understood; cf. 421, 426.
374. **ualeat pater** 'deuce take his father!' cf. Amph. 928 *ualeas, tibi habeas res tuas, reddas meas*, Hor. Epist. II 1, 180 *ualeat res ludicra*.
375. **ualet...disperii. CA. bis**

peristi? It is impossible to render the puns adequately: in *ualet* ('is very well') Phil. plays on *ualeat*, in *bis peristi* the drunken Call. misunderstands *disperii*.—**qui potest?** = *quomodo pote est?* 'how is it possible?' cf. 396 *potest*, Aul. 270 *non potest*, and Most. 758, 1051.
377. **quid**, etc. 'What business had he to': cf. 6 and 34.—**etiam** 'pray' cf. on 383.

PHILO. quíd ego agam ? pater iam híc me offendet
          míserum aduenicns óbrium,
aédis plenas cónuiuarum et múlierum. miserúmst opus,
ígitur demum fódere puteum, úbi sitis faucés tenet : 380
sícut ego aduentú patris nunc quaéro, quid faciám
                        miser.
TR. écce autem *iterum* hic déposiuit cáput et dormit.
                        súscita.
PHILO. étiam uigilas ? páter, inquam, aderit iam híc
          meus. CA. ain tú, pater ?
cédo soleas mihi, ut árma capiam : iám pol ego
                occidáṃ patrem.
DE. pérdis rem : tace amábo. *PHILO.* abripite hunc
          íntro actutum intér manus. 385
CA. iam hércle ego uos pro mátula habebo, nísi mihi
              matulám datis.
PHILO. périi.
    TR. habe bonum ánimum : ego istum lépide
              medicabó metum.

378. *patĕr iam hĭc* cf. *patĕr párcerem* Trin. 316 and Intr. to
Capt. A (ii) ; Wagn. Intr. to Aul. xxxiii says the word drops the
final *r* ; Lor. regards the word as monosyllabic (by syncope, =
patr). *offendet* FZ, edd., **offendit** M.
    380. This line is only found in B. *fodere* Cam., edd., **todere
fondere** B. *cubi* Rl. (Opusc. III 140), to avoid hiatus.
    382. *iterum* Müll., Leo, om. in M. *Eccere aut. h.* Rl., rec. edd.,
Ecce hic autem Guy., Bent. *deposiuit* Cam., Bent., edd., **deposuit** M.
    383. *aĭn* (2 sylls.), cf. 593.
    384. *Soleas cedo mi* Rl., Lor., Bug., to avoid the proceleusma-
tic ; but cf. Truc. 363 *cedo soleas* (MSS. including A), Br. on Trin.³
934, Capt.⁴ 493, and Introd. p. xxi.
    385. *DE.* (**PHILO.** M), ... *PHILO.* Seyff., who argues that *amabo*
is a phrase only used by women ; so 343, but cf. 324. Men. 678.
    387. Either *Péri'. ha ,bé* or *Périi . hábĕ* with hiatus.
meditabor B (from next line), **medicabor** D², Bent., edd. antiq.

380. **igitur demum** cf. on   cf. Catull. xxxiv 8.
132.   383. **etiam uigilas?** ' *Will*
    381. **sicut** = ' for instance',   *you wake?*' an impatient com-
'I mean to say' (application   mand 'Wake up!' cf. Trin. 514
of a general principle) ; cf. Men.   *etiam tu taces?* For the present
588, Mil. 518 etc.   tense cf. further 887a *manesne*
    382. **deposiuit** = *deposuit* ;   *ilico?* (= *mane*).

PHILO. núllus sum.

TR. taccás : ego, qui istaec sédem, ıncditabór tibi.
sátin habes, si ego úducnientem íta patrem faciám
                                                    tuoɪn,
390 nón modo ne intro eát, uerum etiam ut fúgiat longe
                                                ab aédibus ?
uós modo hinc abíte intro atque haec hínc propere
                                                amolímini.
PHILO. úbi ego ero?
TR. ubi máxume uis ésse, cum hac, cum istác eris.
DE. quíd si igitur abeámus hinc nos ?
                    TR. nón hoc longe, Délphium.
nam íntus potate haúd tantillo hác quidem causá
                                                minus.
395 PHILO. eí mihi, quam, istaec blánda dicta quo
                            éueniant, madeó metu.

389. *pauefaciam* or *terrefaciam* (for *faciam*) Bent. (deleting
ego), in order to avoid hiatus.
391. *propere hinc* Rl., Lor.¹, Bug. But the conjunction of
haec hinc lends force, as Br. (Trin.³ 683 crit. note) says.
392. *ego ero ergo* Müll., Bug., in order to avoid hiatus (cf. on
567). *uis esse* Bo., Rl., Lor., *esse uis* M, *esse te uis* Müll., Bug.
393. *si* Bo., rec. edd., **est** M: Bent. simply deleted *est*. But
cf. passages quoted in explan. note.
394. Hiatus after *tantillo* in diaeresis, cf. 389.
395. *quam istaec* Cam., edd., **quom ista haec** M.

388. **nullus sum** 'it is all up
with me'.—**taceas**=*tacc*, cf. on
1129. —**qui istaec sedem** 'how I
may settle that business quietly'.
389. **patrem faciam** ... **ne**
'prevent your father from', with
transference of the subject of
the subordinate clause into the
principal clause: cf. 661, 811.
390. **ne**=*ut...non* cf. Capt.
iii 5, 80.
391. **uos** addressed to the
slaves.—**haec** cf. 371.
392. **hac, Delphium, istac**
Philem., who may be supposed

to be standing near Philol.
393. **quid si igitur ?** 'how
would it be then if we?' etc.; for
igitur in protasis cf. 1093, Merc.
421 *quid si igitur reddatur?*
ibid. 578 *quid si igitur cenam
faciam ?* and on 132.—**non hoc
longe** 'not an inch!' cf. Trin.
483. The phrase is accompanied by an appropriate gesture (δεικτικῶς) : cf. **haud tantillo** (394) 'not ever such a little
bit.'
395. **madeo metu** 'I sweat
with fear'.

TR. pótin animo ut siés quieto et fácias quod iubeó?
                PHILO. potest.
TR. ómnium primúm, Philematium, íntro abi, et tu
                Délphium.
DE. mórigerae tibi érimus ambae.
                TR. íta ille faxit Iúppiter.
ánimum aduorte núnciam tu, quaé uolo accurárier.
ómnium primúmdum *ut* aedes iám face occlusaé sient. 400
íntus caue muttíre quemquam síueris.
                PHILO. curábitur.
TR. támquam si intus nátus nemo in aédibus habitét.
                PHILO. licet.
TR. neú quisquam respónset, quando hasce aédis
                pultabít senex.
PHILO. númquid aliud?
       TR. cláuem mi harunc aédium Lacónicam
iám iube ecferri íntus: hasce ego aédis occludam
                hínc foris. 405
PHILO. ín tuam custodélam meque et méas spes
                trado, Tránio.
TR. plúma haud interést, patronus án cluens. † pro-
                prior sciet 407

396. *sies* Cam., Rams. (cf. Intr. p. xxi), **sis** M, *ut animo sis*
Bent., rec. edd.
399. *nunciam tu* Lor., Bug., **nunc tu iam** M.
400. *ut* Bent., om. in M, *haec* Rl., Lor., Bug. *face*, Rl., rec.
edd., **fa.** . B, **fac** M.
406. **custodelam** Bo., Rl., rec. edd., **custodiam** M. *spes meas* Rl.,
Rams., (M ? cf. Uss., Lor.).
407. **an** B²DF, **ac** B¹. **propior siet** B². After this line there
is vacant space for one verse in M, which however may have
been due to the change of metre.

396. **potin**=*potis*(*pote*)*ne est*
=*fierine potest ut*, cf. on 375.
398. **ille Iuppiter** ' great
Jove', cf. Amph. 461, Virg. Aen.
II 779.
401. **caue siueris**=*caue ne*
sinas cf. 523, 808.
402. **natus nemo** 'no mortal
creature (mother's son)', cf. 451.
—**licet** 'very good', cf. 930, 1153.

405. **intus** 'from within',
foris 'from the outside' (cf. 426
hinc 'from this side').
407. The last part of the line
is corrupt: **pluma** prob. abl.
cf. Ter. Adelph. 76 *hoc* ('in this
respect') *pater et dominus inter-*
est. In 406 Phil. says 'I put
myself under your guardian-
ship'; and the general sense of

*   *   *   *   *   *   *

409 hominí, quoi nulla in péctorest audácia.
410 nam quoíuis homini uél optumo uel péssumo,
quamuís desubito fácilest facere néquiter:
ucrum íd uidendumst, íd uiri doctíst opus.
quae díssignata sínt et facta néquiter,
tranquílle cuncta ut próueniant et síne malo,
415 ne quíd patiatur, quam ób rem pigeat uíuere.
sicút ego ecficiam, quaé facta hic turbáuimus,
profécto ut liqueant ómnia et tranquílla sint,
neque quícquam nobis páriant ex se incómmodi.

409 looks very much like a gloss on *homini pessumo*: the *homo pessumus* is to Tranio the *coward* or the *fool*. Lor.[2] reads *multa* (for *nulla*), connecting with 411, and striking out 410 (as Rl.).
411. After this line M have 425, which occurs again in its proper place: Acid. made the correction.
413. **dissigna(-ni)ta** M, Uss. (so Keller in Hor. Epist. I 5, 16, and Brambach; cf. *dissignator* [M] in Poen. Prol. 19), *designata* Rl., Rams., Lor., Bug. *nequiter* Dous., Bent., Rl., rec. edd., **nequitia** M.
414. So Bent., Rl., rec. edd., **et ut proueniant sine** M. M invert order of this and following line.
415. **ni** B[1]D (= *ne*). **patiatur** B[2], edd., **potiatur** B[1]CD, Bent.
416. *turbauimus* Lamb., Rl., rec. edd., **turbabimus** M (but confusion of *b* and *u* is common in M, cf. 1032, Asin. 224).
418. *se* Cam., edd., **eis (ei)** M.

407 may have been, 'it does not matter whether you call yourself patron or client'. In 746 Phil. calls Tran. *patronus*, prob. with reference to this line.
409 is of course unintelligible without the lost line.
411. **quamuis desubito** = *tam desubito quam uis* 'on the shortest notice'. —**facere nequiter** 'play a deep game', cf. *malus*, *scelestus* = ' cute ' (170, 1071, 1107).
412. **uiri docti** 'a man of genius', cf. 186, 279, 1072 etc.
413. **quae dissignata sint** 'his bold schemes': cf. *quid non ebrietas dissignat* Hor. Epist. I 5, 16 *modo quid dissignauit?* Ter. Ad. 87, where

Donatus remarks ' *Designare* (i.e. *dissignare*) est rem nouam facere; in utramque partem et bonam et malam'. Thus **nequiter** is not to be taken with *dissignata*.
414. **tranquille proueniant** 'have a happy ending'.
416. **sicut** cf. on 381.—**turbauimus**, as so often, of the intrigue or mischief of slaves, cf. 546, 1032, 1053, Capt. I 2, 18; trans.: the storm which we have raised'. Similarly in Tac. Ann. IV 1 *turbare Fortuna coepit*, Virg. Aen. VI 858 *magno turbante tumultu*.
417. **profecto** 'positively', 'actually'.
418. **incommodi** cf. on 255.

sed quíd tu egredere, Sp*h*aério?
            Pver. em *clau*im.
                        TR. óptume
praecéptis pares.
      PVER. *ipsus* iussit máxumo   420
opere órare, ut patrem áliquo apsterrerés modo,
ne introíret ad *se.*
      TR. quín etiam illi hoc dícito:
factúrum *me,* ut ne etiam áspicere aedis aúdeat,
capite óbuoluto ut fúgiat cum summó metu.
clauím cedo atque abi hínc intro: occlude óstium, 425
et ego hínc occludam. iúbe uenire núnciam:
ludós ego hodie uíuo praesenti huíc seni
faciám: quod credo mórtuo numquám fore.

419. *egredere, Sphaerio? PV. em clauim* Scyff., Lor.², **egrede-
res perio iamiam** M, *egredere? perii . eho iamiam* Rl., Lor.¹, *egredere puere?* (but cf. on 308) *PV. fero clauim* Bug., *egredere sic
per ianuam?* Uss. According to the old reading, the slave, in reply
to Tranio's question, *shows the key* without answering in words;
but this is scarcely in Plaut.'s manner: besides *iamiam* is unintelligible.
420. *pares. PV. ipsus* S., **paruisti PV.** M, Bent., Lor.² (with
Philolaches und. as subject), *pares* (*paret* Bug.) *PV. erus te* Rl.,
Lor.¹, Bug.
422. *ad se* Pyl., Uss., Lor.², **adest** M, *aedis* Cam., Bent., Rl.,
Bug.
423. *me* Pyl., rec. edd., om. in M.
425. *occlude* Rl., rec. edd., **atque occlude** M.
427. *huic* Pius, Bent., Rl., Lor., Bug., **hic** M, Rams., Uss.

423. **ne etiam asp.**=*ne asp.
quidem.*
424. **capite obuoluto,** a sign
of terror or despair; cf. 523.
426. **iube,** a formula for a
challenge, cf. Rud. 708 *iube
modo accedat prope,* Ter. Ad.
914 *iube nunciam dinumeret;*
similarly Most. 11 *sine modo
adueniat senex.—et:* cf. on 529.
427. **ludos alicui facere** is
'to play a comedy to divert
anyone' ironically (cf. Rud. 593,
Merc. 225 *miris modis di ludos*

faciunt hominibus) with an allu-
sion in the next line to funeral
games; cf. Cas. IV 1, 4 *nec pol
ego Nemeae credo, neque ego
Olympiae | neque usquam ludos
tam festiuos fieri | quam hic intus
fiunt ludi ludificabiles | seni
nostro.* [Hence 'to make a scene
for' Truc. 759 *iam hercle ego tibi*
(so MSS.) *ludos faciam clamore
in uia*]: cf. on Arg. 7.   Similar
jokes in Amph. 458 f., Aul. 251 f.
428. **quod** (=*id quod*) **credo**
etc. 'I take it there is no chance

concédam a foribus húc : hinc speculabór procul,
430 unde áduenienti sárcinam inponám seni.

THEOPROPIDES (CVM PEDISEQVIS). TRANIO.

TH. Habeó, Neptune, grátiam magnám tibi,
quom méd amisisti á te uix uiuóm domum.
uerúm si posthac mé pedem latúm modo
scies ínposisse in úndam, haud causast, ílico
435 quod núnc uoluisti fácere quin faciás mihi.
apage, ápage te a me núnciam post húnc diem :
quod créditurus tíbi fui, omne crédidi.
TR. edepól, Neptune, péccauisti lárgiter,
qui occásionem hanc ámisisti tám bonam.
440 TH. triénnio post Aégypto aduenió domum :

432. *Quom med* Guy., Bent., Rl. (Neue Plaut. Exc. i 49, B),
Bug., Lor.², **Quom me** M, *Quoniam me* Rl.   *domum* Lor.²,
modo M.
434. *causast, ilico* Bent., Rl., Lor., Bug., (cf. Amph. 714),
causa ilico est M.

of his having games at his
funeral;' i.e. he will die a poor
man (owing to the recent extravagance of his son).—**numquam** = an emph. *non;* cf. on
164.
430. **unde** 'to see whence'
viz. *sarcinam imponam.*—**ad-
uenienti** 'on his arrival', as
aduenio = 'I am come'.—**sarcinam imp.** = 'cajole' cf. 778 *uehit
hic clitellas*, Mil. 985 *probe oner-
atum*, Bacch. 349 *illest oneratus
recte.*
Enter Theopropides (left; cf.
ii 1) with attendant slaves; he
offers ironical thanks (cf. 435
quod nunc uoluisti facere) to
Neptune for his safe return.
For similar addresses to Neptune cf. Trin. 820 ff., Stich. 403.
432. **quom** with indic., cf.
on 29.—**amisisti** 'let me escape'

(= *dimisisti*) cf. 439, Capt. Arg.
7, ii 2, 82.
433. **pedem latum** (prop. an
adverbial accus. of extent) is
here a lax object after *inposisse*,
'set one foot's breadth'.
434. **scies** 'find out', cf. on
149.—**inposisse** = *inposiuisse* (cf.
382) = *inposuisse.*—**haud causast**
...**quin** 'I give you leave to'.
437. **crediturus fui** ' ever
meant to entrust'.
440. **Aegypto** = *ex Aeg.*, cf.
Ponto 'from P.' Truc. 540, *Alide*
'in Elis' Capt. ii 2, 80, *Alidem*
'to Elis', ib. iii 4, 41. Conversely names of *towns* are sometimes constructed with a prepo-
sition e.g. *in Ephesum* Mil. 113.
This vagueness, which in the
time of Plaut. was becoming an-
tiquated, is not unknown even
to later writers; thus we have

credo, éxpectatus uéniam familiáribus.
TR. nimio édepol ille pótuit exspectátior
ueníre, qui te núntiaret mórtuom.
TH. sed quíd hoc? occlusa iánuast intérdius.
pultábo. heus, ecquis ístas aperit mí*hi* foris?   445
TR. quis homóst, qui nostras aédis accessít prope?
TH. meus séruos hic quidemst Tránio.
                    TR. o Theópropides,
ere, sálue : saluom te áduenisse gaúdeo.
usquín ualuisti?
            TH. usque, út uides.
                    TR. factum óptume.
TH. quid uós, insanin' éstis?
                    TR. quidum?
                    TH. síc, quia   450
foris ámbulatis : nátus nemo in aédibus

444. *sed quíd hŏc*, cf. 293, 310, 444, 459, 742.
445. *mihi* Cam., edd., **in** M.
447. *seruost hic quidem* Lor.²
449. *usquin (usquen) ual.* Bent., Rl., rec. edd., **usque inual.** M.

in Sallust (Jug. xxviii 5) *Rhe-
gium atque inde Siciliam*, in
Virg. (Aen. i 2) *Italiam...uenit*,
and in Ovid (Met. xiii 156)
Phthiam hacc Scyrumueferantur.
441. **familiaribus** 'the in-
mates of my house' including
the slaves as in Mil. 183, 262,
Asin. 743, Amph. 127, 146 etc.;
sometimes the word denotes the
slaves excluding relatives Men.
611, Amph. 359, etc.
442. **exspectatior.** The comparative is anteclassical; so *oc-
clusior* Trin. 222, *factius* ib. 397,
confossior Bacch. 889, *confiden-
tior* Amph. 154, *lubentior* Asin.
268, etc.; cf. Most. 150.
444. **occlusa ianua.** It was
of course unusual to lock (*oc-
cludere*) the house-door (*ianua*,
fores cf. Truc. 254 f., Stich. 308)

during the day; but we need
not infer that it was usual to
leave it *open:* see a good article
by Mr Hartley in Hermathena
viii p. 303 ff.—**interdius** 'in
broad daylight' an old adv.
containing, acc. to Büch. L.D.
§ 158, the gen. of *dius* (4th Decl.
=*dies*); we have *dius* opposed
to *noctu* in Merc. 862: cf. Aul. 72.
449. **usquin ual.** 'have you
kept in good health?' cf. Epid.
305 *EP. ne abitas, priusquam
ego ad te uenero. AP. usque
opperiar.*—**factum** cf. on 33.
450. **sic, quia** 'why, because'
lit: 'in this way (you are mad)
that ..' ; so Pareus in Lex.
(=*ideo*), cf. too Pseud. 336.
451. **ambulatis** 'are pro-
menading'.—**natus nemo** cf. on
402.

68　　　　　MOSTELLARIA.　　[II. 2. 22—34.

seruát, neque qui reclúdat neque respóndeat.
pultándo paene cónfregi hasce ambás *foris.*
454, Tr. eho, an tú tetigisti hasce aédis?
455　　　　　　　　　　Th. quor non tángerem?
quin púltando, inquam, paéne confregí foris.
457 Tr. tetigístin?
　　　　　Th. tetigi, inquam, ét pultaui.
　　　　　　　　　　Tr. uáh.
　　　　　　　　　　　　Th. quid est?
459 Tr. male hércle factum.
　　　　　Th. quíd est negoti?
　　　　　　　　　　　　Tr. nón potest
460 dicí, quam indignum fácinus fecisti ét malum.
465 Th. quid iám?
　　　　Tr. fuge opsecro átque apscede ab aédibus.
466 fuge húc, fuge ad me própius. tetigistín foris?
458 Th. quo módo pultare pótui, si non tángerem?
462 Tr. occídisti hercle—
　　　　　Th. quém mortalem?
　　　　　　　　　　Tr. omnís tuos.
463 Th. di té deaeque omnes fáxint cùm istoc ómine—
464 Tr. metuó, te atque istos éxpiare ut póssies.

452.　*neque resp.* Bent., Bo., Rl., Bug., Uss., **neque quis resp.** M.
453.　*Pultando* Bent., Rl., rec. edd., **Pultando pedibus** M. *joris*
Rl., rec. edd. (cf. Capt. iv 2, 51), om. in M, (*hasce ambas*) *TR.* eho
(from next line) Guy., Bent., Bo.
454.　hasc*e* Schmidt, Lor.², has M.
457—467.　I have followed the order of M, with Rams. and rec.
edd.; Rl. rearranges the passage in the order indicated by the
numerals in the margin, substituting *tene terram manu* in 466 (cf.
469, but *tene* seems the wrong word) for *tetigistin foris?* which he
regards as repeated from 457.

452.　**seruat** 'is attending to
the door', cf. Aul. 81 *redi atque
intus serua,* etc.—**neque...re-
spondeat** loosely, for *qui aut
recl. aut resp.*
457.　**uah** cf. on 256.—For
quid est after **uah** cf. Mil. 1139.
460.　**fecisti** cf. on 149.
465.　**quid iam?** 'Why so?'

cf. 1081 and on 365.
458.　**si non tangerem** 'if I
was not to touch them'.
463.　**faxint** sc. *ut pereas.*
'*Faxint* occultius id notat quod
perduint apertius'. Bent. on
Ter. Hec. i 2, 59.
464.　**istos** prob. the *pedisequi,*
who are again referred to in 467

Th. quam ob rem? aút quam subito rém mihi
adportás nouam? 461
Tr. ere heús, iube illos íllinc ambo apscédere.   467
Th. apscédite.
Tr. aedis ne áttigatis.   tángitin'
nos quóque etiam?
Th. opsecro hércle, quin ei tángerent?
Tr. quia séptem menses súnt, quom in hasce aedís
pedem 470
nemo íntro tetulit, sémel ut emigráuimus.
Th. elóquere, quid ita?
Tr. círcumspicedum: númquis est,
sermónem nostrum qui aúcupet?
Th. tutúm probest.

467. *Ere* rec. edd., **Et**...M.   *illim* Bo., Rl., Bug., Uss.
ambo Scal., Lor.², Scyff., **amabo** M, Rl., Bug., Uss.
468. *attigatis* Diomedes, edd., **atigate** B¹CD, **attingite** B²F.
tangitin' S., **tangite** BD, **tangere** C.
469. *etiam* S., **terram** M. This word has hitherto remained
unquestioned. Lor. explains 'do you also touch the earth (as I am
doing)': but we are not told before that Tranio had touched the
earth. Touching the earth edd. explain as a sign of appeal to the
Manes, and cf. Hom. Il. ix 567 ff., Cic. de Har. Resp. xi 23, Ma-
crobius Sat. i 10, 21.   *ei tangerent* S., **eloquere** M (which
does not scan, and is probably taken from 472), *eloquere iam* Pyl.,
eloquere rem Bo., *intro imus huc* Rl., Lor., Bug.

(**illos**): Lamb. explains *istos* as
=*omnis tuos* 462.
468. **attigatis**(ante-classical)
=*attingatis*, cf. Bacch. 440 *si
attigas puerum manu*, 445 *ne
attigas puerum*, Truc. 276 *ne
attigas me*, etc.; similarly *tā-
gere* = *tangere* Mil. 1092 (*tāgax*=
tangax).—**ne attigatis**=*ne atti-
geritis*. For the ante-class. form
of prohibition with pres. subj.
cf. on Capt. ii 2, 81 *ne duis*=*ne
dederis*.
469. **quoque etiam** : for the
pleonasm cf. on Men. 1160 *uenibit uxor quoque etiam*, Pseud.

932 *te quoque etiam*, Epid. 234
*cani quoque etiam ademptumst
nomen*, 589 *hanc quoque etiam*
etc.
471. **nemo** '(it is seven months
since) *anyone*' cf. Amph. 302
*iam diust quod uentri uictum
non datis*' since you have given '.
—**tetulit**. This is the predo-
minating form of the perfect of
fero in Plaut., and is occasionally found too in Ter., Lucr.,
Catull.
473. **aucupet** cf. on 166.—
probe cf. on 4.

Tr. circúmspice etiam.

         Th. némost: loquere núnciam.

475 Tr. caputális caedes fáctast.

         Th. non intéllego.

Tr. scelus ínquam factumst, iám diu antiquom ét
                                       uetus,

id ádeo nos nunc *démum* factum inuénimus.

Th. quid istúc est sceleris aút quis id fecít? cedo.

Tr. hospés necauit hóspitem captúm manu:

480 iste, út ego opinor, qui hás tibi aedis uéndidit.

Th. necáuit?

         Tr. aurumque éi ademit hóspiti,

eumque híc defodit hóspitem ibidem in aédibus.

Th. quaprópter id uos fáctum suspicámini?

Tr. ego dícam: ausculta. út foris cenáuerat

485 tuos gnátus, postquam rédiit a cená domum,

abíimus omnes cúbitum, condormíuimus.

475. *non* Cam., Bent., Uss., **quid est? non** M. *Caputale factumst. TH. quid id est? non intellego* Bo., Rl., Lor., Bug.
     477. So Leo, **Antiquom id adeo nos nunc factum** M, *TH. An-
tiquum? TR. id adeo* etc. F, Uss., Lor.[2] (cf. *Necauit?* 481).
     478. *est sceleris* Bent., Speng., rec. edd., **est sceleste** M, *est
scelesti* Dissald., Bent. (in his copy of Par.), *scelestist* Lor.[1], Reid.
     481. *ei* Sciopp., Uss., Lor.[2], et M, *eidem* Rl., Lor.[1], Bug.—
Scan *ēi* (two syllables) as 947, 986.
     484. *ausculta tu* Bent.; but the hiatus may be justified by the
pause: cf. 498, 1127.
     485. *rediit* Dous., Bent., Rl., rec. edd., **redit** M.
     486. *Abiimus* Weise, **abimus** M, edd.; but the tense is prob. in
any case perfect, and it seems better to write, as Umpfenbach
does, uniformly with *ii*: cf. Eun. 539.

474. **etiam** 'again'.
     475. **caputalis** 'atrocious'.
     476. **iam diu** etc. 'now long
past and forgotten,' cf. 494 *abhinc sexaginta annis*: for the
combination of *uetus* and *antiquom* cf. Trin. 381, Mil. 751,
Cic. Phil. v 17, 47 etc. The
phrase is here (perh. intention-
ally) scarcely consistent with
480.
     477. **id adeo** 'it is this,

which': *adeo* lends emphasis to
id, as in Amph. 952 *is adeo*,
Aul. 288 *ei adeo*, 615, 732; similarly Mil. 1192 *ego adeo*, Rud.
731 *uos adeo*, Pseud. 143 *nunc
adeo*.
     478. **quid sceleris**, cf. Ter.
Eun. 326 *quid hoc est sceleris*,
cf. Epid. 350 *quid istuc est uerbi?*
     484. **ut foris cen.** 'haviug
dined out' cf. on 268.

lucérnam forte oblítus fueram extínguere:
atque ílle exclamat dérepente máxumum—
TH. quis homo? án gnatus meus?
          TR. st', tace: auscultá modo.
ait uénisse illum in sómnis ad se mórtuom.   490
TH. nempe érgo in somnis?
          TR. íta: sed auscultá modo.
ait íllum hoc pacto síbi dixisse mórtuom—
TR. in sómnis?
          TR. mirum, quín uigilanti díceret,
qui abhínc sexaginta ánnis occisús foret.
intérdum inepte stúltus es, *Theópropides.*   495
TH. taceo.
          TR. sed ecce, quae ille† inquit * *

489. *meus gnatus* Bo., Rl., Bug., Lor., to avoid the spondaic
word in the second foot; but cf. *nunquám* Capt. I 2, 9, *nullús*
Poen. 991 etc.   *st! tace* Cam., edd., **si tace** M.
493. *quin* Pyl., edd., **qui** M.
495. *Theopropídes* Lor., Uss. (*Theurópides* Rl.).
496. The line is corrupt; *quae illi ille inquit mortuos* Rl.,
(495) *interdum ineptis. TII. taceo. TR. sed ecce, quae ille ait* Bug.
(uniting the two lines).

487. **oblitus fueram**=*obl.
sum* cf. 519, 821 (note).
488. **atque...derepente**'when
all of a sudden'.—**ille**, vaguely,
as Theopropides' question (489)
shows. Tranio has not quite
made up his mind who shouted
out, and refuses to commit himself when asked.
491 **nempe ergo in s.** 'it
was in sleep then, if I understand you?' i.e. it was only a
dream after all.—**ita** 'yes'.
493. **mirum quin** 'he could
hardly have' etc., 'voudriez-
vous que...?;' lit. 'it is strange
why not'; the phrase is always
ironical, and = 'of course...not',
cf. Trin. 495, 967, Rud. 1393,
and the instances quoted by

Ramsay (Most. p. 148 f.); for
mirum est (mira sunt) ni (='I
shouldn't wonder if...') see on
Capt. IV 2, 25.—**uigilanti** 'when
wide awake'; the meaning is
that the dead can only hold
converse with the living *in sleep*.
494. **abhinc sex. annis**,
'sixty years ago': the more ordinary expression would have
been *abhinc sex. annos* (cf.
Bacch. 388, Stich. 137, Truc.
341); but cf. Cic. Verr. II 52,
130 *comitiis iam abhinc diebus
xxx factis*.
495. **inepte stultus** cf. 316
(note), 952 *erras peruorse* 'you
are very much (preposterously)
mistaken'.

'ego tránsmarinus hóspes sum Diapóntius.
hic hábito : haec mihi déditast habitátio :
nam me Áccheruntem récipere Orcus nóluit,
500 quia praémature uíta careo. pér fidem
decéptus sum : hospes me híc necauit, ísque me
defódit insepúltum clam in hisce aédibus,
sceléstus, auri caúsa. nunc tu hinc émigra :
sceléstae haec aedes, ínpiast habitátio.'
505 quae hic mónstra fiunt, ánno uix possum éloqui.
st st !
Th. quid ópsecro hercle fáctumst ?

Tr. concrepuít foris.

498.   *dedita haec mihi est* (*mihist*) Bo., Rl., Bug.   But cf. 484.
499.   **nam me** BD[1], **nam me in** D[2]F, **nam ine** C.   Acheruntem
M, but cf. Trin. 525 (Rl. Praef. Trin.[2] p. lxvi).   Orchus M, and
again in Asin. 606.
501.   *me hic* Guy., edd., **hic me** M.
502.   *clam* Bent., Rl., rec. edd., **clam ibidem** M (cf. 482).
504.   *haec* Guy., Bent. (*haecc*), Rl., Lor., **hae sunt** M, Rams.,
Bug., Uss.

497—504, uttered by Tranio
in a sepulchral tone.
497.   **Diapontius**, a proper
name, which Tranio invents to
suit the occasion [διαπόντιος =
transmarinus].
500.   **praemature.**   Those
who died before their appointed
time found no abode in the
nether regions prepared for
them, but were compelled either
to roam about on earth or to wait
at the entrance to Tartarus
(cf. Virg. Aen. vi 426—429, 434
—436) ; here the body had also
been buried without due funeral
rites, cf. 502 (**insepultum**).—**per
fidem deceptus** 'the victim of
treason' lit. 'betrayed under
promise of protection', cf. Livy
i 9, 13 *per fas ac fidem decepti*,
Cic. de Invent. i 39, 71 *qui nos
per fidem fefellerunt,* Cic. pro

Caecina iii 7 *qui per tutelam
aut societatem fraudauit quem-
piam.*   In these phrases *per* may
possibly mean 'in violation of',
cf. *perfidus, periurus.*
504.   **scelestae**'under a curse',
so again 532, 563, Rud. 502 *quid
mihi scelesto tibi erat auscul-
tatio?* etc. : so in Capt. iii 5,
104 *scelus = infortunium.*   This
sense is peculiar to Plaut.; cf.
170.—**haec** the regular form of
nom. pl. fem. before a vowel or
h cf. 640.
506 ff.   A noise is heard
within ; Philolaches and his
guests are not supposed to be
aware of the conversation which
is going on outside the house
(cf. 515).   This inopportune
episode Tranio cleverly turns to
his advantage.

hicíne percussit! TH. gúttam haud habeo sán-
guinis:
uiuóm me accersunt ád Charontem mórtui.
TR. perii: íllisce hodie hanc cónturbabunt fábulam. 510
nimis quám formido, né manufesto hic me ópprimat.
TH. quid tú*te* tecum lóquere?
TR. apscede ab iánua:

508. ¡Warren, Leo (see explan. note), ? M, edd. Rl. (reading
Haecine percussast?) and Uss. give 508—510 to Tranio.
509. *ad Charontem* S., **adcheruntem** CD¹ (the second hand in
D adding a above the line), **adacheruntem** B, *Acheruntem* Bent.,
Herm., Rl., Uss., *Accheruntem* Spong., Bug., Lor². (cf. above on
499), *ad Acheruntem* Stud., Müll. See further in Excursus I.
510. *TR.* Cam., Rams., Lor., Bug., om. in M. *Perii* Cam.,
edd., **Per** M.
512. *TH.* Cam., edd., **TR.** BFZ. *tute tecum* Z., edd., **te tu
cum** M. *TR.* Cam., edd., om. in M.

508. **hicine perc.** 'It was
he (i.e. Theopr.) who knocked!'
cf. 516. This is spoken to the
pretended ghost. The existence of an asseverative enclitic
particle -*nĕ* (ultimately identical with the interrogative -*nĕ*,
but entirely distinct from *nē*=
val, which is never enclitic) has
been proved by Minton Warren
(American Journ. of Phil. II.
pp. 50—82). It is attested by
Priscian, who speaks of a '*ne
confirmatiua*' and it is found in
the MSS. in a number of passages from which it has been
violently expelled by editors.
Perhaps its most characteristic
use is in answers, confirming a
previous question, e.g. Trin.
634 *L V. egone? LE. tune! 'I?*—
Yes, you', Capt. IV 2, 77, Epid.
575, Stich. 635 *egone? tune!
mihine? tibine!*, Pers. 220 *itanest? itanest!*; so Most. 580, 955;
but it is also found in exclamatory sentences, e.g. the present
passage, with which compare

Epid. 541 *plane hicine est qui*
etc.; and in conditional sentences e.g. Mil. 309 (*hocine si
miles sciat*), 936 (*at egone hoc
si*), etc., etc.
510. This and the next line
as said *aside*.—**illisce** 'those fel-
lows in the house': for this form
of the nom. pl. (=*illi-ce*) cf.
935, 1098, Capt. III 4, 120;
similarly we have *hisce* (=*hi-ce*)
in Capt. Prol. 35 (note), Men.
877 (note), etc.
511. **nimis quam** 'exceeding-
ly', cf. Capt. I 1, 34 *nimis quam
misere cupio*, and the phrases
*mirum quam, sane quam, mirum
quantum*, ὑπερφυῶς ὡς, θαυμασ-
τῶς ὡς.—**manufesto** cf. on 679.
—**hic** i.e. Theopropides.
512. The suspicions of Th.
are aroused and Tr. sees that
his only chance is to get rid of
his master. His *abscede ab
ianua* is said with an affectation
of extreme terror.—**tute** an emphatic *tu*.

fuge, ópsecro hercle.

      Tн. quó fugiam? *Tr.* ctiam tú fugis?
nihil égo formido: páx mihist cum mórtuis.
515 INTVS. hcus, Tránio.

      Tr. non mc áppellabis, sí sapis.
nihil égo commerui, néque istas percussí foris.
Tн. quaesó quid *istuc est, quór sermonem* ségrcgcs?
*   *   *   *quaé* res te agitat, Tránio?
quicum ístaec loquere?

      Tr. an quaéso tu appelláueras?
520 ita mé di amabunt, mórtuom illum crédidi
expóstulare, quía percussissés foris.
sed tu étiamne astas, néc quae dico optémperas?
Tн. quid fáciam?

      Tn. caue respéxis: fuge, operi caput.

513. *quor* Bo., Rl., Uss. *TR.* Bo., Rl., om. in M.   *fugis?*
Cam., Rl., **fugies (-ges)** M, *fuge* Scal., rec. edd. (cf. 527).
515. *INTVS* Rl., rec. edd., **TH.** M.   *TR.* FZ, edd., om. in M.
517. So Rl. (with *segregas* for *segreges*), Lor., Bug.,; M have

     Queso .... **Quid segreges.**

518. *TR. Caue uerbum faxis. TH. quae res te agitat, Tranio?*
Rl., rec. edd.; but this seems improbable. It is more likely that
the two lines belonged entirely to Theopr.
519. *TR.* FZ, edd., om. in M.
521. *percussissem* Acid., Rl., Lor., Bug.
523. *operi* Guy., Bent., Rl., rec. edd., **operi atque** M.

513. **etiam tu fug.?** cf. on 388.
515. A voice calls from behind the door. Tranio, sup-
posing that Theopr. had heard
it, and again equal to the occasion, uses a form of reply (uttered in a voice of terror) which
gives the requisite hint to the
person behind the door and at
the same time sounds to Theopr.
like an appeal to the ghost.
517. **sermonem segreges**
'break off the conversation',
cf. Mil. 651, Poen. 349.
519. **quicum** interrogative,
cf. on 174, and Mil. 424, 425.—

an...appellaueras? 'Was it you
that called?' For the tense cf.
on 821. Tran. now sees that
Theopr. has not heard the words
spoken from within (515).
522. **etiam** 'still', so 851;
etiam uigilas 383 is quite different.—**quae dico**; for the omission of the antecedent (*eis*) cf.
Amph. 449 *non ego illi obtem-
pero quod loquitur,* and on Capt.
v 1, 20.
523. **respexis, curassis** (526)
are old fut. perfects = *respexeris,*
curaueris, cf. on 212.

TH. quor nón fugis tu?
       TR. páx mihist cum mórtuis.
TH. scio : quíd modo igitur? quór tanto opere ex-
                                              tímueras ? 525
TR. nil mé curassis, ínquam : ego mihi prouídero.
tu ut óccepisti, tántum quantum quís fuge,
atque Hérculem inuocá tibi.
                           TH. Hercles te ínuoco.
TR. et égo, tibi hodie ut dét, senex, magnúm ma-
                                                  lum.
pro di ínmortales, ópsecro uostrám fidem,   530
quid égo hodie negóti confecí mali.

527. *fuge* FZ, Bent., edd., **fugis** B, **fui** CD.
528. *inuoca tibi* S., **inuocabi** B[1]CD[1], **inuocabis** B[2]D[3]FZ, Rams.,
Ell., *inuoca bis* Scal., *inuoca* Bent., Rl., Lor., Uss., *inuoca*. TH. *mihi*
Bug.   *Hercles* Br. (Men.[3] crit. note on 202), **Hercules** M, Bent., Rl.,
Lor., Uss., *Herculĕ* Scal., Bo., *Herculem* Bug., Ell.   *ted inuoco*
Bent., Fl., *te ego inuoco* Rl., Lor., *inuoco* Bug., *uoco* Ell. In support
of *Hercles* Brix compares Stich. 223 *Herclés te amabit...*, Epid. 179
neque séxta aerumna acérbior Hercli..., Men. 201 *Haud Hercles*
(so B) [*ad*]*aeque....* A dissyllabic *Hercules* is also attested by a
few inscriptions (see Rl. Opusc. II 475, IV 85), and is easily paralleled
by other syncopated forms in Plaut., e.g. *anglos* Aul. 434, *uehicla*
Aul. 498, *benficio* Asin. 673, *periclo* (Bacch. 827 and frequently),
manuplares Most. 312, besides *nosti*, *dixti*, *fexti*, *aduexe*, etc.
Something might also be said in favour of *Herculĕ* as a voc.; cf.
Callidamatĕ (MSS. but?) 1130, *Palamedĕ* Nemes. Aucup. 15, *Achillĕ*
(abl.?) Prop. IV 11, 40 : other vocatives in -e quoted by Neue Formenl.
pp. 295, 296, e.g. *Achille, Hippomene, Ulixe* (so common in Ovid
and Seneca), are either long or doubtful. But *hercle*, which is in-
variable as the interjection, is evidence against *Hercule* as the
vocative.
529. *tibi* FZ, edd., **ut ibi** M.
531. Scan *quĭd ĕg' hŏ | diĕ | etc.   *mali* Guy., edd., **malum**
M, but cf. Trin. 847.

525. **scio** 'so you said before',
half ironically.
526. **prouidero** is here hardly different from *prouidebo*, cf.
on 590 and on Capt. II 2, 65.
527. **quis** = *potes*.
528. **Herculem** i.e. as 'Aλε-
ξίκακος.—With the invocation to
Hercules, exit Theopr. Enter

the money lender from the direction of the forum (town), i.e.
by the stage-door to the right of
the spectators (cf. II 1). He
does not see Tranio till 560.
529. **et** = 'and...too'; trans.
'and so do I': so in 397, 426,
cf. on 569.

DANISTA. THEOPROPIDES. TRANIO.

DA. Sceléstiorem ego ánnum argento faénori
numquam úllum uidi, quam híc mihi annus óp-
tigit.
a máni ad noctem usque ín foro degó diem:
535 locáre argenti némini nummúm queo.
TR. nunc pól ego perii pláne in perpetuóm modum.
danísta adest, qui dédit *argentum faénori*,
qui amícast empta quóque *opus in sumptús fuit.*
manufésta res est, nísi quid occurró prius,
540 hoc né senex rescíscat. ibo huic óbuiam.
sed quídnam hic sese tám cito recipít domum?
543a, metuó ne de hac re quíppiam indaudíuerit.
545b accédam atque adpellábo. utut res sése habet,

534. *mani* Rl. (cf. 767), rec. edd., **mane** M.
537, 538. B gives two half lines (completed by Cam.), which
CDF have united.
539. *quid* an early correction, Rl., rec. edd., **quod** M.
540. *Hoc ne* Bo., Bug., Lor.², **Ne hoc** M, Uss., *Ne hoc nunc*
Cam., Rl., Rams.
542. *indaudiuerit* Bo., edd., **inaudiuerit** M.
543—545. M. have

Accedam atque adpellabo. et quam timeo miser.
Nihil est miserius quam animus hominis conscius,
Sicut me habet. uerum utut res esse se habet.

532. **Scelestiorem** 'unlucky'
cf. 504, 563.—**argento faeno-**
ri 'for money (put out) at interest', =*argento faenori collo-*
cato. For **faenori** cf. 1140
(*faenori sumere*), 918 (*dare arr-*
aboni), 1092 (*quaestioni acci-*
pere): sometimes we find the
form **faenore** (602, 917, Epid. 53)
which may perh. be a dative also,
cf. the phrases *iure dicundo*
(=*iuri d.*), *lex opere faciundo*
(=*l. operi f.*), *triumuiri aere*
argento auro flando feriundo etc.,
so common in inscriptions.
535. **nummum argenti** 'one

silver didrachm' cf. *argenti num-*
mos Aul. 108 and note on 115.
536. **in perpetuom modum**
'every inch of me'=*perpetuo*
(550), *perpetuos,* cf. 147, 1035.
538. Note **qui** (abl.) and **quo**
in the same line.—**in sumptus**
cf. on 122.
539. **nisi quid** occ. pr. **ne**
'unless I am beforehand with
some move to prevent', etc.
540. **huic** i.e. the money
lender: **hic** (541) Theopr.
542. **indaudiuerit** 'got wind
of' cf. on Capt. Prol. 30.

pergám turbare pórro: ita haec res póstulat.   546
unde ís?
TH. conueni illum, únde hasce aedis émeram.
TR. numquíd dixisti de íllo, quod dixí tibi?
TH. dixi hérclc uero, ómnia.
                    TR. ei miseró mihi:
metuó ne techinae méae perpctuo périerint.   550
TH. quid túte tecum?
                    TR. níhil enim. sed díc mihi:
dixtíne quaeso?
                    TH. díxi, inquam, ordine ómnia.

(543 *ei* for *et* Rl., edd.; 545 *mi* Bo., Rl.; *ututi* Bo., Rl., Ell., *res sese*
rec. edd., *res ea sese* Ell.). I have followed Langen in regarding the
passage from *et* to *uerum* as an interpolation: (1) the sentiment of
544 is scarcely suitable in the mouth of Tranio; (ii) *conscius*
nowhere else in Plaut. or Ter. has the sense 'conscious of guilt':
it means merely 'in the secret', cf. Aul. 38, Rud. 926 etc.; (iii)
sicut me habet must be explained *sicut me conscium* (or *miserum*)
habet animus, 'as mine keeps me', which is scarcely sense.
    549. With hiatus justified by the slight pause: cf. too for
non-elision of *o* (here before another *o*) Gellius VI § 20, quoted in
Intr. to Capt. p. 15 f., and Ell.'s Excursus on Catull. XXVII 4.
uero ei Rl., Lor.², *uero ea* Bug., *uerod* Rl. (Neue Plaut. Exc.
p. 86), *uero omne ordine* Müll. (cf. 552).   *ei* D³, Rl., rec. edd., *uae*
B, *et* CD¹. After this verse M have 553, 557, 558, 559, which also
occur in their proper places: deleted here by Acid., edd.
    552. *Dixtine* Bent., Rl., Rams., **Dixtin** M, *dixtin quaeso hercle*
Müll., rec. edd.

546. **pergere porro** 'to go
on', as in 963, Trin. 162, *perge
porro proloqui*, 777, Amph. 803
perge porro dicere, Asin. 472
perge porro 'go on!'; similarly
pergunt turbare usque Most.
1053.—**turbare** cf. on 416.
    547. **is**=*uenis*, cf. *exi* 1.—
unde emeram=*a quo em.*, (Fr.
dont = *de unde*) cf. 997; so *huc* =
ad hunc 689, *hinc*=*ab hoc* 596,
inde=*ab eis* 879 (cf. Fr. *en*).
    550. **techinae** a latinized
form of τέχναι, supported by the
MSS. here and in Poen. 817
(by *J* in Capt. III 4, 112); cf. the
gloss *techinis: fraudibus, dolis*

(Anal. Plaut. p. 211); similarly
mina for μνᾶ 627, *drachuma* for
δραχμή, *Alcumena* (in Amph. regularly) for Ἀλκμήνη.
    551. **nihil enim** 'nothing, I
assure you': *enim* is not an in-
ferential but an asseverative
particle in Plaut., cf. Langen
Beiträge pp. 261—271, and
Trin. 1134 *enim* ('why') *me no-
minat*, Capt. III 4, 60 *enim iam
nequeo contineri* 'I declare I can
no longer contain myself'; see
also on 828, Capt. III 4, 36.
    552. **dixti** =*dixisti*, cf. *e-
munxti* 1109.—**ordine** 'from
beginning to end'.

Tr. etiám fatetur de hóspite?
                                        Th. immo pérnegat.
Tr. negát?
     Th. negat, inquam.
                    Tr. quám sit iniquom cógita.
555 non cónfitetur?
     Th. dícam, si conféssus sit.
quid núnc faciundum cénses?
                              Tr. egon, quid cénseam?
cape, ópsecro hercle, aéquom cum eo iúdicem:
sed eúm uideto ut cápias, qui credát mihi:
tam fácile uinces, quám pirum uolpés comest.
560 Da. sed Philolachetis éccum seruom Tránium,

554, 555.   M give incomplete lines: TH. negat inquam Cam.,
quam sit ini- Uss., non confitetur Cam.
     556.   ego Bo., Rl., rec. edd.
     557.   aequom cum eo S., with hiatus, in caesura, after the
interjection, cum eo (meo) una M, cum eo actutum Lang., Lor.²,
cum eo me una Bent., te, una cum eo Rl. (after Pyl.), cum eod una
Rl. (N. Pl. Exc.), cum homine una Bug., Uss.   Lang. shows
clearly that una is unsuitable.
     560.   eccum seruom Tranium Pyl., Rl., Lor., Bug., seruom
eccum Tranium M, Rams., Uss., eccum seruus Tranio Scal., which
violates usage; see on 804.

555. dicam...sit for dicerem
...esset; cf. Asin. 393 si sit domi,
dicam tibi, Epid. 331 si hercle
habeam, pollicear lubens, Bacch.
635 pol si mihi sit, non pollicear,
followed immediately by the reply scio, dares (imperf.), Ter.
Andr. 310 tu si hic sis, aliter
sentias (cf. Roby § 1532).
     556. egon, quid censeam?
'I?' What I think?' Cf. the
French 'ce que je pense?'; for
the subjunctive in a question
which repeats the question or
command of another cf. 906 f.
TR. ecquid placent? TH. ecquid placeant, me rogas?, Aul.
543 ME. quid est? EV. quid sit,
me rogitas?, Most. 577 f. TR.
gere morem mihi. DA. quid tibi

ego morem uis geram?, which
instances doubtless explain the
origin of the subjunctive as dependent on some verb like rogas,
uis understood.   Thus quid cen-
seam? above=rogasne quid cen-
seam? and in 579 abeam?=uisne
abeam?, so 620: cf. note on 301.
     557. cape cum eo iudicem
'choose an arbitrator between
you', cf. Rud. 1380, Truc. 629,
and the verse discovered by
Stud. in A (after Cas. v 4)
nunc ego tecum aequom arbitrum
extra consilium captauero. With
capere cum aliquo cf. cauere cum
aliquo 1142 and note.
     558 f. are an 'aside'.
     560. eccum seruom. Eccum,
eccam, eccos, eccas, eccillum, ec-

qui míhi nec faenus néc sortem argentí danunt.
TH. quo té agis?
                 TR. eccum, quo ábeo.   ne ego súm miser,
sceléstus, natus dís inimicis ómnibus.
iam illó praesente adíbit. ne ego homo súm miser:
ita et híuc et illinc mi éxibent negótium.   565
sed óccupabo adíre.
             DA. hic ad me it. sáluos sum:
spes ést de argento.
                TR. hílarus est: frustrást homo.

---

562. *eccum quo* Uss., Lor.², **nec quoquom** (**-quam**) M, *nequo-
quam* Z, Fl., Rl., Bug. ('nowhere'?).
564. *ne ego sum* Herm., Rl., Lor. (omitting *homo*).
567. *TR.* Cam., edd., om. in M; B gives the whole line to
Tran. After *argento* hiatus with change of speakers, as so

cistum etc., when not used pa-
reuthetically as interjections
(cf. 83 and note), are either followed by an accus. (so here,
Mil. 1216 *era, eccum praesto
militem*, Bacch. 568 *duas ergo
hic intus eccas Bacchides*) or else
stand alone (1127, Pers. 739):
see further in Brix, Capt.³ 1005.
—**Tranium** (nom. *Tranius*) is
prob. a mere bye-form of *Tranio*
(so Büch., Fl., Uss.); although,
as Uss. says, 'miramur Plautum
uersus causa Tranionis nomen
mutasse'. Fl. compares *archi-
tectus* (Mil. 915), a bye-form of
architecto (ibid. 919, Most. 760).
Rl. regarded *Tranium* (nom.
Tranium) as a diminutive of
Tranio 'my little Tr.' and called
it 'ὑποκοριστικόν': but anything
'endearing' seems to be out of
place.
561. **qui danunt** 'a pair
who give', referring to both
Philol. and Tran.; for similar
irregular plurals in relative
clauses cf. Amph. 731 *te heri me
uidisse, qui* ('when we') *hac*

noctu in portum adluecti sumus
Aul. 435.
562. **quo te agis?** Tran. and
Theopr. are on one side of the
stage, the *danista* on the other:
Tran., now between two fires
(565 *et hinc et illinc*), is bound
at any price to prevent explanations passing between his two
enemies, and leaves Theopr. in
order to attempt to pacify the
money lender (cf. 568, 574) and
induce him to go away: 562
(*ne ego*)—567 and 569 (*abi sis*)
—571 are 'asides'. By talking
in a loud tone the money lender
at last succeeds in attracting
the attention of Theopr. (610):
and it is only then that Tran.
informs him who Theopr. is.—
quo=*ad quem* cf. on 547.—**ně**
cf. 75.
563. **scelestus** cf. on 504
and 532.—**dis inimicis** cf. Hor.
Sat. II 3, 8 *iratis natus paries
dis atque poetis*.
565. **ita** cf. on 56.
567. **frustra est** 'is out in
his reckoning', cf. the common

saluére iubeo té, Misargyridés, bene.
DA. saluc ét tu.   quid de argéntost?
                           TR. abi sis, bélua:
570 contínuo adueniens pílum iniecistí mihi.
DA. hic homóst inanis.
                    TR. híc homo certest áriolus.
DA. quin tu ístas mittis trícas?
                         TR. quin, quid uís, cedo.
DA. ubi Phílolaches est?
                    TR. númquam potuistí mihi

frequently in every place of every kind of verse, cf. 392, 398, 586,
673, 718, 742, 798, 821, 948, 952, 977, 1175.
    568.   *Misargyrides* Donatus, edd., **misarcirites** M.
    569.   **Salue et tu** M, Uss., Lor.[2], *Salueto* Lachm., Rl., Bug.
Lachm. disbelieved that *et* ever means 'also' in Plaut. or Lucr.
(cf. on Lucr. vi 749); see on the other side Vahl. in Hermes xvii
pp. 441 f., and Brix on Capt.[3] 1009.   No doubt in the common
formula for returning a greeting and in introducing replies
generally, *et* is often strictly a conjunction and='and...too',
e.g. Trin. 49 *CA. o amice salue. ME. et tu edepol salue* 'and
good morrow to you too, from my heart'; so (without the verb)
Aul. 174 *ME. uale.   EVN. et tu frater,* 'and farewell to you too',
Capt. v 4, 12 *PH. salue Tyndare. TY. et tu,* etc., Men. 1108
*MES. patrem fuisse Moschum tibi ais? MEN. I. ita uero.   MEN. II.
et mihi* 'and he was mine too': cf. ibid. 652, 1094, Most. 529.
Similarly (though not introducing a reply) ibid. 397, 426, Curc. 493,
Rud. Prol. 8.   But such instances as Amph. 266 f., Poen. 142,
Capt. iii 4, 30 (quoted in explan. note) cannot be explained like
this; cf. Most. 296.
    571.   *est inanis* Pyl., edd., **inanis est** M.   *certest* Rl.,
edd., **est certe** M.

ne frustrā sis 'don't you make
any mistake', e.g. Capt. iv 2, 74,
Men. 692.
    569.   et=*etiam*: cf. Amph.
266 f., *enimuero quoniam formam
cepi huius in med et statum,
Decet et facta moresque huius
habere me similes item,* Poen.
141 f. *haud uidi magis.   Et ego
nunc pereo amore,* Capt. iii 4,
29 f. *haud uidi magis.   Et quidem Alc.* etc., cf. ibid. 42.   The

et in Most. 397, 426, 529 is
different.
    570.   **pilum iniecisti** 'opened
fire'.
    571.   **inanis** 'empty-handed',
so Pseud. 256 *surdus sum profecto inani logistae,* 308, 371;
cf. Trin. 701 ('penniless'), Asin.
660 ('unburdened').   The common classical meaning of 'vain'
is, as Lang. shows, not found in
Plaut.—**certest** cf. on 369.

magis ópportunus áduen*ire quam* áduenis.
DA. quid ést?
              TR. concede huc.
                        DA. *quín mihi fuenus* rédditur? 575
TR. scio té bona esse uóce : ne *clamá nimis.*
DA. ego hércle uero clámo.
                    TR. ah, gere morém mihi.
DA. quid tíbi ego morem uís geram?
                        TR. abi quaeso hínc domum.
DA. abeám?
          TR. redito huc círciter merídiem.
DA. reddéturne igitur faénus?
                        TR. reddetúrne: abi.   580
DA. quid ego húc recursem, aut óperam sumam
                              aut cónteram?
quid, si híc manebo pótius ad merídiem?
TR. immo ábi domum : uerum hércle dico. abi módo ⎫
                                    domum. ⎬583
ait híc tibi *   *   *   *   *   *   * ⎭

574—576. M have lacunae, thus filled up by Cam., Rl.
579. *meridiem* FZ, edd., **meridie** M. An M is visible at the
end of the verse in A, which from this point becomes available.
580. *reddeturne: abi* Leo, **reddetur nunc abi** M, *reddetur tibi*
Rl., Lor. *abi*, as in 585: but *abí* 583, cf. 8: cf. Intr. to Capt. A (i).
583 *a*. **ABIMODODOMUM** A, Ri., Rams., Bug., Lor.², abi
modo M.
583 *b*. The commencement of a new verse discovered in A by
Gepp.

574—610. In 574—592 Tra-
nio tries to get rid of the *danista*
by coaxing him, and promises to
pay first the interest (*faenus*
580), and then the capital (*sors*
583 *b* [?], 592), hoping that by this
pretext he may gain time. In
593 he adopts an abusive and
threatening tone, and refuses
to pay the interest, holding out
at the same time (599), as a sop,
the promise of paying the *sors*:
after 600 he loses his temper
and defies his opponent until
Theopr. interferes (610).

576. **bona** 'powerful'.—**ne
clama.** *Ne* with the pres. imperative is common in Plaut. cf.
643, 1105 : cf. on 468.
577. **ah, gere m. m.** 'ah now,
do listen to me'.
579. *abeam?* cf. **iubeam?**
620 and on 556. The *danista*
is naturally surprised at the
request *abi domum*, after 574.
580. **reddeturne** cf. on 508.
583 *b*. The lost verse prob.
contained the promise (repeated
in 592, 599) of paying the *sors* :
hic is prob. Philol.

DA. quin uós mihi faenus dáte.   quid hic nugá-
mini ?
585 TR. *heu*, hércle *nunc* tu abí modo : auscultá mihi.
589 DA. multós me hoc pacto iám dies frustrámini.
590 moléstus si sum, réddite argentum : ábiero.
respónsiones ómnis hoc uerbo éripis.
TR. sortem áccipe.
           DA. immo faénus, id primúm uolo.
TR. quid aís? tu*n*, omnium hóminum *homo* tactér-
rume,
uenísti huc te extentátum ? agas quod ín manust.
595 non dát, non debet.
               DA. nón debet ?
                     TR. ne frít quidem

585—610. In this passage I have, in part, adopted the order
of verses suggested by Rl. in his Praef. xi—xiv, but not introduced
by him into the text. It appears necessary that vv. 586—588 (which
follow 585 in M) should stand immediately before 666 in order to
explain the interposition of Theopr. Rl.'s other changes are not
adopted : 601 with its refusal to pay (*nemo dat*) and defiance (*age
quod lubet*) comes too soon if placed after 589.

585. *heu* Schneider, Rl., Lor., Bug., Lang., Br., eu M, Rams.,
Uss. Cf. on 339.   *nunc* Fl., Rl., Lor., Bug., ne M, Rams.,
Uss. But *ne* (asseverative particle) with the imperative seems
impossible.

591. ERIPIS A, edd., eripit M.

593. So Br., Lor.², QUIDA.S..UOMNIUM.OMI.UM TAETERR...
A (see Rl. Parerga p. 502), quid tu hominem omnium teterrime M.
quid ais, tute homo h. o. t. Scal., *quid ais tu? tun', h. o. t.* Rl., *quid
ais? o tu h. o. t.* Speng., Bug. But Br. shows that *omnes homines*
is the regular order, like *omnes mortales*.

595. Note the change of accent in the reply non *débet*—*nón
debét;* cf. on 12.   *ne frit* Ell., neo erit M, *ne γρῦ* Acid., edd.

590. ablero 'I will go away
at once' cf. 921, 1174 *subegero*
'I will soon...', Mil. 863 *iam huc
reuenero*, Asin. 446 etc.; cf. on
526, 687, 1152 for various uses
of the fut. perf.
591. hoc uerbo i.e. *reddendo*.
592. The *danista* sees that
this is a mere ruse, and delivers
his answer in a loud and angry
tone.
594. te extentatum 'to test
the power of your lungs', cf.
Bacch. 585 *uires extentare* =
'practise your strength'.—quod
in manust 'all that is in your
power' cf. Asin. 86, 94, Rud.
983 etc.
595. frit 'a particle' cf.
Varro R. R. i 48, 8 *Illud summa*

ferre hínc potes. an métuis, ne quo abeát foras
urbe éxulatum faénoris causá tui,   597
quoi sórtem accipere iám licet?
               DA. quin nón peto 599
sortem: ílluc primum, faénus, reddundúmst mihi. 600
TR. moléstus ne sis: némo dat; age quód lubet.
tu sólus credo faénore argentúm datas.
DA. cedo faénus, redde faénus, faenus réddite.
datúrin' estis faénus actutúm mihi,
datúrne faenus?
       TR. faénus illic, faénus hic.   605
nescít quidem nisi faénus fabulárier
unóse: neque ego taétriorem béluam
uidísse me umquam quémquam quam te cénseo.

596—599, 600, 607 are given as restored by Stud. (see 'Fest-gruss' pp. 61—65) from A; so rec. edd.

596. **HINC** A, hoc M.   **METUISNE** A, om. in M.   **ABEAT** A, habeat M.

597. **URB..XOLATUMFAENORIS** A, Vrbem exsul.........his M.

599. sortem M, **OR..M** A.   **AC...ERE..M** A, om. in M, *licet* Stud., **LICEB..** A, ..cebit M. (No trace of a lost line—assumed by Rl.—between 597 and 599 in any of the MSS.)

600. So A, om. in M.

605. *daturne* Rl., Lor., **DATUR** A acc. to Rl. and Gepp.; acc. to Schwarzm. **DATURIN**, which Bug. and Uss. adopt, date M.   *faenus?* *TR.* Rl., rec. edd., **FAENUSMIHI** A (acc. to Schwarzm.), mihi fenus M.

607. *Vnose* Stud., rec. edd., **UNO..** A, Vetro te M, *Vltro te* Seyff.

608. **quam** M, om. in A.

---

in spica iam matura, quod est minus quam granum, uocatur frit.

596. **f. hinc** 'get out of him' cf. on 547.

602. **solus a. d.** i.e. one would think there was no one else to lend us money in the town.—**datare**, frequentative of *dare.*

607. **unose** [prob. from *uni-uorse:* cf. *unorsum* 'all at once',

Lucr. IV 262 and note of Lachm.; for the termination cf. the forms *dextrosus, sinistrosus, prosus, susum, rusum* etc., so common in MSS.] 'from first to last'. The word is extant only here and in Pacuvius (Frag. 213) quoted by Nonius *occidisti, ut multa paucis uerba unose obnuntiem*, where Non. explains it to mean *simul.*

609 DA. non édepol nunc med ístis ucrbis térritas.

586 { iam hercle égo illum nominábo.   *   *   *
{ *   *   *·   *   *   TR. cuge, strénue.

588 beátus ucro es núnc, quom clamas.

                             DA. méum peto.

666 TR. calidum hóc est; etsi prócul abest, urít male.

610 quod illúc est faenus, ópsecro, quod illíc petit?

TR. pater óccum aduenit péregre non multó prius
illíus: is tibi et faénus et sortém dabit,
ne incónciliare quíd nos porro póstules.
uide núm moratur.

             DA. quín feram, si quíd datur.

609. *med istis* Rl. (Neue Pl. Exc. ı p. 49), Bug., Lor.[2], **MEISTIS**
A, **me tu istis** CD, Rams., Uss., **me tu tuis** B.
586. * * * Müll., Bug., Uss.; Rl., Lor. suppose a lacuna *after*
cuge strenue. For position of 586—588 cf. on 585—610.
588. *DA.* Cam., edd., om. in M.
666. *abest, urit male* Pius, edd., **habes turitamale** M. This
v. Acid. placed after 665, and so Rl. who declared it to be spurious:
so Lor., Bug.
610. **ILLUC** A, **illud** M.
612. **ETFAENUS** AM, *faenus* Rl., Lor.[2] (Fl. regards the *et* as
having arisen from an old spelling **TIBEI**, which however is not in
the MSS.).   Scan *tib' ĕt f.;* Stud. prefers *illíus* | *is tibi* | *et faen-*ˈ,
with hiatus after *tibi*, a scansion ridiculed by Rl. Opusc. ıı p. 680.

608. **quisquam** as a fem. is
very rare; cf. *quemquam anum*
Rud. 406, *q. alia mulier* Cist. ı
1, 67, *quemquam porcellam* Mil.
1060.
586. **nominabo illum** ' I'll
call the fellow's name', cf. Aul.
443 *hic pipulo te differam ante*
aedis.—In the lacuna the *dan.*
shouts out the name of Philolaches, as is proved by 616.
666, an *aside:* **calidum hoc**
est etc., 'this is warm work:
although it does not touch me,
I feel it pretty hot'.
613. **inconciliare**, an exclusively Plautine verb, which occurs again Trin. 136, Bacch.
551, Pers. 834. Lang. regards

it as compounded of the negative *in-* and *conciliare* 'to unite',
hence 'to cause division', comparing *ignoscere = non nouisse,*
improbare = non probare, inde-
cet = non decet (Plin. Epist. ııı
1, 2). He therefore translates
here *inc. nos* 'to pick a quarrel
with us'. The generally accepted
sense 'to cause trouble' 'in
angustias urgere' (Uss.) is suitable in most of the passages, as
Rams., Lor. and Wagn. (on Trin.
136) say.—**postules** cf. on 259.
614. **moratur** sc. *te* 'keeps
you waiting'; cf. 794, 803.
For the indic. see on 149.—
quin feram etc. (*aside*) 'Nay,
I'll take anything that's offer-

TH. quid aís tu?
    TR. quid uis?
    TH. quís illic est?   quid illíc petit? 615
quid Phílolachetem gnátum compcllát *meum*
sic ét praesenti tíbi facit conuícium?
quid illí debetur?
    TR. ópsecro hercle *té*, iube
obícere argcntum ob ós impurac béluae.
TH. iubeám — ?
    TR. iube homini argénto os uerberárier. 620
DA. perfácile ego ictus pérpetior argénteos.
TR. audín? uidetur*ne*, ópsecro hercle, idóncus,
danísta qui sit, génus quod improbíssumumst?
TH. non égo istuc curo quí sit *ille uut* únde sit:
sed íd uolo mihi díci, id me scire éxpeto,   625
quod illúc argentumst.
        TR. huíc *quod* debct Phílolaches

616. *meum* Cam., Bent., edd., om. in M.
618. *TR.* edd., om. in M.   *te, iube* Cam., Müll., rec. edd.,
iubi M, *te, obici* Rl., *iuben ibi* Ell.
619. *Obicere* Müll., Bug., Lor.[2], **Obi** M, *Iube* Rl., *Obtrudi* Pyl.,
Uss., *Obfundi* Reid (cf. Asin. 216).
620. *homini* Pyl. (from his MSS.), Rams., rec. edd., **in ho-**
mine(-i) M.
621. *perpetiōr*, see Intr. to Capt. B., Aul. 214.
622—628 in this order Rl., rec. edd.; in M 622—625 follow
628.
622. *uideturne* Cam., Rl., rec. edd., **uidetur** M.
624. *ille aut* Müll., rec. edd., *ego nunc* Rl., Rams., om. in M.
625. *Sed* Müll., Bug., Lor.[2], om. in M.   *mi actutum dici* Rl.
626. *illuc* Rl., Lor., Bug., **illud** M.   *huic quod* Müll.,
Bug., Lor.[2], **est huic** M, *huic enim* Uss.

ed'; the *dan.* now sees some
chance of payment.
615. **quid ais tu?** 'I say' cf.
quid nunc? 172.
616. **compellat** 'is dunning'
cf. Hor. Epist. I 7, 34 *huc ego si
compellor imagine* 'am brought
to book', Sat. II 3, 297.
617. **praesenti** 'to your

face'.
619. **obicere ob os** 'to fling
into the face'; cf. on 371.
620. **os uerb.** cf. Capt. IV 2,
36.
622. **-ne** = *nonne*, cf. 660,
850, 887 a, Trin. 129, 136.
625. **me scire** cf. on 259,
Trin. 365.

paulúm.
  Th. quantillum?
    Tr. quási quadragintá minas,
nc sáne id multum cénseas.
     Th. paulum id quidemst.
Da. adeo étiam argenti faénus cedit. *Th.* aúdio.
630 Tr. quattuór quadraginta ílli debentúr minae,
633 dic té daturum, ut ábeat.
     Th. egon dicám dare?
Tr. dic.
  Th. égone?
    Tr. tu ipsus. díc modo : auscultá mihi.
635 promítte, age inquam : ego iúbeo.
     Th. respondé mihi :
quid eóst argento fáctum?
     Tr. saluomst.
      Th. sóluite
uosmét igitur, si sáluomst.
     Tr. aedis fílius

628. So Uss. (in note), **DA. Ne** and **TR. paullum** M, *TH.*
Paulum id quidemst? TR. ne sane id multum censeas Acid., Rl.,
Lor., Bug.
 629. So Palmer, **credit audio** M (giving whole line to *TH.*),
faenus creditum argenti audio Rl., Lor., Bug.
 630. After this line Rl., Lor., Bug. insert 631, 632 which in
MSS. (including A) appear after 652 *b* (652 *b* = 630). Uss. deletes
630 ; Rl., Lor., Bug. delete 652 *b*.

627. **quasi** 'a matter of' cf.
on Capt. Prol. 20.
 628. **ne** final, cf. 613, 1023.
—**id** i. e. *quad. minae* cf. Trin.
405, Asin. 90. 398. The answer
of Th. is ironical.
 629. **adeo cedit**=*eo accedit*
(Palmer) ; cf. Aul. 519 *ibi ad
postremum cedit miles.*—**audio**,
impatiently, as often in Plaut.
and Ter., 'So you have said'
equiv. to 'Have done!'; cf. Mil.
798 *audio: ne mi ut surdo
uerbera auris*, Phorm. 160.

633. **dicam dare** cf. on 17,
55.
 636. **eo est argento factum**
'has been done with (become of)
the money' for this abl. after
facere, fieri and *esse* cf. Mil.
459 *quid facies ea (machaera)?*
'What will you do with it?'
Capt. v 1, 31 *meo minore quid sit
factum filio*, Mil. 299 *quid fuat
me nescio*, Trin. 157 *siquid eo
fuerit* 'if anything happens to
him', and Most. 231, 346, 1166.

tuos émit.
   TH. aedis?
      TR. aédis.
         TH. euge, Phílolaches
patríssat: iam homo in mércatura uórtitur.   639
ain tu aédis?
     TR. aedis ínquam. sed scin quóiusmodi? 642
TH. qui scíre possum?
     TR. uáh.
        TH. quid est?
           TR. ne mé roga.
TH. nam quíd ita?   644,
    TR. speculicláras, clarorém merum. 645
TH. bene hércle factum. quíd, cas quanti déstinat?
TR. taléntis magnis tótidem, quot cgo et tú sumus.
sed árraboni has dédit quadragintá minas: 648

639. After this line Rl., Lor., Bug., insert 640, 641, which appear after 650 in M: Uss. inclines to reject them altogether as disturbing the sense in either place.

642. q͡uoius-, one syll., cf. 817 f., 903; monosyllabic *eius*, *huius*, *quoius* are frequent in Plaut.

644, 645. *TR.* Cam., edd., om. in M. *speculiclaras* Ell., **speculo claras** M, Rl., rec. edd. (assuming that a line has been lost after *nam quid ita*; but not so Uss.). *clarorem* Cam., Rl., Rams., Lor., Bug., **canorem** M, *candorem* (cf. Men. 181) Speng., Uss.

648. After this v. Rl., Lor., Bug. suppose a line to have fallen out which would have explained *ei* (650).

638. **euge...uortitur** (639), an aside; after which Theopr. resumes the dialogue.—**uortitur** = the classical *uorsatur;* **iam in m. u.** 'is already in the trading line'.

643. **uah** 'whew!', an expression of admiration; cf. on 256.—**ne roga** cf. on 576.

645. **speculiclaras** 'mirror-bright', agreeing with *aedis* (acc.) in 642.—**claror** is formed from *clarēre*, on the analogy of *candor* [*candēre*], *liuor* [*liuēre*], etc., etc.

646. **quid**, 'harkye'.—**desti-**

nat. Lang. has shown that this verb means simply 'to buy' in Plaut., cf. 974, Rud. 45, Epid. 487. The **tense** is usually taken to be present (historical); but perh. we have here an instance of the contracted perfect in -*at* cf *perturbat* 656, and cf. Lucret. I 70, V 396 (note of Lachm.), VI 587: see too Munro on III 1042.

647. **talentum magnum**, an Attic talent (again 913) = 60 minae; cf. *octoginta minae* 918 (2 × 60 = 120 – 40 = 80).

648. **arraboni** (1013 = *pignori* 978) 'part payment'. The

650 hinc súmpsit, quas ei dédimus.   satin intéllegis?
640 nam póstquam haec aedes íta erant ut dixí tibi,
641 contínuost alias aédis mercatús sibi.
651 TH. bene hérele factum.

　　　　　　　　　　DA. heus, iam ádpetit merídies.

652 { TR. apsólue hunc quaeso, uómitu ne hic nos énecet.
　　 { quattuór quadraginta ílli debentúr minae,
631 et sórs et faenus.

　　　　　　　　DA. tántumst : nihilo plús peto.

632 TR. uelím quidem hercle ut úno nummo plús petas.
653 TH. aduléscens, mecum rém habe.

　　　　　　　　　　DA. nempe aps té petam?

TH. petitó cras.

　　　　　DA. abeo: sát habeo, si crás fero.

655 TR. malúm quod isti dí deaeque omnés duint:
ita méa consilia pérturbat paeníssume.

650. *Hinc* Pyl., edd., **Hic** M.　　　　　**quas ei** B, **quasi** CD.
651. *DA.* Pyl., edd., om in M.　　　　　*meridies* Saracenus,
edd., **meridie** M.
652a. *uomitu* Bo., Rl., rec. edd., **uomitum** M.　652b. See on 630.
656. *paenissume* Prisc., edd., **plenissume** M.

word is prob. Phoenician (Heb.
'êrâbhôn).
　650. **hinc** = *ab hoc* (*danista*)
cf. on 547.—**ei** 'sc. *qui uendidit,
quod facile intelligitur*' Uss.;
cf. 628, 788, Capt. II 1, 30 *si
id palam prouenit* for similarly
vague uses of the pronoun.
　632. **uelim** etc. 'I should
like to see'.—**uno nummo plus**
'a single farthing more': cf.
Cic. pro Rosc. Com. IV 10 *Hic
tu si amplius H. S. nummo pet-
isti, quam tibi debitum est, causam perdidisti.*
　653. **adulescens**, without reference to age: 'my good fellow', cf. Trin. 889, Rud. 941
etc., and note of Rams.—**mecum rem habe** 'you may apply

to me': cf. Pers. 576, Truc.
152.
　655. **quod** puts the curse in
relation to the last speaker's
remark : ' wherein may the
Gods confound you?' cf. Amph.
563, Pseud. 1130. Lor. and
Uss. say *quod = aliquod*, for
which Ter. Eun. 252 might be
compared: *negat quis, nego; ait,
aio* (where *quis = aliquis*).
　656. **ita** cf. on 56.—**paenissume** a humorous superlative
of *paene*, also in Aul. 463, 660:
cf. *pectore penitissumo* Cist. I 1,
65 from *penitus*; cf. *ipsissumus*
Trin. 988, and the comparative
in Poen. 991 *nullust med hodie
Poenus Poenior.*

nullum édepol hodie génus est hominum taétrius
nec mínus bono cum iúre, quam danísticum.
TH. qua in régione istas aédis emit fílius?
TR. ecce aútem perii.
       TH. dícisne hoc quod té rogo? 660
TR. dicám : sed nomen dómini quaero quíd siet.
TH. age cómminiscere érgo.
       TR. quid ego núnc agam,
nisi *id unúm* ut *nostro dé* uicino hoc próxumo,
eas émisse aedis húius dicam fílium ?
calidum hércle audiui esse óptumum mendácium. 665
quidquést dicundumst ét decretumst dícere. 667

657. GENUSESTHODIE A, acc. to Schwarzm.
661. *quod* Z, cf. Pers. 623, *quod nomen tibist?* (A, *quid* M),
and again in 700.
663. nisi ut in (DF om. *ut*) uicinum (uitiunum B) proximum
mendacium M. Rl. perceived that *mendacium* had crept in from
665, and proposed *nisi ut in uicinum hunc proxumum rem conferam*
(leaving asyndeton between 663 and 664; so too rec. edd.); my
emendation is based upon the similarity of *id unum* to *uicinum* :
cf. too 669. Ell., retaining *mendacium*, suggests *proximem* (from
proximare, as trans. verb).
664. Eas M, *Eius* Rl., Lor.
665. After this v. Acid. inserted the v. which in M follows 609.
667. *Quidquest dicundumst et* S., Quidquid dei dicunt id M,
Quicquid dehinc dicam, nunc id Rl., Lor., Bug., *Quicquid dein fiet,
id* Rl. (in crit. note), Uss. For *quidquest* cf. Truc. 254.
decretumst CD, Uss., rectum est B, Rams., *certumst* Rl., Lor., Bug.

657. hodíe 'non tempus significat, sed iracundam eloquen-
tiam et stomachum' Donatus
on Ter. Ad. 215; cf. 1073 and
nunquam as an emphatic *non*,
cf. on 164, Capt. II 3, 48.
658. minus b. c. iure, 'more
unreasonable'.
660. dicisne, cf. on 622.
661. nomen quaero, cf. on
389.
662. comminiscere 'try and
think': cf. Trin. 915 *litteris
recomminiscar*.
663. nisi id unum ut cf. on 278.
665. calidum 'served up hot',
i. e. from over the way, as hot

food is served straight from the
kitchen : similarly *calidum consilium* Mil. 226, Epid. 256, 141,
calide, quidquid acturu's, age,
ibid. 256; cf. Most. 666.
667. quidquest dicundumst
'I must say the first thing that
turns up': *quidque = quidquid,*
so *quemque = quemquem* Mil. 156,
160, Capt. IV 2, 17, 18. The
clause *quidquid est* is often thus
used as the object or subject of
a sentence; cf. Men. 1153 *uen-
dam quidquid est* 'all I have',
Mil. 1372 *iam patiar quidquid est,*
ibid. 37 *PY. quid id est? AR.
quidquid est* 'anything you like'.

Th. quid ígitur? iam comméntu's?

    Tr. di istum pérduint.
immo ístunc potius. dé uicino hoc próxumo
670 tuos émit acdis fílius.

    Th. bonán fidc?
Tr. siquídem es argentum rédditurus, túm bona:
si rédditurus nón es, non emít bona.
Th. bono ín loco emit, pérbono.

    Tr. immo óptumo.
Th. cupio hércle inspicere hasce aédis. pultadúm foris,
675 atque éuoca aliquem *huc* íntus ad te, Tránio.
Tr. ecce aútem perii: núnc quid dicam néscio.
iterúm iam ad unum sáxum me fluctús ferunt.
quid núnc? non hercle, quíd nunc faciam, réperio.
manuφésto teneor.

        Th. éuocadum aliquem ócius,

671. *si quídem ĕs* S. (in spite of the length of *ĕs* in Plaut. and
Ter.; *quíd' ĕs* is like *quód ĕst* Trin. 630 etc., Intr. to Capt. A (i):
cf. *si quídem hĕrcle* 229 and note), *si quidem ĕs* Rl., Lor., Bug., *si
quidem tu argentum redditurus's* Uss. (so A acc. to Gepp.).
    673. *Bono* Madvig, **Non** M, *Sane* Uss. It is clear throughout
that Theopr. is quite satisfied with the bargain.   *perbono* is
by Madv. made part of TR.'s speech, in which I have not followed
him: ACD indicate no change of speakers, B has the symbol **SI.**
(in other places **S**=Tranio i.e. *Seruos*) before *immo* (*TR. immo* FZ).
    in optumo Rl. (so A acc. to him, **OPTUOPTUMO** acc. to
Gepp.), Lor., Bug.; I scan with hiatus at the change of speakers:
cf. on 567. (Is it possible that *optuoptumo* is a humorous superlative, ='best of best'? If so, perh. read *immo in optuoptumo*,
striking out *perbono* as a gloss.)
    675. *huc* Rl., Bug., Lor.², om. in all MSS.
    676. *perii* Rl., A (acc. to Gepp.), rec. edd., **iterum** M.
    679. **OCIUS** A, edd., **foras** M.

668. **di ist. perduint,** 'Bother
the name!' (lit. 'the man'): similarly the Sycophant (Trin. 923)
on recovering the name Char-
mides *qui istum di perdant*.
    669. **immo ist. potius,** an
aside, to the audience, 'or rather
the *man*' i.e. Theopr.; for the
ambiguity of *istunc* cf. 540 f.

670. **bonan fide?** 'honour
bright?', which Tr. pretends to
misunderstand as = *bonan fide
emit*.
    677. **unum** 'the same' i.e. as
before. For *unus*=*idem* cf. Capt.
Prol. 20 *una aetas*, III 1, 28 *una
res est*, Men. 56, 1122 etc.
    679. **manufesto** 'in the act',

roga círcumducat: heús tu.
    TR. at hic sunt múlieres: 680
uidéndumst primum,utrum éac uclintnc an nón uelint.
TH. bonum aéquomquc oras. pércontarc *ergo* ét roga:
ego híc tantispcr, dum éxis, tc oppcriár foris.
TR. di té deaeque omncs fúnditus pcrdánt, senex :
ita *me* ét mea consilia úndique oppugnás malc.   685
eugé, eccum optumc aédium dominús foras
Simó progreditur ípsus. huc concéssero,
dum míhi senatum cónsili in cor cónuoco.
igitúr tum accedam huc, quándo, quid agam, inuénero.

681. **uelintne an** M, **UELINTAUTNON** A (acc. to Rl., **UELINT-NEAUTNON** acc. to Schwarzm.).
682. **oras** M, **ROGAS** A (acc. to Schwarzm.)   *percontare ergo* Guy., Uss., **percontare** M, **PERCUNCTARE** A, *i percontare* Rl., Lor., Bug.
685. *me et* S., om. in M.   *tu undique* Rl., Bug., Lor.[2], *cundique* Rl. (Opusc. III p. 142).   **MALE** A, cdd., **mala** M.
686. *Eugé, eccum optume* (with hiatus after the interjection) S., **EUGAE** A, **Fuge optume eccum** M, *Euge eccum huc opt.* Rl., Bug., Lor.[2]
689. **HUC** ACD, **hunc** B, cdd. (but this seems questionable in the face of MSS. and the fact that Plaut. regularly uses *accedere*, as a verb of motion, either absolutely, cf. 543, 717, or else followed by *ad* e.g. Mil. 494 *accedam ad hominem*, Pscud. 312 etc.; in Epid. 149 *accedam periculum* the verb is metaphorical.

ἐπ' αὐτοφώρῳ, cf. Trin. 911, Pseud. 747, 1160, Most. 511 *man. opprimere*, Aul. 465 *fur manufestarius.—* **ocius** is a positive, as in Truc. 803, Pscud. 758, Virg. Acn. v 828.
680. **heus tu** 'do you hear?'
682. **orare** here = 'to say', as in *orator, oratio;* cf. Men. 156, Rud. 184, Virg. Acn. VII 446 *iuueni oranti*, x 96 *Talibus orabat Juno.*
683. **hic**, a place off the stage. Exit Thcopr.—**dum** 'until', cf. 688.
686. **optume** ' in the nick of time'.—**dominus** ' owner'.

687. **huc** i.c. into the *angi-portus* cf. 1046.—**concessero** 'meanwhile I will retire': the same sense attaches to the fut. perf. in Trin. 625, 1007, Aul. 658 (with *tantisper*), Pscud. 573 (with *interea*): cf. on 590.
688. **senatum cons. conu.** 'summon my thoughts to meet in council', cf. 1049 f., Aul. 541 *quid tu te solus e senatu seuocas?* 'from the consultation', Epid. 159, Mil. 592 *redeo in senatum rusum.*
689. **igitur tum** cf. on 132. —**huc** = *ad hunc* cf. on 547.

SIMO. THEOPROPIDES. TRANIO.

690 SI. Mélius anno hóc mihi nón fuít domi,
néc quod una ésca me iúuerít magis.
prándium uxór mihi pérbonúm dedit;
núnc dormitúm iubet me íre: minume.
nón mihi fórte uisum ílicó fuit,
695 mélius quom prándium, quám solét, dedit.
uóluit in cúbiculum abdúcere me anus:
nón bonust sómnus de prándio: apage.

690—746. The THIRD CANTICUM falls into two sections: A
(690—717) cret. dim. + *either* ⌣⌣⌣⌣ (=108), *or* ⌣⌣⌣⌣ (=336),
or ⌣⌣⌣ | ⌣⌣⌣ (=cret. tetram.).
691. So A, edd., **ne (nec) quod esca una meruerit** M.
695. *quom* Gulielmius, edd., **QUAM** AM.   **SOLET** A, edd.,
solum M.
697. *bonust somnus* Rl., rec. edd., **bonus somnus est** M; A has
BONUMSTSOMNIUM (acc. to Rl.), **BONUMESTOMNUM** (acc. to
Schwarzm.).

Enter Simo from his house.
Tranio listens to his soliloquy.
690. **Melius non fuit domi**
'I have not been so well enter-
tained at home'; cf. the opening of I 2. For *bene (male) esse*
cf. 52, 710, Men. 603; sometimes personally, e.g. Men. 485
minore nusquam bene fui dis-
pendio.
691. **nec quod** etc. with
slight anacoluthon, =*et (iam*
annus est) quod ('since')...non,
cf. on 158, 471.—**una esca** 'any
single meal' (here almost=*ulla*
esca), cf. Pseud. 76 *non queo la-*
crumam exorare ut exspuant
unam modo 'a single tear', Aul.
Prol. 23 *huic filia unast* (=*uni-*
ca), 77 *unam litteram longam,*
Asin. 421, Bacch. 968, Truc.
490, Ter. Andr. 118 *forte unam*
conspicio adulescentulam 'one
particular girl'. Slightly different uses of *unus* are: (ii) 'one
and the same', see on 677; (iii)
'only', 'alone', Stich. 617 *tibi*

uni, Curc. 495 *quibus sui nihil*
est nisi una lingua, Trin. 166
unos sex dies, Bacch. 832, Pseud.
54; (iv) the word becomes
weakened so as to be almost
=*aliquis* (τις) or even the indef.
article; Most. 983, 1002, Capt.
III 1, 22 *dico unum ridiculum*
dictum, Epid. 453 *ego magis*
unum quaero, meas (sc. *pugnas)*
quoi praedicem, Stich. 153 *unus*
seruos.
694. **non forte** 'not acci-
dental'=*non temere,* cf. Aul. 616
non temere est quod coruos can-
tat, Bacch. 921 *quos non dabo*
temere etiam, priusquam...; so
non temerarium est 'not for nothing', Aul. 182.—**uisum fuit,**
Plautine for *uisum est,* cf. 994
Aul. 454 *coctum ego conductus*
fui, Mil. 118, Amph. 457; cf. on
821.
695. **quom** with indic., cf.
on 29.
697. **de prandio** 'immediately after luncheon'.

clánculum ex aédibus mc édidí foras:
tóta turgét mihi uxór, sció, domi.
TR. rés paratást mala in uésperum huíc seni: 700
nam ét cenandum ét cubandúmst *eí* male.
SI. quóm magis cógito cúm meo animo:
sí quis dotátam habet úxorem átque anum,
néminem sóllicitat sópor: ibi ómnibus
íre dormítum odiost. uélut*i* núnc mihi   705
éxsequi cérta res ést, ut abeam
pótius hinc ád forum, quám domí cubem.
átque pol néscio ut móribús sient
nóstrae: *de* hac, sát scio, quaé *me* habét male,

699.   **SCIO** A, Rl., rec. edd., **scio nunc** M.
700.   **MALE** Al'.
701.   **et cubandumst** M, **STET**(or **EIET**)**CUBANDUMST** A.
ei male Rl., rec. edd., **MALE** A, **ni trahis male** M (perh.=*si
intrabit*, a gloss).
703.   So Speng., Lor.², **UXOREMATQUEANUMHABET** A, ux-
orem......habet (with lacuna) M.
704.   *sublicit* (=*sublectat* Mil. 1066) Speng., to avoid the
choriambus ; see Intr. p. xxvi.   **SOPORIBIOMNIBUS** A, edd.,
sopo......M.
705.   *ueluti* Rl., rec. edd., **UELUTNUNCMIHI** A, **ue......**M.
709.   *de hac* S., **HAEC** AM, Uss., *at haec* Rl., Lor., Bug. (with
anacoluthon in 710).   *quae me* Lor., **quam** M, *quam me* Rl.,
Bug., and (with .) Uss., *quamquam* Speng.   *habet* Herm., rec.
edd., Speng., **habeat** M.

699.   **tota turget** ' is in a perfect fury ', cf. Merc. 959 *tota in
fermento iacet.*
700.   **res mala** ' trouble ', cf.
on 61.—**uesperum** 'supper', cf.
on 67.
702.   **cogitare cum an.** cf.
inuestigare cum an. Aul. 707.
703.   **si quis...habet, neminem**, loosely for *neminem eorum
qui...habent.*
704.   **sollicitat** ' troubles with
its visits ', cf. Cas. ii 3, 10 *my-
ropolas omnes sollicito.*—**ibi** 'in
such cases ' cf. 109.
705.   **ueluti** 'for instance';
cf. on 159, 299 (*uel*).

706.   **exsequi** pleonastically,
as in Merc. 934.—**certa res est**
=*certum est;* cf. Trin. 270,
Amph. 705 etc.
708.   Familiar addresses to
the audience were common on
the Plautine stage, cf. 280 f.,
and on Capt. Prol. 10. The ty-
ranny of rich wives is also a
favourite theme with Plaut. cf.
Aul. 169, 526 f.
709.   **de hac** 'owing to her ,
cf. Truc. 741 *de eo (argento)
nunc bene sunt tua uirtute.*—**me
habet male** ' is the plague of my
life', cf. Men. 569 *male habeas.*

710 péius posthác fore, quám fuít, mihi.

TR. si ábitus tuos tíbi, senex, fécerít male,
níhil erit quód deorum úllum accúsites:
te ípse iure óptumo mérito incusés licet.
témpus nunc ést senem hunc ádloquí mihi.

715 hóc habet : répperi quí senem dúcerem,
quó dolo a mé dolorém procul péllerem.
áccedam. dí te ament plúrumúm, Simo.
SI. sáluos sis, Tránio.
                TR. út uales?
                           SI. nón male.
quíd agis?
            TR. hominem óptumum téneo.
                           SI. amicé facis,

720 quóm me laudás.
          TR. decet cérte.
                  SI. at hercle haúd bonum

721 teneo seruom   *   *   *   *   *   *

710. **PEIUS** AB²D²F, **Peiius** (i.e. the archaic *Peiius*) B¹CD¹.
fore = ‿‒ in caesura : cf. Intr. p. xxix.
711. *Si* Cam., edd., om. in M, *Abitus si tibi* Speng.
712. **ULLUM** A, edd., **nullum** M.
718—746. SECTION *B*. Cret. tetram. except 728, 737, 740
(=troch. sept.), 731=108, 742—745=iamb. octon., 746=iamb.
sept.
719. *amice* FZ, edd., **ua amice** M, *uah, amice* Speng.
720 f. So Rl., Lor.; **hercle te habeo hau | Bonum teneo
seruom** M.

714. **adloqui**=*adloquendi* (*ut
adloquar*).
715. **hoc habet** 'I have him!'
'a palpable hit!' lit. 'he has
it!' (metaphor from the arena):
cf. Mercutio's 'I have it! and
soundly too' Rom. and Jul. III
1. Tran. is triumphing in ima-
gination at the success of his
stratagem, as in Rud. 1143
Gripus anticipates the discom-
fiture of his opponent with *hoc
habet* 'she's in for it'.—**ducerem**
'lead by the nose' cf. *ductare*

845. For the sequence of tenses
see on 89 *b.*
716. **dolo—dolorem**, a pun
like *pessumis pessum* 1171. Perh.
'stroke of wit'—'strokes of the
whip'.
719. **quid agis**? prop. 'how
do you do?' cf. Hor. Sat. I 9, 4
quid agis dulcissime rerum?
Tran. plays upon the phrase, as
in 868.—**teneo** 'am holding by
the hand'.—**amice** f. ironically.
741. Theopr. gets impatient.
—**isti** =*istic.*

TH. heía, mastígia, ad mé redi.

                      TR. iam ísti ero.   741

SI. quíd nunc? quam móx—?   721

           TR. quid est?

              SI. quód solet fíeri hic 722

† intus. *TR.* quid id est?   *SI.* scis ibi quod solet fieri.

†   *   *   *   *   * loquar.

† sic decet   *   *   * morem geras.   725

† uita quam sit breuis simul cogita. * quid *

TR. ehem,

uíx tandem percépi super his rébus nostris té loqui. 728

SI. músice hercle ágitis aetátem ita ut uós decet:

uíno et uictú, piscatú probo, eléctili   730

cólitis uitam.

           TR. ímmo uita ántidhác erat:

núnc non est, cum ómnia haec éxciderúnt *bona.*

SI. quídum?

           TR. ita *hic* óppido occídimus omnés, Simo.

741 was transposed by Rl. from this, its place in the MSS, to a
position (after 740) where it is as little suitable to the context as
here.   *TR. iam isti ero* Herm., Rl., Lor., Bug., **eram istic
ero** M, **CUMERO** A.

    722. *SI., TR., SI.*; so Rl., Rams., Lor., Uss.   **FIERIHIC**
A, Rl., rec. edd., **fieri** | **Hic** (723) M.

    723—726. This passage cannot be restored unless further
light is thrown upon it by a renewed collation of A.   723. So
A, except that it omits *TR., SI.*, and has **TIBI** for *ibi* (Ell.); M
have a lacuna followed by **quid id est** at end of line; 724—726 are
given as they stand in M.

    731. *Colitis uitam* Rl. (in crit. note), **Vitam colitis** M, *uita*
FZ, edd., **uit (ut)** M.   *antidhac* Rl. (ibid.), **antehac** M.

    732. *non est* S., **nobis** M.   *cum omnia* Ell., **communia** M.
bona Rl. (ibid.), Speng., Lor.², om. in M.

    733. *hic* Herm., Rl., om. in M.

    722. **quid nunc** 'I say': cf.
172.—**quam mox?** i.e. *continua-
bitur quod solet fieri hic :* trans.
'how much longer?'—**quid est?**
'what do you mean?'—**quod
solet f. h.** 'the usual goings on
here'.

    729. **musice** ἅπαξ λεγ. 'in
fine style', =μουσικῶς cf. ὄψον

σκευάσαντα μουσικῶς Trag. Com.
Gr. IV 583.

    730. **uictu** cf. on 45.—**pis-
catu** cf. 67.—**probo, electili.** For
the asyndeton cf. on 104: for
sense of *probus*, on 241.

    731. **uita** 'a life worth
living'.

SI. nón taces? próspere uóbis cuncta úsque adhuc
735 prócesserúnt.
            TR. ita ut dícis facta haúd nego.
nós profectó probe ut uóluimus uíximus:
séd, Simo, ita nunc uéntus nauem *nóstram* deseruít—
                              SI. quid est?
quó modo ?
      TR. péssumo. *SI.* quaéne subdúcta erat
túto in terra ? TR. eí !
        S. quid est ?
                  TR. mé miserum ! óccidi.
740 SI. quí ?
      TR. quia uenit náuis, nostrae náui quae
                              frangát ratem.
742 SI. uell*em* út tu uelles, Tránio. sed quíd est negoti ?
                              TR. éloquar :
crus peregre uenit.
              SI. tunc †............ cor tenditur :

737. *nostram* Rl., Speng., Lor.², om. in M.
738. *TR.* and *SI.* Bo., edd., om. in M.   *quaene* Pyl.,
Bent., edd., **quae nec** M.
739. With hiatus after *me miserum!* which = an interjection.
740. *nostram ui* Acid., Uss.   **ratem** M, *trabes* Lor., *tra-
bem* Speng.
742. *Vellem* Bo., Rl., Lor., Bug., **Velim** M.
743. *tunc tibi actutum* (with hiatus in diaeresi) Rl., Lor., *tunc*

734. **non taces** 'tush!' 'how
can you say so?' cf. Asin. 931,
Bacch. 470, 627.
737. The consecutive *ut*
clause is suppressed by the in-
terruption of Simo.
738. **pessumo** sc. *modo*,
'most vilely'.—**quaene** i.e. *eamne dicis quae* 'do you mean the
one which etc '; so Mil. 13 *quemne ego seruaui in campis Curcu-
lioniis?* Trin. 360 *quin* (=*quine*)
comedit quod fuit?, Rud. 1019
quemne ego excepi in mari?
740. **quae frangat** ' to
smash'.—**ratis** ' est, ut uidetur,

πλάτη, (oar)' Rl., and so Lo-
beck in Paralipp. p. 439, who
compares a fragment quoted by
Festus p. 273 M (from Attius?)
repercutio ratibus mare (cf. Trag.
Rom. Rell.² p. 235). It is perh.
more likely that *ratem* here =
' the timbers' of the ship.
742. **uellem ut tu uelles** 'I
could have wished as you' i.e.
I sympathize with you: cf.
Seneca Epist. LXVII 13 *utrum
tandem illi dicturus es 'uellem
quae uelles' et 'moleste fero' an
'feliciter quod agis?'*

.

inde férriterium: póstea—
    TR. *pol pér tua te genua* ópsecro,
ne indícium ero faciás meo.
             SI. e me, né quid metuas, níl sciet. 745
TR. patróne, salue.
             SI. níl moror mi istíusmodi cluéntis.
TR. nunc hóc, quod ad te nóster me misít senex—
SI. hoc míhi responde prímum, quod ego té rogo:
iam de ístis rebus uóster quid sensít senex?
TR. nil quídquam.
             SI. num quid íncrepauit fílium? 750
TR. tam líquidust, quam liquida ésse tempestás solet.
nunc te hóc orare iússit opere máxumo,
ut síbi liceret ínspicere hasce aedís tuas.
SI. non súnt uenales.
             TR. scío equidem istuc: séd senex
gunaéceum aedificáre uolt hic ín suis   755
et bálineas et ámbulacrum et pórticum.

flagrum tergo tuo Uss.   *chorda tenditur* Cam., Rl., Rams., Lor.,
Bug. (but *chorda* is not elsewhere used of a rope for binding a
slave), *portenditur* Uss.
    744. *TR. pol per tua te g-* Rl., Rams., Lor., Bug., om. in M.
    747. Senarii follow (to v. 782). **meme misit** M.
    750. *numquid* FZ, edd., **unum quid** M.

    744. **ferriterium** a humorously formed word equiv. to *ergastulum:* cf. *ferritribaces uiri* 356, *Ferriterus* as name of a slave Trin. 1022.—**per tua te g.** cf. on 222.
    747. **hoc, quod m. m. s.** 'as to the business on which old master sent me'. The sentence is not finished owing to the interruption of Simo: for *quod misit* cf. *quod me miseras* 786.
    749. **quid**=*aliquid*, cf. Pseud. 29 *an habent quas gallinae manus?*, Rud. 487 *siquis cum eo quid rei commiscuit*, Ter. Eun. 252 *negat quis, nego*.
    751. **líquidus** 'quiet', cf.

Epid. 643 *animo liquido et tranquillo's*, Catull. LXIII 46 *liquida mens*.—**tempestas** trans. '*fine* weather', although the word *tempestas* does not in itself mean this (cf. 108): cf. Mil. 661 *leniorem dices quam mutumst mare* ('than a *calm* sea is silent').
    755. **gunaeceum** 'a set of women's apartments': the Greek word commonly used was not γυναικεῖον but γυναικωνῖτις.
    756. **balineae.** This fem. pl. (of *balneum*=βαλανεῖον) is the only form employed by Plaut. for 'a bath' whether public or (as here) private.—**ambulacrum**, cf. on 817.

Sɪ. quid *sómni* somniáuit?

Tʀ. ego dicám tibi:
dare uólt uxorem fílio quantúm potest:
ad eám rem facere uólt nouom gunaéceum.
760 nam síbi laudauisse áit hasce architéctonem
nescío quem exaedificátas insanúm bene.
nunc hínc exemplum cápere uolt, nisi tú neuis.
†Sɪ. nam *quór* ille ex malo hínc opere exemplum
                                        *éx*petit?
Tʀ. quia esse aúdit aestate íbidem uictum pérbonum,
765 et cólumem sub sole, úsque perpetuóm diem.
Sɪ. immo édepol uero, quom úsquequaque umbrást,
                                        tamen
sol sémper hic est úsque a mani ad uésperum.
quasi flágitator ástat usque ad óstium:

757. *quid somni somniauit* Müll., Bug., Uss., **quid consomniauit** M, *hem quid consomniauit* Rl., Lor.
759. *gynaeceum nouom* Guy., Bo.; but *gynaecĕum* (=γυναικεῖον)
is like *platĕa* = πλατεῖα Trin. 840, *Seleucĭa* = Σελεύκεια Trin. 901.
760 f. are given as restored by Stud. from A : **laudasse hasce
ait** M (760); **esse aedificatas has sane bene** M (761).
763. The reading in this line is quite uncertain; further light
may be expected from A. I have followed Bug.   **NAMILLEEO-
MALUMHINCOPERE.........A, Nam ille eo malo.........opere ex te
exemplum petit** M.
764 f. So Ell., **QUIAESTAUDITUMESSEAESTATEIBIDEMUIC-
TUMPERBONUM** A, **Quia hic............esse aestate perbonam** M.
    ibidem always in Plaut.; cf. on Trin. 203.
765. **TESUBSOLECOLUMEMUSQUEPERPETUUMDIEM** A, **Sub
diu col... ....perpetuum diem** M.
767. **HUC A.   USQUEAMANIST** A (acc. to Gepp.), Uss.

758. **quantum potest** 'as
soon as may be' prob. imper-
sonally as Pers. 51 *sed recipe te
quantum potest*, ibid. 142, 578,
cf. *qui potest* 375: but it might
also be the personal constr., cf.
Aul. 119 *me rursum quantum
potero tantum recipiam* and
note.
761. **insanum bene** 'awfully
well'; *insanum* is an adv. in

Plaut.; so Mil. 24 *epityrum illi
estur insanum bene* 'eats à ravir'
(Tyrrell), Trin. 673 *insanum
malumst hospitium*, Most. 908.
762. **neuis**, cf. on 110.
763. **exemplum expetere**, cf.
103, 1116.
765. **columem** = *incolumem*,
as in Trin. 743; cf. Loewe Act.
Societ. Philol. Lips. ɪɪ p. 466.
768. **flagitator** 'a dun'.

ncc mi úmbrast usquam, nísi si in puteo quaépiamst.
TR. quid? Sársinatis écquast, si Vmbram nón habes? 770
SI. moléstus ne sis: haéc sunt sicut praédico.
TR. attámen inspicere uólt.
                              SI. inspiciat, sí lubet.
si quíd erit, quod illi pláceat, de exempló meo
ipse aédificato.
          TR. cón? uoco huc hominém?
                                    SI. uoca.
TR. Alexándrum magnum atque Ágathoclem aiunt
                                    máxumas 775
duo rés gessisse: quíd mihi fict tértio,
qui sólus facio fácinora inmortália?
uehit híc clitellas, uéhit hic autem altér senex.
nouícium mihi quaéstum institui nón malum:
nam múliones múlos clitellários   780
habént, ego homines hábeo clitelláríos.
magní sunt oneris: quícquid inponás, uehunt.

769. *umbrast usquam* Bug., **UMBRA..USQUAMST** A, umbra
usquam est M.
774. *i uoca* Acid., Rl., Rams., Lor., Bug.
775. *Alexándrum:* cf. *Alexandér* Bacch. 947.
781. *homines habeo* Pyl., Rl., Bug., Lor.², **HABEOHOMINES** AM.
After 782 M begin a new scene, but not A.

770. **Vmbram**, a pun on
umbra (769): 'if you don't keep
any *shade*, perhaps you keep a
maid from Sarsina?' Sarsina,
a town in Umbria, was the
birthplace of Plaut.
773. **de exemplo meo** 'after
my pattern', 'on the model of
mine'; cf. Mil. 1029 *de meis
uenator uerbis* i.e. 'take your
cue from me', Asin. 210 *meo de
studio studia erant uostra omnia.*
774. **eon?** = *eamne?* as *quid
ago?* 368 = *quid agam?*
775. Monologue of Tranio,
as.he crosses the stage in order
to find Theopr.

776. **duo gessisse** 'were two
men who did', cf. Epid. 626
*quem Apella atque Zeuxis duo
pigmentis pingent ulmeis.*—**quid**
etc. 'how about a third, myself?'
Note the difference between *quid
mihi fict* and *quid me fict* (explained on 636); cf. 435.
777. **solus** 'single-handed'
(= *sine exercitu*).
778. **uehit hic clit.** 'here's
one old fellow heavily saddled',
cf. 430 and note.—**autem** like
καί...δέ, cf. *neque autem* 'no
more does' Aul. Prol. 29.
782. **magni sunt oneris**
'they have broad backs': for

nunc húnc hauscio án conloquár: congredíbor.
heus Théopropides.

　　　　　　Tʜ. hém, *nam* quis híc nominát me?
785 Tʀ. eró seruos múltimodis súo fidus.

　　　　　　　　　　　Tʜ. únde is?
Tʀ. quod mé miserás, adfero ómne inpetrátum.
Tʜ. quid ílli, opsecró, tam diú destitísti?
Tʀ. sení non erát otium : íd sum opperítus.
Tʜ. antíquom optinés hoc tuóm, tardus út sis.

783—803. Fourth Canticum: bacchiac tetram.
783. **hauscio** M, Rl., rec. edd., **HAUDSCIO** A.　　*congredibor*
Rl., Bug., Lor.², **CONGREDIAR** AM.
784. *nam* Bug., Lor.², om. in M. Ell. would scan *Heus
Theoprop* | *ides hem* | etc., allowing - ˘ ˘ ˘ , in the case of a proper
name, to stand for ˘ - - .
785. **MULTIMODIS** A, Rl., rec. edd., **multum** M.　　*suo fidus*
Rl., rec. edd., **FILIUS** A, **suo fidelis** M.　　　**UNDEIS** (with space
for name of speaker) A (acc. to Stud.), Rl., rec. edd., om. in M.
786. **MISSERAS** A, Rl.
787. *illi* Bo., Bug., Lor.², **illic** M.　　　*restitisti* Lamb., Rl.,
Lor.
788. **ERATOTIUM** A, edd., **otium erat** M.　For *erāt* cf. Intr.
to Capt. B; Intr. to Aul. p. xix.
789. **sis** M, edd., **SIES** A.

the gen. of quality cf. Men. 100
escae maxumae, Hor. Sat. ɪ 1,
33 *magni formica laboris.*
　783. Dialogue of Tranio and
Theopr.; the latter has been
waiting in the neighbourhood
of the house, and is in a bad
temper.
　784. **nam quis,** cf. on 191.
　785. **multimodis,** cf. on 54.
　786. **quod,** cf. on 747.
　787. **illi,** cf. on 315.—**desti-
tisti** ' absented yourself', lit.
' stood aloof '; ' *desistere : disce-
dere, recedere*' Bodl. Gloss. The
word is prob. extant in this
sense only here and Men. 777
*quid ille autem abs te iratus
destitit,* and ibid. 810.
　788. **id** i.e. 'his convenience',
cf. on 650.

　789. **optines hoc tuom** ' you
stick to your old habit', cf. Trin.
123 *non istuc meumst* 'that is
not my way', 445 *hau nosco
tuom* ' this is not like you', Hor.
Od. ɪɪɪ 29, 57 *non est meum, si
mugiat* etc.—**ut sis.** A noun
clause standing in apposition
to some word in the principal
clause, or as subject or object of
the same (except after ' uerba
sentiendi uel declarandi' etc.),
is regularly expressed by *ut*
with subj. : cf. 992, Asin. 190
*non meumst...ad te ut mittam
gratiis,* Capt. ɪɪɪ 4, 51 *est miser-
orum ut maleuolentes sint.* But
the acc. with infin. is also sometimes used, e.g. Stich. 716 *haud
tuom istuc est, uereri te,* Poen. 572
haud uostrum est, iracundos esse.

Tr. heus tú, si uolés uerbum *unum* hóc cogitáre: 790
simúl flare sórbereque haúd factu fácilest:
ego híc esse et illi simítu haud poté *fui.*
Th. quid núnc?
                    Tr. uise, spécta tuo úsque arbitrátu.
Th. age *í,* duce mé.
                    Tr. num morór ?
                                    Th. supsequór te.
Tr. senéx ipsus ánte ostium éccum opperítur.   795
sed út maestus ést, se hasce *aedís* uendidísse !
Th. quid tándem ?
                    Tr. orat út suadeám Philolachéti,
ut ístas remíttat sibí.
                    Th. haud opínor.
sibí quisque rúri metít. si male émptae
forént, nobis ístas redhibére haud licéret.   800

790. *unum* S., om. in M, *hoc uerbum* Rl., Bug., Lor.²
792. **SIMITU** A (acc. to Gepp.), Rl., rec. edd., **simul** B, **simulet**
CD.   *pote fui* S., **POTUI** AM, *simitur hau potui* Rl. (Opusc. II
p. 258).
793. **uise specta** M, edd. (except Uss.), **UISAGE....ASPECTA** A
(acc. to Gepp.), *uis? TR. age, aspecta* Gepp.   **USQU.** A, edd.,om. in M.
794. *Age i, duce* Rl., Lor.², Speng., **AGE DUC** AM, Uss., *Age,
age, duce* Bug.   *TR. num* Cam., edd., **nunc** M.
795. **IPSUS** A, rec. edd., **ipse** CD, **ipse te** B.   **eccum** M,
ILLUD A (acc. to Rl.).
796. **UT** A (acc. to Stud.), Rl., rec. edd., om. in M.   **se** M,
SE. A.   *aedis* Rl. (in crit. note), rec. edd., om. in M; the form
hasce (found in A and M) shows that a word beginning with a
vowel or *h* has dropped out.

790. **si uoles,** cf. 239.
791. Instead of the regular
apodosis (*reperies haud facile
esse* etc.), we have a clause ex-
pressing simply the *result* of
enquiry: cf. 702 f., and Propertius, *si uerum excutias, facies
non uxor amatur.*
793. **tuo usque arb.** 'just
as long as you like', cf. 767, 957.
797. **quid tandem ?** expresses
some impatience: 'what is the
matter now?' cf. 1000 ('Really?

what was it?'), 1108 ('you don't
say so?').
798. **ut remittat sibi** 'to let
him have back'; *remittere =*
redhibere (800), for which cf.
Merc. 422 *dixit se redhibere, si
non placeat.*—**haud opinor** 'I
think not', cf. on 197.
799. **sibi quisque r. m.** 'in
the country they make hay
while the sun shines', 'charity
begins at home'.—**male emptae,**
cf. on 298.

lucrí quicquid ést, id domúm trahere opórtet.
miséricordiá *stultum haud ésse* hominem opórtet.
Tr. moráre hercle; *uérba facis.* súpsequere.
                                                    Th. fíat.
dó tibi ego operám. *Tr.* senex illic ést. em, adduxi
                                                    hominém tibi.
805 Sı. sáluom te aduenísse peregre gaúdeo, Theópro-
                                                    pides.
    Th. dí te ament.
        Sı. inspícere *iste* aedis te hás uelle aiebát mihi.
    Th. nísi tibist incómmodum.
        Sı. immo cómmodum. i intro atque ínspice.
    Th. át enim mulierés—
                Sı. caue tu ullam flócci faxis múlierem.
    quálibet perámbula aedis óppido tamquám tuas.
810 Th. támquam?
        Tr. ah, caue tu illíc obiectes núnc in aegritúdine,

802. *stultum haud esse* after Rl.; M have lacuna in this and
foll. line.   *frangi nullum* Uss.
    803. So Uss., Lor.², *TH. immo tu facis.* *TR. subsequere* Rl.,
Lor.¹, Bug.
    804. *TR.* Cam., Uss., om. in M.; Bo. and others give whole line
to *TR.*   *ille eccumst* Rl., Lor.; but *eccum* never stands thus with
the verb *est* alone as predicate of the clause; this would be as
harsh as *ecce me sum*; see Brix on Capt.³ v 4, 8 and cf. on Most.
560.   *adduxi hominem tibi* Aldus, Rl., Lor., Bug., **tibi adduxi
hominem** M.
    806. *inspicere iste* rec. edd., **inspicere . te** B, **inspicerent** CD,
inspicere hic Rl.
    807. *tibist incommodum* Bo., Rl., rec. edd., **tibi incommodum
est** M.
    808. *TH.* Rl. (in ed. min.), rec. edd., **TR.** M.
    810. *illic* Jörgensen (cf. Luchs, Herm. VI p. 276), **illi** M, *illice*
Fl., *id illi* Rl., Lor., Bug.

801. **domum trahere** 'keep
it for ourselves'.
    804. **do t. e. operam** 'I am
at your service'. In 1009 the
phrase means 'to listen to' as in
Trin. Prol. 5, Capt. Prol. 6, 54,
III 4, 85.—**em**, cf. on 9.
    806. **iste** 'your slave': cf.
335 *b*.

808. **mulieres**; the objection
of Tr. (680). The subject is
an unpleasant one to Si. and
he answers with some warmth;
cf. *uoltu tristi* (811).—**caue faxis**,
cf. on 401.
    810. **ah, caue...ingeni** (814)
is spoken in a low tone.— **illic** =
illi-ce (dat.), cf. Aul. 663, Men.

te hásce emisse.   nón tu uides hunc nóltu ut est
                                          tristí senex?
TH. uídeo.

TR. ergo inridére ne uideáre et gestire ádmodum,
nóli facere méntionem te *hásce* emisse.
                                          TH. intéllego,
ét benc monitum dúco, atque *esse* exístumo humani
                                                   íngeni.
quíd nunc?

SI. quin tu is íntro atque otióse perspecta, út lubct. 815
TH. béne beni*gn*eque árbitror te fácere.
                                          SI. factum edepól uolo.

811. *hasce* Schmidt, Bug., Lor.², **has** M.   *ut est tristi*
Bo., Vahl., **ut** (ut...*f* B) **tristi est** M, *ut tristi sit* Fl., Uss., Lor.²,
uti tristist Rl., Lor.¹, Bug., *ut sit tristi, senem* Becker.
813. *hasce* Stud., Rl. (Opusc. III p. 123), Lor.², om. in M (B
has space after *emisse*), *ted emisse* Bo., Bergk, Uss.
814. *atque esse* Z, rec. edd., **atque se** M, *teque* Bent., *et te esse*
Rl.   *ingeni* Par., Bent., rec. edd. (*ingenii* Z), **ingenio** M, *hu-*
mano ingenio existumo Rl.
815. *tu is* Par., Vulg., Rams., rec. edd., **tu TR. is** M, *tu i* Rl.
perspectas Cam., Par., Vulg.   *intro: otiose perspecta aedis* Rl.
816. *benigneque* Cam., Bent., edd., **benique** M.   *SI.* Cam.,
edd., om. in M.   After this v. M have

Vin qui perductet?   **Apage istum perductorem. non placet**
Quid est?   errabo potius quam perductet quispiam,

which occur again in a different form after 844.   They were prob.
transferred by mistake to this place and then adapted to the
context.

304, 828, 842.—**oblectes** 're-
mind'.
811. **hunc,** cf. on 389.
812. **gestire adm.** 'be very
elated'.
814. The subject of **esse** is
'so to act' und.—**humani.** This
is the only passage in Plaut. in
which *humanus* has the ethical
sense, = 'humane' 'considerate',
which however is common
enough in Ter., cf. Andr. 113
haec ego putabam esse omnia
humani ingeni, Mansuetique
animi officia, ibid. 236, Hec. 553,

Haut. 99 (*humanitus*).
815. Note the copulative
conjunction, uniting heterogeneous expressions (*quin tu is?*
and *perspecta*); cf. Truc. 631
datin soleas? atque me intro
ducite (*ducitis* Schoell), Asin.
254 *quin tu...reice,...amoue, at-*
que te recipis? (*reicis...amoues*
Gz., Lö.), Most. 1038 f. *lora mihi*
cedo...eademque opera narrane-
ro, Pseud. 277 f. *audio: atque*
in pauca confer quid uelis.
816. **factum edepol uolo,** i.e.
'you are quite welcome'.

TR. uíden uestibulum ante aédis hoc et ámbulacrum,
                             quoíusmodi?
TH. lúculentum edepól profecto.
             TR. age spécta postis, quoíusmodi,
quánta firmitáte facti et quánta crassitúdine.
820 TH. nón uideor uidísse postis púlcriores.
                            SI. pól mihi
éo pretio empti fúerant olim.
                  TR. aúdin 'fuerant' dícere?
uíx uidetur cóntinere lácrumas.
                  TH. quanti hosce émeras?
SI. trís minas pro istís duobus praéter uecturám dedi.
TH. hércle qui multo ínprobiores súnt, quam a
                             primo crédidi.
825 TR. quápropter?
      TH. quia édepol ambo ab ínfumo tarmés secat:

817. So M, Rams., Uss., Lor.[2], *hoc ante aedis uestibulum* Rl.
quoius- monosyllabic as in 642.
820. *SI.* Acid., edd., om. in M.
821. *audin fuerant* F, edd., **auti(e)nfuerant** M.
824. *multo* FZ, Rl., Lor., Bug., **multum** M, Rams., Uss.
825. *TR.* Cam., Rl., Rams., Lor., Bug., **S.** B, *SI.* Uss.

817. **uestibulum, ambula-crum** are prob. two words for the same thing, a space in front of the house, large enough to take a walk in; cf. *ante aedes*, Varro L. L. VII 81 *uestibulum, quod est ante donum.*
820. **non uideor,** cf. on 197.
821. **eo pretio** etc. 'I once paid a fine price for them'; *eo* (emphatic) i.e. *ut pulcrae essent,* 'a suitable price'.—'**fuerant**'. Simo's *empti fuerant* was merely meant as the equiv. of *empti sunt* (cf. 519 *appellaueras = appellauisti,* 822 *emeras = emisti,* 487 *oblitus fueram = oblitus sum,* Aul. 627 *quod abstuleras = quod abstulisti,* ibid. 672, 759, Amph.

383 *peccaueram = peccaui,* Asin. 715, Stich. 251; cf. too on Most. 694); but Tr. seizes on the word *fuerant,* as if Si. had meant that the house *had been* his, but was so no longer.
823. **tris minas,** a humorous exaggeration. — **uectura** 'carriage' 'freight', cf. Asin. 432.
824. **qui,** an old asseverative particle often joined to *hercle,* as here, Trin. 464 *hercle qui dicam tamen* (see note), Men. 428 *hercle qui tu recte dicis:* similarly we have *ut qui* e.g. Capt. III 4, 21 (note), *quippe qui* Aul. 346 (note), *ecastor qui* Asin. 930, *pol qui* ibid. 823, *edepol qui* Mil. 779.

íntempestiuós excisos crédo; id eis uitiúm nocet.
TR. átqui etiam nunc sátis boni sunt, sí sunt inductí
pice.
nón enim haec pultúfagus opufex ópera fecit bárbarus.
uíden coagmenta in fóribus?
TH. uideo.
TR. spécta quam arte dórmiunt.

tarmes secat Scal., edd., **tramisecat** M, *trami secant* Loewe (Prodr.
p. 288), quoting a gloss '*tarmus: uermes in carne*'.
    826.   Cam. gives the line to *TR.* and so edd. (except Uss.).
    827.   *TR.* S., *SI.* Uss., om. in M.   *Atqui* rec. edd.; **Atque**
M.   *sint* Cam. Might we not read *erunt* with hiatus after
monosyllable (*si*)?
    828.   **PULTUFAGIS** A (acc. to Schwarzm.), *pultufagus* Bug.
    829.   *cŏagmenta* trisyllabic by synizesis.

    826.   **íntempestiuos** ' out of
season': cf. Plin. H.N. xvi 39,
189 *robur uere caesum teredinem
(=tarmitem) sentit; bruma autem neque uitiatur neque panda-
tur*, Isidorus Orig. xii 5, 10 *Ita
(i.e. termites) apud Latinos ligni
nermes uocantur, quos tempore
importuno caesae arbores gig-
nunt* (=Servius on Georg. i
256).
    827.   **sunt inducti**, a loose
use of the perfect for the future
perf., perhaps by attraction to
the present (*satis boni*) *sunt*,
which is also used loosely (for
erunt).
    828.   **enim.** See note on 551.
This is one of the few passages
in Plaut., in which *enim* seems
to approach very nearly to the
meaning of 'for'; cf. 926, Capt.
iv 2, 80, Truc. 908, Poen. 286,
604: but even in these cases it
may be trans. 'look you', as
Lang. says.—**pultufagus** 'pot-
tage-eating', a humorous hy-
brid, like *pergraphicus* Trin.
1139, *semisonarius* Aul. 509,

subbasilicanus Capt. iv 2, 35.—
barbarus 'from foreign parts'
i.e. either *Roman*, as so often in
Plaut., cf. Trin. Prol. 19 *Plautus uortit barbare* i.e. *latine*,
Capt. iii 1, 32 *barbarica lege
=Roman law*, ibid. iv 2, 104 :
Lor. refers to Varro L. L. v 105,
Plin. H. N. xviii 8, 19 [83] to
prove that *puls* or *pulmentum*
was the main diet of the early
Romans; or *Carthaginian* (so
Uss., who compares Poen. Prol.
[unplautine] 54 where *Pulti-
fagonides* = Carthaginian, and
shows from Cato R. R. 85 that
puls was also well known at Car-
thage).
    829.   **quam arte dormiunt**
'what fast sleepers they are'.
Dormire is also applied to an
inanimate object in Curc. 153,
ut dormiunt pessuli pessumi, but
Tr. employs the word here as
descriptive of the unsuspicious
state of the two old men. For
similar intentional and self-
corrected mistakes cf. Mil. 27,
819, Rud. 423, Amph. 384 etc.

830 TH. dórmiunt?

TR. illúd quidem, ut coníuent, uolui dícere.
sátin habcs?

TH. ut quídquid magis contémplor, tanto mágis
placet.

TR. uíden pictum ubi ludíficat una córnix uolturiós
duos?

TH. nón edepol uideo.

TR. át ego uideor: nam ínter uolturiós duos
córnix astat: éa uolturios dúos uicissim uéllicat.

835 quaéso huc ad me spécta, cornicem út conspicere
póssies.

iám uides?

TH. profécto nullam equidem íllic cornicem íntuor.

TR. át tu istoc ad uós optuere, quóniam cornicém
nequis

832. *ludificat* Bent., Rl., Stud., Uss., **LUDIFICATUR AM.**
UNACORNIX A, **cornix una** M.   **DUOS** A, **duo** M.   *Vide*
ubi ludificatur Guy., Lor., Bug.
833. So A (acc. to Stud.), but without space for *TR. ; at ego*
uideo rec. edd.   The whole line is omitted in M.
834. **DUOS** A, edd., **duo** M.
835. **POSSIES** A, Cam., edd., **possis** M.
836. **INTUOR** A, edd., **intueor** M.
837. *istoc* Fl., Rl., rec. edd., **ISTO AM.**

830. **illud quidem** etc.
'What I meant to say was, how
impenetrable!' Tr. again uses
a word of ambiguous sense:
coniuent = (i) 'to close up' (generally), (ii) 'to blink with the
eyes'.
831. **quidquid** = *quidque*, as
frequently in old Lat. cf. on
Aul. 196; conversely *quidque* =
quidquid, see on 667.
832. **ludificat** = *ludificatur*,
cf. 1151, Capt. III 1, 27, and on
Most. 166.—**cornix**, a type of
sagacity (cf. the proverb *cornici*
oculum configere), **uolturius** a
type of rapacity, cf. Trin. 101,
Capt. IV 2, 64. The imaginary

picture is supposed to be a
fresco, like those so common on
the walls of houses at Pompeii.
833. **uideor** (ambiguous) =
(to Theopr.) *uideor mihi uidere*
'I think I do', (to audience)
passive of *uideo.*
835. **ad me** 'in my direction'.
836. **intuor**: cf. *optuĕre* 837,
contui 838, *tuĕris* Trin. 708, *in-*
tuitur Capt. III 4, 25 ; on the
other hand we have *optuĕrier* 840,
Amph. 900, *optuetur* Mil. 1271,
intueor Rud. 449 : cf. on 42 (*olĕre*
and *olēre*).
837. **istoc ad uos** corresponds
to *huc ad me* (835) : note the

cónspicari, sí uolturios fórte possis cóntui.

TH. ómnino, ut te apsóluam, nullam píctam conspicio híc auem.

TR. áge, iam mitto. ignósco: aetate nón quis optué-
rier. 840

TH. haéc, quae possum, ea míhi profecto cúncta
uehementér placent.

SI. látius demum óperaest pretium iuísse.

TH. eu: recte edepól mones.

SI. eho, istum, puere, círcuinduce hasce aédis et
concláuia.

nam égomet ductarém, nisi mi esset ád forum negótium.

TH. ápage istum a me pérductorem : níhil moror
ductárier. 845

842. *operaest* Bo., Rl., Lor., Bug., **est operae** M.   *eu* Bo.,
Rl., Lor., Bug., e. B, et CD[1].
843. *puere* Bo., Rl., rec. edd., **puer** M.   **hasce** M, **HOC** (or
HOS) A (acc. to Stud.), possibly for *huc*.
845. So A (acc. to Stud.), Cam., Rams., Uss., **Apage istum
me......nihil moror ductarier** M. Bug., Lor.[2] (after Rl.) amal-

combination of the second pers.
sing. imperat. with **uos**, ' you
and your friend '.
839. **ut te apsoluam** 'to have
done with you ' 'pour en finir ',
Th. is getting irritated: for
apsoluere in this sense cf. 652,
Aul. 512; rather differently
Epid. 465 *te apsoluam breui*
'I will not detain you long';
Capt. III 5, 72 *non uno apsoluam
die.*
840. **age** 'well, well ', cf.
Mil. 1024.—**ignosco** 'I make al-
lowances (for you) '.—**aetate** =
prae, aetate, cf. Capt. IV 2, 28.
On the sense ' old age ' cf. on
196.
842. **latius demum** etc. i.e.
*quom latius iueris, id demum
operae pretium est* ' it's not
worth your while until you have

gone further '; Lang. comp.
Merc. 907 *seruata res est demum,
si illam uidero* i.e. *tum demum
s. r. e., si i. u.* etc., Bacch. 271 f.
*damnatus demum......reddidit =
tum demum r. postquam d. est.*
—**latius** for *longius intro* is, as
Lor. says, very strange.
843. **puere** (cf. on 308), addressed to a slave in the house.
—**circumduce**, cf. on 60.
844. **ductarem** almost = *ducerem.* Plaut. is very fond of
frequentatives, cf. *uictitare* 54,
mantare 116, *rogitare* 368, *re-
cursare* 581, *datare* 602, *territare*
609, *obiectare* 810.—**ad forum**,
cf. on 352.
845. **perductor**, with innu-
endo : the word, in its secondary sense, means 'seducer '; cf.
perducere Hor. Sat. II 5, 77.

847 quídquid est, errábo potius quám perductet quíspiam.
Sɪ. aédis dico.
Tʜ. ergo íntro eo igitur síne perductore.
                                        Sɪ. í, licet.
Tʜ. íbo intro igitur.
        Tʀ. máne sis uideam, né canis—
                        Tʜ. agedúm uide.
850 Tʀ. st! ábi canis, st! abi díerecte: st! ábin hinc in
                                        malám crucem?
át etiam restát: st! abi istinc.
        Sɪ. níl periclist: áge *modo*.

gamate the lines which occur after 816 (see crit. note there) with
the present passage; giving

TH. Apage istum circumductorem : nil moror ductarier.
SI. Vin qui perductet? TH. apage istum perductorem : non placet.

and then 847.
    847. So A (acc. to Stud.), **Quidquid est**............**perductet quis-**
piam M; but M have the complete line before 817; see on 816.
    849. *igitur* FZ, edd., **igitur est** M, *igitur TR. st!* Grut.
    850. So M (with **est** throughout for *st!*, which Bug. retains;
Est abi canis est. TR. abi dierecta B[1]), *TR. Ést. TH. ubist?*
TR. abi hinc dīerecte Rl., *TR. Śt, canis, st, abi! ábi dīerecte*
Lor. For the scansion of *dīerecte* see on 8. We might in this
place scan as three syllables with the ictus on *abĭ*.
    851. **restat** B[1], rec. edd., **restas** B[2]CD, Cam., Rams., Rl.
Speng. and Uss. give *At etiam restat* to *TH.*   *SI.* F, Cam., edd.,
om. in M.   *modo* Rl., Lor., Uss., om. in M.

847. **quidquid est** 'in any
event', cf. Mil. 311 *hercle, quid-*
quid est ('come what may'),
mussabo potius quam interean
male, Truc. 254 *sed fores, quid-*
quest futurum, feriam, Curc. 694;
cf. for a different usage of *quid-*
quid est, 667 and note.
    848. **ergo......igitur**, again
Trin. 756 (note).
    849. **mane uideam** with o-
mission of *ut*; so after *fac* 854,
faxo 68, 1133, *cedo* 373, *uis*
578, *roga* 680 etc. For a different explanation of the subj. as

hortative (acc. to Greek usage)
see Br. on Trin. 1136.—**uideam**
ne, cf. 966, Capt. ɪ 2, 18 *uisam*
ne...turbauerint.
    850. Dogs were commonly
kept at the door of a Roman or
Greek house; but perh. the fun
of this passage consisted in
having not a real dog, but the
figure of a dog represented on
the threshold, like that in the
house of the Tragic Poet at
Pompeii.
    851. **etiam** 'still', cf. on
522.

tám placidast quam est *ágna*: quamuis íre intro
                                        audactér licet
éo ego hinc ad forúm.
                TH. fecisti cómmode: bene ámbula.
Tránio, age canem ístam a foribus *áliquis* abducát face,
étsi non metuéndast.
        TR. quin tu illam áspice, ut placide áccubat. 855
nísi molestum uís uideri te átque ignauom.
                                TH. iam út lubet.
séquere hac me igitur.
        TR. équidem haud usquam a pédibus apscedám
                                                tuis.

852. *quam est agna : quamuis eire* Leo (*agna* Bent.), **quam..a
qua . uis . ire** B¹, **quam est aqua uise ire** B², **quam feta qua uis
eire** C, **quam feta quauiscire** D, *quam est agna quaeuis : eire* Palm.,
quam feta: quamuis eire Büch. ('significatur κύων κυοῦσα, praeg-
nans').
853. *Ego eo* Z, Rl., Lor., Bug. **EGOAD** A (acc. to Schwarzm.).
854. *aliquis* Rl., Rams., rec. edd., om. in M.

852. **agna**, cf. Ter. Ad. 534
*quom feruit maxume, tam placi-
dum quasi ouem reddo*, Ovid
Met. XIII 927 *placidae oues*. In
Poen. 1236 a quiet dog is compared to oil, *ita hanc canem
faciam tibi oleo tranquilliorem.*
853. **commode**, cf. on 255.—

bene ambula 'bon voyage!' cf.
Capt. II 3, 92. Exit Simo.
856. **molestum** 'tiresome',
ignauom 'timid'.
857. **haud usquam** lit. 'no-
whither'=*nusquam* Capt. I 2,
64 (note); cf. Trin. 314 *ne pe-
netrarem me usquam.*

ACTVS IV.

PHANISCUS.

PH.   Seruí qui quom culpá carent tamén malúm
                                        métuont,
hí solent esse éris utibiles.
860 nam ei quí nil metuont póstea quom súnt malúm
                                        mériti,
stúlta sibi expetúnt consilia.

858—884. FIFTH CANTICUM. 858, 860 iamb. dim. + iam. dim.
cat. (syncopated) ⏑⏒⏑ | ⏑⏒⏑‖ ⏑⏒⏒ | ⏒⏑, 859, 861 troch. dim.
⏒⏑⏑ | ⏒⏑⏑, 862 + 863a troch. octon., 863b + 864 troch. septen.,
865 bacch. tetram., 868 two 'iambica cola semiquinaria'
⏑⏒⏑⏒ | ⏑⏒⏑⏒, 869 bacch. dim. cat. + bacch. dim. acat., 871
—873 bacch. tetram., 874 two iamb. dim. cat. (syncopated), 875
f. bacch. tetram., 877 troch. octon., 878 f. cret. tetram., 880 = 858,
881 f. cret. tetram., 883 f. troch. septen.
    In the first four vv. and in 874, 880 I have been guided by
Stud. (Festgruss p. 55 f.) and, except where otherwise expressly
stated, have adhered closely to the division of lines indicated by
M: so too rec. edd.   Rl. reduced 858—876 to bacchiac tetrameters.
Mr R. Ellis has kindly expressed his view of this and the following Canticum in Excursus II at the end of this volume: cf. Intr. p. xx.
The immense difficulty of constituting the metres of this scene is
increased by the fact that the part of A containing it is lost, with
the exception of v. 858 (which agrees exactly with M).
    860. *ei* Stud., Bug., Lor.², illu M.   *postea quom* Bug.,
Lor.² (after Stud. *postea quam*), **postquam** M.

Soliloquy of Phaniscus, who
has come to fetch his master
home (cf. on 313 f.), upon the
difference between a *seruos frugi*
and a *seruos nequam:* cf. Aul.
IV 1, Men. v 6.

858. **carent**, cf. on 29.—
malum = *mala res*, cf. on 61.
    860. **qui nil metuont** i.e.
who are too audacious.
    861. **expetere**, cf. on 763.

éxercent sese ád cursuram : fúgiunt. sed si súnt 862,
reprensi, 863*a*
fáciunt c maló peculi*um*, *é bono* quod *nón* que- 863*b*,
unt. 864
augént ex pauxíllo : *thensaúrum inde* páriunt. 865
mihi in pectore †consilii * * * malam rem prius
†quam ut meum * * * * *
ut adhúc fuít mi, corium ésse opórtet :
sincérum atque utí uotém uerberári
* * * * * * * * *
si †huic imperabo, probe tectum habcbo : 870
malúm quom inpluít ceterís, ne inpluát mi.
nam ut sérui uolúnt esse erum, íta solet *is ésse* :

862. *si sunt reprensi* Lor., Bug., **hii si reprehensi sunt.**
864. *e malo peculium, e bono* Uss., Bug., *quod non queunt* S.,
a malo peculio quod nequeunt M, *de malo peculium, quoniam
nequeunt de bono* Lor. (after Rl.).
865. *thensaurum inde pariunt* Herm. (after Cam.), Bug.,
......**deparant** M.
866 f. Rl. (after Herm.), Lor., Bug. give
*Mihi in pectore id consilist, praecauére
Malúm rem priús quam ut meúm tergum dóleat.*
but this seems open to both grammatical and prosodical objections,
as Rothe and Seyff. have shown.
869. *uerberari* Pyl., edd., **uerberare** M.
871. *ceteris* Lamb., Rl., rec. edd., **ceteros** M.
872. *is esse* Bergk, Lor., Bug., om. in M.

862. **reprensi** 'caught and brought back again'. The word prop. means ' to seize from behind' (by the *pallium*), cf. Trin. 624.
864. **faciunt e malo peculium.** This obscure phrase, which sounds like a piece of slaves' slang, seems to mean ' they get perquisites in the shape of (lit. 'made out of') punishment' (but the reading is doubtful); cf. Asin. 277 where after Leonida has ironically offered to make a present of the stripes that he has received,

Libanus remarks : *largitur peculium: omnem in tergo thensaurum gerit.*—**e bono** 'in the shape of pelf', in antithesis to *e malo*.
869. **sincerum** 'unbroken' 'whole', cf. Rud. 756 f. The rest of the line is connected with the lost line or lines.
870. **si huic imperabo**, etc., if genuine, perh. means 'if I make this (my back) obey me (by avoiding the whip), I shall get a nice roof to cover it'. Or *huic* may be his master, and the sense 'if I humour him so as to rule him'.

boní sunt, *bonúst*; inprobí sunt, malús fit.

874 {nam núnc domí nóstrae

{tot péssumí uíuont,

875 pecúli suí prodigí, plagigéruli.

uelút ubi aduorsum út eant eró *suo* uocántur:

'nón eo: moléstus ne sis: scío quo properas: géstis

aliquo :

iam hércle *tu*, múle, uis íre pastúm foras.'

béne merens hóc preti inde ápstuli : abií foras.

880 solús nunc *ego* eo aduórsum ero ex plúrumís séruis.

hóc di*e* crástini quóm crus rescíuerit,

873. So Bergk, rec. edd., **Bonis (-ni) sum improbis (-bi) sunt malus fuit.**

874 is written as one line in M: I follow Stud., Bug., Lor.[2]

875—878 form in M three lines ending with *eant, sis,* (*foras*) *pastum* respectively.

876. So Lor., Bug., **ubi aduersum ut eant uocantur ero** M.

877 f. The quotation is marked by a new metre; so a letter that is read aloud (e.g. Pers. 501, Pseud. 998, Bacch. 997, 1007 etc.) or an oath that is recited (Rud. 1338); cf. Intr. p. xviii.

877. So Herm., Rl., Lor., Bug.   **quod properas** M, Uss.

878. So Ell. **iam hercle ire (tire D) uis mula foras pastum** M.

879. *preti* Rl., rec. edd., **pretium** M.   *inde apstuli: abii* Bo. (after Cam.), edd., **unde abstultabi** M.

880. So Stud., Bug., Lor.[2] (with hiatus after the iamb. dim.), *ego* om. in M.

881. *die* Pyl., edd., **di** M.

874. **nam,** cf. on 133.

875. **peculi** here in the proper sense, 'savings'.—**plagigeruli,** cf. Pseud. 156 *plagigerula genera hominum,* ibid. 181 *munerigeruli,* Truc. 551 *damnigeruli,* Cas. ii 3, 46 *scutigerulus.*

876. **uelut** 'for instance', cf. on 159.—**uocantur** i.e. by a brother slave.

878. **mulus** 'dolt' is here a term of abuse, as in Cat. LXXXIII 3 *mule nihil sentis.* Here perh. trans. 'swine', cf. 888.

879. **bene merens** 'for my services'.—**hoc preti,** cf. *hoc negoti* Trin. 580, *hoc operis* Amph. 463.—**inde,** cf. on 547.

881. **crastini** (abl.)=*crastino,* cf. on Men. 1156 *die septimi* where Wagn. compares *qui*=*quo* and quotes Gellius to show that *diequinti* or *diequinte* (pronounced as one word)='on the fifth day' was the regular phrase in the time of Cicero. Similar expressions are *die pristini, die proximi;* cf. *postridie*=*postero die.*

mále castigábit eos éxuuiis búbulis.
póstremo minóris pendo térgum illorum quám
meum :
illi erunt bucaédae multo pótius quam ego sim
réstio.

ADVORSITOR.   PHANISCUS.

ADV. Mané tu atque adsiste ílico,	885a
Phanísce, etiam réspicis?	885b,
Pn. mihí molestus né sis.	886a
ADV. uide út fastidit símia.	886b

882. *Male* Rl., rec. edd., **Mane** M.   *exuuiis bubulis*
Herm., Rl., Bug., Lor.², **bubulis exuuiis** M, see Intr. p. xxvi.

884. B gives the line to *Danista*, this and the following line
standing between 841 and 601 (which are brought together in M);
on the shifting of scenes in M cf. Introd. p. xv.

885—903. The SIXTH CANTICUM falls into two parts: 885
—896 SECTION A: 885 a iamb. dim., 885 b + 886 a iamb. septen.,
886 b iamb. dim., 887 a anap. dim., 887 b + 888 anap. tetram.,
889 anap. dim., 890, 891 a bacch. tetram., 891 b + 892, 893 = 858,
894 iamb. septen., 895 + 896 anap. tetram. The whole of this
section was reduced to iamb. septenarii by Herm. and Rl.; I
have in the main followed Stud. and Lor.², observing the division
into lines indicated by M. It should be observed that M omit
names of speakers throughout (except B in 885 a).

885 a. *ADV.* Cam., edd., **TR.** B: cf. note on last line.
Manē, cf. Intr. to Capt. A. (i) and on *abi* Most. 580.

885 b. *respicis* S., *respice* M. With the imperative, *etiam* is
explained by Lor. as = 'again'; cf. 474. Note hiatus after the
vocative, which involves a slight pause: cf. 739.

886 b—889. In this order Acid., Rl., rec. edd. (but not
Stud.); M have the following order: 886 b, 889, 887 a, 887 b + 888.

882. **male** cf. on 316.—
exuuiis bubulis 'cowhide', cf.
censione bubula Aul. 593.

883. **postremo** 'in a word',
to cut the argument short, cf.
198.

884. **bucaeda** ought prop. to
mean 'butcher' cf. the gloss
quoted by Loewe (Prodr. p.
267) *bucidae: qui boues caedunt;*
Phan. here uses it with comic
effect = *qui boue* (i.e. *loris bubulis*) *caeditur*, as if to be flogged

were a trade. Similarly *restio*.
'They shall go in for tanning
much sooner than I take up the
rope business'.

One of the other slaves
changes his mind and follows
Phaniscus. Catching him up
at the door of the house, he
gives vent to his jealousy and
hatred.

885 b. **etiam respicis?** cf. on
383.

886 b. **ut fastidit** cf. on 149.

887*a* manen ílico, parasite ínpure?
887*b*, 888 P*ii*. qui párasitus sum?
      A*dv*. ego ením dicam: cibo pérduci poterís
                              quouis.
889 P*ii*. mihi súm, lubet esse: quid íd curas?
890 A*dv*. ferócem facís te, quia érus tuos *te* amát.
                                     *P*ii. uah!
891*a* oculí *mi* dolént.
      A*dv*. quor?
            P*h*. quia fúmus moléstus*t*.
891*b*, 892 A*dv*. tace sís, faber, qui cúdere soles plúmbeós
                                     númmos.

887 *a*. So Speng., Bug., Lor.[2], **Manesne ilico impure para-site?** M.
887 *b* + 888. *poteris* Cam., edd., **poteres** M, *potis es* Grut.
889. *Mihi* FZ, edd., **Milis** M.   **sum** M, *si* Uss.
890. *facis te, quia* S., **facis quia te** M, *te facis, quia te* Rl., *facis te, quia te* Uss., *facit. quia te* Lamb.   *erus tuos te amat.*
PH. uah! S.; (without *te*) Stud., rec. edd., **eratus amatuha** M.
891 *a*. *mi* Speng., Lor.[2], om. in M.   *molestust* Rl., Lor., Bug., **molestus** M.
892. **nummos** DFZ, edd., **mummos** C, **numbos nos** B.

888. **enim** 'Why', cf. on 551.—**perduci** cf. on 847.
889. **mihi sum** lit. 'I am so for *myself*', i.e. 'that is my affair'; so again Bacch. 73.— **esse** may be = *edere* cf. on 12.
890. **ferocem facis te** 'you give yourself airs', cf. Mil. 1034 *face te fastidi plenum* 'pretend to be fastidious', Asin. 351, Curc. 538, Catull. xcvii 9 *se facit esse uenustum.*—**uah** cf. on 256.
891 *a*. **fumus** prob. a trans. of καπνός, in the sense of 'foolish chatter' 'fumes of the fancy' cf. Plato Repub. ix 581 D καπνὸν καὶ φλυαρίαν ἡγεῖται, Aristoph. Plut. 821 ἐμὲ δ' ἐξέπεμ-ψεν ὁ καπνός· οὐχ οἷός τε γὰρ ἔνδον μένειν ἦν· ἔδακνε γὰρ τὰ βλέφαρά μου. But instead of

calling the taunts *fumus* at once, Phan. first pretends to cry (**oculi dolent** 'my eyes are smarting') and then brings in his repartee *fumus* (cf. Hor. Sat. i 5, 80 *lacrimoso non sine fumo*) as an explanation; cf. Mil. 324 ff. *SC. abi ludis me. PA. tum mihi sunt manus inquinatae. SC. quidum? PA. quia ludo luto.* There is a similar joke about tears and smoke in Asin. 619 f. *LI. num fumus est haec mulier quam amplexare? ARG. quidum? LI. quia oculi sunt tibi lacrumantes.*
892. **plumbeos nummos** 'base coin' i.e. bad jokes; or perh., as Casaubon said, 'false arts' (by which to impose upon your master).

Pн. non mé potes tu cógcre, ut mále tibí dícam. 893
nouít erus me.
    Adv. suám quidem pol cúlcitcllam opórtet. 894
Pн. si sóbrius sis, male nón dicas.   895,
    Adv. tibi optémpercm, quom tu míhi nec eas? 896
Pн. át tu mecum, péssume, ito aduórsus. quaeso
                          hercle ápstine *
iám scrmonem de ístis rebus.
               Adv. fáciam et pultabó foris.
heus, écquis hic est, máxumam qui iniúriam
foribús defendat? écquis has*ce* aperít foris?   900
homo némo hinc quidem foras éxit.   901*a*
ut esse áddecet nequam hominés, ita sunt.   { 901*b*,
                                       902*u*
sed eó magis cauto opus ést, ne huc   902*b*
exeát qui male mc múlcet.   903

893. *me potes tu cogcre, ut male tibi* (with hiatus as in 880)
S., **potes tu cogere me ut tibi male** M, *pol potes tu cogere med ut
tibi male* Bug., Lor.² (after Rl.).
896. *nec eas* Rcid, **neque eas** M, *nequeas* FZ, edd.
897—903. Section *B.* 897, 898 troch. septen., 899, 900
iamb. trim., 901 *a* paroemiacus, 901 *b* + 902 *a* anap. dim., 902 *b*,
903 paroemiaci.
897. *pessume, ito* Rl., Spcng., rcc. edd., **pessimi tu** M.
899—903 *b.* So Stud. (with hints from A), Lor.²   M have

Heus ecquis hic est maximam qui his iniuriam
Foribus defendat hecquis hecquis huc exit atque aperit?
Nemo hinc quidem foras exit ut esse addecet nequam homines
                                   ita sunt.
Sed eo magis cauto est opus Ne huc exeat qui male me mulcet.

Acc. to Stud. A has in 900 **ASAPER..FORIS**, in 901 *a* a spacc
before *nemo*, in 901 *b* **UT** at beginning of line, which ends with
MAGISCAU.

894. **nouit erus me** so Asin.
456 'I havc Mastcr's confi-
denco'.
896. **mihi nec eas** 'I can't
get you to go' cf. Festus p. 162
neceunt: non eunt, ut nec pro

non, cf. *non eo* 877.
901 *b.* **addecet** i.c. as one is
not surprised to find them.
902 *b.* **eo magis** i.e. becausc
they are *nequam.*

Tranio. Theopropides. Phaniscvs. Advorsitor.

Tr. Quíd tibi uisumst mércimoni*um* ésse?

                    Th. totus gaúdeo.

905 Tr. núm nimio emptae tíbi uidentur?

             Th. númquam edepol ego mé scio

uídisse usquam abiéctas aedis, nísi modo hascc.

                      Tr. ecquíd placent?

Th. écquid place*a*nt, mé rogas? immo hércle uero

                      pérplacent.

Tr. quoíusmodi gunaéceum? quid pórticum?

                      Th. insanúm bonam.

nón equidem ullam in púplico esse máiorem hac

                      exístumo.

910 Tr. quín ego ipse et Phílolaches in púplico omnis

                      pórticus

súmus commensi.

        Th. quíd igitur?

                 Tr. longe ómnium longíssumast.

Th. di ínmortales, mércimoni lépidi! *si* hercle núnc

                      ferat

Cam. placed this scene after III 2: it was restored to its present position by Rl.; cf. Intr. p. xv.

904. *mercimonium esse* Reid, **mercimonii** M, *mercimoni hoc esse* Rl., rec. edd.

905. *scio* Pius, edd., **scito** M, *puto* Koch.

906. *usquam* Dous., Rl., rec. edd., **umquam** M.   *abiectus*. D³, edd., **ablectas** M, Scal.

907. *placeant* Cam., edd., **placent** M.

912. *si* Cam., edd., om. in M.

Enter Theopropides and Tranio, from Simo's house. They converse without observing the *aduorsitores*, who remain in the background.

904. **quid ... mercimonium** ('purchase'; cf. 915 *istoc mercimonio*). Cf. Ter. Eun. 273 f. *sed quid uidetur hoc tibi mancupium?* Cic. Fam. ix 261; Att. xiii 10, 1.

907. **ecquid placeant** cf. on 556.

908. **quid porticum** 'What do you think of the portico?':

censes must be supplied; cf. Trin. 811 *quid illum putas natura illa atque ingenio?* Ter. Andr. 583 *quid illum censes?*— **insanum bonam** cf. on 761.

909. **in puplico** 'on the piazza', cf. Capt. iv 2, 29 *in puplico* 'in the street', Stich. 614 *in puplicum* 'into the street'.

911. **longe** = *multo;* cf. on 316.

912. **mercimoni** l., gen. of exclamation, in imitation of the Greek idiom e.g. τῆς τύχης.

séx talenta mágna argcnti pro ístis praescntária,
númquam accipiam.
   TR. si hércle accipere cúpias, cgo numquám
                        sinam.
TH. béne res nostra cónlocatast ístoc mercimónio.   915
TR. mé suasore atque ínpulsore id fáctum audacter
                           dícito,
quí subegi faénore argentum áb danista ut súmeret,
quód isti dedimus árraboni.
             TH. sérnauisti omném ratem.
némpe octogintá debentur huíc minae ?
                    TR. hau nummo ámplius.
TH. hódie accipiat.
               TR. íta cnimuero : né qua causa súpsiet. 920
uél mihi denumeráto : cgo illi pórro dcnumeráuero.
TH. át enim ne quid cáptionis míhi sit, si dederím tibi.

    914. *accipiam* Cam., edd., **accipiem** M.   *cupias* Cam.,
edd., **cupies** M.
    920. *TH.* Pyl., cdd., om. in M.
    922. *captionis* S., **captioni** M. Plaut. uscs the word *captio* in
five other placcs, and always in the scnsc of 'trap', 'quibble': Epid.
297, 701, Most. 1144, Truc. 627, Asin. 790. Lor. and Uss. cxplain
the dat. (which might perh. be rctained in the above sense) as =
fraudi, detrimento, a very rare sensc (cf. Cic. Att. v 4, 4, Gaius
Dig. xxix 3, 7, Lex Rubr. col. 1, v. 45) and not so suitable to thc
present context as 'trap'.

    913. **talenta magna,** cf. on
647.—**istis** vaguely, for *eis* or
illis, cf. 335 *b,* 669. For similar
vagueness of *hic* cf. on 540.
In 918, 919, 921 the same person is described as *iste, hic, ille ;*
in 1155 by *is* and *ille:* cf. on
Capt. III 4, 15 f.
    917. **subegi** sc. *filium tuom.*—
faenore cf. on 532.
    918. **istb** ' the man who sold
it ', cf. on 913.—**arraboni** cf. on
532, 648.
    920. **ita enimuero** ' let it be
so '.—**ne qua causa sups.** ' that
there may be no excuse for

demur in the background '.
    921. **uel** ' or rathcr ', cf. on
299.—**denumerauero** cf. on 590.
    922. **at enim ne...sit** ' but
perhaps there may bc '. The
phrase may be cxplaincd by the
ellipsis of *cauendum est* or *metuo ;*
cf. Aul. 639 *ne inter tunicas
habeas,* Stich. 600 *at ille ne
succenseat.* So in Grcek μή
often = δέος ἐστὶ μή.—**quid captionis** 'somc trap ', cf. Cic. pro
Quinct. xvi 53 *si in paruola re
captionis aliquid uererere,* and
on 1144.

TR. égone te ioculó modo ausim dícto aut facto
fállcrc ?

TH. égon' aps te ausim nón caucre, né quid commit-
tám tibi ?

925 TR. quíd? tibin umquam quídquam, postquam túos
sum, uerborúm dedi ?

TH. égo enim caui a te: eám *mi* debes grátiam
atque animó meo.

sát sapio, si aps té modo uno cáueo.

TR. tecum séntio.

TH. núnc abi rus: dic me áduenisse fílio.

TR. faciam út iubes.

930 TH. cúrriculo iube in úrbem ueniat iám simul tecúm.

TR. licet.

núnc ego me illac pér posticum ad cóngerrones cón-
feram:

924. ni M (=*ne*), cf. 415.
925. *Quid? tibin' umquam* Rl., Lor., **Quia tibi umquam** M,
Quin (i.e. *Quine*) *tibi numquam*......? Pyl., Bug.
926, 927. *a te: eam mi debes* Palmer, **recte eam debis** (corr.
to **debes**) B, **recte eam debis** CD, *recte TR. eandem inis FZ, recte
TR. eam mihi debes* Cam., *recte: eam mihi debeo* Acid., *recte TR.
meam habes* Ell. (=*mihi debes* 'it is I to whom you are indebted
for the favour'). Rl. and Lor. consider that two half lines have
been lost between *recte* and *eam*, and give 928 to *TH.*
929. **ABIRUS** AFZ, edd., **abi i rus** M.   **IUBES** A (acc. to
Stud.), rec. edd., **uoles** M.
930. **IUBE** A, edd., **ubi iube** CF, **tibi iube** D, **.ibi** B.
TR. Cam., edd., om. in M.
931. **ILLAC** A, edd., **illa** M.

923. **ioculo modo** 'even by
way of a joke' 'even in fun',
cf. Rud. 729 *occupito modo illis
adferre uim ioculo pauxillulam.
ioculo* again Stich. 23, Merc.
933.
925. **postquam sum** cf. on
156.
926. **enim** cf. on 828, 551.
928. **sat sapio** 'I show my
good sense'.—**tecum sentio,** an
ironical *aside.*

929. **rus.** The statement
that Philol. is in the country,
has nowhere been made in the
text as we have it; perh., as
Uss. says, Theopr. is supposed
to draw this inference for himself, believing, as he does, that
the town house has been sold.
930. **curriculo** cf. on 362.—
licet cf. on 402.
931 f. an *aside,* after which
exit Tranio.—**illac** with a ges-

dícam, ut hic res sínt quietae atque húnc ut hinc
amóuerim.
Pii. híc quidem neque cónuiuarum sónitus*t*, item ut
antehác fuit:
néque tibiciná*m* cantantem néque aliu*m* que*m*quam
aúdio.
TH. quaé illacc res est? quíd illisce homines quaérunt
apud aedís meas? 935
quíd uolunt? quid íntrospectant?
ADV. pérgam pultarc óstium.
heús, reclude: heus, Tránio, etiamnc áperis?
TH. quae haec est fábula?
ADV. étiamne aperis? Cállidamati nóstro aduorsum
uénimus.
TH. heús uos, pucri, quíd istic agitis? quíd istas
aedis frángitis?
ADV. * nec quid tu percunctator * * * 940

932. **hic** M, edd., **HINC** A. **quietae** M, edd., **QUAESITAE** A
(acc. to Gepp.). *hunc ut* Guy., Rl., Lor., Bug., **ut hunc** M.
After this line M begin a new scene: but not A.
933. *PII.* Rl., Rams., rec. edd., om. in M. *sonitust* Rl.,
Lor., Bug., **sonitus** M. *item* Bo., Rl., rec. edd., **itidem** M.
935. **ILLISCE** A (acc. to Stud.), Rl., rec. edd., **illic** BF, **illis** c
CD.
936. *ADV.* Rl., rec. edd., om. in M, *PII.* Cam.
937. **ETIAMNE** A, edd., **etiam** M.
938. *ADV.* Rl., rec. edd., om. in M, *PII.* Cam.
940—945. So Gepp. from A; M omit the six verses.

ture.—**per posticum** cf. 1045 f.
Tran. desires to release his
friends from the 'state of siege'
1048. — **congerrones** (again
1049) seems to mean 'boon
companions': Ter. Haut. 1033
has the uncompounded *gerro*=
nugator. Varro, Festus and
Nonius derive from *gerrae*=
nugae.
934. **cantantem** sc. *fidibus*
i.e. 'performing'.
935. **illisce** cf. on 510.
937. **etiamne** cf. Men. 697
etiamne astas? etiam audes mea

reuorti gratia? and on 383.—
fabula 'mystification','comedy',
cf. 510.
939. **aedis frangitis**; cf. 453,
899 and Shaksp. Taming of
Shrew v 1 'What's he that
knocks as he would beat down
the gate?'
940—5. In these vv. the
aduorsitor seems to have in-
dulged in pleasantries at the
expense of Theopr.; cf. 949
where the latter calls Phan.
'*puer probus*'.

*   *   *   *   * prae triennio bonus

*   *   *   * quae *   * audias

*   quid uis animule   *   *   *   *

*   *   *   * huc quidem est   *   *

945 *TH.* *   *   * séd quid uobis ést negoti hic?

PH. éloquar.

érus hic noster pótat.

TH. erus hic uóster potat?

PH. íta loquor.

TH. púere, nimis es délicatus.

PH. éi aduorsum uénimus.

TH. quoí homini?

PH. ero nóstro. quaeso, quótiens dicundúmst tibi?

TH. púere, nemo hic hábitat: nam te esse árbitror
puerúm probum.

950 PH. nón hic Philolachés adulescens hábitat hisce in
aédibus?

TH. *hábitauit*: uerum *émigrauit prídem ille ex* hisce
aédibus.

ADV. sénex hic elleborósust certe.

PH. érras peruorsé, pater :

947. **PUERE** A, Acid., edd., **puer** M, *nimis es delicatus* S.,
NIMI .. SDELICATUS A (acc. to Gepp.), **nimium adelicatus** M, *ah
nimium delicatu's* Müll., Bug. (cf. Rud. 681), *nimium es delicatus*
Cam., Uss., *nimium delicatu's* Rl., Lor.   *ēi* cf. on 481.

948. *Quoí hŏmĭnĭ ? ĕrŏ*, with hiatus after *Quoi* (cf. Trin. 604,
Men. 474, Intr. to Aul. p. lxii [68]) and after *homini*, at the change
of speakers (cf. on 567). With *ĕrŏ nóstr.* cf. *ĕrĭs* 859.

949. **PUERENEMOHIC** A, edd., **puer hic nemo** M.

950. **HISCINAEDIBUS** A, Pyl., edd., **hiscedibus** M.

951. So Rl., rec. edd., from A (.**ABI.M.U.BUM...C.....R
.....L...HISCEAEDIBUS**); M om. the line.

952. *Sĕnĕx* cf. 804 *sĕnĕx ill.*   **ELLEBOROSUSESTCERTE**
A (acc. to Gepp.), Rl., Lor., Uss., **cerebrosus est certe** M.

947. **nimis es delicatus**
'you're too fond of joking', cf.
Mil. 984 *uah delicatu's*, Rud. 465
sed ubi tu's delicata 'playful
one': so *delicias facere* = 'to

jest' Men. 381 etc.

949. **nam** i.e. 'I don't mind
telling you: for' etc., cf. 133.

952. **elleborosus** 'a confirmed
maniac' lit. 'a subject for hel-

nám nisi hinc hodie émigrauit aút heri, ccrtó scio
híc habitare.
TH. quín sex mensis iam híc nemo habitat.
ADV. sómnias.
TH. égone?
ADV. tune.
TH. tún molestu's: síne me cum pueró loqui. 955
némo habitat.
PH. habitát profecto: nám heri et nudiustértius,
quártus, quintus, séxtus, usque póstquam hinc peregre
eiús pater
ábiit, numquam hic tríduom unum désitumst po-
tárier.
TH. quíd ais?
PH. triduom únumst haud intérmissum hic
esse ét bibi,

953. HINC A, Cam., edd., hic M.
955. tune. TH. tun Warren, tu tu ne M, tu. TH. tu ne
Rams., Uss., tune TH. ne Fl., Rl., Lor., Bug.
956. So FZ, Rl., rec. edd., habitat haec tat CD, habitat. A.
hem ita. B.   nam M, edd., IAM A.   nãm hĕr. with hiatus: cf.
on 133.   nŭdĭūstértius, in spite of the derivation from nunc
and dius (cf. on 444); cf. on Trin. 727, Intr. to Capt. A (ii).
957. PEREGREIEIIUS A (acc. to Stud.).
958. DESITUMESTPOTARIER A, edd., desitum esse et bibi est
(bibiss.) M (transferred from 959).
959. esse M, essi Bug. (a clever conjecture in Opusc. ad Madv.
miss.), Uss., edi Bug. (in ed.), Lor.[2]

lebore', cf. Rud. 1006 TR. sum
elleborosus GR. at ego cerritus.
—erras peruorse cf. on 495,
316.—pater is not disrespectful
here: cf. Trin. 877, 884.
953. certo scio cf. on 303.
954. habitare sc. eum cf. on
55.—somnias. For metaphorical sense cf. 1013, Rud. 343,
1327.
955. tun cf. on 508. War-
ren here trans. 'I forsooth?'
'You forsooth!' 'Sooth you're
troublesome'.
957. quartus etc., cf. Truc.

509 nudius quintus, Trin. 727
nudiussextus.—usque postquam
'ever since the time that' cf.
767 usque a mani.
958. triduom unum 'for a
single period of three days'.—
desitumst is followed by the
pass. infin., as coeptum est,
(Madv. § 161 obs.).
959. esse et bibi. The combination of active and passive
infinitives, in this and the following line, dependent upon
intermissum est (cf. on desitum
est 958) is lax writing (so too

960 scórta duci, pérgraecari, fídicinas, tibícinas
dúcere.
 TR. quis istaéc faciebat?
  PH. Phílolaches.
   TH. qui Phílolaches?
PH. quoí patrem Theópropidem esse opínor.
   TH. ei *mihi*: óccidi,
si haéc hic uera mémorat. pergam pórro percon-
tárier.
aín tu istic potáre solitum Phílolachem istum, quís-
quis est,
965 cúm ero uostro?
  PH. hic, ínquam.
   TH. puere, praéter speciem stúltus es.
uíde sis ne forte ád merendam quópiam deuórteris

---

961. *Conduci* Rl., Lor., *Audiri* Bug., Uss. For *Dúceré* cf. on 256.
962. **Quoi** M, edd., **CUIUS** A (acc. to Schwarzm.). *ei mihi* Cam., Rl., Lor., Bug., et CD, **S. . B.**
964. *istic potare* Vulg., edd., **istuc portare** M. **SILITUM** A (acc. to Schwarzm.).

the repetition of **ducere** after **duci**), but similar awkwardnesses are not unexampled in Plaut.; cf. 199.
960. **duci** cf. on 36.—**pergraecari** deponent, as in 22, 64; though there would not be much difficulty in regarding it as passive, cf. on 166, 371.
961. **istaec** 'what you say'; cf. *istic* (964) 'in that house (by which you stand)'.
963. **pergam porro p.** cf. on 63 and 32.
965. **praeter speciem stultus** 'more of a fool than you look'.
966. **uide ne** 'I suspect'.—**merenda** is generally regarded as another word for *prandium*:

so Festus 250 *b* 8 f., Marc. Aurel. in Fronto (Epist. IV 6). Nonius however says *merenda dicitur cibus post meridiem qui datur,* and so Isidor. xx 2, 12 *merenda est cibus qui declinante die sumitur...unde et antecenia a quibusdam uocantur:* Calpurnius Idyll. v 61 speaks of the *serae hora merendae.* On the whole it seems more prob. that, like the modern Italian *merenda* it was a light extra meal taken between midday and evening. A certain time may well be supposed to have elapsed since the interview with the *danista* (*iam adpetit meridies* 651) and the *prandium* of Simo 690 ff. took place.

átque ibi *ampliúscule*, quam fúerit sat, biberís.
PII. quid est?
TH. íta dico: ne ad álias aedis pérperam nunc uéneris.
PH. scío qua me ire opórtet, et quo uénerim, nouí
locum.
Phílolaches hic hábitat, quoius ést pater Theópropides : 970
quí, postquam pater ád mercatum hinc ábiit, hic
tibícinam
líberauit.
TH. Phílolachesne ergo?
PH. íta: Philematiúm quidem.

967. *ibi ampliuscule quam* S., **IB . . PLIUSQUAM** A (acc. to
Gepp.), **ibi melius cuiquam** BC, **ibi melius culiquam** D¹ (corr. to
-**cule quam** D³), *ibi amplius quam* Uss., *ibi ne meliuscule quam* Bug.
(after Cam.), Ell., *ibi ne pluscule quam* Gul.   *fuerit sat* S.,
satis fuerit M.
968. *nunc ueneris* Bug., Uss., **ne ueneris** M, *deueneris* Cam.,
Rl., Rams., Lor.
969. **LOCUM** A, edd., **loqui** M, *loci* Gul.
971. **HINCABIITHIC** A (acc. to Stud.), rec. edd., **abit hinc**
M.
972. **PHILOLACHESNE** A, edd., **Philolaches** M.

967. **ampliuscule** 'somewhat
too freely'. The adverb is used
by Sidonius Epist. III 16, and
the adj. by Appuleius, a great
imitator of the language of
Plaut. (De Magia p. 322, 19):
it does not occur elsewhere in
Plaut., but may be paralleled
by *meliusculus* Capt. v 2, 6, 15,
Curc. 489, *plusculus* Pers. 21.—
fuerit subj. by attraction to
biberis.
968. **ne** i.e. *uide ne*, 'I suspect'.—**alias aedis** 'the wrong
house'.—**perperam** 'by mistake'.
969. **qua oportet...quo uene-**
rim. For the change of mood
cf. Amph. 17 *quoius iussu uenio*
et quamobrem uenerim, ibid. 346,
Bacch. 736 and on Most. 149.—
locum is added exegetically to
quo uenerim, and is not the
antecedent to *quo*.
972. **Philolachesne ergo?**
'What, Philolaches?': *ergo* em-
phasises the question: cf. Trin.
901 *ergo ubi?* 'but where?'.
Pers. 18 *satin ergo ex sententia?*
'well but (are you getting on)
as you wish?'—**ita Philematium**
quidem 'yes: and she is called
Philem.'

973*a* TH. quánti?

    PH. trigintá—

      *T*H. talentis?

        PH. μὰ τὸν 'Απόλλω, séd minis.

973*b* TH. líberauit?

    PH. líberauit, *inquam*, trigintá minis.

TH. aín minis trigínta amicam déstinatam Philo-
                          lachi?

975 PH. áio.

    TH. atque eam manu émisisse?

      PH. aio.

        TH. ét postquam eius hínc pater
sít profectus péregre, perpotásse *usque* adsiduó simul
túo cum domino?

    PH. aió.

      TH. quid is? aedis émit hasce hinc
                        próxumas?

PH. nón aio.

    TH. quadráginta etiam dédit huic, quae
                    essent pígnori?

973 *a.* *PH. triginta TH. talentis?* Uss. (A has a space between *triginta* and *talentis*), ADV. triginta talentis M, edd. (except
Uss.).   SED A, edd., sex M.
   973 *b.* This line is found only in A: Rl., Rams., Lor., Bug.
treat it as spurious.   For *inquam* (Uss.) A has ILLAMCE
(acc. to Schwarzm.), or SCILICET (acc. to Gepp.).
   974. *destinatam* Gul., destinatum M, *destinasse* Rl., Rams.,
rec. edd.   *Philolachi* Gul., PHILOLACHEM AM.
   976. PERPOTASSE AM, *tum perpotasse* (spoiling the alliteration; cf. on 32) Rl., Lor., Bug.   *usque adsiduo simul* S.,
A.SIDUOAC....L A (acc. to Rl.), A.SIDUOACSIMULTIM A (acc.
to Schwarzm.), assiduo M (omitting the rest).
   977. *hasce hinc* Stud., Uss., Lor.², HAS HINC A, hic M.
   978. So Cam., edd., HUICQUAESSENT A, huc quae est M.

973 *a.* talentis ironically.
974. destinatam cf. on 646.
976. usque adsiduo simul
cum cf. Truc. 421 *postid ego
tecum, mea uoluptas, usque ero
adsiduo,* and Most. 450, 767,
793; *usque* was the word used
by Phan. in 957.

977. quid is? emit...? 'Tell
me, has he bought?' cf. Mil.
958 *quid hic? undest?,* ibid. 961,
1021, and on *quid nunc?* Most.
172.—hinc prox. 'next door to
my house'.
   978. non aio 'I don't say
that'= 'I say no', cf. on 197.

PH. néque istuc aio.
TH. ei, pérdis.
         PH. immo súom patrem illic
                            pérdidit.
TH. uéra cantas.
    PH. uána uéllem. pátris amicu's uídelicet. 980
TH. heú, edepol patrem eíus miserum praédicas.
           PH. nihil hóc quidemst,
tríginta minaé, prae quam alios dápsilis sumptús
                            facit.
TH. pérdidit patrem.
    PH. únus istic séruos est sacérrumus,

979. *istuc* Schmidt, Lor.², **istud** CDF, **illud** B.
980. *amicu's* Madv., Lor.², **amicus** M, *amicus's* Uss.
uīdĕlicet, as if it were two words (for *uīdĕ* cf. 254, 309, 966, 1109) :
cf. Capt. ii 2, 36, Stich. 555, etc.
981. *heu* Rl., Rams., Lor., Bug., **eu** M, Uss.   **EIUS** A
(acc. to Schwarzm. and Gepp.), Lor., **meum** M.
982. *praequam* Lamb., edd., **praeterquam** M.
983. *PH.* Rl., rec. edd., om. in M. ·   **ESTSACERRIMUS** A,
edd., **si acerrimus** M.

—**huic** 'the man who lives here',
with a gesture.
    979.   **neque istuc aio** ' I
don't say that either'.—**perdis**
sc. *me.*
    980.   **uera cantas** ' your tale
is true', cf. Rud. 478 *eapse can-
tat quoia sit* ' it tells its own
tale, as to who is its owner',
Bacch. 985 *metuo ne idem can-
tent* (' tell the same tale ') *quod
priores.*—The whole truth suddenly dawns upon Theopr.
    981.   **heu** etc. 'Alas! his
father, according to what you
say, is wretched indeed'. *Prae-
dico*, as Lang. shows, does not
here mean 'to call', but 'to
speak of': cf. Aul. 312 *edepol
mortalem parce parcum praedicas*, Rud. 654, Mil. 968; similarly Mil. 471 *edepol ne tu tibi*

*malam rem repperisti, ut prae-
dicas* ' according to what you
say', Pseud. 749.—**hoc** i.e. *triginta minas*, cf. on 628.
    982.   **prae quam** etc. ' in com-
parison with the other extrava-
gant expenses which': for *prae
quam* see on 1146; cf. too *dapsiles dotes* Aul. 165.
    983.   **unus seruos sacerrumus**
' one particular rascal of a slave':
cf. Truc. 251 *sed est huic unus
seruos uiolentissumus* and on 691.
Lor. takes *unus* as merely in-
tensifying the superlative, acc.
to the well-known classical
idiom, as in Capt. ii 2, 28, Asin.
521 *unam mulierem audacissu-
mam*, Mil. 52 f. *unum inuictis-
sumum.*—**istic** vaguely for *illic*,
cf. on 669, 913.

Tránio : is ucl Hérculi contérere quaestum póssict.
985 édcpol nc mc eiús patris misere míseret : qui quom
                            istaéc sciet
fácta ita, amburét miscro ei córculum carbúnculus.
TH. sí quidem istacc uéra sunt.
            PH. quid mérear, quam ob rem méntiar ?
ADV. heús uos, ecquis hasce áperit ?
            PH. quid istas púltas, ubi nemo íntus est ?
álio credo cómissatum abísse : abeamus núnciam.
990 TH. puere * tq *   *   * sequere hac me *
púere, iamne abís ?
           PH. libertas paénulast tergó tuo :
míhi, nisi ut erum métuam et curem, níhil est qui
                           tergúm tegam.

984. *possict* Cam., edd., **potest** M, *pote siet* Ell.
985. **MISERE** A, Rams., rec. edd., om. in M, *nunc misere* Rl.
986. **ita** M, edd., **ISTAEC** A (acc. to Gepp.).   **misero ei** M,
Rams., rec. edd., **MISEREI** A (acc. to Gepp.), *ei misero* Rl.
ēi cf. on 481.
988. For *ěcquis* cf. on 210.   **hasce aperit** M, rec. edd.,
APERITHAS A, *aperit* Rl.   **ISTAS** A, Cam., edd., ista (istac) M.
For *quǐd ǐstas* cf. on 47.
990. Traces of a lost line in A (acc. to Gepp.); om. in M.
991. *PH.* Rl., rec. edd., om. in M.
992. **UTERUM** A (acc. to Rl.), edd., **erum ut** M.   **tegam**
M, edd., **TERGAM** A (acc. to Rl.).

984. **conterere uel Hercoli quaestum** 'squander the gains of Hercules himself'. For **uel** cf. on 299. *Herculis quaestus* is a proverbial expression for ' great wealth': it was customary to offer a tithe (*decuma*) of any windfall to Hercules, who thus became the god of gain, cf. Bacch. 665 f. *si frugist, Herculem fecit ex patre: decumam partem ei dedit, sibi nouem apstulit,* Stich. 233, 386, Hor. Sat. ii 6, 12 *diues amico Hercule.*
985. **misere miseret** cf. on 362.—**qui...ei** (986) cf. on 250.
986. **corculum** ' his poor heart': cf. Cas. ii 6, 9.

989. **abisse** sc. *eos,* cf. on 55.
990. The sense of the lost verse can only be conjectured. Theopr. appears to be desirous to detain Phan., in order to learn further details from him, or perh. to bring him face to face with Tranio: but Phan. cannot afford the time; he must go to find his master. The words *sequere hac me* perh. belong to the *aduorsitor.*
991. **paenula** i.e. protection: cf. Non. 304a *paenulam abusiue ad omne, quidquid tegit, nobilissimi ueteres transtulerunt.*
992. **ut...curem** 'by fearing my master and minding my busi-

THEOPROPIDES.   SIMO.

TH. Perii hércle. quid opust uérbis? ut uerba aúdio,
non équidem in Aegyptum hínc modo uectús fui,
sed étiam in terras sólas orasque últumas   995
sum círcumuectus : íta, ubi nunc sim, néscio.
ucrúm iam scibo : nam éccum, unde aedis fílius
meus émjt. quid agis tu ?
                    SI. á foro incedó domum.
TH. numquíd processit ád forum hodié noui ?
SI. etiám.
          TH. quid tandem ?
                    SI. uídi ecferri mórtuom.   1000
TH. hem,
     nouom.
          SI. únum uidi mórtuom ecferrí foras :   1002 *a*
modo éum uixisse aiébant. TH. uae capití tuo.   1002 *b*
SI. quid tu ótiosus rés nouas requíritas ?

993. *uerba* Cam., edd., **uerbera** M.
996. *circumuectus* F, edd., **circumuentus** M.
998. *agis* Ald., edd., **ais** M.
999. Scan *hŏdie* (cf. 174), *hic hodie* Rl., Lor., *hocedie* Bug.,
Bergk.
1000. *mortuom* Rl., rcc. edd., **mortum hem** M (*hem* coming
from 1001).
1002 *a, b* are reduced to one line by Rl. and Uss.
1003. *tu* Z, edd., **tu ut** M.

ness'. For the noun clause cf.
on 789 and Cic. Att. XII 4 *quic-*
quamne putas me curare nisi ut
ei ne desim?—Exeunt *aduorsi-*
tores.
   993—998. Soliloquy of Theopropides.
   993. **ut uerba audio** 'according to what I hear'; cf. Trin.
729 *ut rem narras*, Mil. 471 *ut*
praedicas (quoted on 981).
   994. **uectus fui** cf. on 694
(821).
   995. **solas** 'desert'; cf. Ter.
Phorm. 978.—**ultumas** 'remote'.

996. **circumuectus** 'cruised
round '.—**íta** cf. on 56.
997. **unde** cf. on 547.
999. **processit** = 'turned up'.
—**ad forum** cf. on 352.
1000. **etiam** 'yes', cf. Ampl.
544. So too Cic.—**tandem** cf.
on 797.
1002 *a*. **nouom** 'unusual!',
ironically and with irritation.
—**unum** = *aliquem* cf. on 691.
1002 *b*. **modo** 'not long before '.
1003. **otiosus** 'like one with
nothing to do '.

Tʜ. quia hódie adueni péregre.

                          Sɪ. promisí foras:
1005 ad cénam ne me té uocare cénseas.

Tʜ. hau póstulo edepol.

                     Sɪ. uérum cras, nisi *quís* prius
uocáuerit me, uél apud te cenáuero.

Tʜ. ne istúc quidem edepol póstulo. nisi quíd magis
es óccupatus, óperam mihi da.   '

                        Sɪ. máxume.
1010 Tʜ. minás quadraginta áccepisti, quód sciam,
a Phílolachete?

               Sɪ. númquam nummum, quód sciam.

Tʜ. quid, a Tránione séruo?

                    Sɪ. multo *hercle* íd minus.

Tʜ. quas árraboni tíbi dedit?

                   Sɪ. quid sómnias?

Tʜ. egone? át quidem tu, qui ístoc te sperás modo
1015 potésse dissimulándo infectum hoc réddere.

Sɪ. quid aútem?

            Tʜ. quod me apsénte hic tecum fílius

1004.   *SI*. Pyl., edd., om. in M.
1005.   *te* Cam., edd., **tue** M.
1006.   *quis* Cam., edd., om. in M.
1009.   *SI*. Ald., edd., om. in M.
1010.   *quadraginta* Pyl., edd., **triginta** M.   *quod sciam* Guy.,
Rl., rec. edd., **quas sciam** M.
1012.   *hercle* Rl., edd., om. in M.
1014.   **te speras** M, edd., **SPERASTE** A (acc. to Gepp.).
1016.   **HICTECUM** A, Pyl., rec. edd., **hic** M.

1004. It was customary to invite to dinner an acquaintance who had returned home from a journey, cf. 1129. Simo excuses himself.—**foras** sc. *me iturum esse*, which words however are always omitted in the phrase *promittere ad cenam (foras)* cf. Men. 794, Stich. 596. Similarly one might in Scotland hear the expression 'to promise out'.

1007. **uel** etc. 'if you like (cf. on 299) I'll give you a turn —as your guest'. For the ἀπροσδόκητον cf. 179, Trin. 991 f. —**cenauero** cf. on 526.•

1009. **operam da** cf. on 804. —**maxume** 'by all means', cf. 1144.

negóti gessit.

Sɪ. mécum ut ille hic gésserit,	1017
dum tu hínc abes, negóti— ? quidnam ? aut quó die?	1018, 1019
Th. minás tibi octogínta argenti débeo.	1021

Sɪ. non míhi quidem hercle : uérum si debés, cedo.
fidés seruandast : ne íre infitias póstules.
Th. profécto non negábo debere, ét dabo :

tu cáue quadraginta áccepisse hinc té neges.	1025
* * * * * * * minas.	1025b
Sɪ. quaeso édepol, huc me adspécta et respondé mihi :	1026
q * * * * argenti minas?	1026b
t * * * * ego dicam tibi :	1026c
ta * * * * * * *	1026d
de te aedis * * * aedis emerit.	1026e
Sɪ. te uélle uxorem aiébat tuo gnató dare :	1027

ideo aédificare hic uélle aiebat ín tuis.
Th. hic aédificare uólui ?

               Sɪ. sic dixít mihi.

1018, 1019. Rl. supposes two lines to have been lost : but unnecessarily.
1025. *te* Lamb., Rl., rec. edd., **ne** M.
After this v. A (acc. to Gepp.) has a v. not found in M, of which however only one word is legible.
1026. After this v. A (acc. to Gepp.) has 4 partially legible vv. not found in M.
1028. *hic* Cam., rec. edd., **hoc** M, Rl., Rams.

1017. **quod negoti**, cf. on 904. —**ut...gesserit**, cf. Pers. 132 *me ut quisquam norit !* 'to think of anyone knowing me!' Cic. Cat. 1 9, 22 *tu ut unquam te corrigas:* cf. too on 301.
1018. **negoti**. The pronoun on which the genitive depends (*aliquid*) is suppressed, as Simo interrupts himself, and turns his exclamation into a question.
1023. **ne** final. '(I say this) that...not', cf. 613, 628.—**postules**, cf. on 259.

1025. **hinc** 'from us', cf. 596, 1039 and on 547.
1026. **huc me adspecta**, cf. Amph. 750 *age me huc adspice.* *Huc* is equiv. to *ad me* (cf. 689 where it = *ad hunc*), so that there is a slight tautology.
1027. **aiebat** sc. Tranio, whose name doubtless occurred in the lacuna.
1028. **ideo** i.e. with a view to the marriage.--**hic** adv.— **aedificare in tuis** (sc. *aedibus*) 'to enlarge your house'.

1030 Tʜ. ei míhi, dispcrii : uócis non habeó satis.
uicínc, perii, intérii.

               Sɪ. numquid 'ránio
1032 turbáuit ?

      Tʜ. immo éxturbauit ómnia.
1034 Sɪ. quid tú ais ?

        Tʜ. haec res síc est, ut narró tibi.
1035 delúdificatust me hódie in perpetuóm modum.
nunc te ópsecro, ut me béne iuues operámque des.
Sɪ. quid uís?

         Tʜ. i mecum, ópsecro, *intro* uná simul.
Sɪ. fiát.

         Tʜ. seruorumque óperam et lora míhi cedo.
Sɪ. sume *á me.*

        Tʜ. eademque ópera haec tibi narráuero,

1031. *Vicine* Acid., Rl., rec. edd., **Vicini** M, Rams.

1032. With hiatus in caesura after *immo*, which is naturally followed by a slight pause, cf. 549.   *immo mi ext.* Bo., Rl., Lor.[2], *immo enim ext.* Müll., Bug., *immo deturbauit* Reid.

After this v. M have **Te ludificatus est (mi) hodie indignisdis**, which Rl. (after Bo.) wrote *Deludificatust me hodie indignis modis:* so Lor. (*med*), Bug. Either this v. or 1035 must be abandoned; and Uss. seems right in maintaining that the latter (correctly written in M) is the more suitable to its context.

1037. With hiatus in caesura justified by the pause. *intro una* Palmer, **una** M, *una nunc* Rl., Lor., Bug., *ad te una* Uss. (in note), *huc una* Reid.

1039. *a me* Palmer, om. in M, *hinc* Müll., Lor.[2]   *eadem ego* Cam., Rl.   *haec intus* Rl.

1030. **uocis** etc. 'I am speechless', ἀφασία μ' ἔχει.

1032. **turbauit**, cf. on 416.— **exturbauit** corroborates *turbauit* (cf. *radicitus, exradicitus* 1112), and at the same time suggests the sense 'turn out of doors (cf. *exturbasti ex aedibus* Trin. 137): trans. 'Was this some mischief of Tranio's?' 'Aye, mischief which has turned us out of house and home'.

1034. **quid tu ais?** seems to express astonishment ('What do I hear?') and is different from the usage in 615.

1035. **deludificor** should be added to Lew. and Sh.—in **perpetuom modum** 'completely' cf. on 536.

1036. **bene**, cf. on 316.— **operamque des**, cf. on 804.

1037. **mecum una simul**, cf. Pseud. 410 *uideo Simonem una simul cum suo uicino*, Poen. 553 *omnes simul didicimus tecum una*, and on Most. 100.

1039. **[hinc]** cf. 596, 1025 and

qui *is* hódie exemplo mé deludificátus *est*.   1040

TRANIO.

TR. Quí homo timidus érit in rebus dúbiis, nauci
nón erit : 1041
nám erus me postquám rus misit, fílium ut suom
accérserem, 1044
ábi*i* illac per ángiportum ad hórtum nostrum clánculum. 1045
óstium quod ·in ángiportust hórti, patefecí foris,

1040. So I propose to write the line (or, *Qui is med exemplo
hodie ludificatus est*), **Quis me exemplis hodie eludificatus** M, *Quis
med exemplis hodie ludificatus est* Bo., Rl. (Neue Pl. Exc. I 37),
Bug., Lor.² *Quis* for *quibus* is quite unplautine; *quibus exemplis*
is a phrase which occurs nowhere else and is very questionable;
for while *miris* (*pessumis*, *plurimis*) *exemplis* are common enough
(cf. on 192), *his* (*illis*, *istis*) *exemplis* are as unexampled as *his*
(*illis*, *istis*) *modis : quibus exemplis* can only be paralleled by *quibus
modis* which occurs Most. 1146, Cas. v 3, 5.

1041. *dubiis* Priscian (VI 3,12), Cam., edd., **dubii sis** M. After
this v. M have

Atque equidem quid id esse dicam uerbum nauci nescio

which I agree with Bonnet and Uss. in regarding as the interpolation of a grammarian without a sense of humour. The line is
quoted by Festus p. 166 b. 14 with the lemma *Plautus in Mostellaria.*

1044. *Năm ĕrus* with hiatus, cf. on 133.   *filium ut* Rl., rec.
edd., **ut filium** M.

1045. *Abii* Cam., edd., *illae* Br., Lor.², **Abilla** M. Br. (on
Mil. 63) compares 931, Asin. 742, Truc. 248.

1046. **horti (orti)** M, *eius* Rl., Lor.

on 547.—**eadem opera** 'at the
same time' cf. Capt. II 2, 43 and
on 259.— -**que**, cf. on 815.—**nar-
rauero**, cf. on 526.

1040. **qui**=*quo*, cf. on 174.—
qui exemplo 'how', cf. Mil. 359
istoc exemplo, Bacch. 540 *more
isto atque exemplo*, Men. 981 *eo
exemplo seruio ut...*, Mil. 726 *uno
exemplo*, and on 192.

Monologue of Tranio.

1041. **non nauci esse** = *nihili
esse*. Cf. Truc. 611 *amas hominem non nauci*, Bacch. 1102
seruom non nauci.

1044. **nam**, cf. on 133.—
For **accersere** cf. 1093 and on
Aul. 605.

1046. **ostium quod** by attraction for *ostii quod*, as often
in Plaut.; so (with antecedent
repeated after rel. clause) 250.

éaque eduxi omném legionem, *quá* maris *qua* féminas.
póstquam ex opsidióne in tutum edúxi manuplarís
                                                       meos,
cápio consilium, út senatum cóngerronum cónuocem.
1050 quóm *eum* conuocáui, atque illi se éx senatu ségregant.
úbi ego omnem uideó rem uorti in meó foro,
                                            quantúm potest,
fácio idem quod plúrumi ali*i*, quíbus res timida aut
                                                  túrbidast:
pérgunt turbare úsque, ut ne quid *póssit* conquiéscere.
nám scio equidem núllo pacto iam ésse posse h*aec*
                                              clám senem.

1047. *qua...qua* Müll. (Koch independently), Bug., Lor.[2], et...
et M; see explan. note.
1049. *congerronum* Cam., edd., **congeronem** M (so the author
of the gloss, quoted by Loewe Prodr. p. 267, *congerronem : conpo-*
pionem [?] *et nugatorem*).
1050. *Quom eum* Rl., rec. edd., **Quom** M.   *se* S., **me** M.
1051. So I write after Pyl. and Palmer; C[1] (acc. to Gertz,
Stud.) has **Vbi ego me uideo uentrem in medio** (meo C[2]D) **fore**
(**foro** C[2]D) **quantum potest**; the line is not found in B.
1052. *alii quibus* Cam., edd., **aliquibus** M.
1053. *possit* Cam., edd., **sit** M.
1054. *haec* Stud., rec. edd., **H**... A, om. in M. After this v.
A (acc. to Stud.) has five lines, which are entirely om. in M : the last

1047. **qua...qua** is found several times connecting *mares...*
feminae (*uiri...mulieres*) Mil.
1113, 1392, *uir...uxor* Men. 666,
Asin. 96, *sacrum...puplicum*
Trin. 1044.
1050. **atque** 'that instant':
cf. Bacch. 278 f. *forte ut adsedi*
in stega, atque ego lembum con-
spicor, Epid. 217, Poen. 650 f.—
se ex sen. segr. 'refuse to take
part in the deliberations' i.e.
either 'leave the meeting' or
'suggest nothing': cf. Aul. 540
quid tu te solus e senatu seuocas?
= 'why are you silent?' For
se segregare cf. Capt. III 3, 2
auxilia a me segregant spernunt-

que se. For the sense of **sena-**
tus cf. too 688.
1051. **uideo**, cf. on 156.—**rem**
uorti in meo foro "'meam rem
agi, meque in discrimen ad-
ductum esse'. Hoc eo referen-
dum est, quod iure ciuili suo
quisque foro iudicium accipere
sine exceptione debet." Lamb.
—**quantum potest**, cf. on 758.
1052. **quibus** etc. 'who have
a case of danger or perplexity'.
1053. **pergunt turb usque.**
'they go on perplexing matters',
cf. on 546 *pergam turbare porro*,
and on 416.
1054. **nullo pacto iam p.**
'cannot any longer possibly'.—

*   *   *   *   *   *   *   * 1055
*   *   *   *   *   *   *   *
pro   *   *   *   *   *   *   *
ille   *   *   *   *   *   *   *
praeóccupabo atque ánteueniam et foédus feriam : mé
moror.
séd quid hoc est, quod fóris concrepuit próxuma
uicínia? 1062
érus meus hic quidémst: gustare ego éius sermoném
uolo.

THEOPROPIDES.   TRANIO.   LORARII.

TH. Ílico intra límen isti astáte, ut, quom extempló
uocem,
cóntinuo exiliátis: manicas céleriter conéctite.   1065
égo illum ante aedis praéstolabor lúdificatorém meum,

is legible. **MET** which Rl. thought he read in 1056 (1057 Rl.) is
denied by Stud.
1061. So Stud., rec. edd., **PRAEOCCUPATOATQ.** A.   *praeoccupabo* is four syllables, by synizesis : so *pracoptauisti* Trin. 648, Ter.
Hec. 532.
1062. Scan *quĭd hŏc ĕst.* **PROXIMAUICINIA** AMF, Rams.,
Büch. (Lat. Decl. § 309), *proxume uiciniae* Rl., Lor., Uss., *proxumae uiciniae* Bug.
1064. *isti astate* Uss., Lor.[2], **ISTASTATE** A (acc. to Gepp.).
extemplo edd., **exemplo** M.
1066. **PRAESTOLABOR** A, edd., **praestabo(r)** M.

clam with acc., as so often in
Plaut. and Ter.
1061. praeoccupabo: the object *aram* prob. stood in the line
before.—foedus feriam i.e. with
Theopr.—me moror 'I am wast-
ing my time' cf. Men.158, Stich.
445, Merc. 468, 930.
1062. proxuma uicinia 'close
at hand'. The more common
phrase is *proxumae uiciniae* (so
MSS. in Mil. 273, Bacch. 205,
cf. Charis. p. 223, 11) or *proxume
uiciniae* as others write it: but,

as Büch. says, the abl. may play
the part of the locative.
Enter Theopropides from the
house of Simo: his first words
are addressed to the *lorarii* :
1066 f. are said to himself, but
overheard by Tranio.
1064. ilico isti ' there where
you are', cf. on 885 *a.*—quom
extemplo, cf. on 101.
1066. ludificatorem meum
...ludificabor etc. 'He has been
chaffing me...I will make chaff
of his hide'.

quóius ego hodie lúdificabor córium, si uiuó, probe.
TR. rés palamst. nunc té uidere méliust, quid agas,
　　　　　　　　　　　　　　　　　　　　　Tránio.
TH. dócte atque astu míhi captandumst cúm illo,
　　　　　　　　　　　　　　　　ubi huc aduénerit.
1070 nón ego illi extemplo hámum ostendam : sénsim
　　　　　　　　　　　　　　　　mittam líneam.
díssimulabo me hórum quicquam scíre.
　　　　　　　　　　TR. o mortalém malum :
álter hoc Athénis nemo dóctior dicí potest.
uérba illi non mágis dare hodie quísquam quam—
　　　　　　　　　　　　　　　　lapidí potest.
ádgrediar hominem : áppellabo.
　　　　　　　　　　TH. núnc ego ille huc ueniát uelim.
1075 TR. síquidem pol me quaéris, adsum praésens prac-
　　　　　　　　　　　　　　　　sentí tibi.
TH. eúge, Tranió. quid agitur ?
　　　　　　　　　　TR. uéniunt rure rústici :

1067.　HODIE A (acc. to Gepp.), edd., hic M.
　1069.　TH. Pyl., edd., om. in M.　　　astu Bo., Rl., rec. edd.,
astute M.　　　ILLO A, Cam., Rl., rec. edd., illoc M.
　1070.　HAMUM A (acc. to Gepp. and Stud.), Kayser (by conjecture), rec. edd., ita mum (meum) M.　　　SENSIM A (acc. to
Stud.), Rl. (by conjecture), rec. edd., sensum M.
　1071.　TR. o mortalem Pyl., edd., o mortale M.
　1073.　MAGISDARE A (acc. to Rl.), edd., mugis M.
　1075.　síquidem, cf. on 229.
　1076.　rure Rl. (ed. min.), rec. edd., ruri M, Rl. (ed. mai.),
Rams.　The MSS. have rure = 'from the country' seven times, =
'in the country' thrice, ruri = 'from the country' thrice (above,

1067.　si uiuo 'as sure as I
live', again 1168, Aul. 565 ego te
hodie reddam madidum, si uiuo,
probe, Bacch. 766 uorsabo ego
illunc hodie, si uiuo, probe :
similarly Aul. 422 si hoc caput
sentit, cf. on Most. 4.
　1069.　docte atque astu, cf.
Rud. 928, Poen. Prol. 111, nisi
astu colas Capt. II 1, 29.—captandumst cum, cf. on 1142.

1070.　Theopr. compares himself to an angler: see on the
name Tranio p. 5.
　1071.　malum ' sly ' cf. 1107
and on 411.
　1073.　hodie, cf. on 657.—la-
pidi humorously, παρὰ προσδοκίαν. A block of stone cannot
be imposed upon; no more can
Theopr.; and for the same reason.
　1076.　ueniunt r. r. sounds

Phílolaches iam hic áderit.
TH. edepol míhi opportune aduénerit.
nóstrum ego hunc uicínum opinor ésse hominem
audacem ét malum.
TR. quídum?
TH. quia negát nouisse uós.
TR. negat?
TH. nec uós sibi
númmum umquam argentí dedisse.
TR. abi, lúdis me : credo haúd negat. 1080
TH. quíd iam?
TR. scio, iocáris nunc tu : nam ílle quidem
datum haúd negat.
TH. ímmo edepol negát profecto, néque se hasce aedis
Phílolachi
uéndidisse.
TR. eho, án negauit síbi datum argentum, ópsecro?
TH. quín ius iurandúm pollicitust dáre se, si uellém,
mihi,
néque se hasce aedis uéndidisse néque sibi argentúm
datum. 1085

*　*　*　*　*　*　*　*

Truc. 669, 693),=‘in the country’ twenty-two times; see Lang. p.
308 f.
1077. opportune mi Rl., Lor.   aduenerit Bent., Bug., Uss.,
aduenies M, aduenit Rl., Rams., Lor.
1078. hunc Z, edd., huc M.
1079. quia Bo., Rl., rec. edd., qui M.
1081. This line is found only in B; Uss. rejects it as a repetition of 1080.   nunc tu Cam., edd., tu nunc tu B.   datum
haud Palmer, haud M, edepol haud Luchs, Lor.², haud edepol Rl.
1084. Quin an old correction, Rl., rec. edd., Qui M.
1085. datum Pyl., Rl., rec. edd., datum est (esse) M.

like a proverbial expression: cf.
799.
1079. nouisse uos ‘that he
has had any dealings with you’,
cf. Pers. 131.—nec. The Eng.
idiom requires ‘and’ here: cf.
1082, Ter. Phorm. 353 GE. negat.
...DE. neque eius patrem se scire

qui fuerit? GE. negat; Madv.
§ 458 c. obs. 2. Cf. too on
471.
1080. abi ‘get along!’ Cf.
Mil. 324, Capt. IV 2, 90 abi
stultu’s etc.
1081. quid iam, cf. on 365,
465.

TH. díxi ego istuc idem ílli.
                    TR. quid ait?
                              TH. séruos pollicitúst dare
súos mihi omnis quaéstioni.
                    TR. núgas : numquam edepól dabit.
TH. dát profecto.
      TR. quín cita illum in iús.   ibo, inueniám.
                                              TH. mane :
1090 éxperiar ; ut opínor, certumst.
                    TR. ímmo mihi hominém cedo.
uél hominem iube aédis mancupáre.
                              TH. immo hoc primúm uolo,
quaéstioni accípere seruos.
                    TR. fáciundum edepol cénseo.
TH. quíd si igitur ego áccersam homines ?
                    TR. fáctum iam esse opórtuit.

1087. A verse appears to have been lost; *istuc idem* must refer
to some previous remark of Tr.
     1089. *TR.* Cam., edd., om. in M.   *cita* Rl., Lor., Bug., et
M.   *in ius. ibo, inueniam. TH. mane* Rl., Lor., **in iussi ueniam
mane** M, *in ius. sine inueniam. TH. mane* Bug.
     1090. *TR. immo* Rl., Lor., Bug., om. in M.   After this v. M
have 1093.   So Rams., Uss.   Acid. (followed by Rl., Lor., Bug.)
transferred it to its present position.
     1091. *mancupare* Uss., Lor.[2], **mancipio poscere** M.
TH. edd., om. in M.
     1093. *iam esse* Cam., Rl., rec. edd., **esse iam** M.

1088. quaestioni 'to be ex-
amined   by   torture'.—**nugas**
'nonsense', acc. of exclamation,
cf. Capt. III 4, 80 (where correct
note), Pers. 718.
     1089.   dat for future.—**inue-
niam.**   At this Tran. makes for
the altar in front of the house
of Simo (cf. on 1061, and 1095),
from which consecrated spot
(*diuinus locus* 1104) it was un-
lawful to drag a refugee by force
(cf. Aul. 598, Guhl and Koner
p. 81 Eng. Trans.).
     1090.   experiar etc. 'I will

put it to the test: I think he has
made up his mind (that he will
submit his slaves to torture)'.
—**mihi hom.** cedo 'leave the
fellow to me'.
     1091.   uel 'or rather' cf. on
299.—**mancupare** 'to make a
formal   transfer'   = *mancupio
dare* Curc. 494, lit. 'to make
over by way of formal seizure ',
Roby § 1243 (where *mancupio* is
regarded as abl.): cf. *mancupio
accipere* Aul. 421, Curc. 495.
     1093.   si igitur, cf. on 393.—
homines i.e. the officers (to ex-

égo interim aram hanc óccupabo.
                              TH. quíd ita ?
                                        TR. nullam rém sapis :
né enim illi huc confúgere possint, quaéstioni quós
                                              dabit, 1095
híc ego tibi praésidebo, ne ínterbitat quaéstio.
TH. súrge.
        TR. minume.
                TH. ne óccupassis ópsecro aram.
                                        TR. quór ?
                                                TH. scies :
quía enim id maxumé uolo, ut illi*sce* ístoc confugiánt.
                                                    sine :
tánto apud iudicem húnc argenti cóndemnabo fácilius.
TR. quód agis, id agas. quíd tu porro sércre uis
                                        negótium ? 1100
néscis quam metúculosa rés sit ire ad iúdicem.

1094. *aram hanc* Rl., Lor., Bug., **hanc aram** M.
1095. *huc* Saracenus, edd., **hic** M.
1096. *ego*, cf. Mil. 142 *in eó conclaui egó perjodi párietem*, and
on Aul. 454. *híc ego intéribi praes.* Reid.
1097. *aram* Pyl., edd., **arma** M.
1098. *illisce* Schmidt, Lor.², **illi** M.
1100. *agis* Pyl., Rl., Rams., Lor., Uss., **agas** M, Müll., Bug.
1101. **metuculosa** D, **metucolosa** C, and this is a spelling
attested by Priscian I p. 138 (Keil), according to many MSS.   B
has **meticulosa** here and so edd.; but in Amph. 293 BCD have
metuculosus, which is adopted by Gz. and Lö. (*mĕtŭcŭlosus*).

amine the slaves). Theopr.
really means the *lorarii.*—**factum esse op.** with irony (i.e. it
is too late now !).
    1094. **quid ita**, cf. on 365.
    1095. **enim** 'to be sure' cf.
on 551.
    1096. **tibi praesidebo** 'I will
take the chair for you', cf. Truc.
715.—**interbitat** = *intereat* ' fall
to the ground'. The verb *bitere*
= *ire* is found four times in
Plaut.
    1097. **occupassis**, cf. on 212.

    1098. **illisce**, cf. on 510.—
sine 'allow me' (trying to move
Tr. from the altar).
    1099. **argenti cond.** 'get him
condemned to pay a fine' i.e.
for causing trouble and loss of
time.
    1100. **quod agis, id agas**
'stick to your purpose' i.e. of
examining the slaves; cf. Mil.
352 *quod ago, id me agere oportet.* For *agas = age* cf. on 1129.
—**porro ser. neg.** 'give occasion
for further bother'.

TH. súrgedum huc igitúr : consulere quíddamst quod
tecúm uolo.
TR. sí tamen hinc consílium dedero ? nímio plus
sapió sedens.
túm consilia fírmiora súnt de diuinís locis.
1105 TH. súrge ; ne nugáre. aspicedum cóntra me.
TR. aspexí.
TH. uides ?
TR. uídeo. huc si quis íntercedat tértius, pereát fame.
TH. quídum ?
TR. quia nil quaésti sit *ei* : *íta* mali hercle ambó
sumus.
TH. périi.
TR. quid tibíst ?
TH. dedisti uérba.
TR. qui tandém ?
TH. probe
méd emunxti.
TR. uíde sis, satine récte : num mucí fluont ?

1102. So Lang., Lor.² (after Servius on Aen. xi 343 *consulere
quiddamst quod tecum uolo*), est **consulere igitur quiddam** M.
1107. *quaesti sit ei : ita* Rl., Lor., Bug., **qua estis id** M.
1108. *TR. qui tandem? TH.* Cam., Rl., Rams., Lor., Uss.,
qui tandem M, *TR. quoi tandem? TH.* Bug.
1109. *Med emunxti* Bo. (after Pius), edd., **Me emunxit** M.

1102. **surgedum huc** 'get
up and come to me' cf. Mil. 81
exsurgat foras. — **igitur** ' do !'
emphasizing the command : cf.
on 132, Capt. ii 2, 43, Aul. 712.
1103. **si tamen ?** = *sed quid
si ?* — **nimio plus**, cf. on 72.
1105. **contra** adv. 'in the
face', as always in Plaut. ; cf.
Mil. 123. — **uides ?** Theopr. assumes an amiable expression of
countenance.
1106. **intercedat** 'put in an
appearance'.
1107. **quaesti.** The gen. in
-*ūs* of substantives of the 4th

decl. is unknown to Plaut. and
Ter. ; cf. Pseud. 1197 where
quaestus is nom. — **mali**, cf. on
1071.
1108. **perii.** Theopr. casts
aside the mask and gives vent
to his suppressed rage. — **qui
tandem**, cf. on 797. — **probe**, cf.
on 4.
1109. **med** old accus. of *me*,
common in Plaut. ; cf. *ted* = *te*
1175, *sed* = *se* (Neue Lat. Formenl. ii p. 181). The same
forms are used for the abl. —
emunxti, cf. on 552. — **num muci
flu.** Tr. plays upon the literal

Th. ímmo etiam cerebrúm quoque omne e cápite
emunxistí meo. 1110
nam ómnia male fácta uostra répperi radícitus:
nón radicitús quidem hercle, uérum etiam exradícitus.
númquam edepol hodié *mi* inultus *uérba* de*d*isti: nám
tibi
iám iube*b*o ignem ét sarmen*ta*, cárnufex, circúmdari.
Tr. né faxis: nam elíxus esse quam ássus soleo
suáuior. 1115
Th. éxempla edepol fáciam ego in te.
Tr. quía placeo, exemplum éxpetis.
Th. lóquere: quoiusmodí reliqui, quom hínc abibam,
fílium?
Tr. cúm pedibus, manibús, cum digitis, aúribus,
oculís, labris.

1110. So Rl., Lor., **omnem e capite munxit (unxti)** M, *omne mi e capite emunxti* Bug.
1112. *exradicitus* Rl., rec. edd., **eradicitus** M. The word is quoted as plautine by Fronto Epist. de Orat. p. 156 *subuertendam censeo radicitus, immo uero Plautino...uerbo exradicitus.*
1113. So I read (after Uss.): **hodie inditus (inuitus) destinant tibi** M, *uerba hodie inultus mihi dedisti: nam tibi* Uss., *tu haec hodie inultus designaueris: tibi* Bug., Lor.² (after Rl.). Possibly *dedisti* should be pronounced as two syllables (*desti*), by syncope, or we might read *dederis.*
1114. So Pyl., Bent., Uss., Lor.², **lubeo (lubo or iube) ignem et sarmen** M.

meaning of *emungere:* 'does your nose run?'
1110. **etiam...quoque**, pleonastically, cf. Amph. 461 *etiam is quoque*, Asin. 502 *etiam tu quoque*, and on *quoque etiam* 469.
1112. **exradicitus** a humorous compound, forming a climax after *radicitus.* Thornton trans. 'not only to the root, but (I have) rooted out the root'.
1113. **numquam.. hodie dedisti,** cf. Rud. 612 *n. h. quiui ad coniecturam euadere*, and on 164 and 657.

1114. The same threat of burning or smoking out the refugee is uttered by Labrax in Rud. 761.
1115. Tran. compares himself to a fish, perh. punning on his name; cf. on PERSONAE p. 5.
1116. **exempla** etc. 'I will make an example of you'.—**quia placeo** etc. 'you like me and so you would make others copy me (as if Theopr. had said *ex te exemplum expetam*). For **exemplum expetere** cf. 103, 763.

Th. áliud te rogo.

　Tr. áliud ergo núnc tibi respóndeo.
1120 séd eccum tui gnatí sodalem huc *ád nos* uideo in-
　　　　　　　　　　　　　　　　　cédere,
Cállidamatem : illó praesente mécum agito, si quíd
　　　　　　　　　　　　　　　　　uoles.

CALLIDAMATES.　THEOPROPIDES.　TRANIO.

Ca. Vbi *somno meam* sépeliui omnem atque édormiui
　　　　　　　　　　　　　　　　　crápulam,
Phílolaches uenísse mihi *narráuit* suom peregre húc
　　　　　　　　　　　　　　　　　patrem,
quóque modo dominum ádu*enientem* séruos ludifi-
　　　　　　　　　　　　　　　　　cátus sit.
1125 aít se metuere ín conspec*tum súi patris* procédere.
núnc ego de sodálitate sólus sum orató r datus,
qui á patre eius cónciliarem pácem. atque eccum
　　　　　　　　　　　　　　　　　óptume.
iúbeo te saluére, et saluos quom áduenis, Theó-
　　　　　　　　　　　　　　　　　propides,

　　1120. *huc ad nos uideo* Rl., Lor., **uideo huic** M, *uideo illic*
Lingius, Uss.
　　1122. *somno meam* Rl., Lor., Bug., **omnium** M.　　*edormiui*
Cam., Rl., rec. edd., **obdormiui** M.　Reid del. *omnem.*
　　1123. *narrauit* Kampmann, Rl., rec. edd., om. in M.
　　1124. *dominum* Bug., Uss., Lor.[2], **hominem** M.　　*aduenien-
tem* Ald., edd., **ad**...... M.
　　1125. *conspectum sui patris procedere* Rl. (after Cam.), rec.
edd., **conspe**.........**ocedere** M.
　　1127. With hiatus after *pacem*: cf. on 484.
　　1128. *aduenis* FZ, edd., **aduenisse** M.

　　1119. **aliud** 'something else'.　　　　1122. **edormiui crap.**, cf. Rud.
—**ergo** 'well' cf. Aul. 320 f. *STR.*　586 *ut edormiscam hanc crapu-*
cocum ego, non furem rogo. CON.　*lam.*
cocum ergo dico 'Well, I am　　　　1126. **sodalitate solus de**
speaking of a cook'. 　 　　　　　　'alone of all my comrades',
　　Enter Callidamates, who du-　　cf. 150.
ring a brief soliloquy explains　　　1127. **conciliarem** 'procure'.
the object of his coming, and　　—**optume**, cf. on 686 : here with-
then crosses the stage to greet　　out a verb. cf. Pers. 738 f.
Theopr.　　　　　　　　　　　　　　1128. **aduenis**, cf. on 29 and
　　　　　　　　　　　　　　　　　　430.

péregre, gaudeo. híc apud nos hódie cenes : síc face.
TH. Cállidamates, dí te ament: de céna facio grá-
tiam. 1130
CA. quín uenis?
TR. promítte : ego ibo pró te, si tibi nón lubet.
TH. uérbero, etiam inrídes?
TR. quian me pró te ire ad cenam aútumo?
TH. nón enim ibis: égo ferare fáxo, ut meruisti,
ín crucem.
CA. áge mitte istaec : te ád me ad cenam díc uen-
turum. quíd taces?
séd tu istuc quid cónfugisti in áram *hanc* insci-
tíssumus? 1135
TR. ádueniens pertérruit me.   *elóquere* nunc, quid
fécerim.
núnc utrisque dísceptator éccum adest : age dísputa.

1129. *face* Sciopp., edd., **tale** M.
1130. *Cállidamates* Rl., rec. edd. (cf. 341, 373), **Callidamate**
M, Rams. (cf. on 528).
1134. *istaec: te* Rl., Lor., Bug., **ista acto** M, *ista, ac te* Uss.,
ista, ac cito Seyff.   *TR. quid* Rl. Lor., Bug. (B has **TR. dic
uenturum quid taces?**): I have followed Loman and Uss. in
giving the whole line to *CA.*
1135. *hanc* Pyl., Lor., Uss., om. in M, *hinc* R., Bug.
1136. *eloquere* Lang., Lor.², **loquere** M.   Lang. shows from
200 passages that *loqui* = 'to give information' (followed by dependent noun clause) is unplautine.

1129. **cenes** = *cena*. The pres.
subj. for imperat. (occasionally
found in the class. period) is
very common in Plaut. ; cf. 47,
388, 594, 718, 1100.—**sic face**
'do !', often used in pressing a
person to accept an invitation
e.g. Stich. 185, 473.
1130. **de cena facio gratiam**
'as for the dinner, I must decline', cf. Trin. 293 *his ego de
artibus gratiam facio*, Rud. 1414
iuris iurandi uolo gratiam facias.
1132. **etiam** 'actually', cf.
Amph. 376, 571 and on 383, 522,

which instances are both different.—**quian** 'do you mean because', cf. on 738.—**ire**, cf. on 17.
1133. **enim**, cf. on 551.—**ferare faxo**, cf. on 68.
1135. **inscitissumus** 'simple-
ton', cf. on 311.
1137. **disceptator utrisque** 'as
umpire between the two parties'
(each party here consisting of
one person). The plural of
uterque occurs also Truc. 152
utrosque pergnoui probe 'both
kinds of land': Amph. 223
should prob. be corrected.

Tʜ. fílium corrúpisse aio té meum.

Tʀ. auscultá modo.
fáteor peccauísse, amicam líberasse apsénte te,
1140 faénori argentúm sumpsisse : id ésse apsumptum
praédico.
númquid aliud fécit, nisi quod súmmis gnati géne-
ribus ?
Tʜ. hércle mihi tecúm cauendumst, nímis qui's
orátor catus.
Cᴀ. síne me dum istuc iúdicare. súrge : ego isti
adsédero.
Tʜ. máxume. accipito hánc *tute* ad te lítem.
Tʀ. enim istic cáptiost.

1138.   *TR.* Cam., edd., om. in M (and placed before next v.).
1139.   **peccauisse** M, Rams., Uss., *potauisse* Acid., Rl., Lor.,
Bug.
1141.   So Bent., Rl., Lor., Bug., **nisi quod faciunt** M. Bo.
and Uss. om. *aliud.*
1142.   *TH.* FZ, edd., om. in M.   *Hercle* Pius, edd., **Erile** M.
   qui's Giphanius, Rl., Rams., Lor., Bug., **quis** M, *quam es*
Cam., Uss.
1143.   *CA.* Cam., edd., om. in M.
1144.   *tute* Rl., Lor., Bug., om. in M, *modo* Uss.   *TR.* Cam.,
Rams., rec. edd., om. here in M and placed before next v.; Rl.
assigns the whole line to *TR.*

1137.   **disputa** 'hold forth',
cf. on Men. Prol. 50.
1139.   **peccauisse** (sc. *eum*),
cf. on 55.
1140.   **faenori**, cf. on 532.
1142.   **tecum cauendumst** 'I
must be on my guard against
you', lit. 'I must use caution in
my dealings with you'. *Cum* is
often used in Plaut. to describe
generally the relation of the
agent to another party: e.g.
orare cum aliquo 'to beseech any
one' Asin. 662, 686 (cf. Eng. 'to
plead with'), *mentionem fac cum
auonculo* Aul. 677 'speak about
it *to* my uncle', *amplexari (oscu-
lari) cum aliquo* 'to embrace

anyone' Mil. 243, 245, *perdere
fidem cum aliquo* 'to break
faith with anyone' Pseud.
376; so even when the relation is a hostile one, *capere iudicem cum aliquo* Most. 557 (cf.
Eng. 'go to law with'), *captare
cum aliquo* ibid. 1069, orig. a
gladiatorial expression (cf. Eng.
'break a lance with' 'try a fall
with').
1143.   **isti**, cf. on 315.—**adse-
dero**, cf. on 526.
1144.   **enim istic captiost** 'I
am sure there is some trap
there': for this sense of *captio*
cf. crit. note on 922. For **enim**
cf. on 551.

fác ego ne metuám *mihi, atque* ut tú meam timeás
uicem. 1145
TH. iám minoris *ómnia alia fácio,* prae quam quíbus
modis
mé *deludificátust.*
TR. bene hercle fáctum, et factum gaúdeo.
sápere istac aetáte oportet *té.* qui's capite cándido.
TH. quíd ego nunc faciám?   *TR.* si amicus Díphilo
aut Philémoni es, 1149
dícito eis, quo pácto tuos te séruos ludificáuerit: 1151

1145. *mihi atque* Rl., rec. edd., om. in M.
1146. *omnia alia fa-* Rl. (after Cam.), rec. edd., om. in M.
1147. *Me deludificatust* S.(cf. 1035, 1040), **Me ludificatus est** M,
Ludificatust me Rl., Lor., Bug.   Scan *bēn' hĕrcle* and cf. on 229.
1148. *te, qui's* Bug., **quis** M, *qui sunt* Cam., Rl., Rams., Lor.,
Uss.
1149. *TR. si amicus Diphilo aut Philemoni es* Leo and Büch.,
si amicus dephilo aut philomontes M, (TH.) *si amicus Demipho aut
Philonides*—Cam., edd., giving next line to *TR.* as FZ (*CA.* B).
Rl. assumed the loss of a v. after 1149.
1151. *pacto* Z, edd., **capto** M.

1146. **prae quam quibus modis** an abbreviated expression
for *prae quam modus est quo.*
Prae quam, prae ut mean lit. ' in
comparison as (how) ': so in 982
*prae quam alios dapsiles sumptus
facit* lit. 'compared with how he
incurs' etc., Mil. 20 *nihil hoc
quidemst, prae ut alia dicam, tu
quae numquam feceris* lit. ' in
comparison how I could tell of
other things' i.e. 'in comparison
with the other things I could tell
of'; in Men. 375 *folia nunc ca-
dunt, prae ut si triduom hoc hic
erimus* we must supply *cadent*
after *prae ut* 'in comparison
with the way in which they will
fall if' etc.; so in Aul. 503 *sed
hoc etiam pulcrumst, prae quam
sumptus ubi petunt* supply *tum
est* 'in comparison with the time
when'.—**quibus modis,** cf. on
54. This and Cas. v 3, 5 are

the only instances of the plural
modis being joined with a pronoun : elsewhere we have *quo*
(*hoc, illo, isto*) *modo.*
1149. Leo regards this passage as coming direct from the
original Φάσμα, in which Philemon, the probable author, mentioned himself and his brother
poet Diphilus.   Tranio then
impudently tells Theopr. to go
to the comic poets—they will
know what to do with him : cf.
Athenaeus XIII 579 f. φυλαττο-
μένη μάλιστα Δίφιλον, μὴ δῶ δίκην
μετὰ ταῦτα κωμῳδουμένη.   This
is one of several passages in
Plautus, in which a character on
the stage makes *the stage itself*
the object of discussion, cf. Mil.
214 *euge, euscheme hercle adsti-
tit et dulice et comoedice,* Rud.
1249 f., Pseud. 1081, 1240, Capt.
III 4, 82, IV 1, 11.

óptumas frustrátiones déderis in comoédiis.
CA. táce parumper: síne uicissim mé loqui. auscultá.
                                        TH. licet.
CA. ómnium primúm sodalem me ésse scis gnató tuo.
1155 ís me adiit: nam illúm prodire púdet in conspectúm
                                            tuom
própterea quia fécit, quae te scíre scit. nunc te
                                        ópsecro,
stúltitiae adulescéntiaeque ut éius ignoscás: tuomst.
scís solere illánc aetatem táli ludo lúdere.
quídquid fecit, nóbiscum una fécit: nos delíquimus.
1160 faénus, sortem súmptumque omnem, quí amica
                                        ste*tit*, ómnia
nós dabimus, nos cónferemus, nóstro sumptu, nón tuo.
TH. nón potuit ueníre orator mágis ad me inpe-
                                            trábilis
quám tu: neque illi *iám* sum iratus néque quid-
                                        quam suscénseo.
ímmo me praesénte amato, bíbito, facito quód lubet;

1153. *uicissim me loqui* Acid., Rl., Rams., Lor., Bug., **me
uicissim loqui** M.   *TH*. Z, edd., om. in M.
1154. *CA*. edd., om. in M.
1155. *me adiit* Guy., Rl., Lor., Bug., **adiit me** M.   *eum*
(for *illum*) Bo., Uss. (keeping *adiit me*).
1156. **Propterea quia fecit (facit)** quae CD, Rams., Bug., Uss.,
Propterea qui (quia B²) fecit qum. B, *Propter ea quae fecit, quom*
Rl., Lor.
1157. *adulescentiaeque ut* Müll., Bug., Lor.², **audlescentiae-
que** M, *adulescentiaiquc* Bo., Rl.   *tuomst* Reid, **tuus est** M.
1159. *nobiscum una fecit: nos* Cam., edd., **una nobiscum fecit
non** M.   *deliquimus* Pius, edd., **delinquimus** M.
1160. *stetit* Palmer (cf. Capt. III 5, 82, Stich. 223), **est** M,
emptast Rl., edd.
1163. *iam* Rl., rec. edd., om. in M.   *quidquam ei* Rl., Lor.,
Bug.

1152. **opt. frustr.** 'the best
story of bamboozling'.—**dederis**
prop. 'you will be found to have
supplied', cf. Trin. 60, Aul. 570;
cf. too on 590.
1153. **licet**, cf. on 402.
1155. **is—illum**, cf. on 913.

1156. **quae**, i.e. *ea quae*.
1158. **ludo ludere**, cf. on
Capt. II 1, 54.
1162. **inpetrabilis** 'effective': for the active meaning
cf. on Capt. Prol. 56, and Merc.
605, Epid. 342.

si hóc pudet, fecísse sumptum, súpplici *ab eo* habeó
satis. 1165
CA. díspudet.
TR. post ístam ueniam quíd me fiet núnciam?
TH. uérberibus, lutúm, caedere péndens.
                                       TR. tamen etsí pudet?
TH. ínterimam hercle ego té, si uiuo.
                            CA. fác istam cunctam grátiam:
Tránioni amítte quaeso hanc nóxiam causá mea.
TH. áliud quiduis ínpetrari pérferam a me fácilius, 1170
quam út non ego istum pró suis factis péssumis
                                       pessúm premam.

1165. *ab eo* Palmer, om. in M, *id mi* Luchs, *iam* Rl., Lor.,
Bug.   Lachm. on Lucr. vi 743 defends the hiatus.
1166. *CA. Dispudet. TR. post istam* Müll. (after Acid., Rl.),
Bug., Lor.², **TR. Dispudet istam** M.
1167. *TR.* Lamb., edd., om. in M.   *tamen etsi* Grut., edd.,
taminestsi M.
1168. *TH.* Lamb., edd., om. in M.   *ego te* Mahler, Lor.²,
ego M, *te ego* Bo., Rl., Bug., Uss.   *si uiuo* Cam., edd., **suibo**
(**siubo**) M.
1169. *Tranioni amitte* Uss., Lor.², **Tranioni remitte** M, *Tranio
remitte* Acid., Bug.   But that the form *Tranio*, so often used as a
nom., should here be a dative is improbable (cf. on 560).
1170. *TH.* edd., om. in M.   *perferam a me facilius* Bo., Rl.,
Lor., Bug., **a me facilius perferam** M.

1165. **fecisse sumptum** is
added exegetically to *hoc.*
1166. **dispudet** 'he is utterly
ashamed of himself': cf. *dis-
taedet, dispereo, discrucior, dis-
cupio.*—**me** cf. on 636.—**nunciam**
cf. on 74.
1167. **lutum** a term of a-
buse : cf. Pers. 406 *lutum leno-
nium*, Mil. 325 (quoted on 891 *a*).
—**pendens**: cf. on Men. 951,
Trin. 247.—**tamen etsi** cf. Ter.
Andr. 864 *SI. ego iam te com-
motum reddam? DA. tamen etsi
hoc uerumst? SI. tamen.*

1168. **si uiuo** cf. on 1067.—
cunctam appears to mean *uni-
uersam*, and the whole phrase to
be = *da cunctis istam ueniam.*
1169. **amitte** = *remitte* (which
however Plaut. does not use with
an abstract object), cf. Poen.
403 *etiam tibi hanc amittam
noxiam unam, Agorastocles.*
1171. **ut...premam** cf. on
789.—**pessumis pessum** a pun :
'get the upper hand of this fellow for his underhand tricks',
cf. 186, 253, 716.

CA. míttc quaeso istum.

TH. *illum ut mittam?* uídcn ut astat fúrcifcr?

CA. Tránio, quiésce; sapias.

TH. tú quiesce hanc rém modo
pétcrc: ego illum, ut sít quietus, uérbcribus subégero.
1175 TR. níhil opust profécto.

CA. age iam sínc ted exorárier.

TH. nólo ores.

CA. quaeso hércle.

TH. nolo inquam órcs.

CA. nequiquám neuis.
hánc modo noxiam únam quaeso *missam* fac causá
mea.

TR. quíd grauaris? quási non cras iam cómmeream
aliam nóxiam:
íbi *tum* utrumque, et hóc et illud, póteris ulciscí
probe.

1180 CA. síne te exorem.

TH. age ábi, abi inpune. em huíc habeto
grátiam.

1172. So Rl., Lor., Bug., **Mitte que sis tume uident ut restat
furcifer** M.
1173. *quiesce; sapias* S., **qui esse sapis** M, *si sapis, quiesce*
Rl., Lor., Bug.
1174. So Acid., Rl., rec. edd., **uerberibus ut sit quietus** M.
1175. *CA*. F, Rl., rec. edd., om. in M (B gives whole line to
CA., and so Rams.).   *ted* Guy., edd., **te** M.   For the hiatus
at change of speakers cf. on 567.
1177. So Rl., Lor., Bug., **unam noxiam unam queso fac** M.
1179. *tum* Acid., Bug., om. in M, *tu* Rl., Lor.

1172. ut **mittam** cf. on 1017.
—**ut astat** 'how he stands care-
lessly looking on', cf. on 149.—
furcifer cf. on 69.
1173. **sapias** 'be wise' (cf.
Rud. 1229 *si sapias, sapias*),
as in Hor. Od. I 11, 6 *sapias,
uina liques.*—**petere** is dependent on **quiesce** on the analogy

of the ordinary construction of
desino, desisto, intermitto, cf.
Gell. II 28, 2 *dei nomen...edicere
quiescebant.*
1174. **subegero** cf. on 590.
1175. **ted** cf. on 1109.
1176. **neuis** cf. on 110.
1179. **probe** cf. on 4.
1180. **em** cf. on 9.

Ω. Spéctatores, fábula haec est ácta : uos plausúm
date.

1181.　Ω Uss., Lor.², om. in M, *CANTOR* Rl., Bug.　It is very
doubtful who is supposed to speak the last line.　In several comedies the appeal to the audience is certainly part of the last speech
of one of the actors (see Pseud., Rud., Men., Poen., Merc.).　I
have followed Uss. and Lor.² in adopting the ambiguous sign
employed in the plays of Terence and in the Trinummus, which
Bentley, prob. wrongly, supposed to be a scribe's error for *CA.*
(*Cantor*) cf. Hor. A. P. 155 *donec cantor 'uos plaudite' dicat:* cf.
note of Wagn. on Andria 980.

1181.　Ω: this line is spoken either by Theopr. or the *domi-nus gregis* [In the Captivi, the Epilogue is assigned by MSS. to the CATERVA] or the *tibi-cen.*

Arg. 1—11 iambici senarii
1—84 iambici senarii
85, 86 bacchiaci tetrametri
89*a* bacchiacus trimeter
89*b* bacchiacus tetrameter
90 iambicus dimeter catalecticus
91—97 bacchiaci tetrametri
98 iambicus dimeter catalecticus
99—101 bacchiaci tetrametri
102 iambicus dimeter catalecticus
103, 104 iambici octonarii
105, 106 cretici tetrametri
107 iambicus octonarius
108 creticus dimeter + trochaica tripodia catalectica
109 = 108
110—112 cretici tetrametri
113 = 108
114 creticus tetrameter
115 trochaicus septenarius
116 = 108
117 trochaicus septenarius
118 iambicus octonarius
119 trochaicus septenarius
120—124 bacchiaci tetrametri
125 iambicus dimeter catalecticus
128—132 iambici octonarii
133—136 = 108
137, 139 cretici tetrametri
140, 141 = 108
142 metrum incertum
143 iambicus octonarius
144 creticus tetrameter
145 trochaicus septenarius
146—148 iambici octonarii
149 = 108
150 creticus tetrameter
{151 = 108
{153 creticus tetrameter

154—156 trochaici septenarii
157—246 iambici septenarii
248—312 trochaici septenarii
313, 314 bacchiaci tetrametri
315 metrum incertum
316, 317 bacchiaci tetrametri
318, 319 anapaestici dimetri
320 creticus dimeter
325 iambicus octonarius
326, 327 metrum incertum
328 iambicus octonarius
329 creticus tetrameter catalecticus
330 bacchiacus tetrameter
333 trochaica tripodia catalectica
334 creticus tetrameter
336 creticus dimeter $+ \perp \smile \smile \smile \vee$
337 = 108
338 metrum incertum
339—341 = 336
342, 343 = 108
344 = 336
345 duae trochaicae tripodiae catalecticae
346 trochaicus septenarius
347 creticus tetrameter catalecticus
348—407 trochaici septenarii
409—689 iambici senarii
690—692 = 108
693 = 336
694, 695 = 108
696, 697 = 336
698—701 = 108
702 = 336
703—705 = 108
706 = 336
707—712 = 108
713 creticus tetrameter
714 = 108
715, 716 cretici tetrametri
717 = 108
718—720 cretici tetrametri
741, 722 cretici tetrametri
723—726 uersus corrupti
727 epiphonema
728 trochaicus septenarius
729, 730 cretici tetrametri
731 = 108
732—736 cretici tetrametri
737 trochaicus septenarius
738, 739 cretici tetrametri

740 trochaicus septenarius
742 iambicus octonarius
743 metrum incertum
744, 745 iambici octonarii
746 iambicus septenarius
747—782 iambici senarii
783—803 bacchiaci tetrametri
804—857 trochaici septenarii
858 iambicus dimeter + iambicus dimeter catalecticus (cum syncope)
859 trochaicus dimeter
860 = 858
861 = 859
862 + 863a trochaicus octonarius
863b + 864 trochaicus septenarius
865 bacchiacus tetrameter
866, 867 uersus corrupti
868 duo iambica cola semiquinaria
869 bacchiacus dimeter catalecticus + bacchiacus dimeter acata-
    lecticus (uel fortasse uersus dochmiacus)
870 metrum incertum
871—873 bacchiaci tetrametri
874 duo iambici dimetri catalectici (cum syncope)
875, 876 bacchiaci tetrametri
877 trochaicus octonarius
878, 879 cretici tetrametri
880 = 858
881, 882 cretici tetrametri
883, 884 trochaici septenarii
885a, 886b iambicus dimeter
885b ⊣ 886a iambicus septenarius
887a anapaesticus dimeter
887b + 888 anapaesticus tetrameter
889 anapaesticus dimeter
890, 891a bacchiaci tetrametri
891b + 892, 893 = 858
894 iambicus septenarius
895 + 896 anapaesticus tetrameter
897, 898 trochaici septenarii
899, 900 iambici senarii
901a paroemiacus
901b + 902a anapaesticus dimeter
903 paroemiacus
904—992 trochaici septenarii (uersus 925, 940—945, 990 sunt
        corrupti)
993—1040 iambici senarii (uersus 1025b, 1026b—e sunt corrupti)
1041—1181 trochaici septenarii (uersus 1055—1058 sunt corrupti).

EXCURSUS I.

Several points are to be observed in regard to the difficult question of reading in 509.

1. *Accheruns* is in Plaut. the name not of a river but of a place, cf. Capt. v 4, 2 *nulla Accheruns* 'no place of torture'; and it is constructed as the name of a *town*, thus *Accherunti* 'at (in) Acheron' Capt. iii 5, 31, v 4, 1, Merc. 606, Poen. 431, Truc. 749 (so *Accherunte* = 'in Acheron' Lucr. 628, 978, 984), *Accheruntem* 'to Acheron' Most. 494, etc., *Accherunte* 'from Acheron' Poen. 344. (It is true that we have *ab Accherunte* in Amph. 1078).

2. The word occurs 16 times in Plaut. (and *Accherunticus* 3 times) and has the first syllable always long [correct Lewis and Short], except in Poen. 831 *quási Ắccheruntem uéneris* (here therefore write with one *c*; the shortening is due to the accent, cf. *quási ipse sit* Poen. 845, *quíd ắpstulisti* Aul. 637 etc., etc.). Poen. Prol. 71 is unplautine; in Poen. 344 we should certainly read as Goetz and Loewe (following A) *quố die Orcus Ắccherunte* (without *ab*); cf. Wagn. Intr. to Aul. p. xlvii; similarly in the tragic verse quoted by Cic. Tusc. i 16, 37 *ắdsum atque aduenio Ắccherunte* (but immediately below *ắltae Ắccheruntis, sắlso sanguine*), cf. Ribb. Trag. Rel. p. 245. In Plaut. then *Ắccheruns* : *Ăcheruns* : : 15 : 1.

3. The accusative occurs 5 times (excluding Poen. Prol. 71).

certum ést hunc Ắccherŭntem praemittắm prius

                                        Cas. ii 8, 12

nam me Ắccheruntem récipere Orcus nŏluit

                                        Most. 499

quóduis genus ibi hóminum uideas, quási Acheruntem uéneris
                                                    Poen. 831
censétur censu ad Ácchcruntcm mórtuos
                                                    Trin. 494

and in Most. 509, the passage in question. In all of these except Trin. 494 the simple accus. is used for 'to Acheron'.
Trin. 494 is a very peculiar instance; Brix translates 'wird
abgeschätzt und geschickt zum Acheron' ('is rated and sent
to Ach.'), remarking that Wagn.'s trans. *ad Acch.* 'in Ach.' is
unplautine. It should be *Accherunti.* Whatever the right
interpretation of this passage may be, the simple accus. (of
motion) would of course have been out of place. It appears
then that whenever Plaut. wishes to express 'to Acheron' he
uniformly says *Accheruntem.* This seems to exclude *ad
Acheruntem* in Most. 509.

4. Are we then in our passage to take no account of the
ad which is preserved in all MSS., and simply to read *Accheruntem?* I have been guided by the curious variant *adcheruntem* preserved by two MSS. to read *ad Charontem;* it
should also be observed that in three passages *B* preserves a
diphthong in the second syllable (*Achaeruns*) Capt. v 4, 1,
Bacch. 198, Poen. 344. There seems in fact to have been some
confusion between *Charon* and *Acheron.* In Pliny II 93, 95
§ 208 we find *Quae spiracula uocant, alii Charonea scrobes
mortiferum spiritum exhalantes,* where a reference to Charon
is quite out of place.

EXCURSUS II.

The Fifth and Sixth Cantica.

The metrical difficulty of these two scenes is well known. Hermann, whose authority in matters of metre is naturally great, must be admitted to have failed in his reconstitution of them as a whole, and even Ritschl's treatment is in many points open to serious question. I have already stated my view of IV. 2 in the *Journal of Philology*. I now repeat it with some modifications, and add what appears to me probably the truth about IV. 1. I follow the numbering of the verses as given by Ritschl. The first four vv. are thus written in B—

858. Serui qui quom culpa carint tamen malum metuunt
Hii solent esse eris utibiles.
860. Nam illi qui nihil metuunt postquam sunt malum meriti
Stulta sibi expetunt consilia.

vv. 859, 861 obviously correspond. Prof. Sonnenschein considers them trochaic dimeters. I hold them to be cretic tripodiac; but the cretic is sometimes replaced by a choriambus, *utibiles, stulta sibi, consilia:* a substitution which is natural and presents no difficulty.

vv. 858, 860 I would write thus as iamb. septen.

Serui qui quom culpa carent, tamen malum [sibi] metuont
Nam illi qui nil metuont [sibi], postquam malum sunt meriti.

In the two following vv. *Exercent sese, Fatiunt a malo*] find no reason for dissenting from the view adopted by Prof. Sonnenschein : and I shall not attempt to fill up the lacunae which the MSS. offer in the three next (865—867). But 868, 869 call for some remark. Ritschl gives the reading of B thus—

868. Ut . adhuc fuit mihi corium esse oportet,
869. Sicerum atque ut uetem uerberare.

I would not lay any stress on the fact that on Ritschl's showing something, seemingly one letter, has been lost between *ut* and *adhuc*. Possibly *uti* may have been written : but the other MSS. have *ut adhuc* with no variation. The really determinative point is that the verse is palpably constituted of two exactly corresponding halves

ŭt ădhūc fū|īt mĭhī ‖ cŏrĭum ēsse ŏ | pōrtĕt,

that is to say, of a paeon followed by a spondee. If anyone asks where I find a parallel, I reply in the Stichus. The opening lines of the Stichus are to my mind as clearly paeonic as anything in Greek Comedy.

Crēdo ĕgŏ fū ĭssĕ mĭsĕ|rām Pĕnĕlŏ'pām
Sŏrŏr sŭo ēx | ănĭmō quū | tām dĭu uĭdŭ|ă

Vĭrŏ sŭō | cărŭĭt nām | nōs eius ănĭ'mum
De nostris factis noscimus ‖ quārūm uĭri hīnc
     ābsūnt
5. Quorumque nos negotiis ‖ ābsēntum ĭta ŭt | ū-
     cūmst
    Sollicitae noctis et dies ‖ sŏrŏr sŭmŭs | sēmpēr.

v. 1 is 2 paeons, an ionicus a maiore, and a catalectic syllable.
v. 2 is 1 paeon, 2 ionici (a min. + a mai.), cat. syllable.
v. 3 is 1 paeon, 2 ionici (a min. + a mai.), cat. syllable.
vv. 4, 5 an iambic dimeter + ionicus a mai. + spondee.
v. 6 is iambic dimeter + paeon + spondee.

I venture to challenge comparison here with the arrangement of these verses adopted by Ritschl or Hermann : and I conceive that they establish the necessity of admitting feet of 4 syllables as standards of measurement in Plautus to a far greater degree than is at present believed. I have already stated my belief that the Sotadic verse enters into the composition of Most. IV. 2.

Returning to Most. 868 I find in it the same combination of paeon with spondee which occurs in v. 6 of the Stichus. There is a careless rollicking lilt in the metre which appears to me to correspond well with the character of the youthful slave Phaniscus.

v. 869 is, I imagine, a dochmiac; though to what extent Plautus admits these is still a question.

Sincerum atque ut*i* | uetem uerberari.

The four next vv. are bacchiac, and the reconstruction of them in the present edition seems highly plausible. Then follow in B —

874. Nam nunc domi nostrae tot pessimi uiuont.
Peculi sui prodigi plagigerali ubi aduersum ut eant
Vocátur ero non eo molestus ne sis.
Scio quod properas gestis aliquo iam hercle ire uis mula foras pastum
Bene merens hoc precium unde abstultabi foras.
Solus nunc eo aduersum ero ex plurimis seruis.

In v. 874 Prof. Sonnenschein follows Studemund and breaks up the line into two so-called *iambic dimeters catalectic syncopated*

nam nunc domi	nostrae
tot pessimi	uiuont
_ ∠ ∪ _	∠ _

I must profess my profound distrust of these *syncopated* iambi, a question however too large to be discussed here. In the present case however everything is in favour of Hermann's view, which Ritschl adopted, that, like the vv. preceding and following it, it is bacchiac, whether as Hermann wrote

nam núnc pessimí tot domí nostrae uíuont

or, as Ritschl preferred and as seems more probable,

nam núnc tot domí pessimí nostrae uíuont.

The five following vv. I would write thus—

876. Vbi áduorsus út eant eró [suo] uocántur
'Nón eo; moléstus ne sis, scío quo properas, géstis aliquo.
Iam hercle [tú] mula uís ire pástum forás.'
Bene meréns hoc preti índe abstulí, abii forás.
880. Solus éx plurimís nunc eo áduorsum eró.

of which 877, 879 agree with Ritschl's arrangement.

876 is bacchiac, 878—880 cretics.

IV. 2.

Following as closely as I can the text of B as exhibited in Ritschl, I would write this scene thus—

Adu. Phánisce etiám respice. Pha. Míhi molestus né sis. 885
Adu. Vide út fastidit símia.
Pha. Mihi súm. Libet esse. Quid íd curas?
Adu. Manésne ilico, ímpure párasité?
Pha. Qui párasitus sum?
       Adu. Ego ením dicam.   889
Cibo pérduci poterís quouis.
Ferócem facís quia te crús tuus amát.   890
Pha. Váh! dolent oculí.
       Adu. Cur?
           Pha. Quia fúmus [est] moléstus.
Adu. Táce si faber, quí cudere plúmbeos solés nos.
Pha. Nón potes tu mó cogere ut[í] tibi maledícam.   893
Nóuit me crus.
       Adu. Suám quidem pol cúlcitellam opórtet.
Pha. Si sóbrius sis, male nón dicas.   895
Adu. Tibi óptemperém, cum tu míhi nequeás?
Át tu mecum, péssime, ito aduórsus.
       Pha. Quaeso hercle ábstine
Iám sermonem de ístis rebus.
       Adu. Fáciam et pultabó fores.
Heus écquis hic est qui máximam his iniúriam
Foribús defendat? Écquis ecquis éxit huc atque
  áperit?   900
Nemó quidem hinc exít foras. Vt esse áddecet ne-
  quam hómiues
Ita súnt, sed eo magis caúto opust, ne exéat, qui
  male me múlcet.

The first verse of the scene is an ordinary Sotadeus.

    Phānĭsce ŏtĭ|ām rēspĭce. |
            Mĭhĭ mŏlēstŭs | nō sīs,

and the same rhythm, if I am right in my conjecture (see *Journal of Philology*, Vol. XI. p. 171), recurs in several other verses, though with less clearness. These are 891, 892, 893, 894. In 891 the first foot is a quinquesyllable *Vah dolent ocu* | i.e. the ionicus a maiore $-\,-\,\smile\,\smile$ is resolved either into $-\,\smile\,-\,\smile\,\smile$ or as is perhaps more probable $-\,\smile\,\smile\,\smile\,\smile$ *-lent* counting as a short syllable. In 892 the first foot is again a quinquesyllable *Tăcĕ si făbĕr*, -*ber* counting as a short. This is a rhythm of which Hermann, in his discussion of the Sotadic metre, *Elem. Doctr. Metr.* pp. 283 sqq. gives several examples. I will quote two, v. 40

$$\text{ὅτι πάντες ὅσοι περισσὸν ἠθέλησαν εὑρεῖν,}$$

and again v. 62

$$\text{τί γὰρ ἐσμὲν ὅλως, ἢ ποδαπῆς γεγόναμεν ὕλης;}$$

where ὅτι πάντες ὅσ- and τί γὰρ ἐσμὲν ὅλ- exactly correspond to *Tăcĕ si făbĕr*. With some hesitation for *qui cudere soles plumbeos numbos nos* of B, *plumbeos nummos* of the other MSS., I have written *qui cudere plumbeos soles nos* in the sense 'you who so often coin us into bad money', i.e. pass us off as cheats. In 893 the epitrite *Nŏn pŏtēs tū*, like *sūūm quĭdēm pŏl* the second foot of 894, is of frequent occurrence in Sotadic verses. Thus v. 29 Herm.

$$\text{ᾱν μακρὰ πτύ} \mid \text{ης, φλεγματίῳ κρατῇ περισσῷ}$$

and its variations $-- \smile -, \quad --- \smile.$

58. δεῖ τὸν φύσει | νικώμενον ἄδικον αὐτὸν εἰπεῖν

67. αὐτάρκεια | γὰρ πρὸς πᾶσιν | ἡδονὴ δικαία.

In the second foot it is even commoner, in the form $---\smile-,$ *e. g.* v. 12,

μιμοῦ τὸ καλὸν καὶ μενεῖς ἐν βροτοῖς ἄριστος

$$- - \smile \smile \mid - - \smile - \mid - \smile - \smile \mid - \smile$$

v. 22. καὶ τὸ μὴ πάρον μὴ θέλειν οὐδὲ γὰρ σόν ἐστιν.

$$- \smile - \smile \mid - - \smile - \mid - \smile - \smile \mid - \smile$$

It must remain a question whether the form which I have adopted of 893 is that intended by Plautus; for -*re* of the infinitive is, as is well known, occasionally lengthened by the comic poets, and possibly

Non potes tu cōgĕrĕ me ŭ tĭ tĭbī mălĕ|dicam

may be the preferable form. In 894 the MSS. give *Nouit erus me*, which is possible ($- \smile \smile \smile -$ for $- \smile --$).

The metres of the remaining verses are as follows :—

886. Iambic dimeter.
887. Anapaestic dimeter.

888.   Bacchiac tripodia hypercatalectic.
889.   Either an anapaestic tetrameter acatalectic or, as I
have written it, two anapaestic dimeters.
890.   Bacchiac dimeter catalectic.
895.   Anapaestic dimeter.
896.   Bacchiac tripodia hypercatalectic.
897, 8.   Trochaic septenarii.
899.   Iambic trimeter.
900—902.   Iambic septenarii.

v. 900 seems to me certain. The thrice repeated sound
ec admirably expresses the impatience of the *aduorsitor*. In
902 the *at* of *exeat* is allowed to count as a short syllable.

I have written for *cauto est opus ne huc exeat* of MSS.
cauto opust ne exeat.

                                        R. ELLIS.

INDEX TO NOTES.

inde = ab eis, 879
Indefinite subject, 73, 197
Indic. = Subjunct., 368, 774
industriae, 348
Infinitive expr. purpose, 67
ingenium, 135
inposisse = inposuisse, 434
insanum, 761
inseruire with accus., 190, 216
interbitere, 1096
interpolare, 262
interpolis, 274
intui, 836
intus, 405
ire = uenire, 547
iste, istic (vague), 669, 913, 983
isti = istic, 741, 1064, 1143
ita, 56, 213, 565, 656, 685, 996
iubere, 426
iuuentute, 30

κατὰ σίνεσιν, 115, 561

late, 842
lauare (intrans.), 157
Lax writing, 199, 959
lectus, 327
licet, 402
liquidus, 751
ludos facere, Arg. 7, 427

male, 316, 882
malum (interjec.), 6, 34, 368
malus, 352, 1071, 1107
mancupare, 1091
manufesto, 511, 679
manumittere, Arg. 1
manuplares, 312
mel, 325
merenda, 966
mirum quin, 493
Misargyrides, p. 6
miseris modis, 54
modestia, 162
modus, 139 ; 54, 1033
mores, 168, 171, 286
multimodis, 785
mulus, 878
musice, 729

nam, 133, 191, 368, 784, 874, 949
ne (interj.), 75, 562
ne = ut non, 390
ne with Pres. Imper., 576, 643, 1105
ne with Pres. Subj., 215, 468
ne = cauendum est ne, 922
-ne (asseverative), 508, 580, 955
-ne = nonne, 622, 660, 850, 887 a
ncuolt, neuis, 110, 762, 1176
nidoricape, 5
nimis quam, 511
nisi, 278, 663
nominare, 586
Nom. for Voc., 311
non, 197, 820, 978
nummus, 115, 535, 892
numquam, 164, 428, 1113
nunciam, 74, 1166

obolere, 39
occlusa ianua, 444
ocius, 679
Old forms: aliqui 174, attigatis 468, contempla 166, 172, 282, congredibor 783, crastini 881, curassis 526, discipulina 154, enicasso 212, haec 504, 640, illisce 510, 935, 1098, inscruibis 216, med 1109, occupassis 1097, puere 308, 843, 947, 949, 990, respexis 523, scibo 997, ted 1175, tetuli 471
opera, 60, 112, 259, 804, 1009, 1039
opes, 348
oppido, 136, 165
optuere, 69, 837
optume, 686
optuoptumo, 673
orare, 682

paenissumo, 656
παρὰ προσδοκίαν, 179, 1007, 1073
Parataxis, 146
patibulatus, 56
peculium facere, 864
pedisequi, p. 6, ii. 2
per, 500

CAMBRIDGE: PRINTED BY C. J. CLAY, M.A. & SON, AT THE UNIVERSITY PRESS.

A CLASSIFIED LIST

OF

EDUCATIONAL WORKS

PUBLISHED BY

GEORGE BELL & SONS.

Cambridge Calendar. Published Annually (*August*). 6s. 6d.
Student's Guide to the University of Cambridge. 6s. 6d.
Oxford : Its Life and Schools. 7s. 6d.
The Schoolmaster's Calendar. Published Annually (*December*). 1s.

BIBLIOTHECA CLASSICA.

A Series of Greek and Latin Authors, with English Notes, edited by eminent Scholars. 8vo.

₊ *The Works with an asterisk (*) prefixed can only be had in the Sets of 26 Vols.*

Aeschylus. By F. A. Paley, M.A., LL.D. 8s.
Cicero's Orations. By G. Long, M.A. 4 vols. 32s.
Demosthenes. By R. Whiston, M.A. 2 vols. 10s.
Euripides. By F. A. Paley, M.A., LL.D. 3 vols. 24s.
Homer. By F. A. Paley, M.A., LL.D. The Iliad, 2 vols. 14s.
Herodotus. By Rev. J. W. Blakesley, B.D. 2 vols. 12s.
Hesiod. By F. A. Paley, M.A., LL.D. 5s.
Horace. By Rev. A. J. Macleane, M.A. 8s.
Juvenal and Persius. By Rev. A. J. Macleane, M.A. 6s.
Plato. By W. H. Thompson, D.D. 2 vols. 5s. each.
Sophocles. Vol. I. By Rev. F. H. Blaydes, M.A. 8s.
—————— Vol. II. F. A. Paley, M.A., LL.D. 6s.
*Tacitus: The Annals. By the Rev. P. Frost. 8s.
*Terence. By E. St. J. Parry, M.A. 8s.
Virgil. By J. Conington, M.A. Revised by Professor H. Nettleship.
3 vols. 10s. 6d. each.
An Atlas of Classical Geography; 24 Maps with coloured Outlines. Imp. 8vo. 6s.

GRAMMAR-SCHOOL CLASSICS.

A Series of Greek and Latin Authors, with English Notes.
Fcap. 8vo.

Cæsar : De Bello Gallico. By George Long, M.A. 4*s*. -
—— Books I.–III. For Junior Classes. By G. Long, M.A. 1*s*. 6*d*.
—— Books IV. and V. 1*s*. 6*d*. Books VI. and VII. 1*s*. 6*d*.

Catullus, Tibullus. and Propertius. Selected Poems. With Life.
By Rev. A. H. Wratislaw. 2*s*. 6*d*.

Cicero: De Senectute, De Amicitia, and Select Epistles. By
George Long, M.A. 3*s*.

Cornelius Nepos. By Rev. J. F. Macmichael. 2*s*.

Homer: Iliad. Books I.–XII. By F. A. Paley, M.A., LL.D.
4*s*. 6*d*. Also in 2 parts, 2*s*. 6*d*. each.

Horace : With Life. By A. J. Macleane, M.A. 3*s*. 6*d*. In
2 parts, 2*s*. each.

Juvenal: Sixteen Satires. By H. Prior, M.A. 3*s*. 6*d*.

Martial : Select Epigrams. With Life. By F. A. Paley, M.A., LL.D.
4*s*. 6*d*.

Ovid: the Fasti. By F. A. Paley, M.A., LL.D. 3*s*. 6*d*. Books I.
and II. 1*s*. 6*d*. Books III. and IV. 1*s*. 6*d*.

Sallust: Catilina and Jugurtha. With Life. By G. Long, M.A.
and J. G. Frazer. 3*s*. 6*d*., or separately, 2*s*. each.

Tacitus: Germania and Agricola. By Rev. P. Frost. 2*s*. 6*d*.

Virgil: Bucolics, Georgics, and Æneid, Books I.–IV. Abridged
from Professor Conington's Edition. 4*s*. 6*d*.—Æneid, Books V.–XII. 4*s*. 6*d*.
Also in 9 separate Volumes, as follows, 1*s*. 6*d*. each :—Bucolics—Georgics,
I. and II.—Georgics, III. and IV.—Æneid, I. and II.—Æneid, III. and
IV.—Æneid, V. and VI.—Æneid, VII. and VIII.—Æneid, IX. and X.—
Æneid, XI. and XII.

Xenophon: The Anabasis. With Life. By Rev. J. F. Macmichael.
3*s*. 6*d*. Also in 4 separate volumes, 1*s*. 6*d*. each :—Book I. (with Life,
Introduction, Itinerary, and Three Maps)—Books II. and III.—IV. and V.
—VI. and VII.

—— The Cyropædia. By G. M. Gorham, M.A. 3*s*. 6*d*. Books
I. and II. 1*s*. 6*d*.—Books V. and VI. 1*s*. 6*d*.

—— Memorabilia. By Percival Frost, M.A. 3*s*.

A Grammar-School Atlas of Classical Geography, containing
Ten selected Maps. Imperial 8vo. 3*s*.

Uniform with the Series.

The New Testament, in Greek. With English Notes, &c. By
Rev. J. F. Macmichael. 4*s*. 6*d*. In 5 parts, The Four Gospels and the Acts.
Sewed, 6*d*. each.

CAMBRIDGE GREEK AND LATIN TEXTS.

Aeschylus. By F. A. Paley, M.A., LL.D. 2*s.*
Cæsar: De Bello Gallico. By G. Long, M.A. 1*s.* 6*d.*
Cicero: De Senectute et De Amicitia, et Epistolæ Selectæ.
By G. Long, M.A. 1*s.* 6*d.*
Ciceronis Orationes. In Verrem. By G. Long, M.A. 2*s.*6*d.*
Euripides. By F. A. Paley, M.A., LL.D. 3 vols. 2*s.* each.
Herodotus. By J. G. Blakesley, B.D. 2 vols. 5*s.*
Homeri Ilias. I.–XII. By F. A. Paley, M.A., LL.D. 1*s.* 6*d.*
Horatius. By A. J. Macleane, M.A. 1*s.* 6*d.*
Juvenal et Persius. By A. J. Macleane, M.A. 1*s.* 6*d.*
Lucretius. By H. A. J. Munro, M.A. 2*s.*
Sallusti Crispi Catilina et Jugurtha. By G. Long, M.A. 1*s.* 6*d.*
Sophocles. By F. A. Paley, M.A., LL.D. 2*s.* 6*d.*
Terenti Comœdiæ. By W. Wagner, Ph.D. 2*s.*
Thucydides. By J. G. Donaldson, D.D. 2 vols. 4*s.*
Virgilius. By J. Conington, M.A. 2*s.*
Xenophontis Expeditio Cyri. By J. F. Macmichael, B.A. 1*s.* 6*d.*
Novum Testamentum Græce. By F. H. Scrivener, M.A., D.C.L.
4*s.* 6*d.* An edition with wide margin for notes, half bound, 12*s.* EDITIO
MAJOR, with additional Readings and References. 7*s.* 6*d.* *See page* 14.

CAMBRIDGE TEXTS WITH NOTES.

*A Selection of the most usually read of the Greek and Latin Authors, Annotated for
Schools. Edited by well-known Classical Scholars. Fcap. 8vo. 1s. 6d. each,
with exceptions.*

'Dr. Paley's vast learning and keen appreciation of the difficulties of
beginners make his school editions as valuable as they are popular. In
many respects he sets a brilliant example to younger scholars.'—*Athenæum.*
'We hold in high value these handy Cambridge texts with Notes.'—
Saturday Review.

Aeschylus. Prometheus Vinctus.—Septem contra Thebas.—Aga-
memnon.—Persae.—Eumenides.—Choephoroe. By F. A. Paley, M.A., LL.D.
Euripides. Alcestis.—Medea.—Hippolytus.—Hecuba.—Bacchae.
—Ion. 2*s.*—Orestes.—Phoenissæ.—Troades.—Hercules Furens.—Andro-
mache.—Iphigenia in Tauris.—Supplices. By F. A. Paley, M.A., LL.D.
Homer. Iliad. Book I. By F. A. Paley, M.A., LL.D. 1*s.*
Sophocles. Oedipus Tyrannus.—Oedipus Coloneus.—Antigone.
—Electra—Ajax. By F. A. Paley, M.A., LL.D.
Xenophon. Anabasis. In 6 vols. By J. E. Melhuish, M.A.,
Assistant Classical Master at St. Paul's School.
—––— Hellenics, Book II. By L. D. Dowdall, M.A., B.D. 2*s.*
—––— Hellenics. Book I. By L. D. Dowdall, M.A., B.D.
[*In the press.*
Cicero. De Senectute, De Amicitia and Epistolæ Selectæ. By
G. Long, M.A.
Ovid. Fasti. By F. A. Paley, M.A LL.D. In 3 vols., 2 books
in each. 2*s.* each vol.

Ovid. Selections. Amores, Tristia, Heroides, Metamorphoses.
By A. J. Macleane, M.A.
Terence. Andria.—Hauton Timorumenos.—Phormio.—Adelphoe.
By Professor Wagner, Ph.D.
Virgil. Professor Conington's edition, abridged in 12 vols.
Others in preparation.

PUBLIC SCHOOL SERIES.

A Series of Classical Texts, annotated by well-known Scholars. Cr. 8vo.

Aristophanes. The Peace. By F. A. Paley, M.A., LL.D. 4s. 6d.
——— The Acharnians. By F. A. Paley, M.A., LL.D. 4s. 6d.
——— The Frogs. By F. A. Paley, M.A., LL.D. 4s. 6d.
Cicero. The Letters to Atticus. Bk. I. By A. Pretor, M.A. 4s. 6d.
Demosthenes de Falsa Legatione. By R. Shilleto, M.A. 6s.
——— The Law of Leptines. By B. W. Beatson, M.A. 3s. 6d.
Livy. Book XXI. Edited, with Introduction, Notes, and Maps,
by the Rev. L. D. Dowdall, M.A., B.D. 3s. 6d.
——— Book XXII. Edited, &c., by Rev. L. D. Dowdall, M.A.,
B.D. 3s. 6d.
Plato. The Apology of Socrates and Crito. By W. Wagner, Ph.D.
10th Edition. 3s. 6d. Cheap Edition, limp cloth, 2s. 6d.
——— The Phædo. 9th Edition. By W. Wagner, Ph.D. 5s. 6d.
——— The Protagoras. 4th Edition. By W. Wayte, M.A. 4s. 6d.
——— The Euthyphro. 3rd Edition. By G. H. Wells, M.A. 3s.
——— The Euthydemus. By G. H. Wells, M.A. 4s.
——— The Republic. Books I. & II. By G. H. Wells, M.A. 3rd
Edition. 5s. 6d.
Plautus. The Aulularia. By W. Wagner, Ph.D. 3rd Edition. 4s. 6d.
——— The Trinummus. By W. Wagner, Ph.D. 3rd Edition. 4s. 6d.
——— The Menaechmei. By W. Wagner, Ph.D. 2nd Edit. 4s. 6d.
——— The Mostellaria. By Prof. E. A. Sonnenschein. 5s.
——— The Rudens. Edited by Prof. E. A. Sonnenschein.
[*In the press.*
Sophocles. The Trachiniæ. By A. Pretor, M.A. 4s. 6d.
Sophocles. The Oedipus Tyrannus. By B. H. Kennedy, D.D. 5s.
Terence. By W. Wagner, Ph.D. 2nd Edition. 7s. 6d.
Theocritus. By F. A. Paley, M.A., LL.D. 2nd Edition. 4s. 6d.
Thucydides. Book VI. By T. W. Dougan, M.A., Fellow of St.
John's College, Cambridge. 3s. 6d.
Others in preparation.

CRITICAL AND ANNOTATED EDITIONS

Aristophanis Comœdiæ. By H. A. Holden, LL.D. 8vo. 2 vols.
Notes, Illustrations, and Maps. 23s. 6d. Plays sold separately.
Cæsar's Seventh Campaign in Gaul, B.C. 52. By Rev. W. C.
Compton, M.A., Assistant Master, Uppingham School. Crown 8vo. 4s.

Calpurnius Siculus. By C. H. Keene, M.A. Crown 8vo. 6s.
Catullus. A New Text, with Critical Notes and Introduction by Dr. J. P. Postgate. Japanese vellum. Foolscap 8vo. 3s.
Corpus Poetarum Latinorum. Edited by Walker. 1 vol. 8vo. 18s.
Horace. Quinti Horatii Flacci Opera. By H. A. J. Munro, M.A. Large 8vo. 10s. 6d.
Livy. The first five Books. By J. Prendeville. 12mo. roan, 5s. Or Books I.-III. 3s. 6d. IV. and V. 3s. 6d. Or the five Books in separate vols. 1s. 6d. each.
Lucan. The Pharsalia. By C. E. Haskins, M.A., and W. E. Heitland, M.A. Demy 8vo. 14s.
Lucretius. With Commentary by H. A. J. Munro. 4th Edition. Vols. I. and II. Introduction, Text, and Notes. 18s. Vol. III. Translation. 6s.
Ovid. P. Ovidii Nasonis Heroides XIV. By A. Palmer, M.A. 8vo. 6s.
—— P. Ovidii Nasonis Ars Amatoria et Amores. By the Rev. H. Williams, M.A. 3s. 6d.
—— Metamorphoses. Book XIII. By Chas. Haines Keene, M.A. 2s. 6d.
—— Epistolarum ex Ponto Liber Primus. By C. H. Keene, M.A. 3s.
Propertius. Sex Aurelii Propertii Carmina. By F. A. Paley, M.A., LL.D. 8vo. Cloth, 5s.
—— Sex Propertii Elegiarum. Libri IV. Recensuit A. Palmer, Collegii Sacrosanctæ et Individuæ Trinitatis juxta Dublinum Socius. Fcap. 8vo. 3s. 6d.
Sophocles. The Oedipus Tyrannus. By B. H. Kennedy, D.D. Crown 8vo. 8s.
Thucydides. The History of the Peloponnesian War. By Richard Shilleto, M.A. Book I. 8vo. 6s. 6d. Book II. 8vo. 5s. 6d.

LOWER FORM SERIES.

With Notes and Vocabularies.

Eclogæ Latinæ; or, First Latin Reading-Book, with English Notes and a Dictionary. By the late Rev. P. Frost, M.A. New Edition. Fcap. 8vo. 1s. 6d.
Latin Vocabularies for Repetition. By A. M. M. Stedman, M.A. 2nd Edition, revised. Fcap. 8vo. 1s. 6d.
Easy Latin Passages for Unseen Translation. By A. M. M. Stedman, M.A. Fcap. 8vo. 1s. 6d.
Virgil's Æneid. Book I. Abridged from Conington's Edition by Rev. J. G. Sheppard, D.C.L. With Vocabulary by W. F. R. Shilleto. 1s. 6d. [*Now ready.*
Cæsar de Bello Gallico. Books I., II. and III. With Notes by George Long, M.A., and Vocabulary by W. F. R. Shilleto. 1s. 6d. each.
Tales for Latin Prose Composition. With Notes and Vocabulary. By G. H. Wells, M.A. 2s.
A Latin Verse-Book. An Introductory Work on Hexameters and Pentameters. By the late Rev. P. Frost, M.A. New Edition. Fcap. 8vo. 2s. Key (for Tutors only), 5s.
Analecta Græca Minora, with Introductory Sentences, English Notes, and a Dictionary. By the late Rev. P. Frost, M.A. New Edition. Fcap. 8vo. 2s.
Greek Testament Selections. 2nd Edition, enlarged, with Notes and Vocabulary. By A. M. M. Stedman, M.A. Fcap. 8vo. 2s. 6d.

LATIN AND GREEK CLASS-BOOKS.

(See also Lower Form Series.)

Faciliora. An Elementary Latin Book on a new principle. By the Rev. J. L. Seager, M.A. 2s. 6d.

First Latin Lessons. By A. M. M. Stedman. 1s.

Easy Latin Exercises, for Use with the Revised Latin Primer and Shorter Latin Primer. By A. M. M. Stedman, M.A. *(Issued with the consent of the late Dr. Kennedy.)* Crown 8vo. 2s. 6d.

Miscellaneous Latin Exercises. By A. M. M. Stedman, M.A. Fcap. 8vo. 1s. 6d.

A Latin Primer. By Rev. A. C. Clapin, M.A. 1s.

Auxilia Latina. A Series of Progressive Latin Exercises. By M. J. B. Baddeley, M.A. Fcap. 8vo. Part I. Accidence. 3rd Edition, revised. 2s. Part II. 4th Edition, revised. 2s. Key to Part II. 2s. 6d.

Scala Latina. Elementary Latin Exercises. By Rev. J. W. Davis, M.A. New Edition, with Vocabulary. Fcap. 8vo. 2s. 6d.

Passages for Translation into Latin Prose. By Prof. H. Nettleship, M.A. 3s. Key (for Tutors only), 4s. 6d.

Latin Prose Lessons. By Prof. Church, M.A. 9th Edition. Fcap. 8vo. 2s. 6d.

Analytical Latin Exercises. By C. P. Mason, B.A. 4th Edit. Part I., 1s. 6d. Part II., 2s. 6d.

By T. COLLINS, M.A., Head Master of the Latin School, Newport, Salop.

Latin Exercises and Grammar Papers. 6th Edit. Fcap. 8vo. 2s. 6d.

Unseen Papers in Latin Prose and Verse. With Examination Questions. 4th Edition. Fcap. 8vo. 2s. 6d.

—— **in Greek Prose and Verse.** With Examination Questions. 3rd Edition. Fcap. 8vo. 3s.

Easy Translations from Nepos, Cæsar, Cicero, Livy, &c., for Retranslation into Latin. With Notes. 2s.

By A. M. M. STEDMAN, M.A., Wadham College, Oxford.

Latin Examination Papers in Grammar and Idiom. 2nd Edition. Crown 8vo. 2s. 6d. Key (for Tutors and Private Students only), 6s.

Greek Examination Papers in Grammar and Idiom. 2s. 6d.

By the REV. P. FROST, M.A., St. John's College, Cambridge.

Materials for Latin Prose Composition. By the late Rev. P. Frost, M.A. New Edition. Fcap. 8vo. 2s. Key (for Tutors only), 4s.

Materials for Greek Prose Composition. New Edit. Fcap. 8vo. 2s. 6d. Key (for Tutors only), 5s.

Florilegium Poeticum. Elegiac Extracts from Ovid and Tibullus. New Edition. With Notes. Fcap. 8vo. 2s.

By H. A. HOLDEN, LL.D., formerly Fellow of Trinity Coll., Camb.

Foliorum Silvula. Part I. Passages for Translation into Latin Elegiac and Heroic Verse. 10th Edition. Post 8vo. 7s. 6d.

—— **Part II.** Select Passages for Translation into Latin Lyric and Comic Iambic Verse. 3rd Edition. Post 8vo. 5s.

Folia Silvulæ, sive Eclogæ Poetarum Anglicorum in Latinum et Græcum conversæ. 8vo. Vol. II. 4s. 6d.

Foliorum Centuriæ. Select Passages for Translation into Latin and Greek Prose. 10th Edition. Post 8vo. 8s.

Scala Græca: a Series of Elementary Greek Exercises. By Rev. J. W. Davis, M.A., and R. W. Baddeley, M.A. 3rd Edition. Fcap. 8vo. 2*s.* 6*d.*
Greek Verse Composition. By G. Preston, M.A. 5th Edition. Crown 8vo. 4*s.* 6*d.*
Greek Particles and their Combinations according to Attic Usage. A Short Treatise. By F. A. Paley, M.A., LL.D. 2*s.* 6*d.*
Rudiments of Attic Construction and Idiom. By the Rev. W. C. Compton, M.A., Assistant Master at Uppingham School. 3*s.*
Anthologia Græca. A Selection of Choice Greek Poetry, with Notes. By F. St. John Thackeray. 4*th and Cheaper Edition.* 16mo. 4*s.* 6*d.*
Anthologia Latina. A Selection of Choice Latin Poetry, from Nævius to Boëthius, with Notes. By Rev. F. St. John Thackeray. Revised and Cheaper Edition. 16mo. 4*s.* 6*d.*

TRANSLATIONS, SELECTIONS, &c.

⁎⁎ Many of the following books are well adapted for School Prizes.

Aeschylus. Translated into English Prose by F. A. Paley, M.A., LL.D. 2nd Edition. 8vo. 7*s.* 6*d.*
—— Translated into English Verse by Anna Swanwick. 4th Edition. Post 8vo. 5*s.*
Horace. The Odes and Carmen Sæculare. In English Verse by J. Conington, M.A. 10th edition. Fcap. 8vo. 5*s.* 6*d.*
—— The Satires and Epistles. In English Verse by J. Conington, M.A. 7th edition. 6*s.* 6*d.*
—— Odes. Englished and Imitated by various hands. 1*s.* 6*d.*
Plato. Gorgias. Translated by E. M. Cope, M.A. 8vo. 2nd Ed. 7*s.*
—— Philebus. Trans. by F. A. Paley, M.A., LL.D. Sm. 8vo. 4*s.*
—— Theætetus. Trans. by F. A. Paley, M.A., LL.D. Sm. 8vo. 4*s.*
—— Analysis and Index of the Dialogues. By Dr. Day. Post 8vo. 5*s.*
Sophocles. Oedipus Tyrannus. By Dr. Kennedy. 1*s.*
—— The Dramas of. Rendered into English Verse by Sir George Young, Bart., M.A. 8vo. 12*s.* 6*d.*
Theocritus. In English Verse, by C. S. Calverley, M.A. New Edition, revised. Crown 8vo. 7*s.* 6*d.*
Translations into English and Latin. By C. S. Calverley, M.A. Post 8vo. 7*s.* 6*d.*
Translations into English, Latin, and Greek. By R. C. Jebb, Litt. D., H. Jackson, Litt. D., and W. E. Currey, M.A. Second Edition. 8*s.*
Extracts for Translation. By R. C. Jebb, Litt. D., H. Jackson, Litt. D., and W. E. Currey, M.A. 4*s.* 6*d.*
Between Whiles. Translations by Rev. B. H. Kennedy, D.D. 2nd Edition, revised. Crown 8vo. 5*s.*
Sabrinae Corolla in Hortulis Regiae Scholae Salopiensis Contexuerunt Tres Viri Floribus Legendis. Fourth Edition, thoroughly Revised and Rearranged. With many new Pieces and an Introduction.
[*Ready immediately.*

REFERENCE VOLUMES.

A Latin Grammar. By Albert Harkness. Post 8vo. 6*s.*
—— By T. H. Key, M.A. 6th Thousand. Post 8vo. 8*s.*
A Short Latin Grammar for Schools. By T. H. Key. M.A. F.R.S. 16th Edition. Post 8vo. 3*s.* 6*d.*

A Guide to the Choice of Classical Books. By J. B. Mayor, M.A.
3rd Edition, with a Supplementary List. Crown 8vo. 4s. 6d. Supplementary List separately, 1s. 6d.

The Theatre of the Greeks. By J. W. Donaldson, D.D. 8th Edition. Post 8vo. 5s.

Keightley's Mythology of Greece and Italy. 4th Edition. 5s.

CLASSICAL TABLES.

Latin Accidence. By the Rev. P. Frost, M.A. 1s.

Latin Versification. 1s.

Notabilia Quædam; or the Principal Tenses of most of the Irregular Greek Verbs and Elementary Greek, Latin, and French Construction. New Edition. 1s.

Richmond Rules for the Ovidian Distich, &c. By J. Tate, M.A. 1s.

The Principles of Latin Syntax. 1s.

Greek Verbs. A Catalogue of Verbs, Irregular and Defective. By J. S. Baird, T.C.D. 8th Edition. 2s. 6d.

Greek Accents (Notes on). By A. Barry, D.D. New Edition. 1s.

Homeric Dialect. Its Leading Forms and Peculiarities. By J. S. Baird, T.C.D. New Edition, by W. G. Rutherford, LL.D. 1s.

Greek Accidence. By the Rev. P. Frost, M.A. New Edition. 1s.

CAMBRIDGE MATHEMATICAL SERIES.

Arithmetic for Schools. By C. Pendlebury, M.A. 3rd Edition, revised and stereotyped, with or without answers, 4s. 6d. Or in two parts, 2s. 6d. each.

> EXAMPLES (nearly 8000), without answers, in a separate vol. 3s.

> In use at St. Paul's, Winchester, Charterhouse, Merchant Taylors', Christ's Hospital, Sherborne, Shrewsbury, and at many other Schools and Colleges.

Algebra. Choice and Chance. By W. A. Whitworth, M.A. 4th Edition. 6s.

Euclid. Books I.–VI. and part of Books XI. and XII. By H. Deighton. 4s. 6d. Key (for Tutors only), 5s. Books I. and II., 2s.

Euclid. Exercises on Euclid and in Modern Geometry. By J. McDowell, M.A. 3rd Edition. 6s.

Trigonometry. Plane. By Rev. T. Vyvyan, M.A. 3rd Edit. 3s. 6d.

Geometrical Conic Sections. By H. G. Willis, M.A. Manchester Grammar School. 5s.

Conics. The Elementary Geometry of. 6th Edition, revised and enlarged. By C. Taylor, D.D. 4s. 6d.

Solid Geometry. By W. S. Aldis, M.A. 4th Edit. revised. 6s.

Geometrical Optics. By W. S. Aldis, M.A. 3rd Edition. 4s.

Rigid Dynamics. By W. S. Aldis, M.A. 4s.

Elementary Dynamics. By W. Garnett, M.A., D.C.L. 5th Ed. 6s.

Dynamics. A Treatise on. By W. H. Besant, Sc.D., F.R.S. 7s. 6d.

Heat. An Elementary Treatise. By W. Garnett, M.A., D.C.L. 5th Edition, revised and enlarged. 4s. 6d.

Elementary Physics. Examples in. By W. Gallatly, M.A. 4s.

Hydromechanics. By W. H. Besant, Sc.D., F.R.S. 4th Edition. Part I. Hydrostatics. 5s.

Mathematical Examples. By J. M. Dyer, M.A., Eton College, and R. Prowde Smith, M.A., Cheltenham College. 6s.

Mechanics. Problems in Elementary. By W. Walton, M.A. 6s.

CAMBRIDGE SCHOOL AND COLLEGE TEXT-BOOKS.

A Series of Elementary Treatises for the use of Students.

Arithmetic. By Rev. C. Elsee, M.A. Fcap. 8vo. 13th Edit. 3*s.* 6*d.*

—— By A. Wrigley, M.A. 3*s.* 6*d.*

—— A Progressive Course of Examples. With Answers. By J. Watson, M.A. 7th Edition, revised. By W. P. Goudie, B.A. 2s. 6d.

Algebra. By the Rev. C. Elsee, M.A. 7th Edit. 4*s.*

—— Progressive Course of Examples. By Rev. W. F. M'Michael, M.A., and R. Prowde Smith, M.A. 4th Edition. 3s. 6d. With Answers. 4s. 6d.

Plane Astronomy, An Introduction to. By P. T. Main, M.A. 5th Edition. 4s.

Conic Sections treated Geometrically. By W. H. Besant, D.Sc. 6th Edition. 4s. 6d. Solution to the Examples. 4s.

—— Enunciations and Figures Separately. 1*s.* 6*d.*

Statics, Elementary. By Rev. H. Goodwin, D.D. 2nd Edit. 3*s.*

Hydrostatics, Elementary. By W. H. Besant, D.Sc. 13th Edit. 4*s.*

Mensuration, An Elementary Treatise on. By B.T. Moore, M.A. 3*s.* 6*d.*

Newton's Principia, The First Three Sections of, with an Appendix; and the Ninth and Eleventh Sections. By J. H. Evans, M.A. 5th Edition, by P. T. Main, M.A. 4s.

Analytical Geometry for Schools. By T. G. Vyvyan. 5th Edit. 4*s.* 6*d.*

Greek Testament, Companion to the. By A. C. Barrett, M.A. 5th Edition, revised. Fcap. 8vo. 5s.

Book of Common Prayer, An Historical and Explanatory Treatise on the. By W. G. Humphry, B.D. 6th Edition. Fcap. 8vo. 2s. 6d.

Music, Text-book of. By Professor H. C. Banister. 14th Edition, revised. 5s.

—— Concise History of. By Rev. H. G. Bonavia Hunt, Mus. Doc. Dublin. 9th Edition revised. 3s. 6d.

ARITHMETIC AND ALGEBRA.

See also the two foregoing Series.

Arithmetic, Examination Papers in. Consisting of 140 papers, each containing 7 questions. 357 more difficult problems follow. A collection of recent Public Examination Papers are appended. By C. Pendlebury, M.A. 2s. 6d. Key, 5s.

Graduated Exercises in Addition (Simple and Compound). By W. S. Beard, C. S. Dept. Rochester Mathematical School. 1s.
For Candidates for Commercial Certificates and Civil Service Exams.

BOOK-KEEPING.

Book-keeping Papers, set at various Public Examinations. Collected and Written by J. T. Medhurst, Lecturer on Book-keeping in the City of London College. 3r.

A 2

GEOMETRY AND EUCLID.

Euclid. Books I.–VI. and part of XI. and XII. A New Translation. By H. Deighton. Books I. and II. separately, 2s. (See p. 8.

—— **The Definitions of, with Explanations and Exercises,** and an Appendix of Exercises on the First Book. By R. Webb, M.A. Crown 8vo. 1s. 6d.

—— **Book I.** With Notes and Exercises for the use of Preparatory Schools, &c. By Braithwaite Arnett, M.A. 8vo. 4s. 6d.

—— **The First Two Books explained to Beginners.** By C. P. Mason, B.A. 2nd Edition. Fcap. 8vo. 2s. 6d.

The Enunciations and Figures to Euclid's Elements. By Rev. J. Brasse, D.D. New Edition. Fcap. 8vo. 1s. Without the Figures, 6d.

Exercises on Euclid and in Modern Geometry. By J. McDowell, B.A. Crown 8vo. 3rd Edition revised. 6s.

Geometrical Conic Sections. By H. G. Willis, M.A. (See p. 8.)

Geometrical Conic Sections. By W. H. Besant, D.Sc. (See p. 9.)

Elementary Geometry of Conics. By C. Taylor, D.D. (See p. 8.)

An Introduction to Ancient and Modern Geometry of Conics. By C. Taylor, D.D., Master of St. John's Coll., Camb. 8vo. 15s.

Solutions of Geometrical Problems, proposed at St. John's College from 1830 to 1846. By T. Gaskin, M.A. 8vo. 12s.

TRIGONOMETRY.

Trigonometry, Introduction to Plane. By Rev. T. G. Vyvyan, Charterhouse. 3rd Edition. Cr. 8vo. 3s. 6d.

An Elementary Treatise on Mensuration. By B. T. Moore, M.A. 3s. 6d.

Trigonometry, Examination Papers in. By G. H. Ward, M.A., Assistant Master at St. Paul's School. Crown 8vo. 2s. 6d.

ANALYTICAL GEOMETRY AND DIFFERENTIAL CALCULUS.

An Introduction to Analytical Plane Geometry. By W. P. Turnbull, M.A. 8vo. 12s.

Problems on the Principles of Plane Co-ordinate Geometry. By W. Walton, M.A. 8vo. 16s.

Trilinear Co-ordinates, and Modern Analytical Geometry of Two Dimensions. By W. A. Whitworth, M.A. 8vo. 16s.

An Elementary Treatise on Solid Geometry. By W. S. Aldis, M.A. 4th Edition revised. Cr. 8vo. 6s.

Elliptic Functions, Elementary Treatise on. By A. Cayley, D.Sc. Professor of Pure Mathematics at Cambridge University. Demy 8vo. 15s.

MECHANICS & NATURAL PHILOSOPHY.

Statics, Elementary. By H. Goodwin, D.D. Fcap. 8vo. 2nd Edition. 3s.

Dynamics. A Treatise on Elementary. By W. Garnett, M.A, D.C.L. 5th Edition. Crown 8vo. 6s.

Dynamics. Rigid. By W. S. Aldis, M.A. 4s.

Dynamics. A Treatise on. By W. H. Besant, D.Sc.,F.R.S. 7s. 6d.

Elementary Mechanics, Problems in. By W. Walton, M.A. New Edition. Crown 8vo. 6s.

Theoretical Mechanics, Problems in. By W. Walton, M.A. 3rd Edition. Demy 8vo. 16s.

Hydrostatics. By W. H. Besant, D.Sc. Fcap. 8vo. 13th Edition. 4s.

Hydromechanics, A Treatise on. By W. H. Besant, D.Sc., F.R.S. 8vo. 4th Edition, revised. Part I. Hydrostatics. 5s.

Hydrodynamics, A Treatise on. Vol. I. 10s. 6d. ; Vol. II. 12s. 6d. A. B. Basset, M.A.

Optics, Geometrical. By W. S. Aldis, M.A. Crown 8vo. 3rd Edition. 4s.

Double Refraction, A Chapter on Fresnel's Theory of. By W. S. Aldis, M.A. 8vo. 2s.

Heat, An Elementary Treatise on. By W. Garnett, M.A., D.C.L. Crown 8vo. 4th Edition. 4s.

Elementary Physics. By W. Gallatly, M.A., Asst. Examr. at London University. 4s.

Newton's Principia, The First Three Sections of, with an Appendix ; and the Ninth and Eleventh Sections. By J. H. Evans, M.A. 5th Edition. Edited by P. T. Main, M.A. 4s.

Astronomy, An Introduction to Plane. By P. T. Main, M.A. Fcap. 8vo. cloth. 5th Edition. 4s.

—— **Practical and Spherical.** By R. Main, M.A. 8vo. 14s.

Mathematical Examples. Pure and Mixed. By J. M. Dyer, M.A., and R. Prowde Smith, M.A. 6s.

Pure Mathematics and Natural Philosophy, A Compendium of Facts and Formulæ in. By G. R. Smalley. 2nd Edition, revised by J. McDowell, M.A. Fcap. 8vo. 3s. 6d.

Elementary Mathematical Formulæ. By the Rev. T. W. Openshaw, M A. 1s. 6d.

Elementary Course of Mathematics. By H. Goodwin, D.D. 6th Edition. 8vo. 16s.

Problems and Examples, adapted to the 'Elementary Course of Mathematics.' 3rd Edition. 8vo. 5s.

Solutions of Goodwin's Collection of Problems and Examples. By W W Hutt, M.A. 3rd Edition, revised and enlarged. 8vo. 9s.

A Collection of Examples and Problems in Arithmetic, Algebra, Geometry, Logarithms, Trigonometry, Conic Sections, Mechanics, &c, with Answers. By Rev. A. Wrigley. 20th Thousand. 8s. 6d. Key. 10s 6d

Science Examination Papers. Part I. Inorganic Chemistry. By R. E. Steel, M A., F.C.S., Bradford Grammar School. Crown 8vo. 2s. 6d.

TECHNOLOGICAL HANDBOOKS.

Edited by H. TRUEMAN WOOD, Secretary of the Society of Arts.

Dyeing and Tissue Printing.   By W. Crookes, F.R.S.   5s.

Glass Manufacture. By Henry Chance, M.A.; H. J. Powell, B.A.; and H. G. Harris. 3s. 6d.

Cotton Spinning.   Bv Richard Marsden, of Manchester.   3rd Edition, revised. 6s. 6d.

Chemistry of Coal-Tar Colours.   By Prof. Benedikt, and Dr. Knecht of Bradford Technical College. 2nd Edition, enlarged. 6s. 6d.

Woollen and Worsted Cloth Manufacture.   By Roberts Beaumont, Assistant Lecturer at Yorkshire College, Leeds. 7s. 6d.

Cotton Weaving.   By R. Marsden.   [*In the press.*

Colour in Woven Design.   By Roberts Beaumont.   [*In the press.*

Bookbinding.   By Zaehnsdorf.   [*Preparing.*

Others in preparation.

HISTORY, TOPOGRAPHY, &c.

Rome and the Campagna.   By R. Burn, M.A.   With 85 Engravings and 26 Maps and Plans. With Appendix. 4to. 21s.

Old Rome.   A Handbook for Travellers.   By R. Burn, M.A.   With Maps and Plans. Demy 8vo. 5s.

Modern Europe. By Dr. T. H. Dyer. 2nd Edition, revised and continued. 5 vols. Demy 8vo. 2l. 12s. 6d.

The History of the Kings of Rome. By Dr. T. H. Dyer. 8vo. 16s.

The History of Pompeii: its Buildings and Antiquities. By T. H. Dyer. 3rd Edition, brought down to 1874. Post 8vo. 7s. 6d.

The City of Rome: its History and Monuments. 2nd Edition, revised by T. H. Dyer. 5s.

Ancient Athens: its History, Topography, and Remains. By T. H. Dyer. Super-royal 8vo. Cloth. 7s. 6d.

The Decline of the Roman Republic. By G. Long. 5 vols. 8vo. 5s. each.

Historical Maps of England. By C. H. Pearson. Folio. 3rd Edition revised. 31s. 6d.

History of England, 1800–46. By Harriet Martineau, with new and copious Index. 5 vols. 3s. 6d. each.

A Practical Synopsis of English History. By A. Bowes. 9th Edition, revised. 8vo. 1s.

Lives of the Queens of England. By A. Strickland. Library Edition, 8 vols. 7s. 6d. each. Cheaper Edition, 6 vols. 5s. each. Abridged Edition, 1 vol. 6s. 6d. Mary Queen of Scots, 2 vols. 5s. each. Tudor and Stuart Princesses, 5s.

Eginhard's Life of Karl the Great (Charlemagne). Translated, with Notes, by W. Glaister, M.A., B.C.L. Crown 8vo. 4s. 6d.

The Elements of General History. By Prof. Tytler. New Edition, brought down to 1874. Small Post 8vo. 3s. 6d.

History and Geography Examination Papers. Compiled by C. H. Spence, M.A., Clifton College. Crown 8vo. 2s. 6d.

PHILOLOGY.

WEBSTER'S DICTIONARY OF THE ENGLISH LAN-GUAGE. With Dr. Mahn's Etymology. 1 vol. 1628 pages, 3000 Illustrations. 21s.; half calf, 30s.; calf or half russia, 31s. 6d.; russia, 2l. With Appendices and 70 additional pages of Illustrations, 1919 pages, 31s. 6d.; half calf, 2l.; calf or half russia, 2l. 2s.; russia, 2l. 10s.

'THE BEST PRACTICAL ENGLISH DICTIONARY EXTANT.'—*Quarterly Review*, 1873.

Prospectuses, with specimen pages, post free on application.

Richardson's Philological Dictionary of the English Language. Combining Explanation with Etymology, and copiously illustrated by Quotations from the best Authorities. With a Supplement. 2 vols. 4to. 4l. 14s. 6d. Supplement separately. 4to. 12s.

Brief History of the English Language. By Prof. James Hadley, LL.D., Yale College. Fcap. 8vo. 1s.

The Elements of the English Language. By E. Adams, Ph.D. 21st Edition. Post 8vo. 4s. 6d.

Philological Essays. By T. H. Key, M.A., F.R.S. 8vo. 10s. 6d.

Synonyms and Antonyms of the English Language. By Archdeacon Smith. 2nd Edition. Post 8vo. 5s.

Synonyms Discriminated. By Archdeacon Smith. Demy 8vo. 2nd Edition revised. 14s.

Bible English. Chapters on Words and Phrases in the Bible and Prayer Book. By Rev. T. L. O. Davies. 2nd Edition revised, in the press.

The Queen's English. A Manual of Idiom and Usage. By the late Dean Alford. 6th Edition. Fcap. 8vo. 1s. sewed. 1s. 6d. cloth.

A History of English Rhythms. By Edwin Guest, M.A., D.C.L. LL.D. New Edition, by Professor W. W. Skeat. Demy 8vo. 18s.

Elements of Comparative Grammar and Philology. For Use in Schools. By A. C. Price, M.A., Assistant Master at Leeds Grammar School. Crown 8vo. 2s. 6d.

Questions for Examination in English Literature. By Prof. W. W. Skeat. 2nd Edition, revised. 2s. 6d.

A Syriac Grammar. By G. Phillips, D.D. 3rd Edition, enlarged. 8vo. 7s. 6d.

DIVINITY, MORAL PHILOSOPHY, &c.

BY THE REV. F. H. SCRIVENER, A.M., LL.D., D.C.L.

Novum Testamentum Græce. Editio major. Being an enlarged Edition, containing the Readings of Westcott and Hort, and those adopted by the Revisers, &c. 7s. 6d. *For other Editions see page 3.*

A Plain Introduction to the Criticism of the New Testament. With Forty Facsimiles from Ancient Manuscripts. 3rd Edition. 8vo. 18s.

Six Lectures on the Text of the New Testament. For English Readers. Crown 8vo. 6s.

Codex Bezæ Cantabrigiensis. 4to. 10s. 6d.

The New Testament for English Readers. By the late H. Alford, D.D. Vol. I. Part I. 3rd Edit. 12s. Vol. I. Part II. 2nd Edit. 10s. 6d. Vol. II. Part I. 2nd Edit. 16s. Vol. II. Part II. 2nd Edit. 16s.

The Greek Testament. By the late H. Alford, D.D. Vol. I. 7th Edit. 1l. 8s. Vol. II. 8th Edit. 1l. 4s. Vol. III. 10th Edit. 18s. Vol. IV. Part I. 5th Edit. 18s. Vol. IV. Part II. 10th Edit. 14s. Vol. IV. 1l. 12s.

Companion to the Greek Testament. By A. C. Barrett, M.A. 5th Edition, revised. Fcap. 8vo. 5s.

Guide to the Textual Criticism of the New Testament. By Rev. E. Miller, M.A. Crown 8vo. 4s.

The Book of Psalms. A New Translation, with Introductions, &c. By the Very Rev. J. J. Stewart Perowne, D.D. 8vo. Vol. I. 6th Edition, 18s. Vol. II. 6th Edit. 16s.

—— Abridged for Schools. 6th Edition. Crown 8vo. 10s. 6d.

History of the Articles of Religion. By C. H. Hardwick. 3rd Edition. Post 8vo. 5s.

History of the Creeds. By J. R. Lumby, DD. 3rd Edition. Crown 8vo. 7s. 6d.

Pearson on the Creed. Carefully printed from an early edition. With Analysis and Index by E. Walford, M.A. Post 8vo. 5s.

Liturgies and Offices of the Church, for the Use of English Readers, in Illustration of the Book of Common Prayer. By the Rev. Edward Burbidge, M.A. Crown 8vo. 9s.

An Historical and Explanatory Treatise on the Book of Common Prayer By Rev. W. G. Humphry, B.D. 6th Edition, enlarged. Small Post 8vo. 2s. 6d. ; Cheap Edition, 1s.

A Commentary on the Gospels, Epistles, and Acts of the Apostles. By Rev. W. Denton, A.M. New Edition. 7 vols. 8vo. 9s. each.

Notes on the Catechism. By Rt. Rev. Bishop Barry. 8th Edit. Fcap. 2s.

The Winton Church Catechist. Questions and Answers on the Teaching of the Church Catechism. By the late Rev. J. S. B. Monsell, LL.D. 4th Edition. Cloth, 3s. ; or in Four Parts, sewed.

The Church Teacher's Manual of Christian Instruction. By Rev. M. F. Sadler. 38th Thousand. 2s. 6d.

FOREIGN CLASSICS.

A Series for use in Schools, with English Notes, grammatical and explanatory, and renderings of difficult idiomatic expressions.
Fcap. 8vo.

Schiller's Wallenstein. By Dr. A. Buchheim. 5th Edit. 5s.
Or the Lager and Piccolomini, 2s. 6d. Wallenstein's Tod, 2s. 6d.

—— **Maid of Orleans.** By Dr. W. Wagner. 2nd Edit. 1s. 6d.

—— **Maria Stuart.** By V. Kastner. 2nd Edition. 1s. 6d.

Goethe's Hermann and Dorothea. By E. Bell, M.A., and E. Wölfel. 1s. 6d.

German Ballads, from Uhland, Goethe, and Schiller. By C. L. Bielefeld. 3rd Edition. 1s. 6d.

Charles XII., par Voltaire. By L. Direy. 7th Edition. 1s. 6d.

Aventures de Télémaque, par Fénélon. By C. J. Delille. 4th Edition. 2s. 6d.

Select Fables of La Fontaine. By F.E.A.Gasc. 18th Edit. 1s. 6d.

Picciola, by X.B. Saintine. By Dr. Dubuc. 15th Thousand. 1s. 6d.

Lamartine's Le Tailleur de Pierres de Saint-Point. By J. Boïelle, 4th Thousand. Fcap. 8vo. 1s. 6d.

Italian Primer. By Rev. A. C. Clapin, M.A. Fcap. 8vo. 1s.

FRENCH CLASS-BOOKS.

French Grammar for Public Schools. By Rev. A. C. Clapin, M.A. Fcap. 8vo. 12th Edition, revised. 2s. 6d.

French Primer. By Rev. A.C. Clapin, M.A. Fcap. 8vo. 8th Ed. 1s.

Primer of French Philology. By Rev. A. C. Clapin. Fcap. 8vo. 4th Edit. 1s.

Le Nouveau Trésor; or, French Student's Companion. By M. E. S. 18th Edition. Fcap. 8vo. 1s. 6d.

French Examination Papers in Miscellaneous Grammar and Idioms. Compiled by A. M. M. Stedman, M.A. 4th Edition. Crown 8vo. 2s. 6d.

Key to the above. By G. A. Schrumpf, Univ. of France. Crown 8vo. 5s. (For Teachers or Private Students only.)

Manual of French Prosody. By Arthur Gosset, M.A. Crown 8vo. 3s.

Lexicon of Conversational French. By A. Holloway. 3rd Edition. Crown 8vo. 4s.

PROF. A. BARRÈRE'S FRENCH COURSE.

Elements of French Grammar and First Steps in Idiom. Crown 8vo. 2s.

Precis of Comparative French Grammar. 2nd Edition. Crown 8vo. 3s. 6d.

Junior Graduated French Course. Crown 8vo. 1s. 6d.

F. E. A. GASC'S FRENCH COURSE.

First French Book. Fcap. 8vo. 106th Thousand. 1*s.*
Second French Book. 47th Thousand. Fcap. 8vo. 1*s.* 6*d.*
Key to First and Second French Books. 5th Edit. Fcp. 8vo. 3*s.* 6*d.*
French Fables for Beginners, in Prose, with Index. 16th Thousand.
12mo. 1*s.* 6*d.*
Select Fables of La Fontaine. 18th Thousand. Fcap. 8vo. 1*s.* 6*d.*
Histoires Amusantes et Instructives. With Notes. 16th Thousand. Fcap. 8vo. 2*s.*
Practical Guide to Modern French Conversation. 17th Thousand. Fcap. 8vo. 1*s.* 6*d.*
French Poetry for the Young. With Notes. 5th Ed. Fcp. 8vo. 8*s.*
Materials for French Prose Composition; or, Selections from the best English Prose Writers. 19th Thous. Fcap. 8vo. 3*s.* Key, 6*s.*
Prosateurs Contemporains. With Notes. 10th Edition, revised. 12mo. 3*s.* 6*d.*
Le Petit Compagnon: a French Talk-Book for Little Children. 12th Thousand. 16mo. 1*s* 6*d.*
An Improved Modern Pocket Dictionary of the French and English Languages. 45th Thousand. 16mo. 2*s.* 6*d.*
Modern French-English and English-French Dictionary. 4th Edition, revised, with new supplements. 10*s.* 6*d.*
The A B C Tourist's French Interpreter of all Immediate Wants. By F. E. A. Gasc. 1*s.*

MODERN FRENCH AUTHORS.

Edited, with Introductions and Notes, by JAMES BOÏELLE, Senior French Master at Dulwich College.

Daudet's La Belle Nivernaise. 2*s.* 6*d.*   *For Beginners.*
Hugo's Bug Jargal. 3*s.*   *For Advanced Students.*

GOMBERT'S FRENCH DRAMA.

Being a Selection of the best Tragedies and Comedies of Molière, Racine, Corneille, and Voltaire. With Arguments and Notes by A. Gombert. New Edition, revised by F. E. A. Gasc. Fcap. 8vo. 1*s.* each; sewed, 6*d.*   CONTENTS.

MOLIERE:—Le Misanthrope. L'Avare. Le Bourgeois Gentilhomme. Le Tartuffe. Le Malade Imaginaire. Les Femmes Savantes. Les Fourberies de Scapin. Les Précieuses Ridicules. L'Ecole des Femmes. L'Ecole des Maris. Le Médecin malgré Lui.
RACINE:—Phédre. Esther. Athalie. Iphigénie. Les Plaideurs. La Thébaïde; ou, Les Frères Ennemis. Andromaque. Britannicus.
P. CORNEILLE:—Le Cid. Horace. Cinna. Polyeucto.
VOLTAIRE:—Zaïre.

GERMAN CLASS-BOOKS.

Materials for German Prose Composition. By Dr. Buchheim. 12th Edition, thoroughly revised. Fcap. 4*s.* 6*d.* Key, Parts I. and II., 3*s.* Parts III. and IV., 4*s.*

German Conversation Grammar. By I. Sydow. 2nd Edition. Book I. Etymology. 2*s.* 6*d.*   Book II. Syntax. 1*s.* 6*d.*

Wortfolge, or Rules and Exercises on the Order of Words in German Sentences. By Dr. F. Stock. 1s. 6d.

A German Grammar for Public Schools. By the Rev. A. C. Clapin and F. Holl Müller. 5th Edition. Fcap. 2s. 6d.

A German Primer, with Exercises. By Rev. A. C. Clapin. 1s.

Kotzebue's Der Gefangene. With Notes by Dr. W. Stromberg. 1s.

German Examination Papers in Grammar and Idiom. By R. J. Morich. 2s. 6d. Key for Tutors only, 5s.

By Fnz. Lange, Ph.D., Professor R.M.A., Woolwich, Examiner in German to the Coll. of Preceptors, and also at the Victoria University, Manchester.

A Concise German Grammar. In Three Parts. Part I. Elementary. 2s. Part II. Intermediate. 1s. 6d. Part III. Advanced, 3s. 6d.

German Examination Course. Elementary, 2s. Intermediate, 2s. Advanced, 1s. 6d.

German Reader. Elementary. 1s. 6d. Advanced (*in the press*).

MODERN GERMAN SCHOOL CLASSICS.
Small Crown 8vo.

Hey's Fabeln Für Kinder. Edited by Prof. F. Lange, Ph.D. 1s. 6d.

Benedix's Dr. Wespe. Edited by F. Lange, Ph.D. 2s. 6d.

Hoffman's Meister Martin, der Küfner. By Prof. F. Lange, Ph.D. 1s. 6d.

Heyse's Hans Lange. By A. A. Macdonell, M.A., Ph.D. 2s.

Auerbach's Auf Wache, and Roquette's Der Gefrorene Kuss. By A. A. Macdonell, M.A. 2s.

Moser's Der Bibliothekar. By Prof. F. Lange, Ph.D. 2s.

Ebers' Eine Frage. By F. Storr, B.A. 2s.

Freytag's Die Journalisten. By Prof. F. Lange, Ph.D. 2s. 6d.

Gutzkow's Zopf und Schwert. By Prof. F. Lange, Ph.D. 2s.

German Epic Tales. Edited by Karl Neuhaus, Ph.D. 2s. 6d.

ENGLISH CLASS-BOOKS.
Comparative Grammar and Philology. By A. C. Price, M.A., Assistant Master at Leeds Grammar School. 2s. 6d.

The Elements of the English Language. By E. Adams, Ph.D. 22nd Edition. Post 8vo. 4s. 6d.

The Rudiments of English Grammar and Analysis. By E. Adams, Ph.D. 17th Thousand. Fcap. 8vo. 1s.

A Concise System of Parsing. By L. E. Adams, B.A. 1s. 6d.

General Knowledge Examination Papers. Compiled by A. M. M. Stedman, M.A. 2s. 6d.

Examples for Grammatical Analysis (Verse and Prose). Selected, &c., by F. Edwards. New edition. Cloth, 1s.

Notes on Shakespeare's Plays. By T. Duff Barnett, B.A. Midsummer Night's Dream, 1s.; Julius Cæsar, 1s.; Henry V., 1s.; Tempest, 1s.; Macbeth, 1s.; Merchant of Venice, 1s.; Hamlet, 1s.

By C. P. MASON, Fellow of Univ. Coll. London.

First Notions of Grammar for Young Learners. Fcap. 8vo.
47th Thousand. Cloth. 9d.

First Steps in English Grammar for Junior Classes. Demy
18mo. 46th Thousand. 1s.

Outlines of English Grammar for the Use of Junior Classes.
71st to 76th Thousand. Crown 8vo. 2s.

English Grammar, including the Principles of Grammatical
Analysis. 31st Edition. 125th to 130th Thousand. Crown 8vo. 3s. 6d.

Practice and Help in the Analysis of Sentences. 2s.

A Shorter English Grammar, with copious Exercises. 34th
to 38th Thousand. Crown 8vo. 3s. 6d.

English Grammar Practice, being the Exercises separately. 1s.

Code Standard Grammars. Parts I. and II., 2d. each. Parts III.,
IV., and V., 3d. each.

Notes of Lessons, their Preparation, &c. By José Rickard,
Park Lane Board School, Leeds, and A. H. Taylor, Rodley Board
School, Leeds. 2nd Edition. Crown 8vo. 2s. 6d.

A Syllabic System of Teaching to Read, combining the advantages of the 'Phonic' and the 'Look-and-Say' Systems. Crown 8vo. 1s.

Practical Hints on Teaching. By Rev. J. Menet, M.A. 6th Edit.
revised. Crown 8vo. paper, 2s.

How to Earn the Merit Grant. A Manual of School Management. By H. Major, B.A., B.Sc. Part I. (3rd Edit.) Infant School, 3s.
Part II. (2nd Edit. revised), 4s. Complete, 6s.

Test Lessons in Dictation. 4th Edition. Paper cover, 1s. 6d.

The Botanist's Pocket-Book. With a copious Index. By W. R.
Hayward. 6th Edition, revised. Crown 8vo. cloth limp. 4s. 6d.

Experimental Chemistry, founded on the Work of Dr. Stöckhardt.
By C. W. Heaton. Post 8vo. 5s.

Lectures on Musical Analysis. Sonata-form, Fugue, &c. By
Prof. H. C. Banister. 2nd Edition, revised. 7s. 6d.

Helps' Course of Poetry, for Schools. A New Selection from
the English Poets, carefully compiled and adapted to the several standards
by E. A. Helps, one of H.M. Inspectors of Schools.

> Book   I. Infants and Standards I. and II. 134 pp. small 8vo. 9d.
> Book II. Standards III. and IV. 224 pp. crown 8vo. 1s. 6d.
> Book III. Standards V., VI., and VII. 352 pp. post 8vo. 2s.
> Or in PARTS. Infants, 2d.; Standard I., 2d.; Standard II., 2d.
> Standard III., 4d.

Picture School-Books. In Simple Language, with numerous
Illustrations. Royal 16mo.

The Infant's Primer. 3d.—School Primer. 6d.—School Reader. By J.
Tilleard. 1s.—Poetry Book for Schools. 1s.—The Life of Joseph. 1s.—The
Scripture Parables. By the Rev. J. E. Clarke. 1s.—The Scripture Miracles.
By the Rev. J. E. Clarke. 1s.—The New Testament History. By the Rev.
J. G. Wood, M.A. 1s.—The Old Testament History. By the Rev. J. G.
Wood, M.A. 1s.—The Life of Martin Luther. By Sarah Crompton. 1s.

BOOKS FOR YOUNG READERS.

A Series of Reading Books designed to facilitate the acquisition of the power of Reading by very young Children. In 11 vols. limp cloth, 6d. each.

Those with an asterisk have a Frontispiece or other Illustrations.

*The Old Boathouse. Bell and Fan; or, A Cold Dip.

*Tot and the Cat. A Bit of Cake. The Jay. The Black Hen's Nest. Tom and Ned. Mrs. Bee.

*The Cat and the Hen. Sam and his Dog Redleg. Bob and Tom Lee. A Wreck.

*The New-born Lamb. The Rosewood Box. Poor Fan. Sheep Dog.

Suitable for Infants.

*The Two Parrots. A Tale of the Jubilee. By M. E. Wintle. 9 Illustrations.

*The Story of Three Monkeys.

*Story of a Cat. Told by Herself.

The Blind Boy. The Mute Girl. A New Tale of Babes in a Wood.

The Dey and the Knight. The New Bank Note. The Royal Visit. A King's Walk on a Winter's Day.

*Queen Bee and Busy Bee.

*Gull's Crag.

*A First Book of Geography. By the Rev. C. A. Johns. Illustrated. Double size, 1s.

Suitable for Standards I. & II.

Syllabic Spelling. By C. Barton. In Two Parts. Infants, 3d. Standard I., 3d.

GEOGRAPHICAL SERIES. By M. J. BARRINGTON WARD, M.A. *With Illustrations.*

The Map and the Compass. A Reading-Book of Geography. For Standard I. New Edition, revised. 8d. cloth.

The Round World. A Reading-Book of Geography. For Standard II. 10d.

About England. A Reading Book of Geography for Standard III. [In the press.

The Child's Geography. For the Use of Schools and for Home Tuition. 6d.

The Child's Geography of England. With Introductory Exercises on the British Isles and Empire, with Questions. 2s. 6d. Without Questions, 2s.

Geography Examination Papers. (See History and Geography Papers, p. 12.)

BELL'S READING-BOOKS.

FOR SCHOOLS AND PAROCHIAL LIBRARIES.

Now Ready. Post 8vo. Strongly bound in cloth, 1s. each.

*Life of Columbus.
*Grimm's German Tales. (Selected.)
*Andersen's Danish Tales. Illustrated. (Selected.)
Great Englishmen. Short Lives for Young Children.
Great Englishwomen. Short Lives of.
Great Scotsmen. Short Lives of.
*Masterman Ready. By Capt. Marryat. Illus. (Abgd.)
*Poor Jack. By Capt. Marryat, R.N. (Abridged.)

Suitable for Standards III. & IV.

*Scott's Talisman. (Abridged.)
*Friends in Fur and Feathers. By Gwynfryn.
*Poor Jack. By Captain Marryat, R.N. Abgd.
Parables from Nature. (Selected.) By Mrs. Gatty.
Lamb's Tales from Shakespeare. (Selected.)
Edgeworth's Tales. (A Selection.)
*Gulliver's Travels. (Abridged.)
*Robinson Crusoe. Illustrated.
*Arabian Nights. (A Selection Rewritten.)

Standards IV. & V.

*Dickens's Little Nell. Abridged from the 'The Old Curiosity Shop.'
*The Vicar of Wakefield.
*Settlers in Canada. By Capt. Marryat. (Abridged.)
Marie: Glimpses of Life in France. By A. R. Ellis.
Poetry for Boys. Selected by D. Munro.
*Southey's Life of Nelson. (Abridged.)
*Life of the Duke of Wellington, with Maps and Plans.
*Sir Roger de Coverley and other Essays from the Spectator.
Tales of the Coast. By J. Runciman.

Standards V. VI. & VII.

* *These Volumes are Illustrated.*

Uniform with the Series, in limp cloth, 6d. each.

Shakespeare's Plays. Kemble's Reading Edition. With Explanatory Notes for School Use.

JULIUS CÆSAR.   THE MERCHANT OF VENICE.   KING JOHN.
HENRY THE FIFTH.   MACBETH.   AS YOU LIKE IT.

London: GEORGE BELL & SONS, York Street, Covent Garden.

www.ingramcontent.com/pod-product-compliance
Lightning Source LLC
Chambersburg PA
CBHW030124030726

47498CB00007B/2545